IMMANENCE

IMMANENCE

J.L. ALDIS, EDITOR

E.E. WEBER, ASSISTANT EDITOR

STORY SPRING PUBLISHING

PEKIN, ILLINOIS

Story Spring Publishing, LLC
3420 Veterans Drive, #325
Pekin, Illinois 61554
www.storyspringpublishing.com

Publisher's Note: This is a work of fiction. Names, characters, places, and incidents are a product of the author's imagination. Locales and public names are sometimes used for atmospheric purposes. Any resemblance to actual people, living or dead, or to businesses, companies, events, institutions, or locales is completely coincidental.

Cover Design: Hilary K. Justice
Graphic: "The Archangel Lucifer by Jacob Epstein," Copyright © 2011 by Marios Hadjianastasis
Graphic: "Discobolus": user: Dorieo / Wikimedia Commons / Public Domain

Ordering Information:
Quantity sales. Special discounts are available on quantity purchases by corporations, associations, and others. For details, contact the publisher at the address above.

Immanence/Aldis, J.L. -- 1st ed.
ISBN: 978-1-940699-09-7

Contents

Foreword

In 2013, Story Spring Publishing bravely exposed the presence of monsters living among us, concealed in our communities, even—dare we say it?—integrated. But *Thoroughly Modern Monsters* was just the beginning. Where monsters lurk, what else might there be? While many of us think we live entirely on the material plane, there are plenty who argue that there is something beyond, and worshippers of every kind demonstrate their belief that the immaterial is present all around, if only we allow ourselves to recognise it.

Every day, we drive past churches, mosques, synagogues, and temples. We don't necessarily think about the cults that have been forgotten in the rush of time and the passing of civilisations. We don't suspect that somewhere quite mundane might once have housed a deity. We don't stop to consider what it might mean if some of those left-behind gods haven't been left so far behind after all. And where there are gods, there will always be demons, those cunning opportunists. Sometimes, for better or worse, there isn't a lot to choose between them.

In the seventeen stories of this collection, a group of talented authors have set themselves to speculating about the consequences when the veil becomes thin enough to let the gods and demons manifest—become IMMANENT—in the world we think we know so well. Whether comic or dramatic, frightening or comforting, each tale offers the reader the chance to become acquainted with someone, or something, that might just show more than a casual interest in their soul.

J.L. Aldis
London, 2016

1

Burning Issues

Antioch Grey

What's the most dangerous thing in the world?

A gun?

A knife?

Some bright lad with an idea?

Some even brighter lad with principles?

It's a bookshop. And it's not just because that's where they keep the books about guns and knives and ideas and principles. It's because that's where they keep the gods.

When Nietzsche said that God was dead, he was wrong. They're not dead, they're just very sick, hanging on to the interstices of life and belief, waiting for the right kind of host—and the right kind of host always turns up in a bookshop.

Well, that and diners. And I'd seen a lot of diners after six months in the U.S.

It's not the clientele that the gods are casting out lures for, like some religious version of a catfish; it's the owners. Anyone who has to work retail will be turning to God before the end of the first week, and that little crack is enough to let the nearest, quickest deity crowbar its way back to full power.

And, of course, the worst-behaved gods have a taste for coffee.

It wasn't the first bookshop I'd been called out to, but it was very nearly my last. I made the mistake of confusing a level three god infestation with a level seven demonic possession and nearly ended up a human sacrifice

3

somewhere between Metaphysics and Self Help.

My first foray into the target shop was on a Monday. Just scoping out the lie of the land, assessing the best way in and out and whether I would need to escalate beyond a couple of pounds of salt and a stern talking-to of the entity in question.

It looked normal. Too normal.

The books were lined up in orderly fashion, perfectly matched in size and then grouped by colour. No one ever stores their books like that. Not anyone sane, anyway.

It had that atmosphere you sometimes get in the suburbs, where unspeakable acts are being performed in the cellar after dark, but the hedges are tidily clipped, the lawn neatly mown, and there's not a leaf or blade of grass out of place, because everything green and growing is too scared to rustle in case . . . *something* . . . gets it.

If you're lucky, it's just a bloke who is too fond of his mum, has never done anything out of the ordinary, and then one day cracks and makes a suit out of human skin.

If you're unlucky, it's something with multiple tentacles and a taste for pain that makes skinning look like the good option.

There was no obvious tentacleness about the place—no sucker marks, no strange tracks in the dust, but then there wasn't any dust, and who had ever heard of a second-hand bookshop without a little bit of dust?

To the right of the floor space stood the counter, manned by a tall, drooping man who looked like he'd been disappointed with life from the moment he was born and had never recovered that level of optimism since. His moustache was eloquent of sadness and soft-boiled egg.

He looked like just the sort of man prepared to swap his immortal soul for a chance at something better.

I headed for the shelves, ducking behind a row of green books, and made a spy hole by sliding a book from its prison and peering through the gap.

The man kept muttering under his breath, repeating some phrase over and over again. Was it an obscure prayer, a sacred mantra, calling upon the power of whatever foul creature had been Summoned to the place?

He took a vessel and filled it with a libation of some fluid that glistened like liquid gold in the dim light.

He wrenched at an arcane apparatus that rattled into life with a deep rumble then finally ground into silence once its awful task was complete. Jets of foul steam rose above the beast, which made a wailing sound like the very souls of the damned.

The man's voice increased in volume as he wrestled with the beast, until I could make out a word here and there.

"Pumpkin spice latte. Pumpkin spice latte, extra froth."

Not a prayer, but a recipe, and even a god of coffee would want something more by way of an appeal than a recitation of a method to make latte macchiato. Even if biscotti were included, gratis.

It wasn't enough to clear him of all suspicion, but he looked like an innocent employee.

I turned away, because even the dullest human can sense when someone is watching them, the way you always get that prickling sensation in the supermarket queue when you know that someone is glaring at the back of your neck for having one item too many for the express lane. It's an instinct wired deep into the brain that kept us alive on the African plains whilst lions tried to creep up on us.

Unfortunately, my own senses failed me.

My watcher coughed twice from behind me, announcing their presence in a way that reeked of silent disapproval.

What are you up to? the cough asked. And, *are you going to buy something? Because if you're going to be weird, there had better be money in it for me.*

I didn't rush to put the book back. If you're caught doing something strange, you should always brazen it out and pretend that you're not doing anything out of the ordinary. Most people won't say anything, either because they're too polite to mock the afflicted or because they think you're one step away from snapping and taking everyone out with a bookmark, some string, and a very sharp pencil.

It's amazing what you can do with a sharp pencil, so it's best to be cautious.

I turned and said, "Have you got anything interesting in steampunk?"

She didn't judge. A short woman of indeterminate age, she wore a sensible checked shirt, a halo of salt and pepper hair, and the numb look of someone who had been asked for too many dreadful books to care any more.

"Classic steampunk, goth steampunk, vampire steampunk, or just how to make your own steam goggles?" she asked.

"I've already got the goggles," I said. "I need something a bit more advanced."

I did have goggles. They were green tinted and polarised to pick up demon spoor, and if you perched them on your head whilst wearing a corset, you could go just about anywhere and be passed over as a cosplayer rather than a demon-slaying operative.

And it couldn't do any harm to have some extra bits and pieces to hide behind.

Yes, I admit it, I like cogs and gears.

"The craft section is over here."

She headed towards the back of the shop, away from the counter and my target.

"I notice that all the books are stacked by colour. That's a little peculiar," I said.

"It's sensible."

"Really?"

"You don't think that people come into second-hand bookshops knowing the author or the title, do you? No, it's 'I read the book twenty years ago, and it was green, and it had a picture of a woman in a red dress on it.' If I want to make the sale, I need to be able to find a green book."

"I can see that," I said slowly. It could be the truth, or it could be some bizarre ritual to Summon a fell creature from the deeps. I couldn't think of a demon with a taste for colour coding, but it was always possible. Start the victim off with something small, something meaningless, like arranging your shelves in a particular way, and then keep escalating until they were slaughtering small animals for your delectation.

"I shelve non-fiction by subject and title, if that makes you feel better. People choose that by topic, not book colour."

The steampunk collection ran to a couple of shelves and then eased into general jewellery-making with a scattering of metalworking. It was a good selection, and there were a couple of books I hadn't seen before.

Perhaps I should have been more careful, but I was expecting demons, and although they may leap out at you with bloody claws, you have to enter into a contract to sell your immortal soul before they can really hurt you. You just have to stand your ground, threaten them with lawyers, and they soon shamble off back to where they came from.

But, as I said before, it was gods. And gods are worse than demons—they don't have any rules to govern them, only rules to govern others.

The technical term is an asymmetrical entity.

The informal term isn't something you can share in polite society; fortunately I don't mix in polite society much, so . . . They're complete bastards.

"Let me know if there's something else you're interested in," she said. "And there's ten per cent off a coffee, if you spend more than twenty dollars."

This wasn't going to be hard. There were good books and an expense account, and I could justify any purchases as necessary for my cover.

Time runs differently in a bookshop. You know how it is: you go in for ten minutes just to pick up a book on making soup and then come out an hour later with three books on soup, a new knitting book, and something on eighteenth-century politics. We were going to run a study on the phenomenon, but the Bosses realised this would mean hundreds of operatives spending expenses in bookshops to prove something that we already know is true—and even they aren't that daft.

By the time I made my way back to the front counter, I had amassed a pile of ten books, a coffee discount, and hopefully the good will of the owner.

The sad man had shuffled off somewhere else in the shop, and the woman had taken his place at the register. "I see you've found a good selection," she said, her manner slightly warmer than before.

"Yes, though I could always buy more," I replied.

"Please, do." She smiled.

"Perhaps I'll go back for another look, after a coffee."

I ordered a flat white, nothing too fancy, so that her attention would be on me and not the mechanics of coaxing some flavoured latte out of the machine and then inscribing it with coffee art. Also, you never know whether the symbol written in the froth is going to turn out to be some arcane sigil Summoning beasts. There's very little difference between a clover leaf and the sign for an unpleasant demon with strong views on humanity's place in the universe being at his feet, licking his hooves.

Best take no chances.

I paid up and then moved to a little table by the side of the counter to peruse my new finds. I sipped at the coffee, which was good, and opened the book on famous local hauntings. There wouldn't be much information in it, just gossip and wild stories. We always make sure that no one ever writes about the true stories. That would lead to panic, speculation, and some daft idiot trying to Summon these things on purpose instead of just stumbling into it.

"I used to live near that house," the owner said. "It was always boarded up and scary looking."

"Did you ever see anything?"

She shook her head. "No, not really."

She paused, and I could tell she wanted to say something more but was worried about what I'd think. They always worry that someone is going to think they're mad, apart from the ones that already are.

"I've seen ghosts," I said.

"Oh," she said and pulled out a chair to join me at the table. "Were you scared?"

I'd been scared spitless, which my Bosses said showed the right attitude to this sort of work, because the scared ones last longer. I nodded. I didn't need to say anything more. My expression said it all. Been there, done that, bought the book.

"So, what happened?"

I wasn't going to tell her the truth. No one needs to know the truth about how close we are to disaster. But mostly, I wasn't going to tell her that I'd saved the world by falling over my own feet at a key moment, spitting out my coffee onto the demonic Summoning circle and managing to break the connection before anything nasty could pop into existence and suck out my eyeballs.

"Well," I said, dropping my voice so that only she could hear. She drew a little closer, anxious not to miss anything. "It was in this little bookshop in England, in a village just outside Oxford . . ."

"Oh, I thought your accent was different," she said. "You don't sound like you come from round here."

"It was a typical country village—church, village green with cricket pavilion, local pub, and a small post office that was open three days a week."

And I felt homesick for England, and warm beer, and proper tea, and all the things you take for granted about your own country.

"I'd stopped off for a very large lunch in the pub, which I decided to walk off around the village green. And there, tucked away in the corner near a large oak tree, there was a specialist antiquarian bookshop. It was one of those shops that has a small frontage, but when you get inside, they seem to go on forever. There was an attic, and a cellar, and an extension that ran back a good fifty feet or so. It had the most books packed into the smallest space I have ever seen."

"It sounds lovely," she said.

"It was. There was treasure after treasure in there, and it was organised so that if you picked up a book here, it led you to a book there, and then you had twenty books you hadn't known you wanted and ten books you knew you wanted but had never been able to find before.

"It was like magic."

It wasn't *like* magic. It *was* magic. It was the worst kind of bait to trap the brightest and most interesting of readers. The eye-sucking was just the precursor, to prepare easy access to the brain.

"I'd poked around most of the rooms above ground, so there was only the cellar left. The stairs were steep and uneven, made of stone worn away by the footsteps of hundreds of years, leading to a low-ceilinged room where I could only just stand up straight. My head was just about brushing the ceiling, and there were a lot of cobwebs, so it felt like something was stroking my hair. All the time."

And the spiders had very definitely been looking at me funnily, lurking in their webs, waiting for something nasty to happen. By this time, I was getting very twitchy. Which, as it turns out, was just as well.

"There was a large bookcase on the far wall, loaded with large, dark leather-bound books. They looked interesting and old—the sort of thing that collectors would travel miles to see."

"There's not a lot of call for that sort of thing round here," she said.

Which she should thank the deity of her choice for. I won't say what sort of leather was used in their making, but it wasn't ethically sourced, is all I am saying.

"I headed straight for that bookcase, and it was only as I got closer that I sensed there was something wrong."

They smelled wrong. The scent of aged leather and old pages is a siren lure to a book-lover. New books, with cheaper paper and flimsy bindings, just aren't the same. If I was being dramatic, I'd say that these books smelled of pain and despair, but I can't put it any stronger than just . . . wrong. Very wrong.

"I could feel the hair on my neck standing up."

That does actually happen. It's a bit of a cliché, but it's a cliché because it's true. It's an early warning system for trouble spotting. There's nothing like the uncanny to make your hair try and separate itself from your body, almost as if it's trying to leave before things get too nasty.

"And then there was this figure," I said. "A tall, dark shape with overly long arms and fingernails that seemed . . . excessive."

Claws. It had claws. And if ever a thing loomed, this thing loomed, which was a neat trick in a room where your head was brushing the ceiling. It sort of created its own space around it, warping reality to give it extra space to loom in.

I damn near widdled myself. I'd left the salt in the car, and suddenly the words to the banishing rituals which I could recite backwards in my sleep deserted me.

"I scurried out of there as quick as I could and made it to the stairs just before it did. I don't know what would have happened if I hadn't made it, but it felt horrible. Like the weight of the world was placed on my chest. I could barely breathe."

I ran, which they said later saved my life, and my back still has the claw-marks to show how close it was. We came back later with the psychic equivalent of an AK47: two experienced ritualists, a very large bag of salt, and the full Book of Unsummoning, with all the indexes.

If all else fails, they say, you can always hit the demon round the head with the thing.

"That sounds . . . scary," she said uneasily.

Bingo.

Something really was going on here, because otherwise she would have laughed in my face. But once you've seen something nasty at the back of the bookshop, when someone tells you a tale like that, you can only think of how scared you'd been, and you weren't inclined to laugh at all.

"Have you seen anything like that?" I asked, trying to be casual.

She narrowed her eyes. "Why do you ask?"

"Have you seen anything?" I pushed her harder. It's important to get that psychological admission that there's a problem before you offer a solution.

She shrugged. "Maybe. Depends what you mean by 'anything'?"

"My employers have sent me here to help," I said, leaving things as vague as possible.

"Who do you work for?"

"I can't say."

"You mean, if you told me you'd have to kill me."

"Oh no, not at all," I replied. "If I told you, they'd have to kill me. They really are very keen on secrecy. But you can think of us as the equivalent of psychic pest control."

That's the lie we tell because no one knows who the Bosses are. We just assume that they're on the side of Right and Good because they're responsible for taking out so much that is Wrong and Bad, but they could just be eliminating the competition. My mentor used to say that and laugh, and then one day, he wasn't there any more, and we stopped making that joke.

She digested the psychic pest control claim with calm consideration. "Could you come back tomorrow?" she said. "It's Bert's day off."

I nodded. "Tomorrow, then."

I swallowed the last of my coffee and headed off with my new books to find a motel for the night.

The motel was clean, bright, and overwhelmingly purple. I like purple in general, but this was relentlessly purple. Purple curtains, purple carpets, purple sheets, purple quilt cover, purple towels . . . I made a note to check whether there was some god or demon with a particular taste for purple in case this was a Sign rather than a sign of bad taste.

I chewed on a sandwich—not purple, though the plate was—and settled down on the bed with my Report Book.

My mentor had always taught me to have a plan, to set out the facts I knew and the inferences I had drawn from them. This was to clear my mind, assess in a detached way what assumptions I had made that could get me killed. I was also supposed to colour code them for easy reading by third parties, just in case I did get killed and someone was sent in to finish the job. I could never be bothered with that. Once I was dead, it wasn't my worry. Not unless they Summoned me for a question and answer session, and I'd done all I could to prevent that happening. I wasn't working for them after death—it was bad enough in life.

I flicked through the reports on Occurrences in the neighbourhood.

One case of Marked for Bad Luck attracted my attention. The man had been caught cheating on his wife, by his wife, had fallen down the stairs chasing after her to apologise, and consequently arrived in the hotel lobby with his trousers round his ankles, showing his rather small penis to his work colleagues, who were there for a team bonding session. Being arrested for gross indecency had probably come as something of a relief by then.

That should have made me stop and think—what kind of demon punishes someone for sinning?

A point the Mop-Up team made at length once they'd cleared away the smoking debris, but as I pointed out to them, when was the last time they had to make that kind of assessment? They always know what they're going to face; they don't go in cold like me. The statistics show that demon activity outweighs god activity about ten to one, which says something about the moral standards of humanity at the moment.

Yes, I concede, it's not like a demon to take such an interest in morality. Normally they're busily egging people on to sin more, sin harder, and sin in ever more interesting and athletic ways, but a vengeance demon is shaped by the preoccupations of its Summoner, and if they take a dim view of extramarital activities, then adulterers in a ten-mile radius should be looking to reform sharpish.

I didn't mention the Unofficial Theory held by most operatives that a god is indistinguishable from a vengeance demon in most circumstances because you never know Who might be listening, and the last person to put forward a practical basis for testing the hypothesis got moved to the arse end of nowhere to file reports on suspicious activities in polar bears.

And it's well known that it's the pandas that are the ones to watch out for. After all, it's the pandas who are living in warm enclosures with all the bamboo they can eat, and it's the polar bears who are clinging to ever-shrinking ice caps, wondering where they can get some eye liner.

The Occurrence reports had traced all of the activity back to the bookshop, a trainee had been sent to take some baseline readings, and the hot spot confirmed, I was sent to expel the entity so that adulterers could continue to fornicate in safety.

Plan A is the salt and the Book of Unsummoning. Plan B is hitting the Summoner over the head so they can be contained in a white room somewhere away from books until we can find a Plan C that works.

The first step was to identify the Summoner.

There were two choices—Bert, the sad man who couldn't operate a coffee machine, and the owner who had carefully not given her name. Bert was my favoured target—demons liked the sad and the barely functional, because they were so easily persuaded and had so much roiling desperation and hope for more than they had.

Ms Nemo shouldn't be disregarded, though. She could have invited me back when Bert wasn't around simply because it would be easier to feed me to the demon without witnesses.

It's not that the job makes you suspicious and cynical, it's just that trusting and naïve gets you killed quicker.

I slept well and ate breakfast off the purple plates with a clear mind.

The bookshop opened at ten, and I turned up at half past. No one likes to be harassed first thing in their working morning when they're coming to terms with their to-do list, but I didn't want her to be too settled.

The coffee machine was hot and running, and Ms Nemo was already clutching a cup like a long-lost friend.

"Do you want one?" she asked.

"Yeah, thanks." I prefer tea, to be honest, but the little rituals of hospitality matter. Technically, I was now her guest and sheltering under her protection. You take what edge you can get where you can get it, even if it does involve pumpkin spice latte.

"Take a seat," she said.

I picked the chair nearest the door, forcing her into the one with the back to the rear wall. "I didn't catch your name yesterday."

"Miranda. And yours?"

"You can call me Susan." It's actually my real name, but no one ever believes me. I could tell Miranda didn't, but that just added to my mystique, which is about all you've got when you work for a shadowy organisation with no flashy badge to wave in people's faces.

"So, Susan, tell me a bit more about this psychic pest control."

I leaned back in the chair a little. "Let me tell you about your pest control problem. You noticed it about six months ago. A customer would come in, they would be annoying in some way—too smelly, too mean to buy books, oversharing about their love lives perhaps—and you'd notice after a while that the next time you saw them . . . Well, something bad would have happened to them."

"Maybe," she said. "But that could be coincidence."

"No. It really couldn't. We checked. The correlation between bad luck and buying books here runs well towards the upper tenth percentile. The odds of that happening by accident are astronomical."

"So?" she said slowly.

"So, someone here is Summoning demons. Probably a vengeance demon, though it might be something worse than that. And then they're setting them on your customer base. And that means you, or your employee."

"I'm not summoning anything, unless you can do it accidentally. It's not something you can do by just wishing or hoping, is it?"

"No, it's not. You have to use precise Words of Summoning and Limitation and make the correct sacrifices, or your brains end up leaking out of your ears, and the demons move on to another target."

"So, not me, then."

"I'll have to take your word on that."

Miranda humphed but accepted the implicit warning. "You're expecting me to take you on faith," she said.

"The worst that can happen to you is that I try and charge you a fee for getting rid of a non-existent entity. The worst that can happen to me is being hit over the head with something heavy and being dragged off to become a sacrifice. On the whole, you do have the better side of the deal."

Especially as I work for free—though if you are thinking of calling in our services, it's as well to check your insurance policy to see what exclusions there are. Things can get . . . messy, and insurance companies are very keen to categorise things as Acts of Gods if it helps them get out of paying for your new house.

"So, what's the plan?" she asked.

"I'll have a poke round and see if I can spot anything that is acting as a focus for this activity—a book, a mysterious crystal, something like that—and then it's the usual—salt circle, words of Unsummoning, and Bob should very much be your uncle."

"And if Bob is not my uncle?"

"We run like fuck and call for back-up. It's a hallowed technique. It's even in the Manuals as plan F."

"You have manuals for this stuff?" she said.

"Well you wouldn't want to make it up on the spot, would you?"

There wasn't anything obvious in the shop. No old books reeking of evil. No dark crystals clouded with malevolence. No pools of blood from sacrifices. No scuff marks from dragged bodies.

Miranda found me in the philosophy section and proffered another cup of coffee. "Found anything?"

"Not a thing. Not even a smudge of chalk from a mystical circle. It's puzzling. Usually there is something to give me a clue as to what's going on—even the most careful Summoner leaves some sort of trace."

"Maybe I'm clean."

"Maybe you are." Maybe the trainee had made a mistake, maybe the centre of the Occurrences wasn't the shop. "Except you were worried enough to let me in here, and you don't strike me as a woman who worries easily. So tell me what it was that convinced you that you had a problem."

"Profits increased, for one thing. A lot. And I noticed that if I really didn't like a customer, they didn't come back, which didn't really square with the higher takings. You'd expect profits to fall. It was just wrong."

"And what about your employee? Did he do anything peculiar at about this time?" I asked. If it wasn't the bookshop, maybe it was the employee who was the focus, and that explained the false positive. If he was in the bookshop when he was doing whatever it was that he was doing . . .

"He did seem more cheerful, but I put it down to the cookbook we found."

"A cookbook?"

"I know. It sounds trivial, so I hadn't mentioned it. It was an old handwritten book of recipes handed down in a family. Bert said that it was his great grandmother's or something. Some obscure connection, somewhere along his family tree, so I let him take it home. I didn't think anyone else would want it. It was in bad condition. He was going to read through it, pick out some recipes, and maybe put them up on the bookstore blog. A bit of a human interest story, maybe get the local paper to run a story on it. It would be good publicity."

"And how long ago was this?" I asked.

"About a month. Maybe six weeks."

"Well now, that sounds like it's worth following up. Can you get him to bring it to work tomorrow?"

"Sure."

It would mean another night in Purpleville, but it was preferable to tipping Bert off that I was interested in his cookbook.

I had purple dreams that night.

Bert's shift didn't start till after lunch, so I spent the morning catching up on my paperwork. Saving the world on a weekly basis generates a lot of forms to be filled in, in triplicate, not to mention the expenses claims.

I managed a long lunch, because if you're going to risk your life, you want to do it on a full stomach. I've no intention of passing into the next world hungry.

Bert was back behind the coffee machine when I arrived. He didn't seem to recognise me from two days before; his attention was focussed on coaxing an espresso from its depths.

Miranda was sorting through a box of books on the table, flicking through them for marks, missing pages, and stray bookmarks.

"Ah," she said. "There you are. Bert, can you bring your cookbook over here?"

Bert looked startled. "What d'you want with it?"

"This lady here collects old recipes. She just wants to have a look at it and see if there's anything of interest in there."

"You said I could keep it," he said slowly, looking between us anxiously. "It's mine."

"I only want to look at it," I said, keeping my voice soothing. "I won't touch it, just look at it."

It did the trick, where arguing about whose book it was would only have put his back up. He nodded and disappeared beneath the counter to fetch out the book. I half expected him to pop back up with a pump action shotgun and dropped my hand into my pocket to grasp the Shortest Book of Unsummoning.

If nothing else, I could always throw it at him to distract him before he could take a shot.

"I never said he could keep it," Miranda hissed.

"The book will have twisted his recollection," I replied. "It's part of its protections."

Bert fetched the book to the table and then hovered near it, hands fluttering in the air as if he was stroking the pages. He'd be calling it his precious next, huddling in corners, clutching it to his breast, and singing songs to it. I'd seen it before, and it had taken a team of three to separate the book from the person it owned.

The book was old and smelly, but the good news was that the leather had come from cows.

"Do you have a favourite recipe?" I asked.

He nodded slowly. "There's one I've been using for the coffees."

"Could you show it to me?"

He clutched at the book, relieved to have it back in his possession again, fingers clasping round the spine like claws. "It's this one." He opened the book to the middle and stabbed a finger at a heading. "It's a gingerbread recipe, and I tried the spice mix in a latte. It was nice."

"You didn't give that to the customers did you?" Miranda asked.

"No, it's a special recipe. It's just for me," he replied. "Would you like to try it?"

"I think that would be nice," I said, before Miranda could say anything. "I'm sure Miranda would love to try it."

The look that Miranda shot me was full of doubt, but she followed my lead. "Yes, I would."

Bert smiled widely and, never releasing the book, started to work the machine.

It steamed, it bubbled, it hissed, there was more steam, and then more steam which rose in billowing clouds around the machine, obscuring the counter and Bert in equal measure.

"I don't like this," Miranda said. "It's never done that before."

"I don't like it, either." I put my hand out to hold Miranda back. I didn't want her disappearing into the cloud, in case there was something nasty lurking in there. "No sudden moves. Don't startle him."

I took out the Salt Grenades and handed her one. "These should disperse the miasma. When I throw mine in, you keep hold of yours. If this all goes wrong, you make a run for it, but if that doesn't work, scatter this round you in a circle and stay in there. No matter what."

"But what if something gets you?"

"Then it gets me. You can't do anything about that, other than make sure that you stay safe."

Because if I let a civilian get hurt, they really would bring me back from the dead to give me a bollocking. It's embarrassing enough getting yourself killed in the line of fire without having to justify it all afterwards, and it takes years to learn to manifest yourself strongly enough to fill out the forms.

I cocked my arm back and let the grenade fly with a muttered Invocation.

Nothing happened.

"Was something supposed to happen there?" Miranda asked through clenched teeth. "A big bang, sparkly lights, something?"

I ignored her and got ready for a second throw, amping up the Invocation to a Force Eight. That should be effective against anything less than a full manifestation of Lucifer, and there really weren't enough flies in the vicinity for it to be him. I hoped.

Again, there was a lack of bangs and sparkling lights, but a voice came from the depths: "Who dares to strike my acolyte?"

And it was then that the penny finally dropped.

"That's not a demon; that's a bloody god. I hate gods!" I shouted.

"And this means what?" Miranda said.

"The Book of Unsummoning doesn't sodding work. Salt doesn't sodding work. The only thing that does work is calling on an even greater power, and then you end up playing God Top Trumps, seeing who has the highest scoring card. If you get it wrong, bang!"

The clouds of steam billowed more impressively and Bert's face was revealed, his mouth open in some holy ecstasy. "Would you like a coffee?" he asked, and I shuddered. There was something about the way he said it that was truly horrible.

"Plan F?" Miranda said.

"If only. But I don't see a back door to this room, which puts a crimp into the idea of making a run for it."

I'd been careless. Bert was between us and the door, and there was no escape. He'd looked harmless, but then they always do, right up to the point they rip your head off.

"There's a store room," Miranda said. "And the door locks."

"It's better than nothing," I said, one eye on the advancing Bert. I really, really didn't want to taste that coffee.

Miranda grabbed my arm and jerked me towards the left-hand stacks. I resisted for a moment, stopping to pick up my bag, and then shot off after her. I could see the door in the corner, and we ran towards it at full speed, slammed it shut behind us, and slumped to the floor, breathing like marathon runners at the end of a race.

"That was close," Miranda said.

There's something about situations like that which encourage you to state the obvious. Somehow the fact that you're still alive to make the comment stops you from not making it.

I leaned back against the box of books on the shelf, and banged my head against the bookcase. "Fuck. Fuck. Fuckity fuck."

A warm orange glow forced its way through the gaps round the door frame, bright as a hundred suns. Whatever was out there was now fully manifesting.

"I hope you've got something in there that will help." Miranda nodded at my bag. "What was so important you had to go back for it?"

"My mobile." It's not big and it's not clever, but if you want to call back-up, a mobile phone is the best tool for the job. Well, it would be if it worked. "No signal. Not sure if it's the room or the god, but there's noth-ing."

"So we're essentially trapped in a small room with no exit, no way of calling for help, and with something peculiar out there that you say is a god," Miranda said. "I thought gods were supposed to be good."

"One word. Tezcatlipoca."

"Oh."

That's the good thing about bookshop owners. They tend to read their own wares and have a bit more about them than your average person. You don't have to fill in the blanks.

"Would you say that Bert was a good man?" I asked. "Kind and forgiving or judgemental and harsh?"

"I've never explored his moral landscape," Miranda said drily. "Why, does it matter?"

"It might give me a clue as to what sort of god is out there. At least we know that it doesn't have a taste for human hearts, or there'd already be a higher body count."

Miranda sighed. "Can it get through the door? Don't we have to invite it in or something?"

"You're thinking of vampires there. It can get through the door if it wanted to. It's just being polite at the moment. It's waiting for an invitation into your heart, but if one isn't forthcoming, then you become a sinner and it'll be a brisk round of smiting. And no locked door is going to get in the way of that."

I scanned the room. There was no window provided for convenient es-cape purposes. There was no access to the roof space, so there would be no crawling to freedom. All there that could be seen was books. Books on shelves, books in boxes, books on the floors: books.

"What sort of books are these?" I asked.

"The ones that don't sell but I can get a bit of money on from internet sales—the heavyweight non-fiction, science, philosophy, and some sex books."

"The sex books don't sell?"

"By mail, in plain brown paper, they sell like hotcakes. Not so much over the counter. No one likes to be judged."

I blinked. That started an idea running. It wasn't much, but it was better than sitting in a trap waiting for conversion or smiting. "I'll need to borrow some books, and when I say borrow, I'm not sure what condition they'll be in afterwards."

She shrugged. "Help yourself."

"Have you got any twine or tape or something to hold some books together?" I opened the first box of books and skimmed the titles. Nietzsche. Perfect. Not Aquinas, he wouldn't do. But Schopenhauer . . . Plato. Socrates the godless. Anyone who doubted in gods or their utility. A second box produced some evolutionary biology; another gave me some atheist authors.

"Miranda," came a soft voice from the other side of the door. "Why are you hiding from me? I mean you no harm."

I piled them up neatly, mixing old and new authors, a bit of science, a lot of doubt, and just a soupçon of sex manual in case it was an easily offended god, and all the while that soft, kind voice was pleading with us to open the door, to open our hearts and just worship and adore.

Miranda had a roll of heavy duty tape on a dispenser, which was usually used for making up boxes. It was strong, brown, and held the bundles together securely. I sat back on my heels and surveyed my work with some pride.

I had created Logic Bombs, and if this worked, it might even make it into the Manuals as a new entry. Of course, we had to live through it first.

"On three," I said. "You open the door, and I'll start throwing."

Miranda placed her hand on the key as I grasped the first bundle. "One, two, three . . ."

She turned the key, the door opened, and I hefted the bundle through. "Nietzsche says that God is dead!" I shouted. "God is dead!"

The voice stopped. There was an awful silence, and it wasn't the silence of a dead god but one that was seriously pissed off. Not one for philosophy then.

I threw out another bundle. "You always were a god of the gaps, the bits in between the explanations. Well, science has filled in all the gaps. There's no more room for you."

The bundles began to smoke.

"Oh, am I supposed to be impressed? That's nothing more than a statistical aberration. Quantum mechanics says that this sort of thing should happen all the time. Is that the best you've got? You can't even pull down a decent stroke of lightning these days, can you?"

The books flared up, bright flames licking along the spines, and a thousand wailing voices chanted . . . something. I'm not a linguist, and I didn't recognise the language, but I recognised the intent. Faith against logic, prayer against reason.

"You can burn the books, but you can't burn the ideas," I shouted over the cacophony.

The sun comes up every day, whether you believe in it or not. The rains come every year, whether you sacrifice a goat or not. The crops grow, whether you make a corn dolly to trap the spirit of the earth or not, and sooner or later humanity notices that a good pile of horse manure does more to keep things green and growing than a prayer.

"You've nothing to offer us any more."

And for good measure, I threw out one of those science books that everyone buys but no one reads beyond the introduction because it's too hard but which nevertheless enter the collective understanding of the world. The ones that tell tales of Schrödinger's cat, and wave particle duality, black holes, and dark matter, and which are stranger than turning water into wine, parting the red sea, or making the rains come.

There was a rumble of thunder, the sharp taste of electricity in the air, and then a large crash of lightning flaring down from the ceiling to hit the carpet just by the biggest pile of books.

"Missed!" I screamed. "You can't hit a barn door at thirty paces."

Miranda laughed, more out of nerves than humour. "Are you trying to make it mad?"

Another flash of lightning hit the door post, throwing me back into the room. "I think it's fading—do you think the voices sound a little quieter?"

"I think so," Miranda replied. "It's working. Whatever it is you're doing, it's working."

"Exhausting the godhead's reservoir of powers," I said, picking myself up and arming myself with another logic bomb.

Bert wasn't visible. I hoped he'd had the sense to duck behind the meagre shelter of the counter.

"Missed again!" I called out to the room. "Once you could have levelled cities, and now you can't even burn down a bookshop."

"Excuse me, that's my bookstore out there!" Miranda said. "I'd like it back in one piece, thank you very much."

I could feel the power building, balls of light forming in the high roof, and then the voices went silent. There was a flash, and then another, and then ten or twenty more in quick succession. Fingers of energy forced their way through the air, trying to find me, touch me, and smite me.

"I've got rubber soles on!" I shouted.

They all missed, earthing harmlessly in the metal bookshelves, driven by science to find the highest points in the room.

"I win," I said softly, offering up one last provocation.

Nothing.

Gods aren't built for cunning, or this one would have pretended to be worn out and saved one last thunderbolt for me. Then he'd have found out the lie about rubber soles.

Smoke hovered in the room, an indoor fog smelling of charred paper and futile anger.

"Are we safe now?" Miranda asked, moving closer to the door.

"I think so."

"Safe from gods, maybe, but those books are still burning," she replied grimly. "So I'd better call the fire department, unless there's something in that bag of yours to deal with flames."

"Only the flames of hell," I replied. "Have you got any fire extinguishers?"

She had, but they were little more than a pool of melted metal.

"We'd better get out," I said.

"Not without Bert."

Bert was behind the counter, clutching his book, still. Miranda took one arm and I the other, and we frogmarched him to the front door and out into the fresh air.

Miranda stood outside the ruin of her smoke-filled bookshop with a resigned expression. "If I'd have known this was going to happen, I would never have let you in. My insurance had better cover this."

"We'll pay for any damage," I said. "And the Mop-Up crew will be here in a bit. You won't have to lift a finger to put things right."

People's gratitude for saving the world never lasted long, but there were few hard feelings that couldn't be helped by the liberal application of money.

"Maybe I'll go into internet sales," she said. "It might be less risky."

I decided not to tell her about the demons haunting the internet. I mean, what were the odds?

Fixation

Lin Thornhill

Mom was right, Yoko thought, winding through the boisterous crowd on East First Street. It wasn't Los Angeles' oppressive summer heat her mother had warned her about, but the size of the crowd gathering for the annual Nisei Week parade in Little Tokyo.

"Daddy!"

The shriek preceded a small child hurtling into Yoko's legs. She stumbled, instinctively reaching out to find her balance, and knocked against the back of a folding chair. "*Gomen nasai!*" She gasped, apologizing to the elderly Japanese woman who was practically launched from her curbside position.

A pinched-mouth glare met Yoko's apology.

Then, preventing a scathing set down, a casually dressed businessman offered the elderly woman a napkin-wrapped pastry. When she snatched it from his fingers, the man chuckled and said, "It's not her fault, Mom."

Yoko paused as the distinctive fragrance of a childhood treat tickled her senses. "Imagawayaki?" she asked.

The man grinned. "Yep. You can get them in the square. It's a little café on the left side facing the Torii gate. You'll see them being made in the window." He pulled another of the sweet pastries from a foil-lined bag and took a hearty bite. "Oh, yeah! I only get these once a year. They're the best."

Yoko smiled before weaving through the compacting crowd, away from the man and his scowling mother. It no longer mattered that it was close to a hundred degrees in the shade; Yoko was determined to find that vendor. Indulging in the treat would be like a taste of home. She was a little homesick for the wide open spaces of her family's orchard.

"The city has changed a great deal since the first time I was there," her mother had said.

As often as Yoko had explored her new home with both mundane and hereditary senses, after a month she was still unfamiliar with much of the sprawling metropolis. She didn't yet have that instinctive feel for the layout of the city as she did her hometown. Thus, instead of finding the heart of Little Tokyo and the mouth-watering aroma of red bean paste and pancake, she discovered the cultural pearl was surrounded by a suffocating mass of ill-kempt inner city muscle.

Cutting through an oncoming wave of people, Yoko took the less traveled path, turning right rather than left. Within a block, she realized she had gone the wrong way. She turned at the next corner into an alley connecting the two main streets. After five steps, she realized she had made a mistake.

"'Sup, pretty mama?" A man stepped away from a corner of the adjacent building.

Every instinct screaming *danger*, Yoko whirled and sprinted back the way she had come.

The man was fast; a meaty hand grabbed for her arm.

Yoko *shifted* enough to evade his grasp, but then he punched her in the back. She staggered, and he shoved her hard.

Falling forward at the juncture between main street and alley, she landed on her hands and knees. Her messenger bag went flying, but the strap remained looped around her forearm. Her attacker yanked at the bag, sending Yoko sprawling face first on the gritty asphalt.

"FREEZE!" The shout acted as a spur to her assailant; he dashed around the corner, spitting profanities at his pursuer, the strap of Yoko's bag slapping at his thighs while he ran. Pounding steps on the pavement passed Yoko at a dead run. The only identifying markers of the chaser were his clean masculine scent—both savory and tropical—and a brief glimpse of the black boots and navy blue uniform of a police officer.

Her immediate need to fight or flee resolved, Yoko remained on the ground for a moment. All her concentration focused on her hands. Anxiety spiked through her, and she panted through her mouth, staring at hands that had begun to transform. In place of day-glo pink fingernails, short black claws had sprouted from her fingertips.

Adrenaline lent her power, and she forced her body back under her control.

Her worst fear was discovery.

Pay more attention to your surroundings! This isn't home.

Shaking her head at her own stupidity, Yoko rose to her feet, brushing hair out of her face before straightening her skirt and assessing the damage. Her legs were grimy, her knees skinned, the left one bloody. Both palms were scraped raw, small bits of gravel embedded beneath the skin in one or two spots. Even worse, her wrist hurt. A lot.

But her fingernails were once more bright pink.

With a heavy, relieved sigh, she removed her diaphanous crimson scarf and held it against her knee, stanching the blood.

The worst damage was the loss of the messenger bag. It held her wallet, her car keys, her phone, her mini iPad—all the necessities of her life. She sniffed back tears. Why hadn't she moved faster, or—

"Are you all right, Miss?"

"Mostly," Yoko replied. The officer's approach had been heralded by his scent, now overlaid with the odor of fresh sweat. Inhaling, she imprinted him in her memory as she finished wrapping the scarf around her knee, tucking the ends to hold it in place. Then she straightened and turned one hand to reveal its gravel-embedded palm. She bit her lip to keep herself from crying.

Then she raised her head to look at him.

Yoko was momentarily incapable of speaking, or taking a breath, or blinking her eyes. She felt dizzy, disoriented.

Standing before her was a living, breathing, physical embodiment of an archetypal hero. Yoko's heart rate escalated, and her eyes never left his.

As expected, he was an LAPD officer. Yoko only noticed his *café au lait* skin tone because it contrasted so vibrantly with the sage green of his eyes. "Let me help you to the first aid station," he said, holding out her messenger bag.

"Thank you," she stammered, "but I heal quickly, and I can clean up at home." She blinked. "Oh! My bag! Thank you so much."

When he stepped closer, her more feral instincts flared to life, that sa-vory tropical scent filling her nostrils. Her heart pounded.

With the knuckle of his bent index finger, he gently raised Yoko's chin, examining her wound. "You're bleeding, Miss. I'd like someone to take a look at your injuries while I get the details of what happened here."

Suddenly, urgently, Yoko wanted to lean into his touch. Only the life-long, mom-ingrained warnings against discovery helped her retain any semblance of appropriate behavior.

Control, Yoko! He's not that hot. Well, yeah, he is, but . . .

"I'll have to insist," he said. "Besides, if you don't come with me, then you can't file a complaint."

She took a deep breath, calming her wildly beating heart, and gazed in the direction her assailant had disappeared. She had marked *his* scent now—distinctive overtones of bad food, artificial patchouli oil, and recreational drugs—and would be able to track him, even in this city with its millions of residents. Reflexive anger quashed her unexpected, overwhelming attrac-tion to the police officer. "I have no idea who he was," she protested. "How can I file a complaint if I can't give you a name?" *Yet,* she added silently.

"It's important to have the complaint on file—even if he's listed as John Doe." The officer flushed beneath his tan. "That guy was fast; he threw your bag at me, and I tripped over it. I hope nothing's broken."

Quelling her fury, her need to track and punish her assailant, Yoko shrugged. "It's just stuff. At least I won't have to replace credit cards or my license."

"I'm sorry I didn't catch him."

She smiled ruefully and glanced at her scarf-wrapped knee. "I'm sorry I didn't wear jeans."

He chuckled, and a quiver of excitement raced along Yoko's spine in re-sponse. Unsettled by her primal reaction, she shifted the messenger bag to her right hand and hissed in pain, dropping it.

"Miss?" He stepped closer, obviously concerned.

"Johnson," she replied, cradling her right arm against her chest. She glanced at him through her lashes.

He gestured. "This way, Miss Johnson. The first aid station shares a tent with the LAPD's community liaison desk. You can get medical treatment and file a report simultaneously."

"I appreciate your help, Officer—" She craned her head to read his name tag. "—Santoro."

"It's only a couple of blocks from here," he said, scooping the fallen messenger bag from the pavement at Yoko's feet and guiding her from the alley toward a street bisecting the outskirts of Little Tokyo.

By the time they arrived at the square, white awning with its distinctive red cross situated on the corner of Traction Street, Yoko's wrist was throbbing in time with her heartbeat. The pain kept her attention on her injuries rather than on her escort's lean physique and strong hands.

Santoro escorted her past a patient being treated by a nurse and settled her on a gurney. He deposited her messenger bag at her side and left her in the care of an EMT.

The EMT was an older man with tousled sandy hair, sprinkled with more gray than sand, and a day's growth of beard. Yoko mentally dubbed him 'Sandy' as he gently unwound the scarf around her knee before poking, prodding, and otherwise examining all of her wounds. He retrieved a chemical icepack, popped the activating element, and carefully wrapped it around her injured wrist. "We'll let that take effect before I examine that wrist," he told her. Next, he swabbed her chin with antiseptic, ignoring her hiss and narrow-eyed glare. "You've got to keep these things clean, Missy. Infection isn't pleasant."

Yoko welcomed the distraction from the young police officer, whose location she could pinpoint even behind her. Her senses seemed acutely attuned to his presence to such a degree that she identified the savory and tropical overtones in his scent as juniper and coconut oil. She was in danger of his becoming too much of a distraction, however welcome.

Instead, she focused on thoughts of her assailant. It was her duty to find him and teach him the lesson he so richly deserved.

Officer Santoro returned with clipboard, forms, and pen in hand. "I've written up your version of the events in the alley. I know your name, but I'll need contact information and ID."

She glanced at her dirty, bloody hands. "My wallet's in my bag. You can take it out."

Instinctively, she turned her head to watch Santoro, but Sandy held her chin in place. "The better you hold still," he said, "the quicker I'll be finished."

"'Kay," she replied, trying not to move her mouth.

"You're from Oroville?" Santoro asked, holding her wallet and reading her driver's license.

Glancing at him from the corner of her eyes, she said, "Yes."

He stepped closer. "Here for a visit?"

Yoko looked at the report Santoro was filling out and read his first name. Matteo. She breathed deeply, marking his scent. "I moved here right after the Fourth of July."

"Great—uh—I mean, you haven't been here long."

"I have a job in the industry." She glanced at him, then quickly away.

"Actress?" he asked.

"Everyone's a wannabe," Sandy muttered, reaching for antibiotic ointment and gauze.

"I design prosthetics," Yoko replied, "and specialized make-up effects."

"Awesome!" Santoro grinned, a dimple showing in one cheek. "My aunt's in the costume department at Warner's, and my cousin's a second AD, but no one else in my family's in the business."

"I'm the only one in my family. There's a lot of room for innovation in my field."

"Where do you work?" he asked, then blushed. "I don't need that information for the report, Miss Johnson. I'm just curious."

Yoko smiled, despite the fact it hurt her chin. "Creature Features in Burbank. I had the job before I moved. There's no way my dad would've let me leave home otherwise, even though my mom was totally behind it."

"My dad's like that with my sisters." Santoro set the forgotten clipboard on the end of the gurney.

"Really? How many sisters? I've only got a brother."

"Two sisters and three brothers. There's a half dozen of us, all twins."

"Wow." She cocked her head; Matteo Santoro had suddenly become more interesting. Three sets of twins in one family. Very lucky.

"And I'm the oldest."

"Me too," she said. "My brother, Rick, hates that."

"Rick? My youngest brother's named Ric. Ricardo, really."

Had Yoko been in her natural form, her furry little ears would have pricked forward with interest. "How old is he? My Rick's nineteen. And he's my best friend."

"Your best friend? Awesome. Luca's mine, but we're twins. I think it's expected. Ric and his twin, Santino, are twenty."

"So pretty much the same age. What about your sisters?"

Sandy cleared his throat. "If you've finished exchanging life stories, I'd like to clean your hands and take a closer look at that wrist."

Embarrassed, Santoro said, "Excuse me," and picked up the clipboard to complete the incident report.

Sandy examined Yoko's wrist. "I doubt it's anything more than a sprain, considering how little swelling there is." The tone of his voice was clinical, and he said, "If that changes, see your doctor. Let me deal with this gravel before wrapping it up." Using a pair of needle-thin tweezers from the sterile tray, Sandy attended to the grit embedded beneath the top layer of skin on her palms and knees.

Fascinated but repulsed by the procedure, Yoko turned toward Santoro. He looked up at her at that very moment; her breath caught in her throat, and her pulse raced. *Wow! He's beautiful.*

He replaced her wallet in her messenger bag. "Aside from little brothers named Ric, we have something else in common."

"We do?"

"Yeah, we've got the same birthday."

"Really?"

"I'm four years older. Before today, Luca was the only other person I knew born that day." Santoro returned his attention to the report, signing it with a flourish. "It's lucky I saw what happened."

Yoko agreed while Sandy applied sterile pads and gauze to her hands and retrieved a compression bandage for her wrist.

"I need to get back on patrol—" Santoro presented the incident report. "—so if you'll read and sign this, I can file it."

The form was filled with neat, block printing in blue ink. "What about finding this guy?" she asked.

His expression turned solemn. "This is a big city, Miss Johnson—"

"Yoko," she said, interrupting him.

"Excuse me?"

"We have the same birthday AND both have little brothers named Rick. I think it entitles you to call me Yoko." *Quit flirting with him!* She mentally screamed at herself.

Santoro's dimple flashed in his cheek. "Well, Yoko, this *is* a big city, and these sorts of incidents occur all too frequently. The perpetrators are rarely caught."

Sandy finished applying bandages to her knees. "You should go home and put ice on your knees and wrist." He helped her off the gurney.

"Thanks, but what about the parade?"

"It's up to you, Miss Johnson, but I would be very surprised if you feel up to it."

"Now that you mention it, maybe I will go home." She was shocked at how much she still hurt. While Santoro held the clipboard, Yoko read and signed the incident report, before collecting her belongings.

As she prepared to leave the shelter of the aid station, Santoro stopped her. "Miss—uh—Yoko—"

Heart suddenly hammering in her chest, Yoko answered, "Yes?"

He held out a business card. She held it gingerly in her bandaged hand.

"North Hollywood Division?"

"During big events like these, officers are pulled in from all over the city. It was my turn." As he replied, they stepped into the unrelieved, hot August day and walked toward the crowds on First Street.

"Lucky for me."

He cleared his throat. "Yes. Well—anyway, you can call me if you have any questions, or if you see that guy again, or—"

Instinct overrode caution, and words spilled from her mouth. "If I'm feeling homesick and want to talk to someone who knows about little brothers named Rick?"

He grinned. "Exactly."

She put the card in the outer pocket of her bag. "Thank you for everything."

As he turned to walk away, she leaned closer to him, arching her back and tilting her head to look him in the eyes. *What do you think you're doing?* Disconcerted by her own boldness, she nonetheless couldn't contain a satisfied smile when she heard his breathing pattern change. She said, "I'd like to show you how grateful I am."

"No! I mean, that's not necessary." Santoro stumbled over his tongue. "It's not that you're not cute . . . I mean, you're really cute, but . . . uh, I'm on duty. Uh—you don't have to do anything like that!"

"Wait! I didn't mean it like *that*," she protested, blushing hotly. She didn't really know what she had meant. "I—I just wanted you to know how much your help meant to me."

"Oh! That's good. Uh, you're welcome." Santoro sucked in a deep breath and took one distancing step.

Yoko was mortified. "I should be going. Nice meeting you."

"It was my pleasure."

She waved one gauze-wrapped hand, turned, and set off on foot toward the parking lot to retrieve her car. She refused to look back. Her thoughts and emotions were a jumble, but she paid closer attention to where she walked and to the people she dodged.

Just south of the Miyako Hotel, Yoko passed a discreet stone obelisk at the corner of an alleyway. Its carved inscription read *Koyasan Buddhist Temple*. A frisson of preternatural awareness rippled along her nerve endings, and the back of her neck prickled. There was no command, but certainly an invitation tickled in her mind.

Wary, Yoko turned into the alley. The further she walked, the fainter the sounds of traffic, both vehicular and foot. The alley was clean, and while narrow, it opened onto a courtyard. The temple itself was a wide, white building whose entrance was a set of wooden doors sporting artfully carved flower emblems.

Scanning the courtyard, she paused in her assessment, recognizing the granite fox statues on either side of the steps. Kitsune, messengers of the goddess, Inari Okami. Yoko smiled and crossed the courtyard to stand in front of one of the fox statues.

"*Konichi-wa*, little brother," she said and bowed deeply before reaching into her messenger bag to retrieve her red scarf and a cellophane package of seaweed-wrapped rice crackers. Wrapping the length of diaphanous chiffon around her hands, Yoko flexed and tore the red cloth in two. She ignored the sharp sting in her injured palms and wrist.

One-half of the scarf she tied around the neck of the first stone fox be-fore opening the package of rice crackers and scattering a handful onto the ground at the statue's feet. After a moment's communion and reflection, Yoko moved to the second kitsune and made her second offering as rever-ently as the first.

A subliminal whisper emanated from within the temple. The hair on Yoko's arms and the back of her neck stood on end. She shuddered, then winced as a needle sharp directive pierced her brain. Yoko accepted the summons as she had the initial invitation at the head of the alley.

Despite never having stepped into this temple before, Yoko was strong-ly reminded of the Buddhist Temple in Oroville, with its distinctive the-matic wood elements and serene atmosphere. As she ascended the temple's five steps, the right-hand door swung open.

No one greeted her; indeed, no one was there at all.

Apprehensive, Yoko hesitated before crossing the threshold. The ache in her head peaked in an undeniable command, and despite her unease, she stepped through the open door. Once inside, she followed the subliminal guidance; her footsteps made no sound.

In addition to the flower symbol from the temple's front door, Yoko noted a more familiar emblem hanging on the wall: the three-fold comma-shaped symbol known as the *mitsudomoe*. It represented different things in the Shinto and Buddhist spiritual paths. In one, it was man, earth, sky; in the other, it was the cycle of life. She remembered her mother's early in-struction in her sometimes broken English. "The goddess cares not what religions worship—only that they do."

The altar was glorious, framed with gilt and crimson cloth. And yet, it was nothing compared to the magnificence of the deity standing on the lower level of the two-tiered dais.

Inari Okami's radiance was so profound it permeated every niche, every darkened corner of the expansive room in which she stood.

Yoko's breath caught in her throat, and she abruptly halted between the rows of padded folding chairs. Immediately dropping to the floor in a full, formal bow, she ignored the bright flare of agony from her injured knee.

Wordlessly, the goddess beckoned her young protégée.

Filled with trepidation and exaltation, Yoko stumbled to her feet.

Hissing as her injured knee straightened, she stepped forward, nonetheless. None in their right mind would ignore such a demand.

Reverently, Yoko bowed her head and approached her goddess.

"Yoko-chan." Inari Okami's melodious voice was soft and gentle. In this manifestation, the goddess appeared in her female form. Her slender figure was clad in a floor-length black silk *yukata* overlaid by an ornate outer robe with exceptionally wide sleeves whose gilt-edged hem circled the immortal being in a wash of color. Unfettered, lustrous black hair hung to her hips, and her features were obscured by a traditional fox mask of gold.

"Inari-sama," Yoko whispered reverently, "you grace me with your presence."

The goddess laughed, the room filling with the sound of her delight. "Look at me, child."

Yoko raised her head, meeting the fathomless onyx eyes through the mask the goddess wore.

Gracefully, a slender hand removed the gold mask, and to Yoko's astonishment, she found herself staring at . . . herself.

She smiled. Or the goddess smiled. Or they both smiled. Yoko was uncertain. Her mother had never mentioned anything like this when speaking of the deity.

Inari Okami's amusement emanated from her like the joy of a spring day during cherry blossom season. "Did you think I would never come?"

Yoko couldn't form a coherent answer, but it seemed one wasn't necessary.

"My kitsune are precious to me, young one," she said in Yoko's voice. "Rare and precious. And today has been a momentous one for you."

Yoko simply nodded.

"As you embark upon your journey, you have a choice to make. There will be many, but you are poised to take the first step. I have come to see what you have learned."

As if she were at home in her parents' kitchen, repeating after her mother, Yoko blurted out, "Test, judge, punish, reward."

The goddess laughed once more. "Yes, young one." A gentle finger touched Yoko's wrist. The compression bandage unraveled and disintegrated as it fell to the floor. Eyes widening in shocked surprise, Yoko bent her wrist to and fro. There was no pain. She opened her mouth to offer thanks, but the goddess spoke. "You might have considered judgment and punishment after your encounter, but it is not those lessons we are *testing* today."

Yoko quickly looked around the large room.

"I assure you, Yoko-chan, we are alone."

More than a little disconcerted, Yoko managed a nod before gathering her concentration for a *shift*. Teeth first, then ears and nose. Her thick black hair—identical to the goddess's—shortened, altered, transformed. Next, with one great shudder, Yoko stood on four dainty white paws. She craned her neck to look at the goddess and sat on her haunches.

Inari Okami traced the edge of Yoko's left ear tuft before circling the small fox. As she walked, the goddess's gilt-edged kimono swept across the floor in a soft hush of sound. "A black-tipped tail, young one?"

Yoko flipped her tail, curling it around her feet. Her eyes followed the goddess's movements.

"I like individuality. It's refreshing." She halted in front of Yoko once more. "Now, the old man."

Swallowing hard, Yoko stood on all fours and shook her head; the fur on the ruff of her neck undulated from side to side. She had never managed the old man successfully. However, as taught, she began teeth first then ears, elongating the lobes and adding wrinkles. Within moments, Yoko was struggling with the masculine bits and the baldness.

Her shoulders slumped.

She had failed.

She wanted to cry.

Inari Okami touched Yoko's head. Instantly, Yoko shifted fully into the stooped, arthritic form of a bald old man.

Delighted, awed, Yoko said, "*Domo arigato, Inari-sama.*"

The goddess no longer looked like Yoko. She, too, had taken the form of an old man. Yoko assumed it was a mirror image of her own transformation.

When Inari Okami spoke, it was in a deep, gruff tone. "It is experience that guides the change, little one. Live longer, and it will come easily to you."

The old man raised his arm, guiding his hand in an outline of Yoko's masculine form as an arc of dazzling golden light leapt from his palm to her chest.

Yoko gasped.

The deity paused, his fingers spread wide.

"Fixation? Some find it a blessing, others a curse." The old man spoke in that rough voice. "You are young; some might say too young. Fixation can serve a purpose, or I can rid you of its yoke." The hand gestured, fingers clenching into a fist as if pulling on a thread. Once more, an arc of light passed between the goddess and her kitsune. Then, with a sub-audible *pop,* the arc exploded in a scintillating array of ethereal sparks.

Yoko's thoughts were a chaotic jumble. The subtle remnants of Matteo Santoro's savory tropical scent dissipated, and she was unable to recall what he looked like. She shivered, suddenly cold, bereft, yearning.

Inari Okami studied her disciple.

Yoko studied her own gnarled and wrinkled old man's hands.

'Who is your mother, child?"

"My mother?"

The goddess narrowed her eyes, nodded her shiny bald head, and said, "Ah. Mitsuko-san. Mitsuko Yamada."

"Johnson." Yoko added, then quailed under the sharp look from the old man's ageless, depthless eyes.

Like water pouring from one glass to another, the goddess shifted to her female form, and Yoko's body shifted along with her. It was the most seamless transition Yoko had ever experienced.

"You have a brother, *hai?*"

"Yes," Yoko replied.

An enigmatic smile graced Inari Okami's lovely features. "*Hai, hai. Kitsune* breed true. It is a sign of superiority." The goddess pulled her golden mask from the loop of her kimono sleeve and placed it atop Yoko's head; it was far heavier than expected, and Yoko shifted her feet slightly, maintaining the mask's balance.

Don't drop it. Whatever you do, don't drop it.

The goddess circled Yoko, cocking her head from left to right.

Yoko held her breath.

"Soon you will choose your path." Inari Okami touched the golden mask.

A sensation unlike anything Yoko had ever felt cascaded from the crown of her head to the soles of her feet, coating every molecule of her being. She was no longer cold, no longer bereft.

Juniper and coconut tickled her senses.

"There. Much better suited for my purposes." The goddess smiled and retrieved her mask. "Learn well, my little ambassador. Remember, every test you administer, every judgment you render is in my name. Choose your path well."

The goddess lightly touched Yoko's cheek, and when Yoko blinked, she was alone in the temple. Later, she would be surprised that she had remembered to bow to the altar before making her way from the temple and into the bright sunlight.

At the bottom of the temple steps, she noticed the norimaki crackers she had scattered at the statues' feet were gone. She took a shaky breath.

A marching band resounded in the near distance, and despite her intentions that morning, Yoko never considered going to watch the parade. Too much had happened in too short a time. The day had been filled with surprises, some pleasant, others disagreeable.

She wanted to laugh and scream and cry.

When she was younger, emotional turmoil had always triggered a shapeshift. Now, Yoko knew she had more control than before.

She resumed her trek toward her car. She would go home to her one-bedroom apartment in Burbank where there was air conditioning, a comfortable couch, and frozen pizza to nuke in the microwave. It wouldn't be as satisfying as fresh imagawayaki, but there was something to be said for the taste of melted cheese and pizza sauce.

Of course, her phone rang the second she opened the door to her apartment.

"Yoko-chan, do you need me to come?"

When they were kids, Yoko and Rick mocked their mother's instincts, but they had learned to respect them. After the day she had experienced, Yoko didn't find her mother's timing quite so remarkable.

"I'll be all right. It's not even as bad as when I fell out of the apple tree."

"Yoko."

Carefully lowering herself onto her couch, Yoko said, "I was mugged, and a police officer got my bag back."

Mitsuko's voice sharpened. "A man?"

"The mugger? Yes." There was silence, and Yoko huffed in irritation. "Yes, Mom. A man. Most police officers are men."

"Don't speak to me in that tone."

Yoko made a face.

"I saw that, young lady."

"We're on the phone. You couldn't have seen that!"

"A mother knows her children." There was a pause. "There's more, isn't there?"

Yoko sat upright. "More?"

"About the young man."

Yoko wondered if she could change the subject. It was a futile hope, so she said, "It may not be what you think."

"What's his name?"

"Do you really need to know? You'll probably never meet him."

"Yoko Madeleine Johnson!"

"Mom!"

"His name, Yoko."

"Fine. It's Matteo Santoro, and he has a twin." Yoko practically bit her tongue for offering that piece of information.

"How very auspicious."

Silence filled the connection for a few moments, but it was relatively companionable. Then, rather abruptly, Mitsuko spoke. "That's not all, is it?"

After a moment, Yoko's mother prompted a reply.

"I don't think I should talk about it," Yoko said softly, perhaps even a little angrily. "It's a kitsune thing."

The sound of a sharp inhalation filled the connection before a whispered response. "Say nothing, my daughter."

"I really didn't plan on it."

Then, because her mother couldn't keep her wet black nose out of other people's business, Mitsuko asked, "And what did you learn?"

Yoko almost growled into the phone. "Mom."

"*Gomen nasai.* Sorry, sorry. I know. But—"

"Test, judge, punish, reward. Everything you've taught us since we were babies. You know, choose the right path."

Again that sharp inhalation. "The light path?"

"The right path. The right path for me."

"*Ah so.*"

"*Hai.*"

Shortly thereafter, the conversation ended, and overwhelmed by the emotional and traumatic upheaval of the day, Yoko was asleep by eight o'clock. By midnight, she had lost control of her human form. Her tail grew, elongated and fluffed out, its furry jet-black tip peeking out from under the covers to tickle her tender chin.

The next few days were extremely uncomfortable for Yoko as her knees scabbed, cracked, and bled, then re-scabbed. The wounds on her chin drew tremendous attention, dismay, and commiseration from her co-workers. Her boss sent her home early on Monday. She went, but not to rest.

Instead, Yoko drove through In-n-Out, ate her favorite fast food burger, speculated about the concepts of fixation and punishment, and turned her RAV4 toward Little Tokyo.

Los Angeles' highways were a snarl of converging, intersecting freeways congested by a metaphorical anthill comprising thousands upon thousands of busily scurrying residents. Within an hour, Yoko was in El Monte, some fifteen miles past her destination. Sighing heavily, she fished the GPS out of the emergency preparedness kit her dad had so carefully packed for her and plugged in her Burbank address. It was almost one in the morning before she crawled into bed.

Tuesday, she found her way back to Little Tokyo.

The area was seedier at night without the crowds and street vendors. She risked altering her ears and nose to take advantage of her heightened fox senses, hunkering down in the driver's seat to avoid undue attention. Regrettably, there were only faint, old scent trails of her assailant, herself, and her savior. Nothing recent enough for a successful hunt, but she would return.

Yoko drove on autopilot, mulling over her reaction to Matteo Santoro.

She pretended excitement didn't skitter along her spine at the thought of him, or worse, that she was aroused by any faint trace of his scent. Being kitsune, she had never engaged in the sometimes wanton sexual behavior of her age mates. Until her control was absolute, she could not risk any potential revelation the emotional high of sexual release with a partner could mean.

Without conscious volition, Yoko had steered her way past the North Hollywood police station with her windows open and her nostrils flaring.

Get a grip!

The phone rang while she ate a late dinner. It was her brother Rick. He teased her about her eating habits, indulging in all the foods their mother wouldn't keep in the house. She rebutted by telling him she was eating salad and broiled chicken, thank you very much. Rick laughed and asked about her work. She asked about his classes. He told her about the babe in Agriculture 101.

Finally, there was a long pause before Rick asked, "You want me to help you hunt this guy down?"

Yoko blinked rapidly against the sudden prickle of tears. "No. I'll be fine."

He wasn't easily diverted. "Yoko, I mean it. If you need me, I'll hop onto I-5 and be there in—oh—eight or nine hours!"

"Thanks. I'm really okay." Her voice reflected all the emotions brought on by the first physical attack she had ever encountered. "It was just a shock, you know."

"You'll take care of it? I don't want to hear that this douchebag hurt you again."

"I'm pretty sure it'll be the other way around this time."

"Good. It's part of our job, you know."

"Yeah," she replied. "Test, judge, punish, reward."

Rick laughed so hard Yoko thought he fell off his chair, and it was so contagious she laughed until tears spilled from her eyes. Later, for the first time since her attack, she fell asleep with a smile on her face.

Wednesday was more of the same: work during the day, a hurried dinner before a drive downtown. Dressed in black jeans, kicker boots, and a black hoodie, she altered her features until her ears poked through her hair and she barely resembled a human, but her senses heightened. Easily, she traced her attacker's noxious odor to Los Angeles' historic Union Station. By a phone booth was a corner littered with detritus reeking of imitation patchouli oil. Her smile was feral, and she ran her tongue along the sharpened points of her teeth.

Test, judge, punish, reward.

Punish.

Considering the scope of acceptable punitive measures, from death, to dismemberment, to soul sucking and mind wipe, to simple verbal chastisement, Yoko's thoughts centered on the more physical. She wanted to crush her assailant.

On her way home, Yoko drove past the police station again.

Santoro still wasn't there.

Thursday night, she discovered an hour-old trace left by her assailant.

Riding that wave of success, Yoko discovered Santoro was at the police station. She drove past the parking lot, turning onto the first residential street. She parked under a tree, opened the window an inch, and hunkered down in the driver's seat.

This is insane! Is this why Inari-sama gave the fixation back?

Suddenly, Yoko giggled at the idea of questioning the rather forbidding deity. In reality, Inari Okami was both more and less. More powerful than any fictional goddess, less terrible than some, and altogether *other*. In fact, irreverence towards her was probably a concept no kitsune could embrace and live to tell the tale.

It also didn't change the fact that Yoko was sitting in her car on a quiet neighborhood street in North Hollywood savoring the faint, enticing aroma of juniper and coconut oil.

With frustrated resolve, Yoko made a decision. She scanned the street and stepped from her RAV4, locking it behind her. She tucked the key fob into her jeans pocket before ducking into the tall hedge between two houses, where she shimmied effortlessly into the form of a small white fox. Exulting in her goddess-found shifting prowess, Yoko turned on dainty paws and trotted to the police station. She reasoned anyone who noticed her would assume she was either a large cat or a very small dog.

At the police station, she counted five cars in the public parking lot, which was separated from the police lot by a tall, rolling gate. Yoko settled at the base of a tree on the verge.

Evidence of Santoro's presence was stronger in closer proximity, and her entire body shuddered in reaction.

She waited. She wasn't terribly happy about it, but it seemed her more feral aspect had taken charge.

A police car pulled into the driveway and waited while the rolling gate unlatched and opened.

Yoko dashed from her hiding place into the inner lot behind the police car. Instinct steered her to the driver's door of a dark blue Jeep where Santoro's scent was strongest. Excitement ruffled her fur from snout to black-tufted-tail. Her tongue darted out, licking the door handle.

EEEW!

Hastily, she backed away. Nostrils flared at a new, stronger whiff of juniper and coconut oil. There. At the back of the vehicle. On the dirty cement, clearly by mistake, lay a half-fingered workout glove saturated in Matteo Santoro's bodily oils and sweat.

His scent triggered a primal reaction.

She whined and snatched the glove in her sharp teeth. *What the hell are you doing?* Whirling, she raced toward the still open gate and sprinted toward her car.

Within five minutes, Yoko was driving eastward. Chagrined by her earlier, arrogant presumption of mastery, she mentally chastised herself for her inability to rein in her instincts.

She felt deviant and a little sick to her stomach.

As soon as she walked through her front door, she stripped. Clothes littered her path to the shower. Her messenger bag landed on the couch, and she flung the glove atop her dresser as if it were dangerous. The water wasn't quite hot, but she didn't care.

Twenty minutes later, Yoko felt better.

Cleaner.

More in control.

She dressed in a pair of boxer shorts stolen from Rick and a camisole which matched the bright green color. Grabbing a bottle from her dresser, she squirted lotion into her hand and slathered her arms and legs.

She tried to remember what the goddess had said, or not said, about fixation.

Then, Yoko glanced at her hand. It was clutching Santoro's well-used glove; she was rubbing it against the skin of her arm. She moaned at the heady fragrance.

Yoko shrieked and dropped the glove.

Eeew! Eeew, eew, eew!

She kicked the glove under her bed and danced spastically around her bedroom for a few minutes before calming down.

This Fixation crap is just freaking weird!

Yoko had barely climbed into bed when the phone rang. Rick's name appeared on the screen of her phone. She snuggled under the covers and answered the cell phone. "Hi."

"Is it true?" he asked with no other greeting.

Bewildered, she replied. "Is what true?"

"Did you fixate?"

Yoko sat bolt upright. "Rick!"

Suddenly, he sounded very young. "I heard Mom and Dad talking. Mom's really worried about this Santoro guy."

Suddenly, overwhelmingly, all Yoko could smell was masculine sweat, coconut-scented sunscreen, and Matteo Santoro's juniper-based aftershave. She held perfectly still. She would not reach under the bed for the glove. She would not.

"Yoko? Yoko!"

"What?" she asked, but her voice cracked.

"Fuck it! I'm coming down. They have colleges in LA."

"No, Rick. I'm okay."

"You don't sound okay." He paused, and the sound of his breathing traveled along the cellular reception between Oroville and Burbank. "You're too young."

"I know," she said quietly. "How do you know his name?"

"You're asking *this*—really?"

She sighed heavily. "Mom."

"Mom."

For twenty minutes, she fended off his suggestion to come south. He was finally persuaded. "Call me if you need me," he said before hanging up.

That night, her nostrils flared, and her whiskers twitched in her sleep.

She ignored the glove.

Saturday found Yoko back in Little Tokyo. This time, however, she was actively tracking her mugger. She missed him by no more than five minutes but was rewarded by discovering the little shop that made fresh imagawayaki. She bought half a dozen and ate two while she strolled through the shops cluttered with uniquely Japanese wares.

At the Buddhist Temple, she replaced her bloodied scarf with proper red bibs and left a steaming hot treat for each of the kitsune statues.

Sunday was a perfect late summer day in Los Angeles. The sun rose high in the sky, the heat index soaring in conjunction.

The only injury still healing was Yoko's chin—it was the most noticeable, so she couldn't do anything to speed it along. She stared at herself in her bathroom mirror, at her piquant face with its too-large brown eyes. She rubbed homemade salve on her chin, braided her long, thick hair, and got dressed for the day.

She ignored the aromatic glove beneath her bed but couldn't bring herself to throw it away. She was almost afraid to touch it.

By mid-afternoon, Yoko was back in Little Tokyo, watching locals and tourists sightsee and window shop.

Her cell phone rang. Predictably, it was Rick. "Catch the douchebag yet?"

Her smile was predatory. "Give me an hour."

"Seriously? Where are you?"

"Eating ice cream in the middle of Little Tokyo."

"Be careful, li'l sis."

Yoko laughed, and a couple of frat boys looked in her direction, but she ignored their incipient interest.

As the sun kissed the horizon, Yoko transformed her ears for more acute hearing and reshaped her nose to enhance her scent receptors' ability.

Her ears pricked forward. She had recognized her target.

Without pause, she worked her way through the thinning crowd. Within the hour, Little Tokyo would be virtually deserted. Past Main Street, she ducked into a doorway. Yoko confirmed there were no cameras or cars or pedestrians to see or record her transformation. She closed her eyes, and between one heartbeat and the next, a small white fox with a black tail tip and too-intelligent eyes stood poised for the hunt.

She raised her delicate snout and inhaled. Layers upon layers of scent clues sparked connections in her brain. As her mother had taught her children, Yoko deftly filtered out extraneous distractions, and there, between her present location and the train station, her prey's odor saturated her nostrils.

Her upper lip curled in a snarl.

Darting across intersections, Yoko sprinted in his direction. She passed a row of cardboard box homes with squatters eating scavenged food.

Three blocks from the train station, Yoko found her prey.

Roberto Anthony lounged indolently against an old brick building near one of the alleys with access to Olvera Street. He was recognizable by the overpowering stench of artificial patchouli oil and drug-infused human sweat.

She didn't bother with the niceties. Following the dictates of her training, Yoko sent a sharp mental probe into her prey's brain before tapping into his life force.

Anthony cried out and slid down the wall until he crumpled into a heap on the sidewalk.

Yoko pranced to and fro, exulting in the triumph of her first capture.

The sounds of the nearby freeway would cover any other noises Anthony might make, but he was firmly under Yoko's control. When he was sufficiently quiescent, she released her mental hold and took her human shape.

He stared up at her, his expression dazed and confused.

"You know," she said, conversationally, holding her anger in check, "I'm young for my kind. I've been well-trained, but I don't have a lot of experience, so I might have totally destroyed your mind just now." Roberto Anthony was incapable of a response. "We have a mandate," she explained. "We have been tasked with testing humanity's moral fiber." Her lip curled in a sneer. "You fail, by the way."

Yoko stepped back and poised her booted foot three inches above his groin. "You hurt me." Vengefully, she kicked him. Hard.

He screamed and curled into a fetal position, his hands clutching his groin.

This man had hurt her, and now she had hurt him. Yoko considered kicking him again. There were other, more painful, more permanent forms of punishment at her disposal. Yet cruelty had never been her way.

She bit her lip, glancing up and down the street, examined the nearby buildings, and looked farther, at taller buildings beyond the freeway. Lights began to gleam in buildings near and far as night descended on the city.

This was the moment. Her first judgment. Her first punishment. Definitely not her first reward.

She thought about what Rick would do.

No. It was her decision.

Her mother had prepared Yoko for it since she was six and shifted for the first time.

Test, judge, punish, reward.

Anthony had failed the test. He had attacked and stolen from what he thought was a defenseless girl. Anthony was vermin.

Extermination was possible. Mind wipe was more viable. It would be seen as an overdose.

The choice was hers.

Inari Okami had told Yoko to choose her path.

Daunted by the enormity of the decision, Yoko wrapped her arms around her torso and inhaled deeply. Trace overtones of coconut-scented oil and juniper soothed her in a gentle reminder of Matteo Santoro. Yoko smiled, her anger tempered by the reminder of the man who had come to her aid.

Inari Okami had anchored Yoko's fixation to Matteo Santoro.

Why?

To serve and protect. The motto of the police department. The ideals my fixation lives by. To serve and protect. I, too, serve. And protect?

Yoko stared at Roberto Anthony.

She made her decision.

"I think we'll take a little trip now," she said. When urged, Anthony rose to his feet, following docilely in Yoko's wake. He climbed into the back seat of her RAV4. Prodded by her mental compulsion, Anthony latched his seat belt before staring out the front window, his brow furrowed, expression otherwise vacant.

In the twenty minutes it took to navigate the late evening traffic from downtown Los Angeles to the quieter suburb of North Hollywood, Anthony uttered not a single word. A wicked, satisfied smile curved Yoko's lips.

Upon arrival, Yoko parked, exited the RAV4 and locked the car behind her, leaving the windows open slightly for adequate ventilation and to dissipate Anthony's rancid body odor.

Her boots made a solid thunk-thunk-thunk as she made her way into the North Hollywood Police Station lobby. Naturally, there was a line at the front desk. Yoko waited patiently, and when it was her turn, the officer seated behind the desk asked, "Yes?"

She pulled Matteo Santoro's business card from her pocket, looking at it briefly. "I'd like to see Officer Santoro, please."

The reception officer—Manning, according to his name tag—moved the mouse linked to his computer, clicked a button twice, and appeared to read a schedule on the monitor. "Santoro's on patrol."

"I see," she said. "I'll wait. Do you know when he'll return?"

Officer Manning narrowed his eyes. "I can't give out that information. Is there a reason you want to see Santoro specifically? We have other available officers."

Yoko imbued her smile with innocence and sincerity. "I can wait for Officer Santoro. He recovered my bag when I was attacked last weekend. He was very helpful."

A knowing expression crossed Manning's face, and he eyed Yoko in a more prurient manner. "I see. I'll be sure to let Santoro know you're waiting, Miss—?"

"Johnson. Thank you." She turned and exited the station, putting a little extra wiggle in her hips. She didn't need Officer Manning to tell Matteo Santoro anything. She would know the moment Santoro was within a mile's radius of her location. Sparing a thought for Roberto Anthony, secured in the back seat of her car, she sent a mental command for him to be quiet and still, and then she moved to a better observation point.

Two hours was a long wait for a young fox, but Yoko philosophically decided it was good practice. Hunting took patience. While she waited, she sent her brother a text: *Bagged in one. I'm turning him in.*

His answer was quick: *Mom would be proud.*

She sent a smiley face in reply.

He responded: *I'm proud of u 2.*

Yoko stared at the message for a long time, her eyes filming with happy tears. She texted back: *Thx lil bro.*

At 11:47 p.m., Matteo Santoro pulled into the police lot. He was accompanied by a heavily muscled officer riding shotgun. Their conversation was easily heard through the car's open windows while they waited for the inner gate to open.

"The paperwork will take at least an hour, Matt."

"We'll be lucky if we get out of here before one."

Santoro pulled the car into the closest parking space, and Brian Sanders hefted his two-hundred-twenty-pound bulk from the passenger seat of the black and white, saying, "I don't know whether to wish for a less boring shift or not."

"On the whole—" Santoro removed his nightstick from its door holster. "—I prefer it quiet. It means fewer people get hurt."

Sanders snickered. "You're such a pussy!"

"Officer Santoro?" Yoko stepped into the light illuminating the back of the station. Her skin tingled from the crown of her head to the tips of her toes. His presence elicited an unanticipated pure, visceral joy. Yoko struggled to keep her expression neutral.

Both men turned quickly, expressions hard, until Santoro recognized her. "Miss Johnson?" he asked incredulously.

"You remember me?" She smiled widely; her entire being thrilled at his proximity.

"You have a brother named Rick."

Yoko's eyes flicked toward Sanders, who had lowered his hand from where it had rested on the butt of his gun.

"Miss Johnson," Santoro said, pulling her attention back to him, "I'm sorry I don't have any news about your assailant. In these sorts of cases, it's highly unlikely—"

"He's in my car," she interrupted.

"Excuse me?"

"The guy who attacked me. He's in my car. If you'd come with me." She turned and sauntered back to the public parking lot.

Santoro and Sanders followed her. Santoro's expression was one of stunned amazement, while Sanders was deeply amused, and his pale blue eyes watched Yoko's ass as she sashayed to her car.

When released from the back seat of the RAV4, Roberto Anthony blinked rapidly and peered at his surroundings.

"I think he might have taken something earlier," Yoko explained reasonably. "He was pretty easy to find, and he's been really docile."

"Miss Johnson," Santoro said, "while I'm glad you've brought him in, it was dangerous—"

"That's very nice of you to say, but I was perfectly safe, I assure you."

Sanders spoke up. "Miss Johnson, you'll need to fill out some paperwork if you plan to press charges."

She frowned. "Oh, yes, I'm pressing charges. That man *hurt* me." Her expression softened when she looked at Santoro. "I'll be happy to sign whatever papers are necessary. I think he needs to learn his lesson."

Anthony whimpered when she said the word lesson, and for a moment, it seemed as if he might make a break for it.

"I'll meet you inside." Sanders nodded, then escorted Anthony into the building.

In what Yoko hoped would become a familiar gesture, Santoro held out his arm directing her toward the entrance to the police station. "I can't believe you tracked this guy down, Miss Johnson."

"I thought you agreed to call me Yoko," she said, "Matt."

"True that." He smiled, and his dimple played peek-a-boo in his left cheek. "Yoko."

She practically radiated light as she entered the station, following in Sanders' and Anthony's path. She stopped dead at the end of the hall. The NoHo police station's 'bull pen' looked exactly as depicted on every police procedural television show she had ever watched. In the far corner, Sanders disappeared with Anthony down another hallway.

She faced Santoro and asked, "Where do you want me?" ignoring the muffled choking and coughing she heard from the officers they passed. Then, like a homing beacon, she turned and crossed the room to a desk she would have been able to find blindfolded. "Here?"

Clearing his throat, Santoro glared at his colleagues before joining her. "If you'll sit here, we can finalize the paperwork and incarcerate your assailant."

"Roberto Anthony," she said.

"Excuse me?"

"That's his name. Roberto Anthony. He's twenty-seven, works at a 7-Eleven, and parties as often as he can. Oh, and he lives with his grandmother and aunt."

Santoro's jaw practically hit the desk. "He told you this?"

"We waited for a couple of hours before you got here. As I said before, I think he took something earlier. I'm not sure he knew what was going on."

"Miss John—uh—Yoko, you're amazing!"

"Thank you." She reveled in the compliment and sat quietly while Santoro linked her complaint to the incident report on his computer.

While Yoko waited, she noted how often the other officers checked her out. In turn, she watched every movement Santoro made, the way the tendons and muscles in his forearms flexed as he worked. She tried not to think about touching him or anything more suggestive.

She failed.

A mischievous smile played at the corners of Yoko's mouth; she enhanced her allure and arched her back slightly. As subtly as possible, she sniffed him, relishing the rich fragrance of man, juniper, and coconut oil.

Seated next to her, Santoro suddenly shifted in his chair, and his cheeks took on a dusky hue.

"After this," she said, "I can thank you properly."

If he had been walking, Santoro would have tripped. As it was, his fingers froze over the keyboard.

"Got the perp Mirandized," Sanders said, sauntering to the desk. "You got the complaint done yet?"

"Uh—yes?"

"Then print it, so we don't inconvenience Miss Johnson any further." Sanders smiled at Yoko, his teeth blindingly white.

"I'll just get it." Santoro crossed the room, discreetly adjusting himself as he walked. There was some *sub rosa* ribbing about his condition, and he punched one of his leering colleagues in the arm.

"So, Miss Johnson, how long have you known Matt?" Sanders leaned forward onto the desk as if the position would allow him to peek down her shirt.

Even secure in the knowledge she wasn't wearing that sort of shirt, Yoko nonetheless leaned back in her chair. "I only met him the day of the Nisei Week Parade when he saved me from that *yatsu.*"

Sanders laughed. "Yutz? You're very surprising, Miss Johnson; I can see why Matt likes you."

"Not 'yutz' like the Yiddish word, but 'yatsu,' y-a-t-s-u. The 'u' isn't pronounced in Japanese." She blushed. "It's a rather rude word used to identify an undesirable person. My mother would scold me for using it."

Sanders leaned closer. "And what is it you do when you're not bringing in desperate criminals?"

"I create complicated make-up for film and television. I specialize in animal transformation. You know, ears, noses, teeth."

At this point, Santoro returned, accidentally-on-purpose shoving his partner out of the way. "Here we are, Yoko. Just sign here." He offered her a pen. "And here." He pointed. "Depending on whether Anthony pleads guilty or not, you might be needed to testify in court."

"Okay." She smiled at him.

"Let me escort you to your car." Santoro cast his eyes around the room, noting the too-interested posture of his colleagues.

Yoko rose to her feet, turning to Matt's partner. "Thank you, Officer—" She peered at his name tag. "—Sanders, for your help."

"And you, Miss Johnson. It's been quite the pleasure," he said, stressing the final word.

She allowed Santoro to escort her to her car. Her human sensibilities informed her that he was perfect mating material. Her kitsune senses concurred. Considering her family's need for secrecy, Mitsuko had preached restraint, but Yoko knew she was now being driven by instinct and very real interest.

Santoro opened the driver's door for her.

As she slid behind the wheel, she asked, "Is it too soon to thank you properly?"

He stuttered. "I'm just . . . it's just . . . we don't even know each other!"

"I know. I want—I don't know many people here, and you've been so nice to me." She bit her lip and looked up at him. He was staring at her mouth. "And we have the same birthday."

He grinned suddenly. "And annoying younger brothers."

Relieved, Yoko laughed and lightly laid her fingers on Santoro's forearm. Every nerve ending fired, and she might have embarrassed herself further, but she had learned restraint from an early age. "Dinner?" she asked.

"Santoro, get your ass in here and finish your paperwork!" Sanders stood in the station's doorway, his arms crossed.

"I have your number, Yoko. When I know my schedule next week, I'll call you."

Yes! Yes, yes, yes!

"Great! I look forward to it." She smiled into his handsome face as he closed the door before stepping back from the RAV4.

Yoko started the engine and lowered the windows before shifting to reverse and driving to the exit. Her preternatural hearing caught the snippet of conversation between Santoro and his partner before the station's door closed behind them.

Sanders' voice easily carried on the night air. "She's gaggin' for it, man!"

Yoko couldn't make out Santoro's reply, only his irritation. He punched his partner in the shoulder. Hard. Knocking Sanders off-balance.

Yoko smirked and drove homeward. She was practically giddy with her accomplishment. Aside from a date with her fixation, she had caught her assailant, rendered a judgment, and chosen her path.

"You have learned well, my little ambassador."

It was the goddess' voice. In Yoko's head. The accompanying, blinding pain was startling in its intensity, and her hands shook as she gripped the steering wheel. Squinting against the spiking agony that apparently characterized any encounter with the goddess, Yoko pulled into the nearest parking lot and the first available space.

"It was the right choice, Inari-sama," Yoko thought. *"It was the right choice for me."*

"It is a good first step."

Yoko sat in her car for another ten minutes, until the urge to vomit passed, and the headache subsided entirely. She realized she was parked outside Toys R Us and laughed at the irony. As of that evening, Yoko was no longer a child.

She started her car and drove home. Turning on the stereo, Ylvis's "What Does the Fox Say?" blared out of the RAV4's speakers. "Ring-a-ding-ding-ding-ding!" she caroled and snickered while watching the yellow-white lights dotting the foothills in the deepening night.

The Last Piece of Fudge in Hell

Wendy Worthington

Frizzle was a demonic possession. Literally. And the demon who possessed her was going to kill her. Also literally. The fact that she hadn't done anything (this time) to provoke him wouldn't matter. He would have preferred Provocation. But Unprovoked Rage was just as horrifying in the end and just as fatal. He would take his time with it, of course, slowly peeling back her flesh and reducing her lung tissue to liquid and generally reveling in the pain and the destruction. The only thing that might speed up the process would be if she could manage to scream loudly enough and with enough agony in her voice to satisfy his bloodlust. But since he usually started by liquefying her lungs, that was probably not going to be an option.

And after she was dead, after the last breath had been drawn from her feeble being and what remained of her heart had pumped its final round of blood and her admittedly underused brain had sent out its ultimate electrical impulse, he would bring her back to afterlife.

That was the worst of all, the Awakening, the return to Hell, the coming back to her miserable existence, tending to a stupid, unimportant demon who made her perform the most menial of tasks and, worse, *repeat* them endlessly, never acknowledging that she might have actually done one or two of them *well* or even simply *right*. He was going to kill her for no good reason, and then he was going to bring her back, just so he could do it all over again.

Frizzle walked into his bedchamber as she did every morning, bearing a cup of coffee and what she hoped every morning would be an acceptable breakfast. She was rarely right. Melchom did not like eating the same thing every morning, but he expected the tremulous creature whose soul he possessed to guess what he wanted without hints or precedence or reason. If she brought cold pizza, that was often the very morning he was craving scrambled eggs or burnt toast or a big slice of road kill. Frizzle's inability to get it right had been a constant irritation and frequent source of death (hers), lo these many millennia.

Today, she had laid her fortunes on a bowl of stale Cap'n Crunch in slightly rancid two percent milk and hoped for the best. And coffee, of course. At least she could always be right about the coffee.

But instead of finding her possessor sitting up and glaring at her, or snoring madly away, or even standing at the window singing *The Beverly Hillbillies* theme song in a high-pitched, off-key tenor, Melchom was curled in a ball in the middle of sodden sheets, whimpering. This was not good.

"Coffee, sir?" Frizzle asked, holding out the cup hopefully.

The whimpering continued uninterrupted. This was not good *at all*.

She should not have cared. Caring was not in her job description. But as she stood there, some tiny thing inside her responded to the sound of suffering. Some tiny voice inside told her this was not an ordinary Very Bad Day. This was Epic.

She took another step toward him, holding the coffee in front of her like a protective shield. "Sir?" she pleaded, thrusting the cup toward him.

Melchom moaned loudly and flung out one of his arms, and the gesture sent the cup flying across the room, where it shattered against the armoire. Steaming coffee dribbled down the cheap veneer. Frizzle shivered. She would be expected to replace that cup out of her own pocket. She glared at Melchom, but he appeared oblivious to her and to her irritation. His head thudded back against the headboard. A great, fat teardrop emerged from the corner of one bloodshot eye and splashed down onto the bedsheets.

"Oh, what *is* the point of any of it?" he wailed.

Frizzle stared at him. Surely this was just one of those rhetorical questions he was fond of asking. But then he so often wanted an answer anyway, if only as an excuse to torment her further. She set down the cereal bowl on the nightstand. She furrowed her brow.

And then she had a Thought. They happened so rarely these days, really. Thoughts usually hurt, so she did not encourage them. But this one had arrived on its own, and it was now knocking insistently on the door to her brain. She opened the door inside her head, and the Thought walked right in.

Fudge! it announced proudly, and then it stood there, maybe waiting for a treat.

She stared at it. She was not about to encourage that sort of thing. She returned her attention to Melchom's pathetic whimpers. This sounded like deep sadness, like the sounds Frizzle herself made sometimes in the middle of the night when she was huddled in her lumpy little bed, feeling cold and lost and miserable and damned for all eternity.

Surely Melchom was not capable of the same degree of sadness. How could he be? He was a demon, a minor one, certainly, but a demon nonetheless, a ruler and possessor of souls. What did *he* have to be sad about? He had no soul to lose, no psyche to injure, no still, small kernel deep within himself to be wounded, and mangled, and isolated. He had a rotten job, it was true, but he had Frizzle to take it all out on, Frizzle to do his grunt work, Frizzle to command and torture and pick on. He had a roof over his head, and food to eat, and an unlimited supply of New York Yankees bobblehead dolls to amuse him. What did *he* have to worry about?

He was gnashing his teeth and gurgling now. This was going to take all morning, and Frizzle had things to do—cleaning and packing and getting him ready to attend the 3,423rd Annual Symposium to Study the Proper Use of Commas-in-Kind, on top of all the usual Friday morning chores. He had refused her efforts the night before to get a jump on the packing, and he would need to leave in an hour, if he was going to arrive at the Seventh Level Marriott in time for the opening singalong. It was the only part of the demonic conference he actually enjoyed, and if he missed it, he wouldn't remember that this had been his fault. He would only remember that Frizzle had, once again, been derelict in her duty, and he would take it out on her.

That was what she told herself, anyway. *It's only a matter of self-preservation. I'm only listening to the Thought so I don't get killed and brought back to afterlife later. It has nothing to do with how pathetic he looks.*

Fudge, replied the Thought with a smug little smile. *Chocolate fudge. And you have some.*

Frizzle stood a moment longer, dithering, then she withdrew from the room and thudded downstairs. The Thought was probably right, and besides, she didn't have anything better to offer. Fudge might indeed help. And she did indeed have some. If she was willing to give it up.

She wrenched open the door to the cupboard under the stairs, the one little sliver of space she called her own. It was dark and musty, and it took her eyes a moment to adjust to the gloom. She thrust a hand under the threadbare blanket and flimsy pallet on which she slept every night, rooting around beneath the slimy straw, until at last, her hand landed on something small and metal. She pulled the tin out into the light, rattled it briefly, and hurried back upstairs.

Melchom had not moved from the middle of the bed, but more tears had joined the first, and snot was beginning to dribble from his nose and down the front of his grey nightshirt. Frizzle sighed at the onslaught of moisture. She would have to do laundry today, on top of everything else. She did not have time to do laundry.

And things were getting even worse. She saw with a terrified shiver that the red of his eyes had begun to glow darkly, the fire seeming to simmer beneath his skin, turning the halfway lowered lids translucent and tracing pathways around the sockets. This was usually a phenomenon discernible only in the later stages of The Rage and only then if she managed to pull her head out of her armpit long enough to look at him closely, as she had dared to do just twice.

She looked down at the treasure she had retrieved, seeing the faint imprint of a grinning reindeer on its scratched and battered surface. She had no certainty that what was inside would do the trick. But she really did need to bring a halt to the pitiful scene before her. Hell was Hell, after all, but it had its degrees, and she could only bear so much of it at a time.

She wrestled the top off the tin. Inside, sat a very small lump. It was crusty and whitened and hardened by the years, quite unpromising to look at, really. Yet Frizzle, who did not exercise her memory often on account of the uselessness of remembering much, remembered the taste of this unprepossessing lump, and it made her salivate.

She realized with a start that she was probably looking at the last piece of fudge in Hell. She couldn't remember where it had come from. She simply knew that this was the last piece and that there was unlikely to be more, it being Hell and all.

And she was about to surrender it, never to taste its creamy, sugary goodness ever again. She hesitated. Maybe this wasn't a necessary sacrifice after all.

She looked back at Melchom. The glow behind his eyes now saturated his entire face, backlighting his lengthening fangs and making his mouth shimmer. His greasy hair stood on end, crackling and sparking. The air in the room was heating up, as well, and the black velvet draperies that covered the walls were already smoking. He was going to start to kill her any minute now. Did she really have a choice?

She lifted the sugary lump out of the tin and held it aloft. She wanted very badly to pop it into her own mouth and pretend it had never existed, pretend she was not seriously considering offering it to the undeserving creature before her.

But then she saw that his head was listing to one side, nearly disengaging from his scrawny neck in its effort to tilt sideways. She had only seen it come unstuck once before, and reattachment had taken an entire week. She was still paying for that one, decades later. If nothing else, the threat of spontaneous decapitation forced her hand.

Oh, what the Hell, she thought, and she thrust her offering toward Melchom—a little knot of crusty fudge waiting to be lost forever.

Melchom, however, was not paying attention. She wiggled it under his hideous nose a few times. Frizzle had never made a habit of being any more helpful than her eternal contract required, so it was not really surprising that he did not immediately grasp that she might be trying to help now.

She shook her head. She took a deep breath. She set the tin down, put two fingers in her mouth, and managed a whistle. The sound stopped him in his tracks.

Melchom squinted at her offering. "What's that?" he grumbled.

Frizzle sighed. "It's fudge, sir. I've been saving it. I thought perhaps it might, um, help?" The word was difficult to pronounce.

Melchom frowned at her, trying to process the curious word. "Help?" he asked, clearly puzzled by her choice of vocabulary. He shrugged, abandoning the effort and moving on to the Thing Itself. "Fudge?" he asked, and he peered at the lump in her hand.

Really, he could not be blamed for doubting her word. The crusted fragment did not look appetizing, and Frizzle found herself almost hoping that he would decline the offer, which she was already regretting profoundly. What had she been thinking? She started to withdraw her hand.

But before she could quite pull out of reach, Melchom snatched it from her fingers. He peered at the hardened lump. He sniffed it. He darted out his scaly, forked tongue and licked it. And again. And then he thrust it between his lips, where it started to melt almost as soon as it made contact with the Hellfire of his morning breath.

Frizzle cringed. Was he just going to swallow the whole thing without even tasting it?

But as she continued to watch through squinty eyes, Melchom's head slowly began to right itself on his neck. The electric crackle of his hair subsided, and the furnace within appeared to tamp down, just a little. All Frizzle needed was a little. Hope rose within her. Yes, the flames within were definitely shrinking ever so gradually back from white hot to red to a deep orange glow.

The air in the room was cooling down, as well, and she saw Melchom's eyes roll back as his expression passed from snarling rictus to a grimace. She saw a ripple of ecstasy infuse his craggy features. His lips smacked together, his mouth starting toward a smile, lurching away from its usual sneering grimace. His head lolled back onto the pillow, and several of his claw-like hands relaxed their grasp on the sheets. He began the humming noises of contentment he usually reserved for savoring a favorite delicacy— a morsel of cheese, perhaps, a juicy clod of mud, or an especially crunchy cockroach.

Frizzle picked up the beat-up tin box from the floor and clutched its desolate emptiness to her chest. She still had things to do, even if the fudge was going to work some magic and buy her a little time.

"Have some breakfast, sir," she urged, pointing to the cereal bowl on the nightstand. "You'll need your strength for the conference."

Melchom clapped one claw over his eyes. "Oh, bother! I forgot about that! Are we packed?"

Frizzle suppressed the impulse to roll her eyes. "We will be, sir." She did not look at the still-empty valise sitting on top of the clothes hamper.

Melchom merely nodded. Then he smacked his lips. "What is that taste?" he asked. "Wait, was that *fudge?*"

Frizzle nodded sadly. "Yes, sir. The very last piece."

"Wait, you had *fudge?* All this time?"

Frizzle nodded again, her shoulders drooping. *Here it comes*, she thought. *Brace for impact.*

Melchom looked at her for a long minute. At last he asked, "And you gave it to *me?*"

She closed her eyes. "Yes, sir. Sorry, sir."

There was a moment's silence. Then Melchom said, "That was very sweet, Frizzle."

She stood quite still. She tried to process his words and the words behind his words. She could not. She sneaked a look at him. Was he making fun of her? Getting ready to pounce? Smirking, at least?

The stretch of his thin lips could, in fact, be seen as smirk-like. But from the angle she was squinting at him, it almost looked like a smile. The demonic version of a smile, anyway. Frizzle trembled. This could not be good. Smiles from a demon, even a minor one, were never good. She tensed her muscles, but she knew there was no running away. He would do whatever he would do, and she would suffer accordingly.

But Melchom spoke again, and the words were strange words indeed. "You know what, my little Frizzly thing?" he asked. "I am giving you the weekend off. You do not have to come with me to the conference this weekend. You may stay here."

Frizzle stood where she was. One piece of her brain had already been running through her To-Do list, longing to scribble things down on her tiny chalkboard before she forgot them again, and that piece was not happy to be dragged away from its job to try to help the rest of her brain figure out just what her possessor had said and just what he might have meant by it.

"Weekend off?" "Stay here?" What was this insanity?

Melchom added, "Just get me packed, wash up, finish your Friday chores, and then you can lie back and enjoy the whole weekend. That is your reward for fudge." He smacked his lips again to emphasize his words, and then he rolled out of bed and padded toward the loo. "Time to make poopy," he announced, and he slammed the door behind him as he exited.

Frizzle stood for a minute more, certain that she must have misheard something, but the *write-things-on-the-chalkboard-immediately!* piece of her brain clapped its hands, and she scurried downstairs while she could still remember a few of the tasks at hand.

By the time Melchom had closed and bolted the door behind him, leaving her locked inside, she had already finished half the list. She decided that he probably didn't really mean it, that he would be retuning early just to catch her taking it easy so he could punish her, and that there was more than enough to accomplish, even if he did stay through Monday morning as planned. But she was determined to carve out even twenty minutes of Alone Time—with a nice cuppa if at all possible—and she became a whirlwind of efficiency.

At last, late on Sunday afternoon, she had crossed off everything on the list. She tried to figure out if she had missed anything, and she finally decided there was nothing left but tea. Nasty, tepid, watery tea, to be sure, but tea nonetheless. She was soon snuggled into her tottery little chair next to the hearth, clutching a mug. She sipped it contemplatively, staring into the flickering flames and indulging in her favorite pastime: feeling sorry for herself.

It had been so long ago, she could barely remember much of anything Before Damnation. But it didn't mean she wasn't able to eke out every possible ounce of self-pity that her sorry state allowed her. It was a miserable lot indeed, and surely no one, no matter *what* she might have done, deserved such misery. She hadn't even indentured herself to an important demon. Melchom was a minor bookkeeper, for Hell's sake. He spent his days recording the contracts of damned souls, endlessly and perpetually, and Frizzle had to pass him each lousy contract and write down the same, damning sentence every week for the same, damning judgments, and then refile every damned one just so they could start all over again. It was enough to drive a demonic possession to distraction.

To judge by Friday morning's hissy fit, the work was starting to get to her possessor, too. That ought to be a consolation, actually. She was miserable, but so was he. Still, he could at least take out his misery on her. She, on the other hand, had no scapegoat, no whipping boy, no object of derision to torment and annoy. She was the low man on this demonic totem pole, and she would be for all of eternity.

She stuck her nose into the mug, allowing a couple of self-indulgent tears to splash down into the watery tea. Their saltiness might just improve its taste. She swished it around, blending her tears with its miserable contents, staring down as if she might see a fortune of some sort in the muddled mess at the bottom.

So she missed seeing how it happened, but when she finally extracted her nose from the tea, something was lying on the floor next to her. She stared at it. It was a Standard Soul Renunciation Contract, and it *should* have been filed in the box next to her tiny desk in Melchom's office, waiting for Monday morning, waiting to be reviewed once more, and noted once more, and filed once more in recognition of the eternal damnation of whatever poor soul it represented. But here it was, lying on the cold stone floor like some ordinary kitchen scrap.

Frizzle picked it up. It read "SF42XR-A," an unnecessarily complex number for such a simple and damning document. She knew this contract as well as she knew the hand now holding it. She had looked at this ridiculous piece of paper every Monday morning since the beginning of Time Eternal. She had passed it to Melchom every Monday, and every Monday he had pronounced it "Fully in Effect" and passed it back to her, and she had duly noted it in her record book and then returned it to her file box and moved on to "19.3LM-821-3/4," and afterlife had gone on.

So what the Hell was it doing here?

She studied it. She realized she had never looked closely at a Standard Soul Renunciation Contract before. They were boring. Damning but boring. They were filled with clauses and fine print, and she had always been too afraid of hurting her eyes and her brain by trying to read one. This was a three-pager, too, which made it especially potentially painful. She peered at the YOUR NAME HERE spot and read "Helen Anne Gabriel." Something about the name tickled a cord deep inside her, but it was probably just because she handled this same stupid contract every Monday, and why wouldn't it have started to settle into her subconscious, if only by osmosis?

She flipped to the last page and looked at the signature scrawled across the dotted line at the bottom. It looked like every other Damned signature—brown and crusted over with age. The blood in which it had been written originally had dried eons ago and was blurry and dull against the parchment.

She started to flip the contract back to page one. But a little wiggle of movement stopped her. She squinted more closely now at the signature. She stared harder. Surely the light in the kitchen, mostly just from the thready fire in the grate before her, was simply inadequate. She held the paper closer, studying the signature. It looked quite strange, now that she was paying attention to it.

The crust that coated the original handwriting was beginning to flake away, and the signature itself, rather than being a single fluid entity, straddled the gaps of the dotted line awkwardly. And, as she watched, the tiniest fragment broke off and slipped down through the dotted line and landed in Frizzle's lap.

She gasped and stared down at her dirty apron where the fragment sat quivering, as though it had become suddenly fearful of its separation. It trembled there for a moment until Frizzle brushed it away with her hand. It tumbled to the floor, and once there, it exploded into brown powder, a tiny puff of dust, followed by nothing.

She looked back at the contract, and now another fragment had broken free and was sliding through the gaps in the dotted line toward her lap. She stood abruptly, forcing it to land directly on the floor, where it, too, puffed into nothingness as though it had never existed at all.

"Stop it!" she squeaked, and she flipped the contract to its first page and then folded it several times, stuffing it into her back pocket and hoping that no more fragments would be able to escape. She looked around the kitchen desperately, but there were no more misplaced contracts to be seen. She still had no idea how this one had gotten here, but she would simply slip it back into the file box, and no one would be the wiser.

Just at that moment, she heard a sound that made her blood freeze.

The front door was rattling. Melchom was coming home from his conference. Early.

She flung her mug into the fire, knowing that it was another piece of crockery she would be obligated to replace, but also knowing that being caught having a sit-down would cost her more. She brushed off her stained apron and patted down her stringy hair, and she hurried from the kitchen, toward the foyer, her arms outstretched to capture Melchom's purple briefcase as he burst through the front door and flung it at her. As he slammed the door shut behind him, he was already half out of his overcoat and was toeing off his muddy boots, releasing the stench of damp socks. Frizzle gathered coat and boots, opened the door to the hall closet, and ditched everything inside just as Melchom pushed past her and headed for the kitchen.

"Good conference, sir?" she squeaked as she tried to keep up with him, not bothering to even try to close the closet door behind her. She couldn't have cared less about the conference, but it was very much in her self-interest to discover her demon's state of mind. She risked a quick glance around the kitchen, hoping nothing was too egregiously out of place, before returning her attention to Melchom.

He had headed straight for the whisky, which was not necessarily the worst sign. Still, it didn't bode especially well, either. He did pause long enough to snatch up a paper cup rather than simply swigging directly from the bottle, and Frizzle took some comfort in that. Once, he had returned home bearing a large straw, which he had stuck into one of the bottles as soon as he had come through the doorway and through which he had proceeded to drain the contents of every bottle he had been able to find as fast as he could suck. That had not been a fun night *at all*. At least tonight he was taking the time to pour himself a cupful before starting on his post-conference bender. Perhaps it had simply been a typical gathering of bureaucrats, and the fudge might even still be having a beneficial effect.

Melchom raised his drink toward the hearth in some kind of silent salute, paying no attention whatsoever to her. He downed the contents in one gulp, and then he crumpled the cup and threw it toward the fire. He missed.

Still ignoring Frizzle, he lurched out of the kitchen and disappeared up the back steps toward his bedchamber. Frizzle hurried after him, cursing now under her breath.

Frizzle's legs were very short, and the steps were purposely built too high for her. By the time she arrived in the bedchamber, she was gasping for air. Melchom had already swept through the room and headed into the bathroom. She hovered in the doorway, listening as he pissed for at least a full minute. But by the time she had finally decided to simply withdraw in the hope that he wouldn't emerge soon and begin bellowing her name, he had lurched back into the bedchamber and was staring at her from across the room.

She held her breath. He held her gaze for a moment longer, then took a few uncertain steps forward and collapsed onto the bed, snoring loudly the moment he hit the sheets.

Frizzle let out her breath in relief. He would likely be out for the whole night. She tiptoed across the room to the bathroom and flushed for him. (*Why is that so hard?* she wondered for the thousandth time.) Then, she flipped off the lights and withdrew for the night.

She rose the next morning before dawn and set about preparing breakfast. Friday's stale Cap'n Crunch had been a hit, but she didn't dare try for a repeat. Melchom very rarely liked the same breakfast twice. She had no idea what he had eaten at the conference, but she hoped it wasn't cold pizza, for that was her Monday morning offering. She made up a tray this time, putting two congealed slices on a plate with a large mug of coffee. She plucked a sprig of unidentified something through the crack in the kitchen window from the tangle of weeds outside that Melchom laughably referred to as the garden. She put the sprig in a bit of water in a shot glass. It made the tray look festive. Or at least it made the tray look less sad than it had without it, and that might be enough to get her through breakfast.

She carried the tray carefully up the back stairs to Melchom's room, nudging the door open with a cautious toe. Melchom was not sniveling this morning, not whimpering, not even snoring loudly. He was instead sitting up in bed, propped by a few of the less lumpy pillows and sort-of smiling at her. She paused in the doorway, suspicious.

"Good morning, little Frizzle O' Mine!" he said perkily. "And what glorious treat do you have for me this fine morning?"

Frizzle clutched the tray in terror. Did he expect fudge *every* morning, now? She did not *have* any more fudge. She thought she had made that perfectly clear. She felt what little enthusiasm she had managed to scrape together for the day flow right back out of her.

Melchom was looking expectantly at her, obviously wanting an answer. She thrust the tray toward him. "Cold pizza, sir," she murmured, but there was no hope in her voice. "And coffee." Even the always-well-received coffee offered no guarantees.

But Melchom's sort-of smile broadened, revealing a fang. "Coffee, eh?" he asked. "*And* cold pizza? What a wonderful combination!"

Frizzle stood where she was, the tray hanging in mid-air in her uncertain arms. So this was going to be a Day of Sarcasm, was it? She felt nauseous. Days of Sarcasm were never fun, and the fact that it was merely Monday, her least favorite day just on principle alone, made it even worse.

Melchom stuck out several of his arms. "Yummy, yummy!" he exclaimed, and he started making *bring it to me* gestures with his talons. Frizzle's head sank lower, but she shuffled forward and placed the tray on his lap. There really was no point in delaying the inevitable.

But Melchom merely picked up the coffee mug with one hand and a slice of pizza with another and began munching and slurping away happily, while he scratched an itch idly with one of the claws on his third hand. Frizzle hovered, unsure now of what he was playing at. He continued to munch and slurp and scratch, making no further comment, and after a moment, Frizzle dared to take a step back, then another, until she had left the room entirely.

She crept down the steps, expecting at any moment to be summoned back for proper punishment. But no call came. She risked a bite of her own breakfast, and still heard nothing. By the time Melchom came clumping downstairs and had marched into his office, she was starting to believe that maybe, just maybe, today might not be so bad after all. She hurried in after him, not daring to wait until he hit the dingly bell on his desk to signal the start of another working day in Hell, and she slid behind her wobbly desk still unmolested and unremarked.

She peered up at Melchom out of the corner of one cautious eye. He was settled behind his desk, spinning a bit in his chair and staring out the huge window at the dead tree that dominated the landscape. She crossed her hands in what she hoped was a properly submissive stance and waited.

After nearly a full minute of silence, Melchom swung round to face her, and the workweek began. "Contract Number One," he commanded, and he waited patiently for her to pluck "Mb7-2.34" from the box and trot across the room to hand it to him. He examined it briefly as she was returning to her desk, waited for her to enter his decision into the record book, and then gave her plenty of time to cross back to retrieve it before requesting the next contract. He was a model of patience, and Frizzle remained deeply suspicious for a good hour and a half.

Things were proceeding so smoothly and efficiently, however, that she relaxed at last.

Just before lunchtime, Melchom requested, "Contract SF42XR-A," and Frizzle recalled suddenly, with an enormous rush of terror, just where that particular contract still was. She bent down to the file box and rustled the contents with her right hand, while her left went to her back pocket and slid the contract out. She stumbled forward, trying to make the switch into the other hand look seamless, and failing. She straightened to see Melchom frowning at her as she arrived at his desk. She held out the contract. He took it from her. He continued to frown, but for a moment she dared to hope that it was simply a variation on his usual unpleasant expression, or perhaps a hunger pang, or maybe only just gas. He directed his frown at the contract, and the possibly-gas wrinkle of his brow deepened into genuine, unmistakable displeasure.

"And what is this?" he inquired.

"It's Contract SF42XR-A, sir," Frizzle replied, trying to look bland.

"It's wrinkled," he observed.

"Yes, sir. Sorry, sir."

"It has been folded," he added.

Frizzle nodded miserably.

"And it was In. Your. Pocket."

Her head dropped to her chest. "Yes, sir," she admitted sadly.

"You have been playing with an official document, my Lowly One. These are not toys. These are extremely important artifacts." His voice was cool, but the rising anger behind was obvious. "You know perfectly well that this is a violation of the Demonic Code, punishable by Unspeakable Death, followed by Painful and Prolonged Reawakening," he pronounced, and he began to cite chapter and verse of the legalese that gave him every right to be a Total Dick.

She contemplated telling him the truth. It wasn't actually her fault that she had ended up with Contract SF42XR-A, after all. She hadn't taken it out of the file box, and it was only because he had come home early that she had not been able to return it to its proper place.

She started to open her mouth, but Melchom was not done. And as she listened to him quoting the painfully detailed laws regarding the care and handling of damnation contracts, she realized that trying to explain herself would just make matters worse.

By the time he had started quoting Volume 845, Subchapter 92, Paragraph 8,743, her eyes were beginning to roll back in her head, but she continued to nod and make subservient noises.

And then, all of a sudden, Melchom's voice stopped. Frizzle glanced up in alarm, and her alarm turned to abject terror as she watched him start to actually *read* the contract, his lips moving silently as he sounded out the words. His eyes flicked up all at once, capturing hers and wrestling them to the mat.

"Just what are you playing at?" he snarled. He raised the contract high over his head and shook it at her. His eyes had become fiery coals, and Frizzle had to take a step back, if only to save her eyebrows from being singed right off.

She gaped up at the contract, and as she watched, she was sure she could see a few more fragments of signature cracking off and landing on the floor next to Melchom's desk in puffs of dust. She wanted to warn him, to point out that the harder he shook it, the more fragments he was releasing, but she had the distinct feeling that even that would somehow become her fault, and she would be punished even for trying to preserve the document. And besides, Melchom was passing the point of no return. He had warned her many times about the dangers of *ira interrupta,* of interrupting the Rage, and she did not have the strength, the know-how, or even the fudge to do anything if his warning turned out to be real. Better to simply let him rage on and deal with the aftermath when it came.

He began to stretch out, to fill the office with his indignation. His being obscured the whole wide window behind his desk, expanding upwards to touch the ceiling and outwards into every corner of the room, a vast canvas on which he could display his wrath. Frizzle stared at the shaking contract a moment longer, and then she shut her eyes and tried to pretend nothing awful was happening, though she knew oh, so much better. She felt the crisping of her flesh, how it began to melt and disintegrate beneath the charred skin, and she sensed the life leach out of her, and she knew oh, so very well that this was not the worst thing. The worst thing was still to come.

Returning to afterlife always hurt, more than dying, even. It was like chewing on tinfoil and scraping a blackboard with fingernail stubs and banging your elbow with a great metal bat, all at the same time. It was worse than thinking, worse than remembering, worse than waking up every morning realizing you had signed away your soul over something petty and idiotic that you couldn't even recall. She longed so desperately to simply stay dead, to drift in the nothingness, perhaps only to bump up against one of those pleasant dreams she had visited once or twice, before Melchom had realized she could still have them and beat *that* out of her. She couldn't even remember any more what any of them had actually been *about*, really, just that they had been nice and hadn't left her feeling nauseous and sad and murderously miserable all the time.

The wash of self-pity felt so good, so comforting, that she nearly missed everything else that came along with it this time. But slowly, slowly she started to be aware of a sound, and then another, and her curiosity, rusty though it had become, shook itself half awake, and she managed to open one eye. She very nearly clamped it shut again, as it was clearly betraying her anyway. But that littlest glimpse had been intriguing. Puzzling, and certainly a lie, but intriguing nonetheless.

She kept the eye open somehow, and her pupil gradually adjusted to the blinding white, irising it down to more of a dingy beige, while her ears sifted through the strange collection of sounds, looking for something familiar. But this was not the shimmering, white-hot fury of unmitigated Hell. It was someplace entirely new.

A murmur of voices washed over Melchom's screechy tenor, drowning out the demonic shrieks. She saw dim figures in blue and green and grey moving around a bed, tending to something lying there. Frizzle craned to see what was in the bed, and suddenly found herself staring down at a very old lady.

The face was an utter ruin, framed by cottony wisps of hair that seemed barely able to maintain their hold on the papery scalp. The woman's eyes were closed, her skin a riot of crevices and wrinkles and valleys and the mottled grey-beige of age and illness. Her desiccated chest, as ruined as her face, had been bared to allow access to a multitude of wires and cables and tubes. But it was clearly a losing fight, and a beeping that Frizzle had barely registered in the background began to slow, surrendering at last to the steady hum of defeat. The activity around the bed slowed and fell into stillness.

Frizzle heard a sigh, and then a single voice said, "That's it, then. Time of death, 12:57."

She gazed down at the face of the woman in the bed, a face ravaged by a lifetime of smiling and frowning and glaring and pouting and wonder and sadness.

So this is what real *death looks like,* she thought.

"Goodbye, Helen," said another voice, and that was the moment at last.

As though her eyes had shifted in her head and were able to actually *see* for the first time, ever, she suddenly recognized her own corpse. Helen Anne Gabriel. AKA "Frizzle," for no reason she could remember. Damned for all eternity. Dead. Lost.

And now, released.

She found herself back for a moment in Melchom's office, before the familiar face of her one-time demonic possessor, stretched wide and furious across the limits of his domain, glowing and deadly, as he held her contract in one clawed talon, shaking its binding-for-all-eternity signature loose from its hold on the dotted line at its conclusion, setting her free at last as the fragments of her eternal commitment scattered from the page and tumbled to the floor and exploded into powdery nothingness.

Then she was back in the hospital room, watching the body she had used up to its very last let go of who she was, as death—real, final death, the actual and ultimate end of things—liberated her with the impossible dissolution of an indissoluble contract.

All because of the last piece of fudge in Hell, given freely.

ReBoot

Murphy McCall

I drive across the state border about an hour after sunset, and it's just after midnight when I arrive at the office in the middle of the national forest. There are no cars in the parking lot, and all the lights are off, but when I turn the knob, the old-fashioned door with the pane of rippled glass opens. There is light in the room, but the pull-down shades hold it all in.

A brawny man looks up as I enter. He's broad through the shoulders, with a barrel chest and heavily muscled arms. He's built more like a stone-mason than an office worker. His curly hair is salt-and-pepper, and he wears readers perched halfway down the bridge of his curved nose.

"Alyssia Sperling?"

I close the door behind me. "Yeah, that's me. Are you Roc?"

"Right."

He doesn't stand but leans forward to shake my hand. His skin feels like sandpaper. What kind of office job gives you hands like a longshoreman?

He says, "The way it works is this. You tell me what you need, and I decide whether or not you speak to the boss. Have a seat."

I sit in the ancient folding chair in front of Roc's desk. There aren't any other chairs. The room is small, a reception area that has been turned into a cross between a supply closet and a file room.

He says, "On the phone, you mentioned something about Biloxi, Tusca-loosa, Joplin, Moore, and Fort Worth. Tell me more about that." Roc is holding a Mont Blanc pen, but even when I start talking, he doesn't take notes. He just rolls the pen between his fingers.

"I volunteer at a no-kill animal shelter called Noah's Haven. We receive a monthly newsletter from the Kill Not Network. One night when I was alone in the office, I read through about five years' worth of the newsletter in one sitting."

I sit forward, and Roc rests his elbows on his desktop, his eyes never leaving my face.

"The first story that caught my eye was about Joplin—you'll remember they had an EF4 tornado in 2011—"

Roc interrupts. "It was an EF5."

I shake my head. "But the National Weather Service—"

"Trust me."

Whatever. If this old guy thinks he knows more than the National Weather Service, let him believe it.

"So after the storm, the Joplin shelters were swamped with displaced pets. But the community stepped up in huge numbers to provide homes for the animals. In fact, within three months of the storm, the pet population levels in the shelters, both government-run and privately owned, were at an all-time low."

Roc sits back and lets the pen drop. He frowns and makes a "hmph" sound. Then he says, "You want to talk to the boss about animal shelters? Seriously?"

I push back. "The animals are only a part of it. It's about the man who took over the no-kill shelter in Joplin after the director died in the storm. The new guy instituted an open door policy, accepted every pet that was brought in, and managed to drive adoptions in record numbers. His marketing campaigns were insanely successful."

A door behind Roc's desk opens, and a man emerges. I have an impression of height and advanced age. He wears narrow, rectangular glasses.

His eyes are the clearest blue I've ever seen.

Roc swivels, his hands raised in a halting gesture. "I wasn't ready for you yet, Boss."

The boss lays a calming hand on his employee's shoulder. "No worries, Pete."

I look from one face to the other. "I thought your name was Roc."

The boss answers. "Same thing." He shrugs.

"She's just babbling about animal shelters," Pete/Roc says, as if I'm not in the room.

The boss moves around the desk and perches on the edge of it. He looks into my eyes as he speaks, but it seems as if he's continuing his conversation with his employee. "No, she's talking about the man who appeared to run the shelter after the storm. Isn't that right, Aly?"

I let out the breath I'd been holding and nod. "Yes, that's right—I'm sorry, I don't know your name."

The boss takes my hand, and I notice that I feel oddly calm and peaceful.

"You can call me Shad. Why don't you come into my office? Pete, bring us some coffee."

Shad seats me on a loveseat, a misfit in the otherwise utilitarian office space, and sits across from me in a creaking office chair. We have our mugs of hot coffee, although Shad abandons his on the small coffee table between us as soon as he sits down.

"Why do you want to see me?" he asks.

I stall by drinking my coffee. It's a good brew, and I savor it. Taking caffeine on board is always helpful, particularly when it's past midnight, and I have a long drive home when I leave this place.

Shad waits patiently, his blue eyes bright behind his glasses. I can feel the weight of his full attention, and it is a pleasant sensation. I have a strong feeling about this man. I find I want to tell him things, and I think he wants to tell me things too.

I've been on fact-finding missions before—I've done a bit of investigative reporting—so I go into my interview mode.

"You're a hard man to find."

This is true. I've been in a few unsavory places, tracking down shelter volunteers in the cities where Lucian Belzar has coordinated pet adoption campaigns. I got the tip about Roc in a dive in Pleasant Grove, Alabama. It's one of the things I like most about researching a story—you never know where the trail will take you.

"You're under a misapprehension, Aly. You didn't find me. I found you."

Well, that's interesting. Apparently, Shad is a turning-the-tables type.

I ditch my coffee mug and take up my pen and notebook. "How did you do that?"

Shad waves a dismissive hand. "I have associates in many different places. One of them told me you'd been asking questions about Lou."

A thought occurs to me. "Are you with the current administration? National security or something?"

He chuckles. "I am not. And I assure you that neither I nor Lucian Belzar, as you know him, have any interest at all in government—yours or anyone else's."

"So you're a special interest group? One of those not concerned with government but well-funded and able to exert influence politically?"

Shad shakes his head once. "Nothing so . . . secular."

"The Roman Catholic Church?" I say. He's dressed in jeans and a button-down formal shirt with the sleeves rolled up, but I can easily see him in a priest's collar. Catholics aren't the only religious group in the world, but at the highest levels, they seem to have very deep pockets.

He looks amused but shakes his head. I'm running out of guesses. "Freemasons?"

"Can we agree that my associates and I are part of no group you've ever heard of? Will that be acceptable, Aly?"

I want to be able to verify the things Shad will tell me, but I can see we've hit a wall. I nod and ask, "How do you know Lucian Belzar?"

A smile curves his lips. "Lou and I go way back—to the beginning, really."

My previous good feelings begin to mutate to annoyance. At this rate, I'll still be trying to make sense of Shad when the sun rises. He must be the kind of guy who radiates kindness and goodwill only as long as everything goes his way.

Focused on me as he is, Shad picks up on my skepticism immediately. He raises a placating hand and says, "May I tell you what I know in my own way, Aly?"

Best to let him have his say, and then I can ask questions. I nod.

"Lou and I are, metaphorically speaking, part of a group of . . . programmers. We write the code that operates the computers that run the world."

Interesting metaphor, but it's not working for me.

"Sorry, but that doesn't make sense. Everyone has a computer. My *phone* is a computer."

He actually looks rueful. "That development caught us by surprise—we never planned for that."

Who does he think he is? Nostradamus? I try to contain my impatience and keep my eyes on his face.

He says, "Programmers are separate from their creations—rather like gods, if you'll pardon the term. Programmers aren't meant to become code themselves, Aly. It's bad system management and bad for the program as well."

Shad pauses for a moment then offers another example, obviously a nod to my hopes and dreams.

He says, "It would be like an author inserting herself into her own novel. If the story can't progress without your physical presence, perhaps you need to rewrite."

Okay, this guy is either nuts or God.

Maybe both.

"Could you forget the comparisons and just tell me who Lou is and what he's up to?"

Shad pulls at the lobe of his ear then seems to make a decision. He leans forward and says, "I always believed what he said to me the last time I saw him. Lou was going to be the agent of irresistible temptation in the world—that was his grand plan. But he gave that up ages ago. He told an associate of ours that people are—and I quote—'no damn good, and they don't need anyone else's help to destroy themselves and everything around them, including Earth itself.' Of course, by then he'd developed certain . . . appetites. And there was no coming back to who and what he was before."

Shad settles back again, and a flare of his nostrils precedes a derisive twist of his lips. "Besides, Lou really loves the little animals. He'd do anything to take care of them—and they adore him."

But I'm getting ahead of myself, as usual. Let me back up.

I'm Alyssia Sperling. Call me Aly. Freelance writer, animal lover, and shit at picking out men.

I only got into a second-rate school with a third-rate Master of Fine Arts program, but I work hard because I love writing. A short story here, a magazine article there, and with Mom's American Express as my ace in the hole, I'm getting by and building a resume. I'm three years out of graduate school, in shouting distance of thirty, but I'm a writer, by God.

There's one other important thing in my life. I love animals. I live in a one-bedroom apartment, and there are rules about how many pets I can keep, but I kind of bend the rules. I have Groucho and Harpo, the two tail-less cats I call the Manx Brothers, and there's Gertie, my Irish Setter. I've had her since I was in high school, and she's old, so I got her a playmate to keep her active. Tewksy is a Yorkie/Chihuahua mix I rescued from the city-run shelter across the tracks.

I have to stay away from that place.

The city shelters euthanize the old and unwanted pets, and it's heart-breaking to walk past the cages of wagging tails and plaintive meows—to see the hopeful eyes—and be unable to rescue them all. Their only crime is to be alive and abandoned by the people responsible for them. They haven't done anything to deserve being killed.

That's more than I can say for most of their human counterparts—but it's not my job to judge.

I volunteer in a no-kill animal shelter here in Arlington called Noah's Haven. The weird thing is we've had a huge upsurge in animal adoptions in the area recently. That's a good thing, because every shelter in the city has been overrun by pets because of the recent storm. You heard about it, right? An EF5 multiple-vortex tornado flattened a mile-wide swath of Fort Worth before rampaging through the middle of Arlington. If you can be-lieve the news reports, there was about three billion dollars' worth of storm damage. Two hundred seventeen people died, one of whom was Frank Gil-land, the director of the no-kill shelter where I volunteer four days a week.

Animal Control hit the streets the next day. Some of the pets were res-cued from the rubble of demolished homes, and others were found wan-dering the devastated neighborhood streets.

The city shelters were overrun the first day, and after that, Animal Con-trol just started coming straight to us. Of course, they came to the intake door in the middle of the night, as if doing their good deeds in the dark would prevent their bosses from knowing how few animals were delivered to the designated shelters.

When we realized the director of Noah's Haven had been a victim of the storm, that's when our volunteer coordinator, Lucian Belzar, stepped up to run things without being asked. He prefers "Lou" to "Lucian," and he has loads of great qualities—one of which is the ability to aggressively promote animal adoptions without making the Haven come off in the least as pushy or desperate. It is remarkable how few visitors leave the shelter without finding a pet to adopt. It's no less amazing how the ones that previously left empty-handed return another day to find the perfect companion.

Another of Lou's fine qualities is his looks. I can't quite pinpoint his age. No one on staff knows him outside of work, and the physical cues are contradictory. His olive skin is unlined, but his eyes—gorgeous green-gray that shift color with his moods—seem older, somehow. There's no gray in his shining black hair, but he is the most self-possessed person I have ever met.

When we were inundated at Noah's Haven, Lou asked me to come in to work as often as I could—and I have a hard time saying "no" to Lou.

All the volunteers are charmed by Lou. He's the sort who's the life of the party, hanging out with the guys at the bar to watch the big game, wolfing beer and nachos—but Lou never accepts an invitation. And he's just the sort women flirt with, regardless of their age. I've seen toddlers throw their arms around his neck as if he's family the first time they see him, teenage girls try out their flirtation skills on him, and grown women who ought to know better act like fools when he smiles at them.

I always tried to avoid him. He's gorgeous, he's charming, he's friendly— I can't help feeling the way I do about him—but I'm not stupid. I'm short, and small tits aren't interesting enough to compensate for my big ass. I'm one of those girls to whom people always say, "Your face is so pretty—"

Yeah, I don't stick around to hear what comes after the "but . . ."

Kind of punny, right?

It was just easier to keep my distance from Lou, because when I got too close, I got really stupid.

It was Saturday night, and the volunteers at Noah's Haven were exhausted. We'd been run off our legs for nearly a month since the tornado, and no one was willing to give up Saturday night to man the intake office.

Of course I volunteered. What can you expect when Lou turned those drop-dead gorgeous, pleading eyes on me and asked me to do it?

The other workers made sure all the animals were fed and watered and the sick ones medicated before they left me alone in the building. I wandered the office, wishing I had something to read, but my e-reader was still plugged into the charger on my bedside table.

I took paper from the copy machine tray and tried to outline the next scene of the short story due next month. But the overhead light was glaring, I didn't have a cup of hot tea to sip, and I missed Gertie's head on my knee and the Manx Brothers batting at the laptop keyboard, trying to displace it so they could curl up in my lap.

I searched through the desk and found nothing to interest me except quarterly newsletters from the Kill Not Network. Desperate for distraction, I began to read.

I read them in reverse order, skimming for the most interesting parts. It was in the newsletter from the autumn of 2011 where I first saw the name "Lucian Belzar." Then I was riveted. I devoured the information, even going back to reread the bits about Lou. They didn't always get his name right—in some places they called him "Lucas" or "Louis"—but the stories were all similar.

He was like an angel in the world of no-kill shelters, stopping in for a few months, helping in times of disruption, making sure the animals were taken care of.

I was so immersed in my reading that when a voice said "Hi" from the doorway, I screeched in panic, adrenaline rushing through my body before I saw the speaker.

Lou laughed, lounging with a shoulder against the door frame, his hands half-tucked into the pockets of his jeans. He wore a Noah's Haven tee-shirt, the perfect foil for his pecs and biceps, and his curly hair looked as if he had washed it and shaken his head like a dog to fling the water off.

It was a good look for him.

But there was something magical about him showing up at that moment—when my mind was full of his heroics on behalf of pets in need. Just seeing him made it a little hard for me to breathe.

"I didn't mean to startle you, Alyssia."

His smile was sweet, his eyes warm as they rested on my face, and I felt my irritation melting. I relaxed, but I wanted to ask him what he was doing here.

He leaned into the hallway and straightened to display a portable cooler. "You agreed to take this shift on the spur of the moment—I thought you might want something to eat."

Before I could answer him, my stomach growled audibly. He looked so pleased with himself that I didn't even feel embarrassed. He laughed, and I laughed too. It didn't occur to me that I was alone with him in a building empty of other human beings. All I cared about was how strongly drawn to him I was.

And how hungry.

He nodded toward the next room. "There are a couple of stools in the intake room. We can put down some paper towels and eat on the exam table."

It wasn't the ideal situation, but I was too hungry to argue with him. He walked past me, and I had a hard time not checking him out. Then the aroma of the food wafted to my nose—he'd brought fried chicken.

I quickly segued from Lou's legs to drumsticks.

He covered the stainless steel exam table with a strip of paper towels, and we ate fried chicken with our fingers, using more paper towels to wipe the grease from our lips and hands. He had brought a tub of deli potato salad and the pink whipped cream and gelatin concoction that tastes so ridiculously good. He even remembered the plastic forks.

There were four cold beers in the cooler as well, and somehow, as we laughed, ate, and drank, he drew me out of my usual reticence. His eyes were unusually green in the fluorescent lighting, and his attentiveness kept me talking.

The three beers I drank may also have had something to do with that.

I seldom have more than one beer, but he kept handing them to me—and we were having so much fun, I didn't want the meal to be over. I was dreading his departure, even though I knew there was no reason for him to stay after we finished eating.

He put the remaining food in the cooler, and I gathered the trash to put in the waste basket. Then I washed my hands at the sink and stood to the side so he could wash his, too. Now I was full and sleepy in addition to feeling sad that Lou was leaving. The long hours until the morning shift arrived at Noah's Haven stretched before me like a blank wall. I wished I was at home with the dogs and the Manx brothers. If I couldn't keep Lou with me, I wanted to sleep in my own bed.

I turned to go back to the office.

"Aly?"

I turned, expecting Lou to ask a question, but instead he kissed me. There was no awkwardness—he just gathered me to him and bent to press his lips to mine. I wasn't thinking about the suddenness of the act, or his position as my supervisor—we were both volunteers, anyway. All I was thinking about was how good it felt to be held, and how he smelled of shampoo and aftershave, and how I wanted to put my hands under his shirt and touch his skin.

He broke the kiss and looked down into my eyes. I wobbled on my feet and realized I had definitely drunk too much. But Lou seemed to take my unsteadiness as a sign of overwhelming passion, because he picked me up and sat me on the edge of the exam table. Then he took his shirt off and tossed it over his shoulder.

My capacity for coherent thought hit the floor with his shirt.

I wish I could say I don't remember how many times we were intimate, but pathetically, I do.

It was five.

The second time was three days after the first. I was at home in my softest sleepshirt and an old pair of shorts, with fuzzy chartreuse socks on my feet. I was cuddled up on the sofa with the Manx brothers, the dogs sleeping at my feet, while I read a trashy romance novel. Mom was supposed to drop off some mail of mine that went to her house, and I'd left the door unlocked for her. But when the knock came, it was nearly ten o'clock—much later than I expected her. I'd just been so caught up in my guilty pleasure I'd lost track of time.

"The door's open, Mom," I called, but she wasn't the one who entered my apartment and closed the door again.

It was Lou. Oh God, it was Lou, looking like the hero of the book I was reading, standing in my living room in jeans and a snug black tee-shirt. I flipped the cover of my e-reader, relieved that I wasn't holding a paperback with a full color picture of a half-naked man on the front.

"Hi," I said, wishing I'd washed my hair—wishing I'd *brushed* my hair.

"Hi," he said, but he wasn't really speaking to me. Gertie and Tewksy were sitting at his feet, tails wagging, eyes trained on his face as if he had doggy treats in his pockets. Groucho and Harpo were twining his ankles, covering his jeans with cat fur. Lou bent to pet each of them, speaking in a quiet voice.

He was gentle and calming and loved animals as much as they loved him. Could there have been a more perfect man?

I stood up, wishing I were fully dressed—I didn't even have a bra on—and trying to remember if I'd brushed my teeth since finishing breakfast twelve hours ago.

"You should lock your door," Lou said, straightening up with Harpo in his arms, the cat purring loudly enough to rattle windows.

"I was expecting my mom to drop by," I said.

He allowed Harpo to leap onto the floor and dusted his hands together. He said, "I'm sorry. I should have called."

I hadn't been ready for him, but I didn't want him to go. I said, "Is everything all right? Trouble at the shelter?"

He flipped the deadlock, then took a step closer, and I took two, moving to stand with him in the circle of approving house pets.

"Everything's fine, Aly. I just . . . wanted to see you."

It was all I needed to hear. We never even made it to the bedroom. We did it right there on the sofa. It was unnerving to open my eyes at the wrong moment and find the cats watching us with half-lidded eyes.

It was only when he'd left again that I realized we should have gone into the bedroom and shut the animals out. As for the animals, they were sitting in a line, staring at the closed door, as if I wasn't even in the apartment.

The next two times we made love were at the shelter, on the very uncomfortable intake exam table. He no longer showed up with food and beer, all charm and seduction. No, when I was there alone at night, he stole into the empty building, cocky and sure of his welcome.

"Maybe next time we can have dinner first," I said, sitting up and refastening my bra.

He was tucking his shirt into his jeans, slightly bent to see his reflection in the metal paper towel dispenser. He didn't respond.

"Lou?"

He turned to me, his fingers ruffling through his disordered black curls, making sure they stayed that way. "Yeah, Aly—look, I'm not boyfriend material."

He smiled, to take away the sting of his words, but the charm bounced off me. It was clear to me that he couldn't wait to escape.

I yanked my shirt down and shrugged, trying to act like it didn't matter to me—that I didn't have a sick feeling in my stomach. "I'm not looking for a boyfriend. Just someplace more comfortable to be with you—and maybe have some conversation or something."

He chuckled, as if I'd said something funny—as if we were sharing a joke together.

I watched him saunter out the door, fearing the joke was on me.

I managed to stay away for almost three weeks. Indignation carried me through the first ten days. I had my pride. I avoided him as much as I could at the shelter, and when he was unavoidable, I made as little eye contact as possible.

When it finally dawned on him that I was pissed off, he started doing little things to thaw me out. One day at lunch, he dropped a fried pie from the burger joint on the corner in my smock pocket—he knew I loved them. Another time, he handed me the clipboard of a client who was there looking for a cat to adopt, and there was a sticky note with a silly face drawn on it. I didn't understand him—he didn't want me, but he wanted me to like him?

Hell's bells. Surely even Lou knew that players do not get everything they want. There are consequences for bad behavior.

Even so, the night came when I gave in. I decided to just show up at his place—but I didn't know where he lived. So I followed him home from the shelter.

Lou lived in a small apartment complex. There were only four buildings, each with four units. The steeply canted roofline meant there was a sleeping loft. People were arriving home from work, some with plastic bags from the grocery store up the street. Others came right back out with dogs on leashes, dutifully giving their pets a bit of a reward for the long hours of incarceration.

I lurked in the parking lot, noting details like a writer, but inwardly squirming like a woman with no—or perhaps just too little—self-worth.

After half an hour, I was brave enough to knock on his door. Lou opened it and broke into a smile. I couldn't decide if he was smugly pleased with himself or—less likely—truly happy to see me.

To be honest, my attention was quickly distracted from his face to his shirtless chest. I wanted to be indifferent to his beauty, but so far, not so good.

He stood aside, and I walked into the apartment. As soon as the door closed, he backed me up against the wall, hands braced on either side of me, bracketing me in.

"So, you're not mad at me?" he said.

There was beer on his breath. He leaned in and nuzzled my ear, his stubble rough against my cheek.

I steeled myself against the urge to wrap my arms around him. I was going to be in full control of this encounter.

I was still trying to decide how to proceed when he turned and walked away, towards the galley kitchen. The smell of simmering spaghetti sauce wafted to me from the pan on the stovetop. My stomach growled, and I pressed a hand against it.

He glanced over his shoulder with a smile. "Make yourself at home. I'll bring a beer."

I watched his muscled back all the way into the kitchen, and then I tore my eyes away.

This was essentially a studio apartment with a loft for sleeping. The room was so crammed with electronics that the air crackled and hummed with it. And on every surface, including the sofa and the desk chair, there were cats. Every single one of them was black. I had never seen so many animals in one house—certainly not in a one-room apartment. I took a quick breath, but all I smelled was meat sauce. There was no hint of litter box odor. I couldn't imagine how he managed that.

There was motion across the room, and another cat came through the slight gap in the curtains. The window was open, and there was no screen to prevent the cats from moving into and out of the apartment at will. That explained the litter box question.

He was back with a can of beer. I took it from him, popped the top, and drank deeply.

"Let's go upstairs," I said and turned to climb up to the loft.

I didn't know what I'd do if he didn't follow, but I didn't have to worry. He was quick to follow. I abandoned the beer can on a cluttered bedside table and gave him a shove towards the mattress. He laughed and dragged me down with him.

Even with less-than-fresh sheets, the bed was more comfortable than the cold exam table at the shelter. I'd thought surprising him at home would put me in charge of things, but he wasn't interested in slowly undressing one another. He got my jeans off in the first minute, and six minutes later, he was flat on his back beside me, slightly out of breath.

If possible, I was more frustrated than I'd been before.

He popped off the bed and grabbed my hands, pulling me to my feet.

"Thanks for coming by," he said, and kissed me with more attention than he had paid to the sex.

I couldn't even call it love-making. Not this time.

Then he handed me my jeans and went downstairs, whistling.

My blood felt like it was boiling under my skin, and my hands trembled as I fastened my jeans. Dressed, I headed down the stairs, but before I reached the bottom, there was a knock on the door.

Lou's eyes met mine, and he gave me a comical look, lips in a circle, eyes wide, as if he was imitating something he'd seen on a sitcom.

"Oops!" he said, and he opened the door.

A girl with long, flame-red hair stood on the other side, a bottle of wine in hand. She was the newest volunteer at the shelter, and I doubted she was more than twenty years old.

"Hi," she said, looking from me to Lou and back to me again.

"Aly just dropped some paperwork by," Lou said. "Come on in—make yourself at home. There's beer in the fridge."

I pushed past her. "Why open another beer? I only had one swallow, and I left mine in the bedroom. You'll be up there in a minute anyway."

I sat fuming for a long time in the parking lot. That was when I remembered the article about the Joplin shelter, from that night at Noah's Haven when Lou first showed up—when every word I read just made him more of a hero to me.

Their shelter director had died in the tornado—just like here. Their number of adoptions went through the roof—just like here. Lucian Belzar stepped up to take over running the shelter.

Just. Like. Here.

I put the car in Drive, already planning my itinerary. It was six hours from here to Joplin, with Moore, Oklahoma at the mid-point. After tha,t I'd head south and visit Tuscaloosa and Biloxi. See their shelters. Interview their volunteers.

Follow Lou's trail.

But first, I had to call Mom and arrange for her to come by to feed the cats and walk the dogs. Hell, they like having Mom around more than me because she ignores my rules and feeds them from the table.

No reason for them to suffer because I can't rest until I get answers.

I don't waste time when I get back from my visit with Shad. After a few hours' sleep, I feed the animals and hit the shower. As I wash, I remember what little I understood of Shad's technical explanation.

"Do you know what a ghost job is in computing? No? It's a program that starts when you boot up your system that runs as a background process, rather than being under the direct control of a user. Well, ghost job isn't the term our group uses for it. We call it a demon."

I look up from my scribbling, and Shad laughs at my expression.

"Yes, it's very much apropos for Lou, isn't it? A primary function of the demon is to dissociate from any controlling terminal. A demon can configure hardware, run scheduled tasks—as well as unscheduled ones, if it's a self-determined demon, like Lou—and make itself invisible to any monitored file system.

"Demons can be the very devil to kill, and Lou is sure, after all this time, that he is invincible—but after eons of trial and error, I believe I have come up with an . . . uninstall program."

Shad smiles at me, still benign, but with a prickling hint of something vengeful in his blue eyes. He holds up a tiny plastic Ziploc bag with a memory stick in it.

Lou is disheveled when he answers my knock, a man who kicks back on Sunday to drink beer and watch the game. But I'd bet money he's on his computer.

"Aly," he says, and I can see his eyes check the parking lot behind me. Guilty, much?

"Lou," I answer.

"You haven't been at the shelter this week."

I give a quick smile. "Yeah, I've been out of town."

He seems to relax. "Wanna come in?"

I follow him into the apartment, glancing around his clutter of electronics with a more knowledgeable eye than the last time I was here. There on the interior wall is the sturdy metal shelving, each shelf containing two or three units that look like desktop computer towers to me, lights blinking merrily. The machines are bolted to the rack and cabled to each other. I understand now I am seeing the network—the file server, the proxy server, and attendant machines—that supports his computing activities.

The screen saver is up on the thirty-four-inch central monitor, but from the position of the desk chair and the sweating can of beer by the keyboard, I know I've interrupted him at work.

"Have a seat," he says, collapsing onto the sofa, displacing cats.

I drag the computer chair over to face him. I have to urge two sleek black cats to vacate before I can sit.

"What's up?" he says.

I extract my notebook. "I've been to see Shad," I say and watch comprehension widen his eyes.

But he's too cool to stay dumbfounded—he seems to glide effortlessly into amused indulgence. "I never took you for a true believer, Aly. Those are the ones Shad usually recruits to do his dirty work." He shakes his head. "You think humankind is the point of all Creation? Get real. They're more like the worst malware infection your hard drive ever had."

He isn't looking at me. Instead, his eyes gaze over my head as if he's watching the Creation take place on the wall behind me. His black hair curls over his head in a way that might have felt familiar to Michelangelo's *David*, but the stern furrow of his brow would have been more at home on the face of Saul of Tarsus. He sprawls on the sofa, one booted foot up on an ottoman, the other thrust out at an angle, a wide-open posture that demonstrates his self-assurance. He has no concerns about Alyssia Sperling.

Arrogant bastard.

I sit quietly in my chair. I never glance up at the loft where he sleeps. Well, only once.

I will not think about that.

How could I have been so stupid? Didn't experience teach me early on that the likes of him have no lasting use for the likes of me? I should never have let my guard down with him. But to be fair, I had no idea who I was dealing with. I hadn't thought I'd find a *being* behind the goings-on in Moore, and Tuscaloosa, and Joplin, and Fort Worth. Highly *unnatural* natural disasters and acts of God—but it's not God that serves his people with devastation and ruin.

I don't know what to say to him. I want him to keep on talking, but there's another part of me that doesn't want to minister to his vanity—not one more sip from my cup of admiration.

Conceited bastard.

He says, "Creation was a game—role playing, of course—that got out of hand." He grins, but it isn't a happy grin. He looks like a wolf just before it goes for your throat. "Shad was always up for a friendly competition, but there are limits to how far you can go before even your friends have had enough."

He crosses his arms behind his head, his ribbed tank top pulling tight across impeccable pecs, his biceps swelling to the size of Texas grapefruit—but I won't fall for it. Not this time. Not again. I keep my eyes on his face just long enough for him to know I'm not going to be distracted by his antics, then I glance at my notebook again. Detachment is still more difficult than I thought it would be, but righteous indignation is a powerful motivator—and I am determined to get as many answers as I can before I end it once and for all.

"So, what did you do?" I meet his eyes again and ask the question quietly, no judgment in my tone. I give him just enough to keep him talking.

He shrugs. "Nothing major. We each had our own hubs, of course, but when we came together to work—or to play—we all linked into the main network. It didn't belong to any of us. The network just made it easier for the computers to communicate. The programs we came up with belonged to all of us—it was shareware." He smirks, pleased with his use of modern slang.

I respond only by twirling my finger in the air. *Get on with it.*

Lou doesn't care for being urged. He heads for the kitchen. "You want a beer?"

He's brushing past me before I can answer. Walking out in the middle of a conversation.

It'll be the last time.

I address the back of his curly head as I rise and move toward the wall of electronics.

"You think you're not created? You think you're a god, like he is? Well, you're wrong. Don't worry, though. You're not little old malware, like me and the rest of humanity. You're a virus—accidental, it's true, but the most virulent bit of code ever written by the Master Programmer. He had no idea what it would do—he was just fooling around, you know, *creating*. He never would have clicked 'execute' if he'd known *you* would spring to life."

It's a good thing Shad drew a diagram for me, or I never would have figured out which machine to access the USB port on. When I repeated back the instructions to him, he covered my hand with his for a moment, filling me again with bone-deep peace. As he led me to the door, he said, "I know I can count on you, Aly."

I insert the harmless-looking little memory stick—one with a rubber guard with the Tasmanian Devil on the end—and poise my finger over the Enter button.

Lou's paying attention to me now—I can tell because I hear the full beer cans hit the linoleum floor, and one of them bursts open and begins to spew beer. He's growling, too angry to even formulate words as he runs for me, but I've finally got the upper hand.

Even a demon can't overcome time and space once he's in human form.

"And you know the best news of all, Lucifer Morningstar? I have the code to unmake you."

He gathers himself for a leap, and I realize my peril. He has the lithe grace and deadly speed of a jungle cat.

His breath is on my face, and feral eyes are staring into mine as his hand closes on my throat.

I push the button.

It would be a lie to say nothing happens—in its way, the unmaking is every bit as cataclysmic as the tornado that so recently flattened much of the city—but the absolute truth is that, despite the tectonic shift in human reality, I am the only human who knows the truth.

Immediately after, I am standing in an empty apartment. There is no furniture, no electronics—just a ratty rental unit with a carpet covered in cat hair. Of the cats themselves, there is no sign.

I pick up my backpack, which is sitting on the dirty carpet rather than on the table where I left it, and walk out into the parking lot. The sunny day I remember has been replaced by a darkly overcast twilight.

I start the car. The apartment complex and the surrounding neighborhood are deserted, but I see lights in windows. The thickly wooded area behind Lou's apartment goes on for a quarter mile or so before the next housing development, and as I drive, I have the eerie feeling I am being watched. I slow down and stare into the trees, and I swear I can see a row of tiny green eyes—but when I blink, the eyes are gone, and I chide myself for being silly.

When I get home, I climb the stairs to my apartment, glad the deed is done. I want a stiff drink, a long, hot bubble bath with a novel to distract me, followed by about twelve hours of uninterrupted sleep.

I unlock the door, but before I can get inside, Gertie, Tewksy, and the Manx Brothers push past me and rush down the steps.

"Hey! Come back here!"

I grab for Harpo, who is at the back of the pack, but he turns on me with a hiss and a flash of unsheathed claws before all of them run down the stairs and into the darkness.

"Mine did that, too."

I glance over at my neighbor, an elderly woman with leathery skin and a smoking habit that has her outdoors frequently. She can see my lack of comprehension, so she explains.

"Just a few minutes ago. I came home early from shopping—the sky got so dark I thought we were in for another storm—and when I opened my door, the cat and dog ran out without even looking at me."

She drops her butt onto the concrete and steps on it. "I don't know what got into them."

She turns to go into her apartment, and I enter mine. Knickknacks and photographs from the tops of the bookcases and mantelpiece are on the carpet. At first I am confused, but then I see the shattered glass on the photographs—one of me with the Manx Brothers in my lap and another shot taken at the groomer's, of me with the dogs on their leashes—and it seems deliberate. Vindictive.

In the kitchen, the pet bowls of food and water are upended, with the contents splattered all over the floor.

I drop my backpack on the sofa and turn on the TV. There is video footage of animals running from humans. Running from houses, from cars, in packs and alone, into fields and up trees, anywhere to escape. I sit on the sofa, staring at the unfolding story. Fleetingly, I wonder about the shelter—about the *zoo*—and I flip from the local channel to CNN.

There is video from Europe—from Asia—from Down Under. All over the world, for some inexplicable reason, animals are in revolt from human-kind.

After ten minutes of watching, I abandon the TV and pour three fingers of Hennessey. I drink half of it before I carry it into the bathroom and fin-ish drinking it in the tub. I have no book to soothe and distract me. There's no remedy for the empty, deserted feeling I have. There's no cat perched on the side of the bathtub, eager to be near the warmth of the water, and no dog lying on the floor, patiently waiting for me to emerge from voluntary bathing.

I am alone, devoid of the companionship I depended on more than I re-alized.

Had Shad known this would happen? Or was it another "surprise" development, like PCs and climate change?

I jerk upright in the cooling water, realization hitting my brain with an impact like an overdose to a junkie.

Mind and stomach roiling, I vomit in the bathwater.

Then I stand beneath the shower, awareness like a scourge thrumming in my body. The sick swirls down the drain, and I wish the truth could be so easily disposed of.

Why did I seek out Shad? Because Lou didn't return my love. I acted like a classic woman scorned. I might as well have walked into Shad's office, wearing a flashing neon sign that said "Use Me."

Had I really imagined I was a player in their game? An equal?

I was nothing but the lowliest pawn.

When the water runs cold, I towel off and pull on a warm bathrobe, stuffing my feet into bunny slippers. Staring at the fluffy pink ears of my house shoes, I wonder. Will the wild animals change? They are already feral, of course, doing their best to avoid humans at all costs. It's the house pets and domesticated animals who have experienced a . . . change of heart.

Too nauseated to eat, I lie down on my bed. I stare at the ceiling, my brain skipping from one thought to the next without giving me a chance to thoroughly think anything through. I skitter from every hint of thought about how I was used. Instead, I concentrate on the pets.

Perhaps it's only this generation of house pets that are in revolt. There may be some kittens and puppies still in utero that will be born still wanting human love. But if they are born to animals that have gone feral, will they be the same sweet baby pets we've always known?

My first tears come then, but there's no purring cat to lodge on my chest and reassure me—no wet doggy nose to push comfortingly into my hand.

I sleep and dream of being in a desert, friendless, thirsty, and alone.

It is three in the morning when I awake to the sound of scratching at the front door. I stumble out of bed, wondering how the dogs got outside.

Then I remember, and I feel a jolt of hope and joy.

Whatever went wrong in the world at the unmaking of Lucifer Morningstar, hater of humans and lover of animals, has come right again.

My babies have come home.

It is only when I open the door and find a legion of black-furred, green-eyed cats crowding the breezeway—*there must be over a thousand of them*, I think—that I realize my error.

I know what—or who—has gotten into them. All of them.

And the largest cat—the one the size of a small panther—leaps at my throat.

Riders of the White Horse

Libby Weber

My friend Adolfo Camarillo, one of the last *Californios,* rode the first white horse to the settlement that bore his name, but he did not know what else that horse carried on its back. How could he? He had only his cross to protect him, and the verses he read to his family at every meal said nothing of such evil things. Though I lost much of the Chumash language after I was adopted by the estimable Ysabel Yorba, the word *nunasus* stayed with me because of the prickling terror the old stories roused in me. Those stories saved my life once.

I first encountered the *nunasus* one July, when I was supervising the men clearing an irrigation ditch in Adolfo's alfalfa field. I spotted a flash of white out of the corner of my eye where a cloud of dust was rising up from a road to the northeast. Even at that distance, I knew it was Adolfo, since he was wearing the pink silk shirt of which he was terribly proud, though I did not know the white horse he rode. Far behind him, I could see his new-fangled automobile chugging over the rise, piled high with purchases from the state fair.

I told the men to finish their work without me and made my way over to the barbed wire fence that separated the land that was once Rancho Callegulas from the road. My crow self perched on the fence and cocked her head at the far-off clouds of dust.

"I do not like what rides that horse," she said.

"You only dislike Adolfo because he drives your kin from his fields," I said, smiling at her ruffled feathers.

"I do not mean the Man," she said scornfully.

95

I shielded my eyes from the sun with my hand, and I could make out my proud young friend's form rising and falling in time with the beautiful horse's gait. He was anxious to return to his wife and children, no doubt, and to give me leave to return to my adobe house on the north edge of Rancho Guadalasca, which had belonged to my mother many years before. But as he drew closer, I saw a shimmer in the air that streamed out behind him like a mirage.

"What is it?" I asked my crow.

She clacked her beak at me. "Call your beast, slow one. We must protect the nest."

With growing unease, I whistled for my mare and mounted her quickly as my crow landed on my shoulder.

We galloped toward the house along the dirt pathways that marked the boundaries between the fields and pastures, and as I neared the stable where Adolfo had dismounted, I saw it. It sat astride the white horse like a man, but it was twice as large and perfectly transparent, invisible but for how the light bent around it. Though it had no eyes that I could see, I felt its awareness wash over me like a January wave. An unnamed fear seized my heart, the same fear that haunted my dreams when I was a child. My fingers flew to the smooth beads of my mother's rosary, which I wore under my blouse.

Wishing to spare my crow self from the terror, I tamped her down into a small, hard stone. As I drew nearer to where Adolfo stood greeting his family, I could feel her wings beating against her prison. I hummed a song from my childhood to calm her, and the fear loosened its grip on me to the point that I could approach my friend and his family.

Adolfo's children swarmed around their father and the beautiful white horse, and his wife Isabella, who was nearing her confinement, watched in amusement as she rested against the fence. None of them seemed to sense the rider on the horse.

"What have you done this time?" she asked her husband fondly.

Adolfo handed the horse's reins to his eldest son. "I have hurried home to my beautiful one on a horse as white as snow," he said, kissing Isabella. "His name is Sultan."

Isabella gave him a wry smile. "I hope you did not pay too much for him. He is too old to be of much use."

"I did not buy him to work. I bought him to sire many white foals for good children to ride."

"His stride is good," said Isabella.

"What do you think of him, Beatriz?" he asked me. "I should like your opinion."

I swallowed my words of warning and approached the horse. I held my hands toward his nose, and one ear twitched forward as he sniffed them. I leaned forward and breathed into his nostrils, and his other ear flipped quickly toward me but then relaxed. I gave him a small apple from my skirt pocket then ran my fingertips along his neck and across his withers. I paused when I neared where the fearful thing sat, but I could sense no tension in Sultan. In fact, other than his perfect white coat, there seemed to be nothing unusual about him.

I cleared my throat, hoping my voice would not shake. "He has an even temper, but his ears tell me that he also has a sense of fun, so watch your fingers when he is feeling playful," I warned the children. I looked at Adolfo. "He has a fine build and will produce many foals."

Adolfo smiled. "I'm glad to hear you say that," he said. "And thank you for taking such good care of the ranch while I was away."

I made a dismissive sound with my lips. "The barley field fence needs mending where the cattle cut through, Mr. Lewis wants to talk to you about that western section of Rancho Las Posas, and Minerva bears watching with the Hernandez boy."

"All business today," said Adolfo, his smile fading somewhat. "But I'm sure you have much to do at home. You will come for supper tomorrow. I have gifts from the fair."

"If I must," I said, feeling a smile on my lips despite my unease.

Adolfo pressed a kiss to my forehead. "Yes, *abuela*, you must."

By this time, the children were clamoring for rides on the new horse, and Adolfo assured them there would be rides after dinner. My own horse's ears were twitching as I approached her. She might not have been able to sense the other presence, but she knew I was frightened, and she didn't like it. The old song was still running through my head, the Chumash words rusty in my memory, but as we began to ride for home, I found that my mouth remembered them. As the music filled me, I found that I could breathe easily for first time since Adolfo's return. I released my crow self from her tiny stone prison, and she beat her wings at my ears.

"Why did you hide me?" she asked. "I would have dived on it from a great height and torn it to pieces!"

"It is not a vole," I said, smiling at her wrath.

"It is an enemy. Enemies are the same as prey, only less good to eat."

"Attacking an unknown enemy is foolish."

She clicked her beak noisily next to my ear. "If it is stronger than we are, then we shall gather others first and then attack."

She leaped from my shoulder, and as I rode toward home, she rose quickly into the sky until I could see all of my ancestral lands, from the mountains all the way to the sea, through her eyes. And yet, it was neither idleness nor the hunt that spurred her to such heights. It was fear.

Josefina was the first of my adopted sisters to respond to my summons. Santa Barbara was a long day's ride to the north, but she arrived three days after I wrote to her, with mother's old carpetbag lashed to the back of her saddle. I took her with me the following morning to Adolfo's while he was out in the fields and the children were at their lessons. She sniffed at Adolfo's extravagant ranch house but seemed satisfied by the number of children Adolfo and his wife had produced, as if it justified the size and beauty of their home. Her fidgeting hands stilled when she felt the presence in the stable, and though she was not as well acquainted with her spirit self as I was, I could feel her close in on it for protection, just as I had.

Dolores arrived next, with her quick smile and infant son at her breast, and she too folded in on herself when she felt the fear. Only Sister Juana—we still called her Jennie in our hearts—faced it unflinchingly, with only a quick sign of the cross to indicate that she was aware of anything out of the ordinary, though she did not speak until that evening when we sat around my table.

"We must cast it out," she said, fingers brushing over the plain wooden cross she wore as a sign of her station. "I have brought holy water and chrism from the mission."

"It is not our place," said Josefina. "A priest ought to perform the rite, and the Camarillos must be the ones to pay for the costly oils. They have money enough."

"But the children!" exclaimed Dolores. "Must they suffer until then?"

"I saw no sign that the children suffer, nor do any of the family," I said. "The rider does not harm them any more than it does the horse. It is waiting, but we must not."

"Beatriz is right," said Sister Juana. "It is clearly an associate of Satan. I have seen such demons possess good people and drive them to horrible acts. We cannot wait until it begins to spread its evil."

"I agree," said Dolores. "Mother would not have refused to help."

Josefina glared at her. "Mother did not work for nothing, nor did she do someone else's work on a whim."

"Adolfo's father was a good friend to Mother," I said, "and Adolfo has been a good friend and neighbor to me."

"He has you riding hither and thither to care for his property when he takes trips for pleasure and gives you nothing in return," said Josefina. "You are not a young woman, Beatriz, and he is not your son."

"Adolfo is my friend," I said. "If you cannot calculate the value of that, then all your investments and accounts have done you more harm than any chore of Adolfo's has done me. Are you so jealous of the Camarillos' wealth that you would refuse to help?"

Josefina's face darkened, and I thought she would shout, but she held herself back. "It is not jealousy," she said at last, her voice strained. "It is the ostentation that angers me. All the fiestas and dinner parties, all the exotic crops he plants for his vanity's sake. If he were not trying to show off with extravagant purchases, he never would have brought the cursed creature here."

I could not trust myself to reply calmly. Fortunately, Sister Juana spoke up.

"It is not for you to decide how a man may spend his money, what crops he may plant, or what horses he may buy," she said. "And if Adolfo is guilty of gluttony, pride, or avarice, that will be a matter for him and the Lord on the day of reckoning."

At last, Josefina fell into chastened silence, or so it appeared.

"When shall we act?" asked Dolores, pulling a wooden whistle from the folds of her blouse.

"Tonight is the hands' night off," I said. "They'll be getting drunk out by the cowshed. Only the dogs can give us away, and they know me. I can keep them quiet."

"I'll need herbs for burning," said Josefina with ill grace. "Show me where they grow, Beatriz."

I recognized the prevarication for what it was, took a sip of mescal for strength, and followed her outside.

"White sage is as common here as it was when we were children," I said when we were out of earshot, gesturing towards a large shrub just beyond my fence.

Josefina rubbed one of the soft leaves between her fingers and sniffed it. "What is it that we go to fight?"

I shrugged, not wanting to voice the worst of my suspicions. "Perhaps the horse's first owner rides him still."

She began pulling large leaves from the ends of the branches. "That creature may ride like a man, but it was never human."

I watched my sister expertly strip the leaves from a new branch. "There are old stories among my people," I said haltingly, "of harmful spirits called *nunasus,* but I have never seen one."

"Sister Juana named it a demon," said Josefina with heavy irony.

"Sister Juana named you a demon when we were children. That does not make it so."

Josefina gave her quick, barking laugh. "Help me with this."

"I must find *momoy.* We will need our spirit selves in this fight."

Josefina frowned. "Dolores is still nursing."

"Gabriela Ruiz has milk from her youngest daughter. She will care for Pedro until the *momoy* has run its course."

"You have thought about this," said Josefina, a trace of accusation in her voice.

"You have had nearly as much time to think of it as I have," I replied mildly, stooping to pick the dark green leaves from where they grew at the side of the road, "yet all you seem to have thought of are reasons not to help."

"I do not want to fight it," said Josefina softly.

"Neither do I," I said, "but the others cannot see what Mother taught us to see. Only we may fight it."

Josefina shoved the sage leaves into her apron. "When your letter came, the first thing I wondered was what could be so terrible that you asked for our help. But now, I've felt that coldness in my bones; I do not wish to see what it will do when cornered."

"I do not believe it can harm our bodies," I said, ripping off a small piece of *momoy* leaf and handing it to her. "But the fear it brings can harm our spirits. We must not let it."

Josefina crushed the leaf in her teeth, spat it out, and swallowed its essence, wincing at the bitterness. "I know," she said. "But knowing it doesn't make fear disappear."

Out of the corner of my eye, I saw her wolf spirit approach us, wary and suspicious, and my heart swelled with fondness for my sister. I took her hand and squeezed it. "I am glad you came."

"I'm not." But she smiled, and her wolf pressed itself against her leg. It was the last time the two of us would speak alone.

That night, guided by the old stories of the *nunasus,* my sisters and I cast out the rider with talismans, fire, and song. But we discovered the next morning that it had taken a victim as we sent it shrieking off into the darkness. It was usual for the ranch hands to get drunk and shoot targets on their night off, but there had been a disagreement, and when the dust settled from the brawl, they realized that Raul Vargas wasn't getting back up. He was twenty-five.

The Camarillos did their best by the Vargas widow and children by giving her a job in their kitchen and sending Raul's sons to school. Sister Juana and I performed our own rituals for the dead man; hers to ensure his entry into heaven and mine to cleanse his spirit, since the gatherings had never turned violent before the rider's arrival. To our great relief, the rider did not reappear, and my sisters soon returned to their homes.

For a time, things were as they had always been. The town that bore Adolfo's name prospered, more automobiles raised plumes of dust on the roads, and the sprawling ranchos that surrounded my adobe sprouted smaller farms and homes.

That winter was wet and cold, but even as the hillsides greened, Sister Juana fell ill, and God, whom she served faithfully, called her home. Josefina wanted to bury her in Santa Barbara next to Mother, but Dolores and I insisted we follow Sister Juana's wishes and bury her at the Mission in San Juan Capistrano, where she lived and worked.

When Dolores and I burned her meager possessions to keep her spirit from being bound to this world, Josefina said that Sister Juana would have cursed our heathen ways and said we dishonored her memory. Kindhearted Dolores bore Josefina's grief-filled spite with patience and understanding. I did not. It angered me to hear her deny Mother's legacy and the very wolf spirit that stood next to her and growled, even as she railed against us. I am not proud to say that I meant to hurt her with my words as badly as she hurt me with hers. Josefina hanged herself in Mother's old office three weeks later, so I never had the chance to take them back. We buried her next to Mother.

Dolores said she didn't blame me, but she flinched when I tried to embrace her, and her cheerful, breezy letters grew somber and less frequent.

The following summer, there were four snow-white foals at the Camarillo ranch, each as beautiful as their sire, and from the first day I saw the foals wobble about their paddocks and beheld the shimmering aura that surrounded them, I knew that they bore riders as well.

I wrote to Dolores at once, but the letter that arrived three weeks later was written in an unfamiliar hand and explained the family had moved to Sacramento where Dolores's husband could make more money working for the railroad. During the move, a wagon had broken its axle, and it fell on Dolores while she assessed the damage. She still lived but would need many months to recover. However, the fear for her that rippled through my stomach fled when I saw that she had sent me her wooden whistle. If she was well enough to include it with the letter, I felt certain that I should see her before long. How I wish that I had been right.

And so it was that I was left to face the four new riders alone, but to my shame, I hid from them, and I forced my crow self to do the same. She cried out from being confined, but I worried that she would draw the riders' attention if I allowed her to fly free, or worse, that she would attack them and provoke their wrath. I mourned her fading, but fading was better than being destroyed.

I reminded myself that the first rider had only caused harm to others when we forced it from Sultan's back. Whatever evil was in the riders' nature, they did not harm their chosen mounts or those who cared for them. Besides, if it took four of us to drive off one rider, what chance did I have alone against four of them?

As the town of Camarillo flourished, so did the white horses and the creatures that rode them. Adolfo's hair began to turn gray. Every now and then, he or one of the children would visit my adobe to drink mescal or lemonade with me, but the riders filled me with such fear that I could no longer bear to visit the Camarillo ranch.

I threw myself into helping my other neighbors with day-to-day problems, like mending fences and assisting with foaling and calving. Though the work I did was much the same as I had done at Adolfo's, my days were never as enjoyable as they had been. I missed seeing my friend nearly as much as I missed my crow's freedom, but I believed the situation to be under control, and I told Dolores so when she wrote to tell me that she was expecting another baby. I told myself that Dolores needed more time to recover, that she needed to be with her family, that in her condition I could not subject her to such powerful evil. In my solitude, I could not see that fear had affected me, as well.

The town of Camarillo continued to grow as the old *ranchos* shrank, and one day Adolfo's daughter Minerva brought news that the State of California had bought part of the Lewis ranch, six miles south of Adolfo's, to build a hospital. It wasn't a hospital for the injured but for those with sickness of the spirit. Yet when I joined the crowd gathered on a nearby hill to watch the dedication ceremony, we saw that it was no prison-like building of brick or cement surrounded by barbed wire; there were neat white stucco buildings with red-tiled roofs surrounded by gardens, trees, and fountains. The town folk milled in the courtyard, straining to catch sight of the shiny cars that deposited dignitaries in front of the main building, all sweating in their Sunday best.

When the clock in the tower struck noon, I felt a sinister chill settle into my bones as I saw a cloud of dust approach from the north. Adolfo's white horses were famous now, and their numbers had increased greatly in the ten years since Sultan's arrival. They were now expected at important events, and Adolfo, who adored pomp and celebration, was always happy to oblige. There were four of them that day, their white coats shining like silk. Each bore a Camarillo in his finest clothes, and the awful riders shimmered behind them.

The ceremony was brief so everyone could escape the midday sun and drink cold lemonade in the shade, and the doctors and nurses returned to their work, for patients had begun arriving earlier in the week. The white horses were hitched to a post beneath an oak tree; Adolfo's eldest grandson fed them treats while the other Camarillos mingled with the local and state dignitaries. It was then that I noticed the riders were moving.

They slid from their mounts and oozed through the dappled shadows of the leaves. To my surprise, the horses' eyes rolled back in their heads, and they cried out. The Camarillos rushed to calm them, but the horses struggled against their harnesses, tossing their heads and attempting to escape.

The riders moved steadily toward the main hospital building into which all the doctors and nurses had gone, and in that moment I grasped the riders' true nature. They needed the white horses to increase their numbers, but they were no more part of the horses than a leech is part of the limb to which it attaches. Now that the riders had found a place full of those who would have no defense against them, they no longer needed to spare the creatures that had unwittingly hosted them. To make matters worse, at the edge of my mind, I could sense the riders back at the Camarillo ranch moving toward the hospital to join the feast.

The realization made me hot with shame. I had thought myself strong for having defeated one of the riders, but my courage had been taken from me that night as surely as Raul Vargas had been taken from his family. Cowardice had made me unwilling to see the riders for what they were, and now the hospital's patients would be at their mercy. For the first time in years, anger burned through my cold fear, and I knew I must do something to stop them.

I reached inside to release my crow self, but she had been confined for so long that she sat listlessly on my shoulder, too weak to fly. I bounced my shoulder, hoping to coax her into flight, but she turned her dull eyes on me.

"What would you have me do, my jailer? Fly in circles for joy at my release?"

"I have been foolish and cruel," I said. "The riders stalk the sick, and we must stop them."

"Would you release me only to draw the wolf away from the lambs?"

"You once advised me to mob the wolf," I said.

"I do not see a mob."

"Not yet," I said, "but you will."

The next morning, I wrote to Dolores. However, the letter I received in return was full of ill news and excuses. I suspected several of her claims were lies, because her normally flowing script grew smaller and her nib had nearly torn through the paper. I wrote her once more, begging her to come, and received a much longer letter that made me see that the first rider had taken something from all of us, after all.

Dolores implored me to leave the riders alone because they had already taken two of her sisters, and she did not wish them to take me, as well. She told me things about Sister Juana's death that I hadn't known, namely that she had gone into seclusion immediately after returning to the mission. She ate little and slept less, refusing to speak, until at last the ascetic life she'd chosen had weakened her enough that when influenza set in, she could not fight it off. Then, Dolores told me of letters that she and Josefina had exchanged after our fight, saying that Josefina's spirit had been broken the night we defeated the rider, but she had been able to fight off the black moods until I broke off contact with her. She told me that I was more important than a hospital full of lunatics and that I should be in the hospital myself, if I really expected her to leave her family to fight a battle that could prove fatal for both of us.

I folded the letter in half, tossed it into the fire, and said a prayer for Dolores's compassion, which I now understood had died that night all those years ago. That night, I drank mescal in memory of the women my sisters and I had once been. Though we had stopped the *nunasus* from taking our lives as we fought it, it had still taken something fundamental from each of us.

I sat by the fire, trying not to think about Dolores's letter or the last things I had said to Josefina. As I absently fingered Mother's rosary, the soft click of beads against beads caught a fragment of memory from my early childhood, and I vividly recalled the feel of the shell beads that decorated the fringe of my grandmother's leather apron, long before I had been taken to the mission to be adopted. I had sat by fire that night, too, and as the healing songs that the village shaman sang for my grandfather echoed through my mind, I thought of the line from Dolores's letter that said I should be in the hospital myself. My path was clear.

The next morning, I rode down to the hospital to ask for a job. They hired me to clean rooms and make patients' beds in the main hospital, and I was to start the next day. My crow self seemed to have recovered from her ordeal, and once more she hopped around the different rooms as I did my work, poking her head into everything and investigating anything that reflected light. To my surprise, I did not see a rider for several days, and when I did, it was gliding across the lawn towards the buildings in the south quad, where I was forbidden to go.

I soon learned that this was because the south quad housed the sickest patients who were not expected to leave after a week, as the main hospital's patients often did. My crow agreed that it would be safer for us both if she did not enter the closed wards, but she could still fly over the locked gates and gaze through the windows, where I could see the riders drifting up and down the corridors and among the patients and staff. Now and again, I would see a rider in the main hospital, which forced me to work through my fear of them, because they struck quickly and without mercy.

Before the end of my first week, a rider took a woman who had been found by the police wandering drunk down the road. Though she was calm when they brought her to the main hospital, she became violent, and it took three nurses to subdue and sedate her. She never woke. It was declared to have been an accident, but I had seen a rider shadowing the night nurse whose syringe had delivered the fatal dose of sedative. I was assigned the task of disposing of the dead woman's belongings, and I burned them while saying prayers to ease her passing into the Upper World.

As the weeks passed, I began to see through my crow's eyes that the patients in the south quad were not the riders' only victims. So many doctors and nurses arrived at the hospital filled with good intentions, but the riders were as dangerous to the unwary as they were to the ill. No person is free from wicked impulses, and watching those who arrived wishing to heal the sick gradually become indifferent to their patients' suffering was awful. But I stayed focused on my paid task of keeping the patients' rooms clean and the more important job of teaching them the old songs and stories to strengthen their spirits.

As the months went by, more riders arrived from the Camarillo ranch as more foals of that cursed line were born, but I and my allies among the patients drove them away from the children's wards and protected those whom we could. I prayed with them, sang with them, and even smuggled in *momoy* tea for those who wished to find their spirit selves. I was careful to give them the smallest amount possible, for *momoy* is powerful medicine.

But in their south quad stronghold, the riders grew more powerful. Only doctors and the strongest aides and nurses were allowed in. It is a great irony that the strongest were so quickly tainted by the riders, because once a person entered the south quad, that person was never again the same.

Those of us who had worked at the hospital for a long time heard tales of what happened in the closed wards. Petty things at first, like stealing gifts meant for patients. But then there were whispers of medical procedures late at night, terrible injuries that had clearly not been accidents, even disappearances—and as the population in the south quad grew, the more time the staff had to spend there. And the longer the staff were exposed to the riders, the more callous and cruel they became.

When the south quad patients' garden privileges were revoked without explanation, we could only see them through the barred windows and locked gates. I watched them pace up and down the hallways and around the courtyards like blind ghosts, withdrawing from the riders as I had once done but without any means of protecting themselves. The shimmering outlines of the riders grew larger and more monstrous as their captives diminished, and though new patients arrived at the south quad every week, none of them left it.

I considered writing to Dolores again for help, now that I had enlisted allies against the riders' influence. But in my pride, I thought I had banished the riders from most of the hospital, and I did not wish to share credit for having done so with anyone, especially not my cowardly sister. I believed that I could drive them from the south quad as well, if I could gain access.

I had been at the hospital for several years the day that Mr. Olsen, the head nurse, caught me giving *momoy* tea to a patient. The patient was returned to his room, but Olsen, who had spent a great deal of time in the south quad, dragged me out of the main hospital, past a locked gate and a guard who looked the other way, into one of the closed wards. It was far worse on the inside than I had imagined. The floors and walls were stained, and the building stank of sickness and chemicals. Olsen led me into a dark office and seated me across the desk from him.

I expected him to shout and dismiss me, but he looked at me as if I were an insect, and his silence was far more unsettling than any threat to my job. I could see the shimmering presence of a rider looming near his head, as if it were whispering in his ear.

"I have decided to keep this matter from the police," he said at last.

"Why should it be a matter for the police? My people have been using *momoy* in healing for centuries. You call it white thorn-apple."

"We also call it datura. It's toxic."

"All medicine is poison in the wrong dose," I said.

His lips tightened. "You knew that Mr. Tims is being treated for opiate addiction," he said. "You could have killed him. According to the law, you should be in jail. But in light of your years of service here, I have decided that it would be in your best interest and that of the hospital to treat you for antisocial behavior instead of involving the authorities. Don't you agree?"

"I have done nothing wrong."

He slammed his fist down on the table and bared his teeth. "You know what would happen if I called the police?" he asked. "You'd be locked up, convicted, and would spend the rest of your life in prison!"

I hid my shaking hands beneath the table while I considered the trap he had laid. If I defied him now, I would lose my ability to protect the patients. If I agreed to treatment, I would be at Olsen's mercy, and I had heard many horrible stories about him and others like him who had been perverted by the riders. But then I realized that if I consented, I would be housed in the south quad—an ideal place to drive the riders away once and for all.

I lowered my head. "I accept."

"Good," he said, unaware that the rider was sliding over him, slithering down his shoulders. "Sign these papers."

I was reaching for the papers to read them when Olsen grabbed my arm and stabbed me with the syringe he had hidden behind his desk. I could hear the riders roaring in triumph as he forced my fingers around a pen. Red and yellow patches expanded in the corners of my vision, and my tongue felt like a sandbag in my mouth. All went black.

I do not remember much of those first days of solitary confinement other than pain, confusion, and terror. I was cut off from my inner self and could do nothing but cry out. When I ceased resisting, they stopped the awful injections, but my memories are far from whole.

Adolfo came. I remember him swearing at Olsen in Spanish, but of course Olsen would not release me into my friend's custody. Adolfo must have contacted Dolores, who visited soon after, but she could not linger in the presence of so many riders, nor could she convince Olsen to let me go. Because I had voluntarily submitted to treatment, there was nothing any of them could do.

When my dosages were reduced enough to allow me to respond to commands, I was led to a dingy room with a large mirror on one wall, which I knew would be used to observe me. A doctor entered with Olsen and a man carrying a clipboard, and the doctor began to ask me questions. Though I understood the questions, the words of my response were jumbled in my head and would not emerge from my lips coherently.

Suddenly, a warning caw sounded in my ear, and to my great joy, I realized that my crow self was perched on the table. I had never been so glad to see her, for the drugs had clouded my awareness, and through her thoughts I understood the danger I was in. Olsen had forced me to give up my freedom for three months of treatment. If during that time I appeared ill, as I most certainly did while under heavy sedation, they could refuse to release me at the end of those three months. My mind had been mired in quicksand, and in struggling against it, I had forgotten that a part of me could fly free.

I limited my answers to nods and shakes of the head, which visibly frustrated my interrogators. Olsen called me horrible names and spat insults at me and finally gave me an injection so powerful that I was unconscious for the rest of the day and did not wake until the middle of the night. My stomach gnawed at me from having missed dinner, but I had also missed my evening pills, so my mind was clearer than it had been since coming to the south quad, and I saw that I was somewhere new.

Not wishing to draw the gaze of anybody who might be watching, I lay still, glancing around the room without moving. There were eleven other women lying on cots, all in varying states of drugged sleep. One had her arms wrapped around herself and was moaning softly.

Since there was no watch-mirror in the wall and no faces lurked behind the thick glass of the door, I slid silently from my bed and crept between the cots to the window. The bars were too thick and close together to allow escape, and the panes were too grimy to see very far, but the window was open enough to allow my crow self to hop through the bars and fly off into the night.

Through her eyes, I could see the half-moon illuminating the courtyards, which meant that I had been in the closed ward for two weeks. I sighed in relief at the simple pleasure of using knowledge and observation to deduce the date. But my relief was short-lived.

As she flew higher, I realized with dawning horror that what I had taken for shadows from the trees were actually riders. Dozens were gliding between buildings, and I couldn't imagine how many others were inside, sapping life and goodness from staff and patients alike.

Back in my human body, I pressed my hand to my heart as I understood what I had done. In my foolish decision to confront the riders in their stronghold, I had only trapped myself and given them free rein over the hospital. I could no longer protect the patients and instruct my allies. It was only a matter of time before the riders did to all the patients and hospital staff what they had already done in the closed wards.

I allowed myself a few moments to weep, in hopes that the last of the poison that the nurses had forced on me would flow out with my frustrated, angry tears. My crow self, sensing my distress, returned through the open window, sat on my shoulder, and began to preen my hair. My despair ebbed into a dull ache in my heart, but I had no idea what to do.

The touch of a hand on my shoulder made me flinch, and I looked up to find a fellow patient standing over me. She sat down by my side, rubbed my back gently, and began to sing a tuneless lullaby. In that moment of kindness, I felt a glimmer of hope, the first I had felt since my arrival. Under the watchful eye of my new friend, my sleep was deep and healing.

The next morning, I awoke hungry for details that might aid my escape from the riders' clutches. I followed my new friend down the hallway until we were herded into line for morning pills. The day nurses knew that I had been difficult during my interview and watched closely to ensure that I swallowed my pills, but they began bickering over which radio program to listen to and did not see me shuffle over to the line for the bathroom and, once I was in the open stall, heave the medicine quietly into the toilet. My mind still felt as though it was suspended in water, but it was far better than before.

I joined my friend soon afterward and found her conversing with two other women on the opposite side of the room from the nurse's station. I learned that her name was Alice, that her husband had had her committed after she'd had several psychotic episodes, but that she was doing well enough. Her companions didn't say much, as they were heavily sedated, but Alice introduced them and spoke to them kindly, and they appeared to respond to her. My crow perched on the back of her chair and preened Alice's hair as I told her as much of my story as I thought she would believe. I didn't mention the riders specifically, but I described my efforts to combat despair while I worked.

Alice nodded sympathetically when I had finished. "Would you teach us the songs you taught them in the main hospital? We may not know our spirit selves, but we used to sing long ago when I first came here, and I miss it. And I happen to know that Izzy here has a lovely singing voice," she said, patting the hand of the black woman seated next to her.

I hid my smile behind my hand so the nurses would not see it. "I would be proud to," I told her, and I began to teach them the words of an old song.

When the orderlies announced it was time for exercise, I left Alice and Izzy practicing my ancestors' language and shuffled out into the courtyard ahead of the others in search of a way out. I sent my crow out over the locked gates and doors, but there was no escape for me. I was about to send her to look for *momoy* growing nearby when I stumbled in surprise. Hopping slowly next to one woman was a spirit jackrabbit. She seemed unaware of it, and as more men and women joined us in the courtyard, I counted nearly twenty men and women among the crowd walking with their spirit selves—tortoises, snakes, several birds, coyotes, raccoons, and even a jaguar.

I lengthened my stride so that I drew up alongside the jackrabbit woman. I began to sing one of the healing songs in a very quiet voice, eyes down and watching the jackrabbit. Its ears twitched. I continued to sing, and to my delight, the woman fell in step with me. Though her eyes were fixed ahead and her expression remained slack, she reached out and took my hand.

Out of the corner of my eye, I glanced at the other people and their spirit selves, but apart from catatonia, they had nothing in common. They were men and women, old and young, and many variations of skin and features. However, when the exercise period was over and a nurse yanked my hand from the jackrabbit woman's, I saw that all of the people with spirit selves were being led into ward twenty-eight, a place whose reputation was terrible, even judged by south quad standards.

I recalled whispered stories about experimental treatments being used on the low-functioning patients in ward twenty-eight, and suddenly Olsen's fury at my having supplied a patient with *momoy* tea began to make sense. Could *momoy* or something similar be part of these experiments? I had to find out.

When we returned to our ward, I sang a song for Alice and Izzy and then excused myself, claiming to be tired. I returned to our bedroom, sat by the wall under an open window, and sent my crow self hopping through the bars. She flew across the courtyard, over the roofs of wards twenty-eight and twenty-nine, and alighted on the sill of an open window. Through it, I could see the common room where the patients in ward twenty-eight gathered. All of them were accompanied by their spirit selves.

Curious, my crow hopped through the window and was immediately distracted by light reflecting off a windowed door that led to an isolation room. Her claws scrabbled against the glass and eventually found purchase in the metal trim surrounding the opening.

Through it I could see a Chinese woman sitting on the floor of a tiny room, curled up next to her spirit deer, stroking the creature's neck. Its head rested on her shoulder, and they rocked back and forth together, as if in time to a lullaby.

My heart leaped. Someone aware of her spirit self could be a powerful ally against the riders. The entire ward might be allies if they could be weaned from their daily doses of poison and convinced to fight. My crow self hopped off the window and fluttered through the ward. None of the other patients looked at her, nor did their spirit selves.

Satisfied, she flew over to the dispensary, where a technician was putting the evening pills into white paper cups. My crow self was interested in the shiny glass bottles, but I noticed that the cups that contained the doses of mind-numbing poison also held some shriveled brown objects that I recognized in triumph.

Teonanácatl, Dolores had called them when we found the little brown mushrooms growing in the wild. She said they were to her ancestors what *momoy* was to mine. I felt tears of joy fill my eyes as I grasped that it meant that the secret treatments in ward twenty-eight included true medicine.

Back in my own body, I could feel my stomach tighten, and before I could help myself I was laughing. To my surprise, I heard laughter coming from the doorway, where a passing patient began to laugh as well. Soon everybody in the common room was laughing, and I felt tears running down my cheeks. In that moment of delight, the riders did not exist, even as the nurses and aides ordered us to be silent.

My crow self gave a few delighted caws and flew around the common room of ward twenty-eight, which to my surprise attracted the attention of several of the spirit creatures. Since the aides in my ward were still trying to quiet the common room, they did not hear me begin to sing, and my crow sang the song in ward twenty-eight. One by one, the spirit creatures began to shake off their torpor, and one of the raccoons approached her.

"Why do you call us, sister?" asked the raccoon.

"Because we are needed," I said through my crow. "There is a wicked presence we must drive out."

"They are already gone," said a magpie, who was preening her tail nonchalantly. "Mostly."

My crow clucked disapprovingly at her. "Some of them left, but that's because they are no longer confined here."

"If they have found better hunting elsewhere, why should we care?" asked a snake, which had been wrapped around a chair leg.

"Sooner or later, they will run out of easy prey in the rest of the hospital," I said. "When that happens, they will return here. Your human selves are weak from the poison they are given with the true medicine."

"What do you believe we should do?" asked the jackrabbit, who had been listening thoughtfully.

"Fight!" shouted my crow, without any prompting from me. "At night we will teach you songs that the riders cannot abide, and you can help your humans light sacred fires so that we may mob our enemies! They will be driven out!"

"Even if we succeed, more arrive every year," snarled a coyote. "Why fight a battle we can never win?"

My crow paused, listening for my words. "More riders may come," I said through her, "but if our humans have the chance to heal for a time without their interference, they may choose to remain dormant until weaker prey arrives."

"That does not give me confidence," said the jaguar, staring at my crow with her hunter's eyes.

"It is not meant to," I said. "The riders may defeat us. But I have seen a strong home keep them at bay for many years. There will always be new riders as long as their chosen vessels thrive, but they cannot grow strong where there are those willing to stand against them."

The jaguar chose this moment to begin cleaning her paws. The seemingly casual gesture revealed sharp claws that flashed in the fading daylight.

The magpie trilled out, "We will fight! We will fight!"

In the weeks that followed, I wrote several letters to Dolores asking for her help. But by the time I judged that my allies in my building and the patients in ward twenty-eight were ready to challenge the riders, I had received no reply. Though I suspected that my letters had never been sent, awful thoughts would visit me in the pre-dawn hours, whispering that my sister no longer acknowledged me because I was in a hospital for the mad, and such people were not talked about. Knowing these thoughts were made stronger by the riders' presence did not make them less painful.

As I busied myself in preparation for our stand against the riders and shared laughter and song with my fellow patients, I also mourned the loss of Dolores's wooden whistle, which had cheered so many when I had worked in the main hospital. It had disappeared along with my other belongings when I was taken to the closed ward.

We decided to act on a Wednesday, ten weeks after my arrival. Though the riders' exodus from the south quad had had dire effects on the rest of the hospital, the ward twenty-eight patients were much improved by prayers, songs, and comfort from their spirit selves. Some even spoke in voices rough from disuse, and all were more alert and interested in their surroundings. They clearly found strength in being united against a common enemy.

One cloudless day in early autumn, we were herded into the exercise yard. I seized the moment that it took our watchers' eyes to adjust to the sunlight to flip open the lighter I had stolen the previous week. When I was satisfied with the flame, dim in the bright sunshine, I tossed it over the wall, where I knew it would fall beneath a row of sage bushes whose roots were protected by a bed of dry mulch.

I slowed my pace to watch my crow self, who had hopped over the far wall, and my heart leaped when I heard her cackle triumphantly at the crackling flames. At that point, I began to sing softly, and the jackrabbit woman, who had once again fallen into step next to me, joined in the song. I could already smell sage burning, and I watched the aides to see how long it would take them to notice. The smell of sage grew strong, and the wind was such that I knew it would blow the smoke to the north, where most of the riders were feeding.

My skin began to tingle as others from my ward began to join the song. Even Olsen sensed what we were doing before he realized that there was a fire burning nearby. He yelled at the jackrabbit woman to shut up, but she kept singing, even more loudly now that she had been noticed. Fortunately, someone sounded the alarm before Olsen reached her.

"This way! Go! Go!" One of the aides shouted as he ran to the gate and unlocked it. At last!

As the nurses and aides ushered us out of the south quad, I and the patients from ward twenty-eight continued to sing amid the hubbub, shouting the sacred words at the top of our voices. I smiled fiercely as Alice took my other hand, and Izzy's powerful voice rang out, bouncing off the buildings like sun off a mirror.

Already I could hear otherworldly shrieks as the less powerful riders were driven out, but I could see four of the oldest and largest massing around the clock tower, forming a wall in front of us. My crow cawed to signal the spirit animals' advance, and the jaguar tore off towards them, teeth bared. The coyotes yipped and sped after her. The birds attacked, shrieking for all they were worth. I was about to follow after my crow when I felt a gentle hand squeeze mine.

"You can see them, too," said Alice, staring at where the riders were scattering under the spirit animals' attack.

"Yes," I said. "Alice, it's important that you keep the others singing. Can you do that?"

I was surprised to see tears trickling down my friend's cheeks. "All this time," she said softly.

"Sing, Alice," I said. "And never stop as long as you can see them."

She met my eyes for one last time. "I won't."

I nodded, then ran off to the gate, which the patients of ward twenty-eight had pulled off its hinges, and charged into the chaos, shouting the song. I ran to the burning sage bushes and was trying to pull a smoldering branch off to use as a weapon, when an arm like iron hooked around my neck and pulled me back.

"You did this," hissed a voice in my ear.

The arm tightened against my windpipe, and I could not breathe. Though I knew the voice to be Olsen's, it was also the voice of the riders. I had just enough time to process this before I felt a needle pierce the flesh of my side. My eyes widened as my heart began to race.

"It ends here," said the voice from somewhere far away.

He was wrong.

Though the stories and songs of my childhood saved my life the first time I faced the *nunasus,* they were not enough to save me a second time. My body was incinerated and the ashes buried in back of the hospital, along with the remains of other patients who had "'disappeared." But my enemies made an error—the staff members, grown greedy under the riders' spell, were allowed to divide my belongings between themselves. Instead of ensuring my passage into the Upper World, as burning my belongings would have done, they made sure that I and my crow self would linger.

That night, Dolores's whistle sang out, and it shook me from the torpor of death and drew me to ward twenty-eight. There, I saw jackrabbit woman in solitary confinement for her suspected part in the afternoon's confusion. As Olsen approached her cell, looking sooty and exhausted, her jackrabbit thumped his foot on the floor, which gave her enough warning to slip the stolen whistle inside her shirt and feign sleep. Olsen went away unsatisfied, and the spirit animals took up her song of triumph.

Emboldened by her resistance, I rose into the sky with my crow, and I saw that though a few riders still remained on hospital grounds, they lurked outside the buildings, unable to enter.

Olsen left the hospital soon after, around the same time that the sedative doses became less frequent and the closed ward patients' garden privileges were restored. Alice's husband soon came to take her away, and I comforted Izzy at night with songs, as our friend had once done for me. I still bore silent witness to hideous acts perpetrated by those under the influence of the riders that lingered. But the long-term patients in the closed wards continued to pray and sing, and in other parts of the hospital, I whispered the old songs to patients as they slept. Slowly, the despair that had blanketed the institution for so many years began to lift.

Televisions, newspapers, and magazines appeared in common areas, and I learned how much the world outside had changed. I also learned of my old friend Adolfo's passing. Though my spirit was bound to the place where I had been murdered, I prayed for his passage to the Upper World and knew he would rise on wings of the love of his family and the residents of the community he so enriched.

As for the white horses, the community's pride, they were expensive to keep. As ranch lands dwindled, so too did the number of white foals being born. From high above the hospital, I sensed each new arrival, but the newborn riders did not stir from their mounts. There they stayed, dormant, until the last of the horses were sold at auction and scattered.

Eventually the hospital closed, but the riders and I linger, for they can no more change their natures than I can change mine. The old buildings and grounds have found a new life as a university, and there are those who sense the riders lurking in the south quad, but I, Beatriz Yorba, will remain to fight them with sacred songs and to sing the spirits of their victims to the Upper Kingdom.

The Semi-Detached of Usher
Episode 1: The Ringer of the Doorbell

Jonathan Waite (with Jae Eynon)

Terminal 5, Heathrow Airport, London.

Among the rumpled passengers staggering off the plane and into the sterile light of the air bridge, a distinguished gentleman, impeccably dressed in a three-piece suit and carrying a silver-knobbed cane and a peculiarly carved box tucked under his arm aroused, strangely, no curiosity at all. He moved with the herd, passed immigration without incident, and continued to the luggage carousel, where he retrieved a small suitcase. At customs, an overzealous officer chose to take an interest in the box, whereupon the gentleman raised his eyebrows and lowered the tip of his cane to the floor. The knob at the top glowed briefly with an eldritch light, and the customs officer forgot why he had called the man over. By the look of him, he had forgotten his own name.

The gentleman nodded and walked away.

He found the taxi rank and asked courteously to be driven into London, quelling the driver's babble with another jab of the cane. An hour later, he was searching the ledgers in the National Archives; some time after that, with a ridiculous coffee confection his passport to a sit-down and free wifi, he slipped a tablet computer from his pocket. A little research, culminating in the horror of National Rail Enquiries, told him what he needed to know.

Hours later, as the afternoon waned, the gentleman emerged, still immaculate, from a provincial railway station. Above his head, a sign in a slightly shamefaced font confessed "Eltdown". He looked around, smiled grimly, and tucked the box away where it would not immediately be noticed. Time enough for that later.

Kevin Usher stuck his key in the lock of his sliding-down-the-property-market semi-detached house on the outskirts of Eltdown.

". . . the simplest thing!" Edwina's voice carried from her car as she yanked her handbag off the passenger seat. "I distinctly remember you saying you had a staff meeting, so—"

"I did. But it got cancelled at the last minute, as usual, and then I remembered your pottery class, so I thought . . ."

He opened the door and walked into the living room, remembering to wipe his feet. They might get another couple of years out of the carpet if they were careful. Tallish, forty-ish, formerly thin, scruffy in a semi-academic way, Kevin didn't glance at the mirror on the wall. He took off his tie and held the door for Edwina. She noticed that he'd forgotten to undo the top button of his shirt but couldn't conjure the energy to mention it. She carefully hung her jacket, three years old but still smart, on a hanger and took off her shoes. Last through the door was a middling-to-small child whose outfit would have been more suited to a middle-aged hippy, had she not worn it with complete self-possession. She fiddled with the bells on her plait and regarded her parents with interest.

"A pottery class I had already cancelled because you told me about the staff meeting. Honestly, Kevin, I wonder sometimes if you pay any attention."

"I do wish you wouldn't go on, Mummy," said the child. "I think it's sweet of you to both come and pick me up."

Edwina closed her eyes for a moment, struggling for a calm tone of voice. "Tara, darling, it is not 'sweet'. It's stupid. Stupid is what it is. Two cars to pick up one child—I felt like a procession. And don't, please, keep calling me Mummy. Okay? I keep telling you that 'Mummy' is twee. My name is Edwina."

"I know, Mummy," said Tara.

"I rang to tell you," said Kevin. "Tried to. You weren't in, and your mobile was switched off."

Tara grinned and marked a 'point for Daddy' in the air.

"That," said Edwina, "is entirely beside the point. Entirely."

"What's the point of having a mobile phone if nobody can call you on it?" said Kevin.

"I just don't like all the not getting work calls all day." Edwina avoided his eyes.

"Shall we call it a draw?" said Kevin gently.

"I'm going to make some tea."

"That would be lovely." Kevin stretched and flopped into an armchair, waggling a foot at Tara, who knelt down and began picking at the laces.

"Anyway, Tara," called Edwina from the kitchen, "I'd have thought you'd be more concerned about the waste of petrol . . . the pollution . . ."

"A drop in the ocean, Mummy. One extra car makes no difference at all."

Tara got the first shoe off and made a start on the other. Edwina reappeared in the kitchen doorway and stood watching.

"You know, darling, your father is quite capable of taking off his own shoes."

"Yes, but it's nice when people do things for you, isn't it, Daddy?"

Kevin opened an eye. "I have to admit there's a certain sybaritic luxury in having one's shoes taken off for one."

"Kevin, you encourage this child. Ten years old, and she's no better than a servant!"

"But Mummy!" Tara opened her eyes wide. "It's good training for later life. I need to learn how to be a dutiful wife and cater to my husband's every need . . ."

"Do I have to make you read Germaine Greer again?" said Edwina, struggling to restrain a twitch of the lips.

"No! Anything but that!" giggled Tara.

"Good. Now, since you're feeling so domestic, come and help me with the tea. You can tell me about your day."

"You haven't asked Daddy about his," said Tara, staying put.

"Boring and tedious," said Kevin.

"At least you have a job." Edwina failed not to sound bitter.

"If you can call it that. Junior clerk. Patronised by the public, condescended to by small boys with degrees in Political Science or Business

Administration . . ."

". . . and forced to be polite to little old ladies who insist on paying their entire year's council tax three months late, in pennies. Yes, I've heard it. Now, Tara, you see why I don't ask Daddy—I mean Kevin—about his day."

"Because you're jealous," said Tara.

"Kitchen. Now."

Tara, recognising the Tone That Must Be Obeyed, scrambled to her feet and followed Edwina into a kitchen as relentlessly clean and intransigently down-at-heel as the living room

"You are, though, aren't you, Mummy?" persisted Tara.

Edwina picked up the kettle and took it to the sink, where she turned on the tap with force enough to send a tsunami of cold water ricocheting back out and onto her blouse.

"Jealous? Because your father gets to earn a wage while I spend my days doing housework?" She slammed the lid of the kettle shut. "Because if I were doing what I'm trained for, I'd be earning more than twice what he is?" She turned round to face Tara. "Why should that make me jealous?"

"You shouldn't let it worry you so, Mummy."

Edwina set the kettle back on its base with extreme prejudice and strove for a level tone.

"Tara, what worries me is that I seem to be the only member of this family who *is* worried."

"Well," said Tara, dragging out the vowel, "if you stop worrying, then you won't be. So you can stop worrying."

"You don't understand, Tara! Kevin isn't earning enough to keep us. We moved out here after I lost my job because we couldn't afford a house in the city, and then I couldn't get a job out here, and Kevin couldn't get a teaching position and had to make do with the job he's got, and—"

"And since then we've just drifted further and further into debt, and the more we try to get out, the worse it gets. I know."

"How do you know?" said Edwina, surprised.

"Daddy explained it all to me the other night. Seriously, though, can I ask a question?"

"Of course you can, darling."

"How exactly does you worrying make it better?"

"Well, it doesn't, of course, but . . ."

"So why do you do it?" Tara's eyes were limpid pools of innocent enquiry.

Edwina made a noise of pure frustration. "Oh, you're as bad as your father!"

"Much worse, Mummy. Much, much worse. By the way, did you know that the kettle boils faster if you switch it on?"

"What? Oh." Edwina deflated. "Your father's like Mr Micawber. He thinks something will turn up—but life doesn't work like that."

"Something did, though, didn't it?"

"Did what?"

"Turn up. For Mr Micawber."

"He was a made-up character in a made-up story, as you very well know. Like those games you play when you pretend to talk to Great-Grandma on the phone. Just pretend. Not real."

"But what is reality, Mummy?" Tara gave an exaggerated sigh and cocked her head. "Am I going to have to make you read Carlos Castaneda again?"

Back in the living room, Kevin also sighed and levered himself up from his semi-supine position in the chair to sit forward and grapple with his other shoe. He tugged at the lace, which promptly and inevitably knotted itself. Kevin prepared to work himself up to another sigh, a really good one full of world-weariness and resignation, but his effort was interrupted by the doorbell. Though he was nearer, he glanced at the kitchen doorway, only to have Edwina's voice return his tiny volley of hope with a backhand "Would you get that, Kevin?"

He rolled his eyes and got up. The uneven gait caused by his demi-shod state struck him as having possibilities, and by the time he reached the front door, he was in full-blown Quasimodo lurch. He undid the latch and opened the door, vocally supplying the horrible screech of ancient hinges that Edwina's assiduous use of WD-40 made a sad impossibility. His terrible hunch forcing him to address the doormat, he produced a voice that could only be the bastard lovechild of Karloff and Lugosi, schooled to maturity by Gollum.

"Welcome to my home . . ."

He caught sight of the highly polished shoes on the mat and straightened, taking in smartly tailored trousers and the waistcoat and jacket that constituted the rest of a suit that had probably cost more than Kevin's entire house, a grey silk tie garnished with a shining gold tie-pin, and, crowning the ensemble, the look of faint surprise that adorned the face of a gentleman of a certain age who was standing at the door bearing a cane and a small suitcase.

"Oh, I'm sorry," said Kevin. "I was expecting, erm . . ." Inspiration struck. ". . . a cat."

"A cat," said the gentleman.

"Yes. You know . . ." He bent down with his hand out and made 'puss-puss' noises. "A cat."

"Do they often use the doorbell?" said the gentleman, elevating his eyebrows just far enough to indicate profound disbelief.

"Oh, yes," said Kevin, by this point somewhat desperate. "Very well brought-up, the cats round here."

"And also very tall."

During the pause that followed, Kevin tried unsuccessfully to toe off his remaining shoe, but it was uncooperative and, under the expressionless gaze of the visitor, Kevin finally gave up the battle for both dignity and pretence.

"What can I do for you?" he said.

"Do I have the honour of addressing Mr Kevin Usher?" enquired the gentleman.

Kevin, unused to having the opportunity to speak with him regarded as any kind of honour, replied cautiously, "That would depend on who was doing the addressing."

"My name," said the gentleman, is "Bal-Shaddath. I am . . . a messenger."

"Oh lord, you're not the Jehovah's Witnesses, are you?"

"Who is it, Kevin?" Edwina called out.

Kevin lifted his foot and yanked the shoe off manually. "Only we really aren't very interested in that kind of thing, you see . . ."

"I assure you, Mr Usher, that Jehovah—" At this point, Bal-Shaddath gave a delicate shudder. "—has nothing whatsoever to do with this."

"Um, Hare Krishna, then?" He surveyed Bal-Shaddath's ensemble again.

"I must say, I like the new look."

"Kevin! Who *is* it?" Edwina shouted louder. "Is it the Jehovah's Witnesses again?"

In the middle of two conversations, Kevin felt not quite up to the task. He handed his shoe to Bal-Shaddath. "Hang on a moment, will you?" Over his shoulder, he shouted, "It's all right, darling, I can handle it." Turning back to Bal-Shaddath, he said, "Right, where were we? Oh yes, erm, insurance, was it?"

A little nonplussed, Bal-Shaddath handed back the shoe and gathered his dignity. "Mr Usher—"

"Right, Mr Sanctimonious God-botherer," said Edwina, shoving Kevin out of the way, "you've picked the wrong house this time."

"Edwina," said Kevin.

Edwina ignored him. Shoving her sleeves up, she stepped forward.

"My husband let you get away with it last time. He can't help it—he's just a weak and foolish man. But now *I've* got you, and *I've* got a little message for God, okay?"

Bal-Shaddath backed up a pace.

"Mrs Usher . . ."

Edwina pressed her advantage and stepped forward again.

"Because we've been calling Him maybe twenty times a day—and that's not counting taking His name in vain—that's genuine attempts to get in touch, make an appointment for a quick consultation, sort things out on a person-to-deity level, you know? And does He ever call back? Fax? Email? Divine revelation? Don't make me laugh," she said, laughing bitterly. "So— since you seem to be in touch with Him on a regular basis, you can just tell Him from me—"

"Edwina," said Kevin, "he's not the Jehovah's Witnesses. He's an insurance salesman."

"Oh. Oh well. Same applies—just change the names."

Bal-Shaddath seized on Edwina's momentary hitch in momentum. "I am not selling anything, Mrs Usher. I have something to deliver to your husband. May I come in?"

Kevin, suddenly wary, pulled Edwina back. "You're not a lawyer, are you?" he said.

Reaching into his inside pocket, Bal-Shaddath gave a minuscule hint of a might-be eye crinkle. "Well, as it happens, I—"

Kevin thrust his shoe into Edwina's hands and made to close the door.

"Stop right there!" he shouted. "I'm not admitting anything and I'm not accepting anything, so—"

After a long and trying day of bad British transport and worse British coffee, Bal-Shaddath's patience reached its end. He jabbed his cane firmly into the doorstep and, once again, the silver end glowed eerily. Edwina's face went slack and her arms fell limply to her sides. The shoe dropped.

"Hear the words of Bal-Shaddath, the Immanent One, the Guardian of the Portal, Destroyer of Millions, the Chaos Out Of Time!" she intoned.

"What?" said Kevin.

"What?" said Edwina in her normal voice.

Bal-Shaddath had somehow managed to move smoothly past them. "If I may . . ." he said, advancing into the living room. He set down his suitcase and eyed the worn-out décor with some distaste. "Hmm. We seem to have lost much over the years."

"Here, you can't just barge in like that!" Kevin protested.

"I am not, as you put it, 'barging in', Mr Usher. Your charming wife invited me in."

"What? When?"

"Just now. Didn't you hear me?" said Edwina.

"You said something like, 'Hear the words of Bad-Shaggit '. . .'"

"Bal-Shaddath, please," said Bal-Shaddath, looking pained.

"Oh, Kevin, do wash your ears out," said Edwina. "I said, 'Well, as long as you're here, you might as well come in.'" She frowned. "Or something like that."

Kevin gave up. "Well, since you're in, what do you want?"

"I must discharge my duty," replied Bal-Shaddath. "I admit I had hoped for something a little more in keeping . . . But in the end, I suppose the bloodline is all."

With something of a flourish, he reached into a nothingness in space located on his person and produced the box, from which he blew invisible specks of dust before proffering it ceremonially to Kevin, who recoiled, his hands behind his back.

"What? But . . . How? What?"

"Your inheritance, Mr Usher."

At that moment bending to pick up the shoe, Edwina also picked up the word and straightened abruptly.

"Inheritance?" she said, and handed the shoe to Kevin.

"That is what I said, Mrs Usher," affirmed Bal-Shaddath with a courteous nod in her direction.

"Hang on," said Kevin. "Does this involve money?"

Bal-Shaddath smiled tightly. "How crass. But yes, there is a substantial sum involved."

Kevin, oblivious to any shame he was obviously expected to feel, narrowed his eyes. "And . . . this wouldn't be one of those substantial sums that has a minus sign in front of it?"

"I assure you, Mr Usher, if you choose to accept the legacy, you will become quite wealthy. As the world reckons wealth."

"Oh, Kevin!" breathed Edwina, hope beginning to spark. Warily, though, she turned her question to Bal-Shaddath. "How wealthy, precisely?"

Bal-Shaddath gave a weary sigh. "Several hundreds of millions of dollars and other stable currencies, mostly in property, funds, and investment portfolios. A percentage of the income is transferred each month into a checking account in a reputable Boston bank," he recited. "This arrangement will, of course, be altered in light of your being resident in this country."

"I didn't know you had any rich relatives, Kevin," said Edwina.

"Neither did I. Hang on . . ." He turned back to Bal-Shaddath. "*If* I choose to accept? Why wouldn't I? What's the catch?"

"There is a precondition," Bal-Shaddath conceded. "You must accept the inheritance in full or not at all. The terms of the will are quite specific."

"Oh, right. And I suppose there's some great old rambling mansion in the swamps somewhere that'll cost more to pull down than—"

"Alas, no. Not any more. The legacy consists of the money, some few goods and chattels from the estate, and . . . this." Once more, he proffered the box.

"Nothing . . . bad?" Kevin said tentatively.

"Kevin, you're a wimp," snapped Edwina. "I'm sorry, Mr Bal-Shaddath, my husband has paralysis of the spine. Can I accept on his behalf?"

"I fear that only the True Heir may accept the legacy." The capitals were audible.

"I'm not a wimp," said Kevin. "I'm just having a hard time with the concept of anything good happening to us. I really think we ought to know a bit more about—"

"Kevin Rodney Usher. If you don't accept this inheritance right here and right now, you can . . . you can . . . Oh, Kevin, can't you see? This is it. Our ship. It's come in at last! It's here if we want it, and I for one do want it, and if you make one of your cheap jokes out of that I'll crown you. I want you to accept this. Right here, right now. Come on!" Edwina panted with the effort of persuasion.

Unhappily, Kevin caved in. "Oh, all right then."

Bal-Shaddath held the box out again, balanced on the palm of his left hand, tucked his cane under his right armpit, and drew a sheet of ancient-looking paper from a pocket, shaking it open. He cleared his throat and read formally:

"Do you, Kevin Rodney Usher, being of the right and true line descended, being sound of wit and knowing whereof you speak, having— hmm, hmm, a lot of antiquated legalese I'm sure I needn't trouble you with—"

"Hang on," said Kevin.

Edwina growled.

Kevin sagged. "Oh, all right. Carry on."

"Do you, Kevin Rodney Usher," resumed Bal-Shaddath, "take unto yourself the inheritance of the line of Usher, all the duties and perquisites thereto appurtenant, and vow to keep the same in trust for your heirs until your death?" He paused. "You should say, 'yes'."

"Er . . .," said Kevin.

"Or 'no', of course, if you . . ."

"Don't even think it," threatened Edwina.

"Yes. I do, I suppose," Kevin said.

He handed his shoe to Bal-Shaddath again and took the box, which he immediately dropped with a loud yelp.

"Kevin!" said Edwina, shocked.

"It moved! It moved!" He shook his hands as though burned.

Bal-Shaddath stood tall and, in a voice that seemed to echo, declaimed, "It . . . is . . . *done.*"

The light in the room dimmed, and Kevin and Edwina watched in perplexed horror as the box began to sink slowly into the carpet. They stumbled backwards as a faint rumbling sound shook the air, vibrating the fabric of the whole house.

"I didn't think the pile was that deep," Kevin said faintly as he watched the box sink lower.

"My carpet!" screeched Edwina, diving forward. Her fingers scrabbled at the edge of the box, but she was too late, and the carpet closed over the top, leaving not a trace. The rumbling and vibration grew stronger.

Bal-Shaddath stood in the middle of the room as unperturbed as though sinking magical boxes and earthquakes were an everyday occurrence for him.

"As it was in the infancy of the cosmos, when the stars swelled and burst forth with unnameable life, as it was when time itself writhed in the birthpangs of matter—" he proclaimed.

The room shook harder. The ceiling cracked and a little plaster fell, pattering to the carpet where Edwina still knelt, vainly trying to discover where the box had gone. Kevin, vaguely remembering a disaster movie he'd once seen, staggered in the direction of a doorway.

"When the Elder Gods bound the Great Old Ones for a time to be imprisoned in domains beyond time and space, till the stars attain once more their age-lost conjunction—"

"Kevin, look!" Edwina shouted, pointing at the wall behind the sofa.

With a deep grating sound, the wall parted, crumbling slightly, as an arch of ancient stone rose majestically into position, its opening filled by a door of wood so old and solid, so scarred and bound with iron straps and bosses, that it seemed ready to repel an army of dragon-riding barbarian warriors. The noise and movement subsided as the arched doorway settled into place with an echoing thud. A picture teetered on its hook and fell to the floor.

Kevin unwrapped his fingers from the kitchen doorframe and wobbled over to help Edwina to her feet.

He looked. "Well, that's a little incongruous," he said.

The house situated at the un-detached side of the Ushers' semi presented a rather different aspect from the unsuccessful battle against challenged finances with which the Ushers faced the world. The garden looked like the front of a packet of grass seed. The edges of the lawn were crisp; there was not a hint of moss in the short, velvety grass—a daisy wouldn't even have dreamed of setting root there; the dead-heading was up to date, and there wasn't even the breath of a hint of a weed amongst the flowers. Behind the faux-lattice windows, the living room's aspect reflected the perfection of the exterior. The precisely-placed brown leather three-piece suite was shiny; the fireplace with its lifelike-flame gas fire was shiny; the horse-brasses decorating the walls were shiny—as were the golfing trophies arranged prominently on a shelf attached to the party wall.

In the midst of all the blindingly polished perfection sat Ralph Furniss in his favourite armchair, a John LeCarré hardback open on his lap. In his fifties and militarily neat, possessed of thick pair of glasses, a thin moustache and a vanishing chin, Ralph favoured zipped cardigans, brown corduroys, and a quiet and orderly existence. Which was, without warning, overturned as the whole room began to shake and rumble.

He clung to the arms of his chair and watched in horror as his beloved shelf of trophies came loose at one end and the entire row of little cups and figurines slid inexorably down the slope and crashed to the floor.

A scream sounded from the kitchen.

"What in heaven's name?" muttered Ralph. He struggled out of his heaving chair and staggered to the window to peer out in search of juggernauts, low-flying aircraft, unexpected oil-drilling, or something else he could write to the papers about. There was nothing in view apart from the Ushers' two unwashed cars parked on the road next to his own waxed and polished Vauxhall, and, as suddenly as it had begun, the noise and shuddering stopped.

"Right," he said. Head thrust forward, he stamped out of his slippers and into his shoes, thrust his arms into his coat sleeves, and seized his stick in one hand and a headless gilded golfer in the other. "This is it," he snapped. "Enough is enough. I'm a patient man, I hope, but somewhere a line must be drawn. I'm just going next door, Emily!" he called into the kitchen.

"What was it, Ralph?" came the shaky reply.

"I don't know, do I? But it's quite clear to me that that Kevin Usher is at the bottom of it. I'm going round now to have it out with him."

"Do be careful," said Emily.

"I'm always careful," said Ralph.

He stamped out, pausing to put the door on the latch.

Next door, Kevin and Edwina, the latter still on the floor, were staring wild-eyed at Bal-Shaddath, who stood arms outstretched, an expression of ecstasy on his face. He had apparently forgotten that he was still holding Kevin's shoe.

"It is well!" he proclaimed joyfully. "My master has accepted his new home!"

"What master? What home? What are you talking about?" stammered Kevin, while Edwina clambered to her feet and tried with less than her usual success to pull her clothes straight.

"I am in your debt, Mr Usher," said Bal-Shaddath with a bow. He looked quizzically at the shoe in his hand and gave it back to Kevin. "Had you not accepted the legacy, my Master and I would have been condemned to wander this unforgiving world until your heir should come of age and find a dwelling place."

"Well," Kevin said, "You can just pack him away again and get back to wandering, because there is no way I am accepting—"

The doorbell rang.

"I'm afraid you have already accepted, Mr Usher. The contract, though verbal, is quite binding under the applicable legal system. Which, I should mention, predates the Babylonian code by a considerable number of years."

"I forgot. You're a lawyer."

Bal-Shaddath reached into his jacket again. "As I started to say earlier, I do happen to be a partner in a quite well-respected practice in Boston." He handed Kevin a card.

The doorbell rang again. Twice.

"Yoth-Garnath, Vul-Shathrion, Bal-Shaddath and McGillicuddy," read Kevin. "McGillicuddy?"

"A very old and distinguished family. And now I must deliver the rest of your legacy." He cleared his throat. "One would suggest that you do not open the Portal just yet, Mrs Usher." Edwina, having approached the new-to-them ancient door, snatched back her hand. "My master," continued Bal-Shaddath, "can be somewhat . . . cranky . . . after long journeys."

"Cranky?" said Edwina, frowning.

"Are you fond of your current shape, Mrs Usher?"

The bell sounded again, followed by a torrent of knocking.

"Well, I could afford to lose a few pounds, I suppose," said Edwina.

"Off which limb?" Bal-Shaddath enquired.

"Look," said Kevin impatiently, "who is your 'Master' anyway?"

Bal-Shaddath closed his eyes and made a reverent obeisance which Kevin knew for certain was not aimed in his direction.

"I am not worthy to utter his name."

"Does there happen to be anyone around who is?" said Kevin.

"He is the greatest of the Fairly Great Old Ones. I have served him faithfully for four thousand years, and—"

"Oh, come off it," Edwina said. "I mean—that's ridiculous!"

"Is it, Mrs Usher?"

"Of course it is!" She gestured impatiently. I've seen four-thousand-year-old people in the British Museum, and you're a lot juicier than they are. You're as normal as I am."

"Am I, Mrs Usher?"

Before Edwina's eyes, Bal-Shaddath's form began to blur and shift. The air around him eddied with a suggestion of thrashing tentacles and glowing eyes in places that eyes had no place to be.

"Am I?" he repeated, his voice distorted, echoing.

Edwina shuddered and closed her eyes. Kevin put his arm round her as she swayed.

"Are you all right, darling?"

She shook him off and lifted her chin.

"Of course I am. What were you saying, Mr Bal-Shaddath?"

"Yeah," said Kevin, giving Edwina another concerned glance before returning his attention to the lawyer, "who are these Fairly Great Old Ones?"

"Long ago, when the Elder Gods crushed the rebellion of the Great Old

Ones, they also worked their will upon the Slightly Less Great Middle-Aged Ones, and the Really, Really Great Decrepit Ones."

"Should I be taking notes?" Edwina said.

"Whose side were we on?" said Kevin.

The knocking at the door was enough this time to rattle it in its frame.

"This was long before your species existed, and the issues involved were too titanic for your petty minds to grasp," sniffed Bal-Shaddath.

Kevin opened the door to find a purple-faced Ralph Furniss gesticulating with a headless gold figurine that had once been his most prized golfing trophy.

"Can you call back another time, please, Ralph? We're a bit busy just now," said Kevin. He absently took the trophy, gave Ralph his shoe, and shut the door in his face.

"The Fairly Great Old Ones were divided." Bal-Shaddath continued as if there had been no interruption. "Some fought for the Great Old Ones, some for the Elder Gods. But all were imprisoned, even the Not Very Great Oldish Ones."

"That hardly seems fair," said Edwina.

The door shook under Ralph's furious pounding.

"Fairness is a human concept, Mrs Usher. But the Elder Gods were merciful, in their way. They set a term on the confinement of their enemies, to be determined by the stars in their courses."

"No time off for good behaviour, then," Kevin said.

"When the conjunction comes, all those who still have gateways to this universe shall be released from durance, and the battle shall resume."

"And this house is now the gateway for your Master," Edwina guessed.

"Indeed," said Bal-Shaddath. "And now I must summon the servants. Excuse me."

He turned smartly on his heel and went to the front door, which he opened to reveal Ralph, still there, still holding the shoe.

"Not today, thank you," he said firmly but politely, and walked past the fuming man, pulling the door shut behind him.

Kevin put the headless trophy on the mantelpiece and noticed that his hands were shaking. Not surprising, really. It was a wonder he could still walk, or think, or even breathe. He joined Edwina at the portal, where they wordlessly examined its time-scarred surface and the heavy iron ring that served as a handle.

"It's pretty convincing, isn't it?" Kevin said.

"Don't touch it, Kevin!"

"Oh, come on, Edwina, it's got to be some sort of trick. I mean, I don't know how he did it—yet—but all this talk of Masters and Grand Old Codgers or whatever. It's just a load of complete and total— Oh, hi. Bal-Shaddath. We were just talking about you."

"I can imagine," said Bal-Shaddath, who seemed to have re-materialised inside the room. "I can assure you, however, that there is no trick. And now . . ."

He opened the door, where they caught a brief glimpse of Ralph, staggering back from their second unexpected visitor of the day. This visitor had to duck his bald head and turn sideways to fit through the doorway. Dressed in homespun and a hairy goatskin jacket, he seemed all shoulders and very little neck and had a face like a brick. He stood awkwardly, taking up what felt like three-quarters of the room and all of their attention, until a wizened gypsy woman shoved him to one side and shuffled forward to stare with bright black eyes at the quivering Ushers.

"This is Tor," said Bal-Shaddath, indicating the giant. "You need not be apprehensive. He is sworn to obey your every command."

"He is?" squeaked Kevin.

"The only thing you cannot do is order him to leave you. He will be in charge of the care and maintenance of my Master's home. And any other little odd jobs you might have."

That brought Edwina out of her rabbit-in-headlights trance. "Pssst. Kevin . . . the porch roof . . ."

"Tor good at roofs," rumbled Tor, seemingly from somewhere in his boots. "Just show Tor where to nick lead from."

The door thundered with knocks once again. Tor turned around and went to answer, Bal-Shaddath stepping smartly aside to avoid being mown down.

"What for all this knocking?" growled Tor, opening the door on a suddenly quailing Ralph. "You want Tor come knock on you door? You go home."

Ralph thrust the shoe at Tor and turned tail, at which Tor let out a satisfied grunt and closed the door, absent-mindedly gnawing on the shoe.

"That's useful," murmured Kevin.

Edwina turned to the old woman. "And who might you be?"

The woman gave a twisted smile. "Many people I might be, mistress. But I am . . . *Malyeva.*"

"Cook-housekeeper, I suppose," said Kevin brightly.

"Maybe. And . . . maybe not. Some things are better left . . . undone."

"Like what?"

Malyeva's hand darted quick as a snake straight for his throat. "Top button of shirt when no tie is worn," she snapped. With a twist of the fingers, she dealt with the button and subsided.

"Ow!" said Kevin before his brain caught up with the fact he was unhurt. "I mean . . ."

"Malyeva is wise in many ways," Bal-Shaddath assured him. "I'm sure you'll get on."

The dubious silence that followed that statement was broken by the rattle of cups as Tara came through from the kitchen, carefully and with some difficulty carrying a large tray laden with teapot, milk, sugar, mugs, spoons and a packet of biscuits.

"Tea, anyone?" she said, as though earthquakes and mysterious portals and the cast of a 1930s horror movie in her living room were all quite normal. "Excuse me," she said to Tor, who obligingly stepped aside, eclipsing the whole front window. "Thank you."

"Tara!" said Edwina, forcing a smile. "I'd forgotten you were in the kitchen. Darling, maybe it would be a good idea if you went upstairs—"

Tara was all composure as she arranged the tea things on a low table. "Oh, I don't think so, Mummy. I mean, if all these people are going to be living with us, I'm bound to meet them eventually, so why not now? How do you like your tea, Mr Bal-Shaddath?"

Bal-Shaddath blinked. "Black, thank you. And you are . . .?"

"More of an orange juice person, actually." She poured for Bal-Shaddath then addressed Tor again. "You look like a milk-and-two-sugars."

Tor looked down at himself, confused.

Malyeva leaned towards Kevin. "I see there is wisdom in your line still."

Tara handed Tor his mug with an admonition that sugar was bad for his health and turned a questioning face to Malyeva, who drew herself up to her entire four feet ten.

"I do not drink . . . tea. I have . . . reasons."

"Is she always like this?" said Edwina to Bal-Shaddath.

"Heavens no," he replied, sipping his tea. "Sometimes she can be quite melodramatic."

"I think I'm getting a headache," Edwina muttered.

"Hang on!" said Kevin. "Somebody said something intelligent just now."

"It was me, Daddy."

"I need an aspirin," said Edwina, and wandered upstairs, absently taking the chewed shoe from Tor as she passed.

"That was it," said Kevin. "You can't all move in here—we've not got the room."

"I don't think you will find any problems accommodating us," Bal-Shaddath assured him.

"No, seriously, I'm talking our room, Tara's room and the bathroom upstairs. That's it."

"What about your den, Daddy?" said Tara helpfully.

"Far too small. And there's no room down here, as you can see. No stables, no outbuildings, no servants' quarters. Just one ordinary semi-detached house, and none too big, either."

"Tor not take up much room," mumbled Tor, hopefully but blatantly economical with the truth.

"We could move, I suppose. Find a bigger house, more rooms. . ."

Bal-Shaddath shook his head slowly, and Kevin began involuntarily to mirror the action, absorbing its import with a sinking heart.

"You're going to tell me we're stuck here now, aren't you?" he said.

"Until your death, or the destruction of this house. I'm terribly sorry. However, as I have been trying to say—"

From upstairs, a loud expletive and the pounding of feet interrupted him. Kevin arrived at the foot of the stairs barely in time to catch Edwina as she pelted down them.

"What's happened?"

Her eyes wider than he'd ever seen them, Edwina stammered, "Kevin!

There's . . . there's . . . There's more upstairs than there used to be!"

"What?" said Kevin. "What do you mean, more upstairs?"

"Great long corridors . . . Come and see!"

Kevin, whose indignation at the way his life was being steamrollered and turned inside-out was finally surfacing through the general haze of surprise, allowed himself to be pulled up the stairs. He stopped at the point where their perfectly serviceable beige carpet morphed seamlessly into an expanse of flagstones where their tiny landing had once been. Ahead and to either side, endless corridors stretched away through perspective-bending dimensions, some lit by flickering torches, some with gas-mantles, some fading quickly into chthonian darkness, and each one lined with doors.

"At least the bathroom's more or less where we left it," said Edwina, pointing to an open doorway about a wicket's length down one of the less terrifying passages, electric light spilling out onto worn stonework.

A nagging worry about heating bills fluttering to one side of his mind, Kevin stamped back down the stairs.

"Your house is quite spacious now," said Bal-Shaddath, "at least on the inside. As I said, I think you'll find that making room for us is not a problem."

"But how . . .? Never mind." Kevin combed his hands back through his hair and bellowed, "You might have told us about that a little earlier! Look what you've done!" He gestured wildly around himself.

To everyone's surprise, Tor growled and hulked forward, shoving his face, at the end of a pile-driver neck, towards Bal-Shaddath, who looked him up and down.

"Dear me," he said. "What's got into you?"

"You make master angry. You bad. Tor punish."

"Oh dear," said Bal-Shaddath, backing away. "He's very loyal, you know. He'll obey . . . you . . . implicitly. You only have to say the word." His legs met the sofa, and he sat down abruptly.

"Yes, I was just beginning to gather that," said Kevin with a grin. "All right, Tor. Leave him."

"Tor not hurt?" said the giant mournfully.

"Not just yet."

"Thank you, Mr Usher." Bal-Shaddath straightened his already-straight tie. "This body is not my only one, of course, but it does feel pain quite effectively."

"I'll bear that in mind." Turning to Edwina, Kevin said, "Are you okay, love?"

"Don't call me 'love', Kevin. It makes me feel like a barmaid. And of course I'm all right—it was just a bit of a shock, that's all."

Seeing that the Ushers were in no immediate need of extreme violence to be performed on their behalf, Tor grunted and turned to go upstairs. "Tor find room," he explained.

"I would say you were handling it very well, Mrs Usher," said Bal-Shaddath from the sofa. Far better than some of your husband's ancestors, in fact."

Edwina preened a little. "Yes, well, I am a legal secretary, or used to be. We have to cope with—"

"Did I understand you correctly? You are—" Bal-Shaddath perked up.

"A legal secretary? Yes, I am. Was. What's wrong with . . . Ohhh!" She grinned suddenly.

"What's going on?" said Kevin, looking from one to the other.

Malyeva, who until now had watched the proceedings with a beady eye from a corner of the room, gave a satisfied nod, stepped forward and announced, "I must go. I have . . . *things* . . . to do." She vanished through the kitchen door and could shortly be heard opening cupboards and tutting loudly.

"Tell me, Mrs Usher," said Bal-Shaddath, looking almost as beady as Malyeva, "Why did you abandon your career?"

"I didn't. It abandoned me. The firm collapsed. Or, to be precise, the senior partner collapsed and the junior partner went to the Bahamas with the contents of the safe."

"I had assumed that I should be compelled to relinquish my practice while my Master remained here," said Bal-Shaddath, "but this changes matters considerably. Do you think, Mrs Usher . . .?"

"Hey!" said Kevin.

"I'll think about it," said Edwina. "I can show you my qualifications and CV."

"I am sure they will be admirable," said Bal-Shaddath. He stood up and held out his hand for her to shake.

"Excuse me? Hello?" said Kevin.

They looked at him. He floundered a little. "Well, what about *his* qualifications and CV? We don't know a thing about him!"

"I think we've seen enough to be convinced he's genuine."

"Genuinely *what*, though?"

Edwina raised an eyebrow. "Really, Kevin. Can't you see this is a great chance for me? I can restart my career. You always said that you'd be more than pleased if I found another job."

"Yes, but I never thought . . ."

"That it would actually happen?" said Edwina sweetly.

"Not that—I knew you'd find something sooner or later, but . . . for *him*? Mr Dark-Magic-And-Mysterious-Portals? I can't believe I'm even saying this," he added.

"Well, now I can go out to work sooner rather than later."

"No need to go out," said Bal-Shaddath. "I shall be living in and can set up an office."

"Even better. Anyway, Tara's at school most of the time and she's pretty self-sufficient when she's at home, and we have, er, *people*—" She gestured towards the stairs and kitchen. "—to look after the house. All however-much-there-is of it. It's ideal!"

"I suppose so."

"You know it is."

"Yes, you're right, as you always are. Love." He looked around. "Speaking of Tara, where is she?"

"In the kitchen, isn't she?"

Malyeva appeared like a wizened genie at the kitchen door. "She is not with . . . me," she said and vanished again to clatter the pots.

"Then where?"

With a mutual look of horror, Kevin and Edwina turned towards the Portal and realised that it was no longer entirely closed. Ripples of coloured light oozed from around it and puddled ominously on the floor.

Some time before her parents took note of her absence, more or less when Kevin started having conniptions about living space, Tara had real-ised that a) what was most interesting in this whole situation was not up-stairs (though that sounded pretty interesting) but was actually behind the Portal, b) Bal-Shaddath wasn't looking, and c) there was no time like the present.

She sidled towards the enormous door and cautiously took hold of the unadorned iron ring that turned the latch. Heavy and cold in her hand, it also felt curiously alive, as though a trickle of electricity were humming through its molecules. She let go of it, just to make sure she could—because she'd read enough fairy tales to know a thing or two—then took a firm hold once more. A glance around the room assured her she was safe from adult interference until, with a shock, she met the expressionless gaze of Malyeva, but Malyeva simply blinked and tilted her head. Tara couldn't tell whether it was curiosity, anticipation, or permission, but clearly the old lady wasn't about to interfere, so she braced herself and turned the ring.

It was somewhat disconcerting that there was neither a deep clunk from the latch nor a rusty shriek from the hinges. Tara paused for a moment, then decided that if the door was aiding and abetting, then that constituted an invitation of sorts. She pushed the door just wide enough to let her pass, and slipped through, pushing it to—but not fully closed, because Lucy Pevensie was something of a heroine to her, and there wasn't really much philosophical difference between wardrobes and mysterious Portals—and taking stock.

Beyond a short landing floored in stone, a flight of ancient steps, their centres worn by the passage of countless feet, descended into darkness. Roughly-hewn walls rose to either side and arched over Tara's head, splotched with lichens and oddly disquieting stains. Though there was no obvious source of illumination, waves of shimmering, coloured light played up the walls, swirling gently in a mesmerising display. An orchestra of drips and strange noises echoing below suggested a cavernous space out of sight. Tara picked up her trailing hippy skirts and made her way carefully downwards, noting how the light swelled and followed her, considerately illuminating the way.

After about twenty steps down, she found that she could make out the bottom of the stairway, as well as a hint of what waited there. She stopped and fastidiously dusted a step, then sat down.

"Hello," she said.

Something shuffled and writhed and came closer.

"I know we aren't supposed to disturb you yet," she continued. "But if I was moving into a new house with a bunch of strangers, I'd be upset if at least one member of the family didn't come and say hello."

The coloured lights swirled faster as the occupant of the downstairs abyss hove into view, dragging a vortex of unspeakable dimensions with it. It glared at Tara. Or at least, that's what she had to assume, from the available evidence, it was doing.

"I hope you've got some kind of voice, or this is going to be a very one-sided conversation," she said.

The air shook and shattered as the thing roared, a weird, distorted howl conveying a suggestion of syllables.

"That's better," said Tara. "Now we can get to know each other."

The Thing roared again.

"That's not a very nice thing to say," said Tara. "If we're going to be friends, you'll have to change your attitude a little."

The Thing roared louder, apparently not accustomed to reproof.

"I'm sure you are. So am I. But it doesn't mean you have to be rude. Now, my name's Tara. Can you say 'Tara'?"

Another roar.

"Well, we'll have to work on that. What's your name?"

ROAR!

"I don't see that that matters. I can't talk to you if I don't know your name, now can I?"

Tara was treated to a longer, more nuanced and involved roar, accompanied by interdimensional thrashing.

She blinked. "I might have to practice that a bit, I think. Do you have a nickname at all?"

"Tara!"

Panicked parental shouts from above caused Tara to roll her eyes.

"Oh, dear. I'll probably have to go now. I'll come back and talk to you whenever I can, all right?"

In a rush, Kevin and Edwina were upon her, grabbing her arms and hauling her to her feet.

"Tara, darling! Are you all right?" panted Edwina, squeezing her all over to check that all limbs were in place.

"Don't go on, Mummy. Of course I am. I was just—"

She was rudely cut off by the sound of retching. Kevin, assured that Tara was in one piece, had looked around and caught sight of the Thing. Edwina turned to see what the cause was and screamed. Overcome with horror and disgust, they bolted up the stairs, hauling Tara with them. She twisted round enough to give the Thing a little wave before they threw her back through the door and into the living room, where Bal-Shaddath sat drinking tea in a disapproving manner. They continued to the kitchen, to retch loudly into the sink, leaving Tara under the cold gaze of their new house guest.

"That," said Bal-Shaddath, "was exceedingly reckless of you."

"I'm a rebel," she said. "You'll get used to it."

"You might have jeopardised my entire mission."

"You said it yourself. Daddy's stuck with you and your Master. And you're stuck with me."

Kevin staggered back in, ashen-faced. "What the *hell* was that?"

"You saw one of the aspects of my Master."

"I said hello, and he told me he wasn't used to food that talked back," said Tara.

"*What?*" shrieked Kevin.

"A natural misunderstanding," said Bal-Shaddath, raising a reassuring hand. "I'll talk with him."

"If that . . . that—" He heaved at the memory. "—thing lays one hand, tentacle, whatever, on my daughter—"

"That is hardly likely, since she is your only heir. At the moment."

"I was . . . I was tricked into this by a . . . a trick," Kevin shouted. "I ought to sue you!"

"In Boston, Mr Usher, we have a saying. 'Never sue a lawyer.' I admit that you were not allowed much time to read the small print, as it were, but I feel quite sure that the advantages of this relationship will far outweigh the drawbacks."

"Oh, you do, do you?" fumed Kevin.

Edwina tottered out of the kitchen, looking pasty. "Where's Malyeva?" she said.

"Here, lady," said Malyeva from right behind her.

Edwina jumped a mile.

"I clean the sink now," Malyeva added.

Tor stumped down the stairs, every tread protesting at his weight. He stopped to bounce on one experimentally.

"Tor found room," he announced. "Tor move stuff in already,"

"Stuff?" said Kevin.

"Goat. Chickens. Block and cleavers. Forge. Hammers." He shrugged. "Stuff."

"I didn't see . . . How did you . . . No—don't tell me. I don't want to know. I just hope you picked a nice big room for all that . . . stuff."

"Nice room. Too much furniture. Had to move furniture. But Tor like rose pink. Chickens like rose pink, too."

"Oh, no . . ."

"Our bedroom!" wailed Edwina.

"It's all right, Mummy," said Tara. "I'm sure everything will be just fine. I think it's quite fun, really."

Speechless, Edwina flung her arms in the air and fell back onto the sofa, where she lay in a pose of dramatic swoon for everyone's benefit.

"Mrs Usher, Mr Usher," Bal-Shaddath said in his most conciliatory tones, "you will adjust, as your daughter is so admirably adjusting already. My Master need not impinge on your daily lives at all. I—" (This, with a hard look at the butter-wouldn't-melt Tara.) "—shall see to his needs. You will find Tor and Malyeva really quite excellent servants when you get to know them."

Kevin stared around him at his extended-in-more-ways-than-one household and shook his head.

"I don't believe this. Half an hour ago I was a nice, normal, poverty-stricken nonentity. Now I'm the head of the Addams family."

"Oh, no. Far more respectable," said Bal-Shaddath. "This is the House—" He looked around him and very, very faintly curled his lip. "The Semi-Detached . . . of Usher."

Diabolus in Musica

Spring Strahm

The asphalt down Sixth Street is soft and sticky, practically melting in the Texas heat. I duck into El Camino Diablo, a devil-themed bar and my preferred spot to meet potential clients. Joel the bartender tosses me a can of whatever beer is on special today, and I claim my favorite table. My back is up against a brick wall, and I've got a full view of the front door. Old habits die hard. Anyone walking in through that door is going to need a couple of seconds to let their eyes adjust to the dim red lighting that's standard at the Camino. It gives me time to decide if I like what I see.

I crack the tab on my beer, toss back a swig, and take stock of the place. The usual group of Camino regulars is milling around one corner of the bar, talking to Joel. Check. Some lost tourists have stumbled in out of the sweltering heat and taken up residence next to the swamp cooler that just manages to keep the Camino unpleasantly humid on days like this. That's unusual but nothing to be concerned about; they're probably in town for the music festival. The nose of a big black tour bus, one of those gigantic land yachts that bands cruise around in, edges up in front of the window. Some of the tourists move up to the front for optimal gawking positions.

A guy wanders into my peripheral vision from the hall leading to the restrooms. He scans the clientele and shoots Joel a look. Joel nods in my direction, but he hasn't got time for an introduction, because there's been a marked increase in the number of heat-shocked and thirsty tourists since the bus pulled up.

"Edward Anders?"

145

"Eddie." I nod and gesture to the bench across from me. "Pull up a seat."

"Tom." He slides into the booth without bothering to pull his hands out of his pockets, which makes the back of my neck crawl. It's been 105 degrees for the last three months; no one in Austin is cold. "How's it go?"

"All right." I extend a hand. He gives me a cordial nod, but his hands stay put. Other than the pocket thing, he scans as a non-threat. I've got about eight inches on him and I'd guess a hundred and fifty pounds. His skin reflects the red lighting so well, I'm betting it's never seen the sun. That same lighting has turned his eyes black. His hair is a pile of messy curls and waves topped with a big pair of sunglasses. A number of piercings on his face and ears mark where jewelry has been removed. He's not from around here—definitely in town for the festival. Tom adopts a quirky grin while I scan him up and down.

"So, what can I do for you?" I prompt him.

"Need a minder."

"Okay." That's a pretty broad job description. "I worked in Protective Services for the Army for the last three years of my service. I'm trained in tactical driving, unarmed combat, and counter-surveillance. I was military police before that, in Kandahar. What kind of minding are you looking for exactly?"

"I'm looking for a blood that's got his head screwed on better than me. I need help with my fans; they're a bit . . . enthusiastic."

"Talent security isn't my usual gig." What this guy wants is a meat shield, and I'm quite a bit more than that. Still, I'm not opposed to getting compensated for a cakewalk, if the price is right. "But I've done a little bit of everything as a civvy."

"Yeah, all right, but can you work with my—eh—personal style, so to speak? I like to enjoy life, make friends, have a naughty now and again." He *actually* winks at me. At least the guy has a sense of humor and isn't afraid to be up front. That's a good thing in a client. "I just need to avoid the kind of friends who cut off bits of my hair."

I look past his ear a moment, noting the crowd of people milling around the tour bus. Does that belong to this guy? I should recognize him if he's that popular, but I can't even place where he's from. He's got a weird accent with something like an Australian twang . . . There's a little Latin thrown in there, too. Maybe Cuban? And a burr in the back of his throat I couldn't reproduce if my life depended on it. And his word choice is . . . strange. I saw plenty of fun travel and adventure in the army, and I've never heard anyone talk like this guy before. I'm intrigued.

"I don't have a problem with that." I shrug, bringing my attention back to him. "I can advise you and watch your back. I'll run background checks on persons of interest, organize security—the whole nine yards—but in the end, I take your instructions. A good bodyguard should blend into the background as much as possible when not needed."

"I want someone bigger than me, too, someone whose sight will stop the scissors before they come out." He looks me up and down, pouting in approval. "Sam said you were built like a brick shit-house, and he wasn't mistaken."

"Thanks." Yes. I am a big guy. I'm too conspicuous for clandestine work, but as a bodyguard, my size is an asset. Guys like me are trained to be gentle from birth, because we don't need much to be intimidating and dangerous. For me, violence is just a tool. "Sorry . . . Who did you say sent you?"

"Samiel. You know. Big basher, rides a Harley."

"Oh." I nod. I do know plenty of Sams, but not one that rides a motorcycle. I moved a lot of spooks back in the day; maybe one of them is going by Sam now. "Can I ask where you're from?"

"Ah, way beyond the black stump." He waves me off. "You wouldn't know it."

I look him up and down. A little voice in the back of my mind is telling me I can trust him. Here lies fortune and fame . . . and girls, girls, girls! But a louder voice, the one that's kept me alive and makes me good at my job, is telling me to proceed with caution. The guy is cagey, and from what little he's told me, he might as well be totally football bats. When the thought crosses my mind, the contents of his pockets become more interesting.

"Mind if I ask you what's in your pockets?" I ask.

"Pay attention, don't cha?" The impish grin on his face spreads out like an oil slick. He jerks his head, indicating we should leave now. "We'll get to that later."

I almost get up and go right then, but survival instinct slows me down.

I look around. I've never seen the Camino this crowded. Not even on a

Saturday night. It's getting loud, too. I wonder if he's trying to isolate me for a reason.

"Now's fine." I cross my arms. "I can't accept you as a client if you don't trust me and vice versa."

"All right, but don't say I didn't warn ya."

He raises his hands, loosely curled into fists, and opens his fingers one at a time. One, two, three, four, five. . . six? Six fingers on each hand? Then he stands and slips the sunglasses down his forehead, exposing the little prosthetic horns hidden behind them. The Camino goes absolutely silent.

The best camouflage is often none. Without the stage makeup, piercings, and horns, I couldn't have recognized him.

"Wadda ya say?" Tomis 'Sixfingers' Smith nods at the thickening mob around us. "Ready to battle?"

The Camino bursts with excitement, and the crowd collapses in around us.

This job is going to be huge—early retirement in Monaco huge—so huge I don't care how off his nut Smith is. I stand up, look big, and get to work.

Let me fill you in on Sixfingers, just in case you've been living in a cave for the last twelve months.

Tomis 'Sixfingers' Smith released his first single, "Heart Surgeon," online, free of charge, and instantly slaughtered the pop charts.

He's a great musician, but he's got three gimmicks that give him a godlike aura in the hard rock/heavy metal industry. First, a birth defect: he's got six fully functional fingers on each hand and flaunts them by playing guitar lightning fast, like Buckethead on steroids. Second, he plays a modified guitar designed to play notes based on irrational numbers, like pi. Tom is eager to tell anyone who will listen that the philosopher who discovered irrational numbers was cast into the sea and drowned by the gods for it. Finally, his composition relies heavily on musical intervals banned by the Church during the Renaissance for being so goddamned awesome they must be evil.

Pop producers everywhere throw their radios out the window when one of his songs comes on.

The music is a bit weird, a little ethereal and other-worldly, but he's anchored his style with the classics: Black Sabbath, Deep Purple, Led Zeppelin, Guns N' Roses, Metallica. It doesn't hurt that the guy knows how to write lyrics with an edge to them.

Early on, some poor kid killed himself while listening to "Heart Surgeon" on repeat. After that, detractors made Sixfingers that much more famous by getting organized. Tom responded by pledging twenty-five percent of the sales from his first full-length album to charities working with at-risk teens and disappeared from the public eye.

A few weeks later, he released *Make the Devil Cry,* and in some small ways, the world changed overnight.

Since then, he's been featured nude on the front of *Rolling Stone,* grinning out from the glossy cover at the world, fig-leafed by his modified guitar. *Time* featured him as Person of the Year, and he was declared the Sexiest Man Alive by *People* magazine. Everywhere you go, there's an image of Tom Smith, half-naked and smiling at you. Dudes have started dyeing their hair red and getting curls put in to affect a Sixfingers look. Women's fashion has changed, too: Tom's got a thing for big, curvy girls.

Some say it's the music. Some say it's his looks and "bad-boy charm." Still others believe it's shrewd manipulation of media coverage. His music has been labeled, censored, or outright banned across the world, and lo and behold, no one can stop him from making his mark. There are cults—actual religious cults—that use his lyrics as their holy texts. The guy has his own protest groups, and he has stalkers. Tom is chaos in a bus, and it's my job to keep him out of trouble.

Tom hits the last chord in "Soul Broker," and The Inferno Hotel and Casino shivers as his fans scream. He stands, illuminated in the spotlight like a holy idol, arms raised and dripping sweat. Maybe an unholy idol—the light is red, he's wearing a cassock studded with metal spikes, his hands and arms are covered in fake blood, and there's green smoke rolling across the stage. Definitely unholy. Either way, I'd say he's earned the right to stand there, soaking it in after the marathon concert he just played.

On the screen behind him, the clock strikes midnight, and confetti bursts from the ceiling.

"Happy New Year, everybody!" He waves to the crowd. He bows to the flock of backup singers-turned-succubi and to the touring band, all of whom are sporting a total black-out, souls-of-the-damned look. Finally, with all the class that an eight-inch hairdo and chain around his neck allow, he sweeps one arm toward the crowd, as if to say (and I've heard him say it) "I am your humble servant" and bows one last time.

"Whoop!" He steps into the wings, and I take up position at his side. "Nice show."

"Yeah, it was okay." He frowns, glancing at his watch. It's a funny contraption with a stationary arm fixed in the middle and rotating rings around the edge that indicate the time. At least I assume it indicates time; the characters are like something out of *The Lord of the Rings*. The thing looks ancient, like an antique, but it never needs to be wound. He always comes backstage, listens to the crowd, and watches the time before doing an encore. He waits until the crowd is on the cusp of despair then strides back out.

Just when I think it can't get any louder.

He waves, blows kisses, and holds his palms up for silence.

"One more," he tells them, swinging his guitar into place.

He plays the album title track, "Make the Devil Cry." It's all instrumental, and it's like the guy is playing kickball with your heart for ten minutes. Even after hearing it played night after night, I still mist up. It makes me think of my dad, fishing, hiking, going to the beach. Then when the notes turn melancholy, I remember how he died: demented and screaming that I was Viet Cong.

I'm not alone here. Tom's put whole amphitheaters in tears with "Make the Devil Cry."

Tonight, Tom's in a good mood and ends it on a cheerful note. The crowd will file out happily, like a bunch of stoners on Bob Marley's birthday.

He comes off stage and does the rounds, shaking hands and doling out sweaty hugs. It's a ritual I have to prepare for in advance. I've run a background check on everyone with backstage access then made sure security checked their bags and gave them a comprehensive pat-down.

Tom could have played anywhere he wanted in the U.S. tonight, but it had to be Vegas. He picked tonight's venue for its after-party possibilities. Where partying is concerned, Tom is one gung-ho mo-fo.

We head down after Tom got his make-up off about two hours later. Fortunately for me, The Inferno has set up a nice, well-controlled venue with plenty of security. I received a complete list of personnel and guests well in advance. Most are celebrities, producers, and industry big-wigs. There's also a selection of attractive women, ostensibly the winners of an "ultimate fan" contest. I've run their backgrounds and memorized their faces, so spotting party crashers won't be a problem.

When we arrive, Tom looks between the bar and the dance floor, caught in indecision. I can see the wheels turning: booze or girls, booze or girls . . . Then a waiter with a tray of glasses and a bottle of champagne offers him a drink. Tom takes the bottle and problem solved: booze *and* girls.

Tom's liver is Teflon-coated.

I take a spot at the corner of the bar, far enough away to be unobtrusive but close enough to keep track of Tom and order an energy drink. Despite my above-average height, it's not easy to pick him out on the mirrored dance floor. They're using black lights, lasers . . . the whole shebang. I lose him once, but he reappears, swing dancing with a pretty girl in the middle of the crowd. And so it goes for about an hour until I spot Tom's horns creeping along one wall toward the door.

I intercept him in the hall.

"Hey, what's going on?"

"This party gives me the yawns," he shrugs. "Crowd's too easy in there . . . I want to be a *person* tonight."

"You're going plainclothes?" I learned pretty early on that talking Tom out of these unplanned diversions was futile. I carry a beanie in my coat pocket as a contingency measure.

"Yes I am." He smiles as we get into the elevator, and I hand over the contingency cap.

"Jewelry." I outstretch my palm, and Tom deposits an assortment of facial hardware in my hand. Ah, the glamor of the music industry. "This would be easier if you took off the prosthetics."

"I keep telling you the horns are sub-dermal. I'm not taking them out."

Tom unbuttons his shirt, revealing a Sixfingers t-shirt beneath. "How do I look?"

"You're kidding."

"What? I have lots of fans in town! One more guy in a Sixfingers shirt blends in perfectly."

I groan, but he's got a point. This is exactly the perverse kind of crap I've come to expect from Tom, but he always manages to surprise me somehow.

"Hey, lighten up. Our cover is a stag night, right? Relax." I take off my tie and unbutton my collar. Tom wraps his arm around my neck. "Besides, the tour's almost over, and I want to see what you're like when you're having fun. Let's bang around town, find a boozer, get pissed, get a couple of girls . . ."

"No, Tom." I shake my head. He's still trying to get me drunk on duty; it's a hobby of his. He's never really grasped the difference between a bodyguard and a companion. Problem is, he's charismatic, persuasive, and I need to keep my head clear. In boot camp, he'd have led his buddies on shit patrol armed with a tooth brush. "That's not my job."

Tom shoves his hands in his pockets and looks at his toes for a second.

"Agh, Eddie. Sometimes I feel emptied, you know . . . jumping from one berg to the next." He smiles and claps me on the back. "You've been a real mate for a turn or two longer than I've had before. Can't blame me for loving you."

Then, he extracts his other hand from his pocket and pops a couple of magic mushrooms into his mouth. My whole body jerks into action reflexively, but it's already too late.

"God damn it, Tom."

Tom smiles at me with all his teeth, and the elevator door opens. "Let's get this party rolling."

The décor on the gambling floor is typical Vegas posh. All glitter, no substance. Within ten minutes, Tom's entranced by a three-story chandelier. The structural supports are mosaicked in tiny mirrors, and I've been watching a couple of ladies in the reflections. I'm pretty sure we're being followed.

"Tom, you expecting to meet anyone tonight?"

"I'd like that." He smiles dreamily.

"Nothing pre-arranged you didn't mention?"

"Naw." He shrugs and starts reaching for a strand of cut glass. It sparkles.

Well. I'd rather get this done before he really starts trippin' balls. I stop and turn around.

"Good evening, ladies. Can I do something for you?" I open my hands and smile big.

The brunette in blue puts her hand to her chest in surprise, and the blonde in black blushes. They're both gorgeous, built big and lush like Valkyries, practically made to order for Tom.

"Oh, um . . ." The blonde looks at her friend, looks back at Tom, and says, "We were just enjoying the scenery."

"You guys have dates?" The brunette smiles bashfully.

Tom turns around and stares at them for a moment. His jaw drops open. I don't know what he's seeing, but apparently it's even better than real life.

"We do now, diamond eyes." Tom swings into action and offers the brunette his elbow.

The blonde comes over and attaches herself to me without invitation.

"What're you going to call me?" she asks.

"Nothing. No offense, it's just . . ." I try to play to my cover. "I'm getting married tomorrow."

The fact is I haven't dated since my ex-girlfriend Dear Johned me while I was in Afghanistan.

"It's all right, lovey; Eddie's a gloomer." Tom turns around and offers her his other elbow. "Now, what mischief should we get up to, do you think?"

"There's a real nice room on the thirteenth floor for high rollers."

That's what this is about. Someone has plans, and these two are bait. The question is if they're equal opportunity or singling out Tom.

"Tom, this is a very bad idea." I take hold of his shoulder gently. For a rock star playboy, Tom is weirdly naïve. "The buy-in is going to be astronomical . . . .. I've got a wedding to pay for."

"The drinks are free," the brunette says hopefully.

"Lady after my own heart." Tom nods in approval. He pauses for a second, and his eyes track across the room jerkily until they land back on my face, and he snaps out of it. There are beads of sweat on his forehead. "C'mon Eddie, I'll buy you in. It's not like I can take it with me, and I'm gonna cark it if I don't get a little action now and again." He turns around with a girl on each arm. "Lead the way, ladies."

On the thirteenth floor, the women are pretty, and the drinks are top shelf. The girls sandwich Tom between them, where he proceeds to get mesmerized by the dealer's trick shuffles. While everyone else is playing, he's entranced by the fancy lighting, which cycles from sunset to sunrise every ten minutes or so, complete with LED stars. Just as often as not, his head is back, his mouth is open, and he's in some totally different universe when his turn comes up. One of his companions gives him a flirtatious prompt, and he does something apparently random with his cards. This goes on for some time, and yet he does pretty well, which strikes me as a bit too good to be true. The jaws of a card shark are opening wide.

"So, how'd you like to play for something a little more interesting?" the blonde asks.

Tom, who's been stupefied by her hair for the last half hour, perks up, but I'm not inclined to let my client begin trading in anything other than money (which he has in abundance) while under the influence of hallucinogens. I've worked for secret squirrels, and I know how that goes.

"All right, that's enough." I step into the light on the table and put a hand on Tom's shoulder. "It's time to go."

Tom blinks at me. The lights are on, but no one's home. I set his arm over my shoulder and start ushering him away. Before we can make it out the door, a couple of guys step through, blocking our path. They're dressed sharp, one with a girl on his arm, the other absently twiddling a poker chip between his knuckles. It's all a little too perfect for Las Vegas. Tom digs in his heels and stumbles backwards a step.

"You all right, Tom?" I ask him.

"Am I hallucinating, or are my cousins standing right in front of us?"

"Looks like there are a couple of sham-urai who want to impress you."

"Ross, Oliver . . . I didn't know you guys were out," he says, sober-ish.

"Hey, Tomis!" Oliver, the gambler, tries to wrap his arms around Tom, but I push myself between them. He shoots me a dirty look. "Your trained monkey is really cramping your style."

"What's the lurk, Oliver?" Tom asks. "Mo got you tending the stock or what?"

"Gambling and girls."

"We're expanding our holdings," Ross says, more interested in his escort's cleavage than anything else. "Mo'll cut you in; all you gotta do is go home and put in a little face time."

"C'mon Eddie, let's blow this anthill." Tom starts pulling *me* through the door.

Ross steps up and blocks the door.

"Uncle Bee wants a word with the prodigal son."

"Go back to Hell, Ross." Tom looks him up and down. "You've got no power over me, and neither does Bee. Now. *Piss. Off.*"

We leave Ross and Oliver glaring at the back of our heads.

"I thought you were the black sheep of the family, Tom," I ask once we're well enough away.

"Yeah," he shrugs, "I am."

The next day, we're out on a two-lane highway in the middle of bum fuck nowhere, winding our way downhill, when three guys on choppers roll up behind us. This is exactly the kind of chokepoint I try to avoid, but a road closure forced my hand. The bikers start buzzing around our wheel wells like horseflies. I'm not big on the idea of being forced off a cliff.

"What do you want me to do?" the driver asks.

"Force them to the left. Don't let them get up beside us." I watch as one of them pulls a hand cannon in the rear view mirror. He's going for a back tire, and the configuration of the bus doesn't give me an angle on him. So the choice becomes stopping and stopping with a flat tire. Neither option is good. "Strike that. Stop."

The driver hits the brakes, and we come to a halt.

"Keep the tires on the asphalt, call for help, and if things go south get Tom out of here." I rip open my packer and slap on my bullet-proof vest. "Run them over if you have to."

I check my sidearm and step into the road, keeping it at the low and ready. These guys ought to be in a roadside bar extorting protection money, not harassing celebrities. I hope to God this is a shakedown and not a kidnapping attempt. Their patches, a pair of wings with a sword and a shotgun crossed in front, identify them as members of "The Saints" motorcycle club. One has a patch reading "V. President" over his left breast pocket. The guy who tried to shoot out our tire is almost as big as I am and has no neck on account of all the muscle. His patch reads "Sgt. at Arms." Number three hasn't got a title.

"Help you guys?" I ask.

"Need a word with Sixfingers," the VP says, pulling off his helmet. No-Neck does likewise and lights a cigarette.

"Whatever you've got to say to him, you can say to me."

"Not bloody possible." No-Neck exhales a puff of smoke.

"Oi!" Tom calls from behind me. I glance over my shoulder. "You fellas want a coldie?"

"Tom, get back in the bus!" I shout. By the time I turn around, biker number three has taken off *her* helmet and is shaking out long locks of golden hair. The Goddess in Leather raises one eyebrow at me.

"It's okay, Eddie, I know these blokes." I'm not distracted that long, but before I know it, Tom's right there, dangling what's left of a six pack in front of him.

Without waiting for a reply, he snaps a beer out of its plastic ring and tosses it to the VP. The Veep reaches up, snags the beer out of the air, and cracks it open. Tom lifts his eyebrows at No-Neck, who crosses his arms and frowns. The GIL sniffs dismissively and busies herself with her gloves.

Tom raises his eyebrows at me. No. I shake my head slowly. Two goons and a lady are threatening him, and he's passing out beer?

"Listen, kid, Mike's got a message." The VP wipes his mouth and leans forward, hanging his wrists over the handlebars casually. "He wants you out of our territory yesterday."

"Yeah, and we're gonna do whatever it takes to make sure you leave, pronto," adds No-Neck.

"Guys, guys." Tom raises his hands and smiles. "C'mon, I want what you want. I'm working on it. We're heading down to the . . . border . . . as we speak."

"Yeah, so we heard. You were supposed to bail after Vegas."

"C'mon, the timing wasn't right." Tom's eyes drift over to me for a moment. "You know I've got to go out with a bang."

"This can be arranged." No-Neck reaches for a shotgun mounted on the side of his bike . . . right next to what looks like a goddamned sword.

I snap my M-9 up and get No-Neck's head in my sights before he can bring it around.

"Why don't we just keep things civil?" I ask him.

I hear a click, and the GIL produces a Glock 17 from I don't know where.

"Cool it, Cam. Eva." The VP puts his hand on No-Neck's arm and he lets the shotgun sink back into its holster. Eva lowers her gun but keeps it in her hand. "The problem, Tom, is that Mike never trusted you, and now you've gone and broken your promise to clear out."

"What does he think I'm gonna do, Gabe? Ravage the countryside?" Tom laughs. Gabe's eyes flicker toward me for an instant. Tom sighs and says, "Eddie, can you wait by the bus?"

"No, Tom," I say, staring at No-Neck Cam. "These dudes are big, armed, and do not like you. I cannot do my job waiting by the bus. I fucking refuse."

"Go on, no need to get so clucky." Tom says, holding up the rest of the beers casually as if to give me something to do other than aiming a gun at the heavily armed biker who moments ago threatened to blow his head off. Tom's eyebrows knit, and the corner of his lip twitches. "Piss off, ya leatherhead! This isn't yer problem."

I've looked down the barrel at some pretty nasty customers and kept it together. I've had my ass chewed by generals. Somehow getting smoked by Tom is worse.

Before I know it, I'm putting my sidearm away and taking the beers.

"No drama, mate." Tom smiles and pats my shoulder, as if to apologize for tearing me a new one moments before. "We're just gonna have a little convo."

"Eva, put your piece away and keep him company." Cam tells the GIL.

I don't stop to wait. I couldn't wait if I wanted to. I've been sent to the kids' table, and I'm angry.

"Hey," I listen to boots on gravel behind me as Eva strides up. "Nothing personal, okay?"

"Sure. Nothing like pulling a gun says, 'Let's make friends.'" I reach the bus and rest a shoulder against the fender. "What do you guys want?"

"Gabe doesn't lie," she says, pulling down her zipper and removing her jacket. She has a star tattooed on one arm . . . actually it's multiple stars: stars within stars within stars, and some old-looking text in a circle on the outside. It's a bit like Tom's watch. "Your boss made a deal and didn't stick to it. He's not what you think, you know. We're the good guys."

"That's news to me." I shrug and smile with just my teeth. Eva sighs and leans against the bus, jacket over one shoulder and helmet dangling from her fingers.

A few minutes later, Tom's smiling, leading Gabe and Cam over to the bus.

"We've got an entourage down to Arizona."

"Eva, start searching the bus," Cam directs her.

"What?" I furrow my eyebrows. "They're just going to do a little Health and Comfort Inspection and convoy with us down to the border? Why the hell would you agree to something like that?"

Tom puts his arm around my shoulders and pulls me in for a quiet conversation. "You got some galbas taking Cam on like that, but scan this, Eddie: you do not want a fight with him."

"These guys aren't just tagging along for the ride," I hiss, getting pretty close to the end of my rope. "They are not nice people. If you invite them along, Tom, I cannot protect you from them."

"Nah, Cam was born with a sneer, but he's not a bad guy. They've got a code." Tom waves it off. "Besides, Sixfingers arriving with a couple of The Saints is totally badass. It'll start a ripper of a party!"

I turn on my heels and go watch Eva's bag drag through the RV. The other two take a cargo compartment each. Between the three of them, I'm not at all convinced I know what they're doing. They turn up nothing of interest and eventually wander out, each holding a beer. They get on their bikes and kick-start their engines. "All right!" Tom claps his hands together, smiling. "Let's get this show back on the road!"

This leaves me no time to check for sabotage, or bombs, or illegal goods they might be piggybacking on us.

It's Situation Normal: All Fucked Up on the Sixfingers tour bus.

Hot wind has been buffeting the side of the bus the entire morning. Outside, cacti are collecting drifts of sand, and long spindly trees trail red flowers like flags in the wind. I've been watching a dark storm cloud rise in the distance while going through a pile of background checks in the passenger's seat. Tom's in the back singing "Highway to Hell" in the shower.

There's a line on the highway where the sunshine ends and the storm starts. We pass across it and SPLAT! It's not a storm; it's a swarm of bugs. SPLAT! SPLAT! SPLAT!

One crunches up against the windshield right before my eyes. It's huge. It's like a locust, but its face, twisted up from the impact, seems almost human. The wiper blade scrapes it away the next instant, leaving a long arc of red ichor along the glass.

The cloud gets thicker, blotting out all visibility on the road ahead. The wiper blades start to strain under the weight of dead bugs. I hear the rocky engines of our escort accelerate, and all three pull alongside us. Gabe gestures us off the road. Eva, riding next to him, has drawn some kind of impossibly large weapon, something I don't recognize. Cam zips past both of them, sword drawn and held aloft. It flickers in the dimness of the cloud. Somehow he's lit the thing on fire. White-hot, it leaves a trail of smoking insects in his wake. The three of them accelerate balls to the wall and disappear into the cloud of bugs.

A handful of locusts drop through the celling vent into the bus. I squeal like a cherry recruit on zero day and start stomping on the things. I jump up on the dining table and wind the vent shut, but not before one crawls onto my bicep and bites.

"Gah!" I didn't even know insects were supposed to have teeth! It's also got a tail which curls around and nails me with a stinger. I can tell from the burn that it's toxic. I brush it off my arm with a little more force than is necessary, and it lands against Tom's chest. He's standing in the middle of the living space, with a towel around his waist and an acoustic guitar in hand. He looks down at the thing. "Don't touch it!" I shout.

Tom disregards my warning, grabs it by the tail, and dangles it in front of his eyes.

His lip curls. "That's disgusting." Then he smacks the thing on the table.

I stand in front of the door, and Tom stands in front of me.

"I can help."

"Don't go out there."

"I need to help."

"You're not going out there." I cross my arms. "Those things are poisonous."

"C'mon, you've seen me drink. You know how resilient I am." He smiles. "Besides, do you hear that?"

"What?"

Tom rolls his eyes toward the ceiling and goes quiet.

He's right. There is a sound, something low under the noise of locusts colliding with the bus, a sort of grinding noise.

"These bities are chewing their way through the walls," he says.

"Holy crap. . .."

There's a crash from the cab that sends me into a crouch. It's been a while since loud noises dropped me to the ground, but I'm all nerves. Assassins I can take. Being out-manned, out-gunned, and cornered isn't fine, but at least there's an obvious enemy and a problem to solve. Even the tension of driving a route laced with IEDs is manageable because there's something to do that makes the situation more tenable. I can't fight a swarm of bugs. I don't even know where to start.

"Stop!" Tom shouts, and I pivot on my heels just in time to see our driver disappear into the swarm. I sprint forward and pull the door shut again. I watch through the window as a grown man is picked to the bone in a matter of seconds. The skeleton is stripped before it hits the ground.

Now I'm crawling in flesh-eating insects, and something in the back of my mind breaks. A great big blubbering sob starts working its way up my throat. I push it back. I've felt this before, during my first real ambush. I might fall to pieces later, but right now keeping my head is the only way to survive.

I start beating the things off of me, but they seem more-or-less paralyzed. After the initial panic fades, I realize Tom is playing. It's soft, something akin to "Make the Devil Cry," but more . . . *soulful.* It rises and falls between joy and despair, and soon I'm stunned, too. I fall back into the driver's seat peacefully.

It must be the insect stings, because my head fills with cotton, and I let Tom walk through the door wearing nothing but a towel.

He steps into the swarm, fingers dancing over the strings. I watch through the windshield as the swarm breaks around him, locusts dropping like hail.

This can't be real. It's got to be the bites, because I've got to be hallucinating. Outside, the insects are breaking up. I see Cam and Gabe hip deep in piles of dead locusts, continuing to do . . . whatever it is they were doing. Somehow, they survived without a scratch, but Eva is gone. Her bike is lying in the road like a dead animal, and she's nowhere to be seen. There's not even a skeleton left.

I rub my arm. It's swollen, hot to the touch, and painful. I'm off-balance and confused, but I need to keep it together until I can get Tom somewhere safe. I wipe my hand over my face, take a deep breath, and get out of the bus.

It sounds like I'm walking on Rice Krispies. I look at my feet and note that the dead insects are still there. If this is a hallucination, it's remarkably complete.

I try to ignore that fact.

Tom is decidedly displeased about the delay while we make our statements to the police who've trucked in from a town fifty miles away. He paces the road, checking his watch every few minutes. Meanwhile, Cam and Gabe make themselves scarce, leaving Eva's bike and a human skeleton behind for me to explain. At the first mention that perhaps we should head over to the station to make statements, Tom gets really friendly and convinces the cops that the skeleton is a prop. After a couple of autographs, they . . . just let us go. No more questions.

Five hours later, we pull into beautiful Ajo, Arizona, population 3,705 and home of the New Cornelia open-pit copper mine (now closed). It's a lovely place for the last concert on the *Make the Devil Cry* tour. Tom's blown a fortune pumping the water out of the bottom, contouring the bulldozer scars into stadium seating, and spreading around the tailings to create parking for the 80,000 guests his agents have sold tickets to.

Tom affectionately calls it: The Pit.

People are already camping out in the parking lot. About an hour ago, Gabe and Cam reappeared in my rearview mirror, and just as Tom predicted, it makes quite a stir. I pull the bus around, taking the spiral road to the bottom of The Pit carefully. The roar of the motorcycles reverberates around the rock walls until it's almost deafening. The acoustics are strangely good down here.

I've been ruminating on the events of earlier today, and I've still got nothing. The bite on my arm is swollen and painful, but I haven't died yet. As soon as we're parked, Tom dives into preparation for this last, big show. I get the security personnel in line and sweep the venue as per usual.

Nevertheless, as sunset fades to darkness, standard operating procedure seems woefully insufficient.

"Okay, Tom, it's show time." I knock on the dressing room door, pause, and let myself in.

I draw my sidearm instantly.

"Drop it!" Tom's backed against the wall, cringing away from his assailant. "I will shoot you!"

"Your boss isn't what he claims to be." It's Eva, bearing down on him with that strange weapon I saw in the swarm. Now, close up, I recognize it: a multi-tank Super Soaker. *What the hell?* "Hand over the astrolabe, demon," she snarls.

"What the fuck? Eva?" I put away my sidearm. I'm not risking a shot at anyone armed with a squirt gun. "I thought you were dead."

She depresses the trigger, releasing a stream of water. Tom yelps and covers his face with his arms.

"Ouch!"

While Eva's distracted, I catch her around the waist. She drops the squirt gun and snaps the back of her head into my nose with a crunch. Hot blood rolls down my upper lip into my mouth. My eyes tear up, and momentarily blinded, all I can do is get her off her feet. I pivot her around my weight, get her off balance, and bring her to the ground with my knee in the small of her back. She flails beneath me, reaching for a real gun on her hip. I rip it out of her hand before she's got a grip and toss it away.

She continues to struggle, but I have her pinned well enough to get a set of disposable restraints on. I stand up, heaving a sigh, and look to Tom.

"Ow, ow, ow. . ." Tom's mincing around the dressing room. . . smoking. Not smoking a cigarette. . . smoking from the places where Eva's Super Soaker hit him. A bolt of lightning hits my spine. Why didn't I think of it sooner? Acid attacks leave a horrific aftermath!

"Tom!" I grab one of the big bottles of water he uses on stage, pull off the cap, and douse him with it.

"Sodding sod of a sod!" he swears, wiping the water from his face and taking half of his makeup with it. "That hurt!"

"Let me see." I inspect the damage: just a few red spots on his cheeks and neck, nothing that won't heal. I heave a sigh of relief. "You're okay."

"Do you know how long it takes to do this whole look?" Tom turns around in the mirror, pokes at a limp chunk of formerly spiky hair, and shoots Eva a scowl. "Bloody puppet," he mutters and starts wiping off the mussed makeup.

"What did you put in that thing?" I turn on Eva.

"Holy water." She looks back at me steadily, cool as a cucumber.

"I'm sorry, what?" I shake my head in disbelief.

"Holy water." She says again slowly, like I'm the crazy one. "Your boss is a demon."

"Oh, Eva." Tom turns away from the mirror, places one hand over his heart, and begins to take long, dance-like strides toward her. "What's in a name? That which we call a rose, by any other name, would smell as sweet. So a demon would, were he not a demon call'd . . .."

He stands there, waiting for a reaction, but Eva simply looks away.

"I'm a showman, Eva."

"Eddie, I know it's easier to tell yourself a story that fits into your every-day expectations, but what you've seen the last few days—it's real," she says to me then looks at Tom with burning hatred in her eyes. "This is the de-mon Asmodeus, and he's going to use the crowd's energy to unleash seven-ty-two legions from Hell onto the Earth."

"Fuck, I'm good!" Tom turns back around, stretches the corner of one eye to the side, and applies an obscene amount of eyeliner. "Fine, so I'm a demon—but the Big Bad is just an act; I'm not Asmodeus."

"Eddie, listen." She wriggles to her knees, and I draw my sidearm again, gesturing her to stay still. She sits back on her heels. "Gabriel and Camael are angels. They can't touch him; it'd be *the* act of war that starts Armageddon. It's down to humans, you and me, to stop him."

"Eva, sweet, I'm the family freak," Tom says, turning back around and resting his weight against the makeup station. "Gramps is running a black one on me, and you know why? I've got free will, and I'm not about to use it to his advantage. I keep running 'cause I'm not that kind of guy—I'd rather make love, not war and all that. I'm not going to open a portal to Hell; Hell bleeds. I know—I've been there."

I check my watch—ten minutes late. I don't know why Tom is playing into Eva's delusions, but I do know the crowd is getting impatient. We're sitting at the bottom of a pit in a structure made of plywood and surrounded by a sea of anxious metalheads who want what's inside. The situation is about to get kinetic.

"C'mon, Tom, she's delusional. It's time to get on stage." Tom turns back around and attends to his eyeshadow.

"Eddie! Remember the locusts, the bite on your arm!" Eva looks at me desperately. I run my hand over the hot welt on my arm. I'm having a hard time calling to memory what the bug even looked like, the place in my memory where it ought to be is sort of . . . fuzzy. "Could a delusion bite you?"

"I . . ." I feel sure that someone else, someone smarter than I am, can explain it. You might even say I have faith.

"You ought to be helping me, Eva. It's like I told The Saints, I'm trying to slip the knot here. If my family catches me, I'm scrubbed, and you lot, well . . . it won't be pretty." Tom swipes on some dark lipstick and turns around with the saddest expression I've ever seen on the guy. "I never wanted to put you in danger; I just like your little sphere, and I'm tired."

"I know the tricks your kind play," Eva spits. "Don't expect sympathy from me."

"Naw, that's all right." Tom drops the frown and points to his watch. *What did she call it? An astro-something . . .* "You'll see. Hades is close right now, and as soon as I cross the Styx, I can give 'em the flick in Elysium."

"Tom, this is seriously not right." I put a hand on his arm and gently try to get him walking. "She's mentally ill, and you're feeding her delusions."

Tom smiles at me a little sadly.

"Agh, Eddie, they should bottle your blood. Wish I could take you with me." Tom claps me on the shoulder and kisses me right on the lips. Then he picks up his guitar, and on the way out nods at Eva. "Be open to her; she's not as cracked as she seems."

"You'll never get away with it!" Eva shouts. "The Saints are watching. The instant your soldiers cross that threshold they go to war."

"They're insurance, lovey, just in case." Tom gives her a cock-eyed grin, then looks at me and waves. "Time to do the bolt."

A few moments later, a wave of applause makes the entire stage shudder. Tom hits the first few chords of "Obsidian Eyes," and the cheering falls to an abrupt silence.

"Eddie, please listen to me," Eva says while I look around for something to keep her ankles together. "My organization has been protecting the world from demons for millennia. We are the angels' proxies; we do what they can't. I know it's difficult to believe, but you have to trust me."

"How'd you make it through that swarm of . . . locusts?" I ask, kneeling next to her with a roll of gaff tape.

"The seal of God." She inclines her chin toward the tattoo on her arm. "It protects me. It will protect you, too, if . . ."

"How'd you get in here without me knowing?"

"Eddie, eighty thousand people are about to die!" she insists, but I just look at her.

"You climbed into one of the cargo hatches during the storm?"

"Yes!" she snaps. "Is it worth even the tiniest risk that I'm telling you the truth?"

"I believe that you believe, Eva, and I'm sorry I have to do this to you."

"He has horns!" she shouts. "No one can be that much of a blockhead."

"It's all part of the act." I sigh, and get her up on my shoulder in a fireman's carry. I pick up a folding chair with the other hand and start humping it toward the stage. "Right now, I'm afraid the best I can do is to let you watch the world not end. Then, we'll get you some professional help."

I set her up in the wings where I can keep an eye on her and Tom at the same time. I work on a round of radio checks to keep myself and the hired security staff on our toes. I've found myself entranced by the music more often than I care to admit and have no expectation that anyone else will do better.

He follows "Obsidian Eyes" with "The Salt Works" and keeps going through his catalog of songs, working from soft to hard, mellow to intense. By the time he hits "Soul Broker" and "Heart Surgeon," the crowd is ecstatic. Security personnel in the bleacher-style seating on the walls of The Pit are having a hard time keeping people out of the aisles. The barricades in front of the stage are getting pushed back a little bit at a time. The guys I've got embedded on the floor keep getting swept up in an expanding mosh pit.

We're starting to lose control.

To make matters worse, a storm's rolling in, and it looks bad. Long tentacles of swirling clouds are beginning to pinwheel over The Pit.

I'm about to call Tom off stage so we can get things straightened out when he transitions into "House of the Fly" without so much as lifting his fingers from the strings. Thunder rolls, and a blast of fire erupts from the clouds.

I glance over at the effects guys, wondering if they failed to notify me about new elements to the show, but they're running around like chickens with their heads cut off.

"It's starting," Eva says, wriggling. "Let me out! We can still stop this!"

"Calm down." I rest a hand on her shoulder, not feeling very calm myself. The excitement in the air is starting to get to me. "Please."

Eva turns her head and bites my arm. I recoil, wrapping my other hand around the bloody tooth marks. She heaves herself around, bringing one of the chair legs down on the instep of my boot. I fall to the ground in agony as the little bones splinter. I'm on the floorboards long enough to feel a high-pitched drone reverberating through them.

A fly lands on the wound on my arm, sucking away at the blood. I brush it off, trying to place the sound, when another lands . . . and another. I cast my gaze over the crowd and see a stream of black flies pouring out of the mosh pit. On the lip of the mine, I see Cam's sword burst into white-hot flame.

I scramble to my feet, just in time to watch Eva swing the folding chair at my face.

"You know that story where the Devil lets you out of Hell if you can make him cry?" Tom shouts to the crowd. Clang! Eva lets the chair go once it connects and darts toward Tom. There's no time to stop and take inventory of which bones in my face are broken; I sprint onto the stage after her. Tom takes a quick step forward and doesn't miss a beat while I get my arms around her and heave her off her feet. "Well, my friends, it's true, and this is how I did it."

He swings into the final number, "Make the Devil Cry," while Eva and I grapple in the background. I really wish he'd run away, but the crowd loves it. They think it's a stage show with crazy effects and mixed martial arts.

I'm finding out pretty quickly that Eva's faster than me, and my shattered foot and broken nose aren't making things any easier. I've got to get in close to use my size and strength before she exhausts me. I quit the hand work, accept a couple of strikes to my face, scoop her up in an under hook, and flip her across my back. Tom takes it in stride and gestures toward us as I begin to haul her off stage. The crowd cheers. "It's all just part of the show, folks!"

Eva hooks her arms under mine, levering herself over my shoulders, and uses her own weight to throw me to the ground. As we roll across the stage, scrabbling at each other, Tom unslings his guitar and backs up. The crowd goes batshit. They know what's coming next and so do I. I've been served a soup sandwich. Tom's going to stage dive, and my hands are too full of Eva to stop him.

The crowd roars with the anticipation of a hungry beast at feeding time, and a thunderclap tears open the air . . . literally. It starts like a golden firework: a sudden flash, a pinprick of shimmering light that expands into a circle. The circle freezes in place, framing a hologram of a landscape: a black sand beach on a misty river, with a lone boatman poling his way toward the shore.

I roll my eyes toward the sky. The stage lights illuminate the storm of flies like big shimmering ribbons. Beyond them, Gabe and Cam circle The Pit on giant wings, watching, bright against the storm above. They become silhouettes in the lightning. Tom's taking it all in, improvising, playing in rhythm to the action, and the crowd is cheering to the most epic finale of all time.

Tom hits a power chord, and I realize . . . this is *real*.

This is not a hallucination brought on by a bug bite. This is not delirium from lack of sleep. It's too weird, too detailed. This is real, Tom's running from something . . .

. . . and I've got to help him.

I heave myself to my feet and lunge across the stage. As the last note comes to an end, Tom takes a running leap. He twists in the air, shouting "Rock on Earth!" I throw myself after him, arms outstretched, and manage to get him in a bear hug the moment before we hit the hologram.

A wave of nausea rolls through me. For a moment, I lose all sense of up and down, and my head fills with pressure.

Then I come to a rest, face first on top of Tom.

"Ouch," he wheezes. "Eddie, you barmy sod, this isn't a healthful place for a mortal."

I roll off of him, rubbing the back of my head.

"What'd you mean, 'mortal'?" I'm dizzy, and my vision is blurred like I took one to the back of the head. All I can tell from this perspective is that my knees are dug into damp black sand.

"Don't lose your monkeys on this." Tom's feet come around into my view. "But I am a demon, like she said. A bit more than that, really. Sort of a . . . prince. Not a very good one, mind . . . but . . . I am."

"You're a prince?" I take a deep breath and start to stand. My broken foot hurts, but the pain seems far away. It's like waking up inside a dream with the real world tucked away in the back of your head. Except I'm pretty sure this is real. Maybe. ". . . from Hell?"

"That's the whisper." He offers me a stabilizing arm. "The sick will get better. Happens to everyone, first time through."

As my eyes begin to clear, I see a black sand beach and a sky like an iron lid. In the distance, a lone figure poles a boat toward us. There is no golden circle. From where I stand, there's no way out. "Where are we?"

"On the bank of the River Styx." He smiles. "I'm happy you came, mate, but now it's me watching you, and you know that's a laugh."

Tom shoves his hands in his pockets. His expression falters.

"What is it?"

"You got some change I can borrow?"

Fame

Matthew Joseph Harrington

Before the universe began to fade, Lee said, "Just once I'd like to go someplace where I got some good news."

He landed, naked and hairless as usual, on a very large and well-kept road, after a drop of perhaps forty feet. A car was about to hit him, so he ran off the road to avoid destroying it. The driver hit the brakes well after the collision would have occurred, but at least there was no following traffic. The car swerved across several aisles—no; his unexplained gift of tongues told him that it was "lanes" in the local usage—and pulled off the road and stopped. The driver got out of the car, faced back toward Lee, and shouted something long, inarticulate, and extremely heartfelt.

Lee ran up to just behind the car (merely doing that would be frightening enough without coming closer, and the man had already had a bad scare) and said in the same language, "I'm sorry about that. I don't get to choose where I land."

The man, who was more pink-skinned than Lee (and closer to red just now), stared for a moment with his mouth still open. He looked up at the sky, all around, then at Lee again. "Did you fall out of an aircraft?"

"No, I was moved to this universe when my job in the last one was done. I'm The Hero."

"Of what?"

"Not *a* hero, The Hero. I'm the original. Proticles Peleides. Sometimes called Achilles. Most people end up calling me Lee."

His real name went right out of the man's memory, also usual, and the

171

man said, "Achilles?"

"I was given the nickname by someone who liked puns. It means 'no destruction' or 'in place of a thousand', depending how you say it."

"I thought Achilles was dead."

"Yeah, I get that a lot. Can you tell me the worst problem in the world you can think of? I get sent places where things are so bad an invulnerable man is needed."

"Meeran," he said, invoking the principal deity, "obsolescence, I guess. It's expensive getting the improved stuff every time. How come you got out of the way if you can't be hurt?"

"Because you can. Invulnerability isn't just about being immune to swords. If I'm in contact with the ground, I'm an immovable object. Your car would have wrapped around me like paper. When you say 'obsolescence', do you mean deliberate manufacture of goods of poor quality that wear out quickly?"

"Uh, no, what kind of idiot would do that? People would change brands like a shot."

"A very common kind. They find others to do the same with their own products, to increase profits."

The man was frowning at this. "But then the reclamation system would be completely swamped."

The gift of tongues told Lee that this was a way of conserving finite resources. Sensible. "I'm accustomed to places where there is no such system. And yes, the garbage that accumulates is staggering."

The man was staring at him now. "I believe you. Why do I believe you?"

"I don't know. People normally do. I think it's because I don't need to lie to protect myself, and somehow people can tell that."

"You never lie?"

"Oh, I've lied. Other people's safety is a concern." Though not the most important.

"Oh." The man thought hard for a moment, then shrugged and said, "Need a lift?"

"I don't know which way I'm supposed to go yet."

"Well, if you're walking down the road naked, you'll be interfered with."

The man just didn't get it. Being interfered with was at worst a way of telling what he had to do. "Sure, thanks."

"Any kind of place you want to be? Are you okay?"

Lee had sagged all over. "I'm okay. There's only one place I want to be, and it doesn't exist anymore. I can go to just short of where you're going. Not all the way, so you don't have to explain."

"Oh, I don't mind explaining," the man said with a grin. "This is too good a story not to tell."

Lee frowned faintly. The man had talked briefly with a naked stranger he'd seen on the road, and he thought that was an exceptionally good story? This place must be very dull. "All right with me," he said.

They got in, and the seat adjusted itself to fit Lee. No centralized economy here, with some minion in a far-away office dictating that one size fits all and tough shit if it doesn't. A restraining harness lowered itself over his torso. "Nice car," Lee commented.

"It was my father's," the man said disparagingly. "I keep meaning to get a new one, but something always comes up."

"Oh, how well I know how that is," Lee said.

"You like music?"

"Most of it. I've heard some that was remarkably bad, mind you."

The man grinned. "As you said: 'How well I know how that is.'" He started the car and touched some things on the wheel, and the voice of a woman who had done a lot of drinking and fighting, probably along with the band, sang feelingly about what she'd like to do with them next. In Lee's experience, music that forthright indicated a highly ambitious culture, boldly seeking new things, not self-satisfied and repressive.

He began wondering what in Tartarus he was doing here.

He calmed himself—not without some pride in being able to do so—and felt for where the worst local example of slavery was.

There was one.

In the world.

One?

It wasn't nearby. And it was . . . odd. He'd encountered a somewhat similar type before, but it had been a while . . . Claudius Britannicus, that was it. Poor kid had barely survived his father's murder and was proclaimed Imperator with the blood of his stepmother and stepbrother literally still on his hands. Lee had found himself in the bizarre position of counselor for over sixty years, only moving on after Britannicus had taken his advice to end all the German raids permanently by setting fire to every mile of woodland along the Rhine in autumn. It surely would have done the job; the firestorm must have burned to the Urals. Britannicus had resented the job more every year, precisely because he'd been right about his father's wish to restore the Republic—a worse civil war than the one Octavian had ended would have erupted the day that happened.

Lee wondered idly which descendant had succeeded him. He'd liked Decimus, himself. As a boy, he'd been a quick study, and he never used more force than necessary—but he didn't hesitate to use that force promptly, since delay would mean using more later. Lee had nicknamed him Lethargicus. He'd outlived his two more active elder brothers, so he was likely. (Actually his oldest sister, Flavia, would have been the best choice—she'd run the Palace household for decades without making anyone miserable, quite a trick—but the Romans didn't do that, silly asses.)

"Do you have a map of the continent?" he said.

"In the food box. What do you need to find?"

"Whatever's that way," Lee answered, aiming a thumb backward, then opening the sort of compartment he'd seen used to hold gloves, guns, books, and, now, underneath a large montagu (no, called a splitloaf here), maps.

"Thessaly?" the man said.

Lee stared at him.

The man glanced at him, flinched, and added, "The nearest big town is Thessaly. You came down in Landing—funny coincidence, huh?"

"Funny, yes," said Lee. Coincidence, he doubted extremely. "Let me look at this quickly, and you can let me off here. I think I'm going the other way."

The characters on the map looked kind of like Hangool, but the names were from all over—except that Chesapik, possibly the best harbor in the world, was named Aegilla, and there was a very big city called Neathenopolis, which was about the right direction and distance for the one slave.

Whatever kept moving him around had, as always, arranged for his arrival right here, right now—and was making an even more heavy-handed point of it than usual, which was saying something, to put it mildly.

"Thanks for the use of the map. I have to go."

"I'll take the next capillary and drop you off."

"No, the window's fine." He ran it down, slipped out, and landed running the other way. The driver had a control that would close the window.

His current situation would be made inconvenient by the fact that the route was entirely through inhabited land, and he didn't want to do any damage . . . except that this road was utterly straight, was set below ground level, had angled concrete revetments on both sides, and, at the moment, appeared to be empty.

He set out running. He'd be able to see bridges and suchlike in time to slow down, so as to prevent the shockwave of his passing from shattering them.

It turned out there wasn't anything that crossed above the road.

Running at full speed shortened a trip of hours to one of a few minutes. There was no traffic at all, on the best-made road he'd ever seen, leading directly to where he wanted to go. As a rule, Olympians were not, in the words of someone he'd met a few Earths back, "the kind of people who keep the Clue Shop on the corner from going out of business," but the only thing that was missing from this message was a Titan holding up a sign that said "THIS WAY, PROTICLES."

Given that *he* never knew where he was going to end up, the question was, who did?

He knew coincidence was a genuine phenomenon, not just some god's idea of a good trick (or at least not usually), but also knew it was something that didn't happen to him. He'd ask the one slave what was going on.

Signs gave him plenty of warning to slow down before reaching Neathenopolis, and he took the capillary that led the right way. He slowed to perhaps the speed of a cheetah, that being safe for traffic, but there still wasn't much: just trucks delivering goods. Some kind of holiday, perhaps . . . established in anticipation of this date.

He *really* wanted to talk with that slave.

He followed the trace to the tallest building in the (remarkably clean) city, labeled in characters that spelled out CROATOAN SPIRE. He knew what a croatoan was: an island-fish. He should know, he'd killed the last one himself, after evacuating the people it was going after. (There had probably been some heart attacks when they all discovered themselves miles inland, but he'd been pressed for time. That thing had been *hungry*.) Somebody was doing more than blatantly attracting his attention; they were having fun with it.

He walked into the lobby, and a couple of guards moved to flank him as he went to the main desk and said, "I believe I'm expected."

The woman there was trying not to stare at his genitalia, and said, "Um, ah, your name?"

"You wouldn't recognize it. I am the son of Peleus." At least his father's name wouldn't be beyond recall.

"Oh, Mister Peleides! Yes, you're the only appointment today. Top floor."

Lee nodded and headed for the elevators. One of the guards said, "This one, sir."

"Thank you."

"I always thought you were one of her stories."

"Until today, I was." The elevator was unlocked for him, and the guards stayed back as he went in. There was only one button, and he pressed it. The doors shut and the elevator rose.

It rose fast, too. A mortal man would have to brace himself against a corner—or better yet, lie down. The question of who used this thing was likely connected to the question of *who could possibly know when and where he showed up?*

It stopped moving, the doors opened, and a petite woman, shorter than he was, glomped onto him naked and kissed him.

She succeeded because he was always as fast as he had to be . . . and he recognized her.

When both their tongues were free he said, *"Cassandra?"*

"Proticles!" she said and set her feet onto the floor again. When she was at half arm's length from him, still holding his shoulders, she grinned and said, "I *don't* think it's about time we finally fucked."

It took him a moment, but then he grinned back and said, "It worked."

"It worked," she agreed. "Come on, we can catch up after." She took him by the hand and led him through a large office and the door of its living suite.

"That'll take some time."

She smiled over her shoulder. "Oh, I have time."

He had still been covered with Ilian blood and innards (he'd quit using a sword because they kept breaking), splinters from the horse he'd burst out of, and moisture that had condensed on his skin when they'd boiled a big pot of water under it for a couple of hours before putting it in the temple of Poseidon. His temper had been worse than usual, and in those days, that had really been saying something.

A girl of about twelve, richly gowned, hair done up, was waiting just outside the back of the temple of Apollo when he'd massacred his way through the soldiers holed up there, and she wasn't afraid of him. This was the biggest surprise he'd had in his life so far, and he stopped to look at her.

"Masonry," she said and took a step closer to him. A chunk of the temple landed where she'd been. Part of it hit him, and he brushed off the bits that had stuck when it shattered.

"Oracle," he said.

"Cassandra."

"They call me Achilles."

"Because mortal men can't remember your name. You're immune to it. You were inside the horse. I told them. I refused Apollo, and he cursed me never to be believed."

"Takes after his father," Proticles said.

She smiled at him then. "But you're immune to that too. You believe me!" She suddenly hugged him.

"I do, but I have a captive to rescue and a rapist to kill. We can talk later."

"I don't think so. I'll die from people ignoring what I tell them."

Proticles thought about that for a while—he was still short of practice in those days—and finally said, "So lie."

"What?"

"Tell everyone the opposite of what you want them to believe. Lie."

Her lips parted, her eyes grew wide, and she clutched her chest. Then she threw her head back and gasped, hard. Then she looked at him in wonderment and said softly, "I am no longer doomed."

Very pleased, he said, "And I have confounded the will of that rapist Apollo. This is turning out to be a good night. Stay safe, and we'll talk some more later."

She looked sad but said, "Yes. Later."

"Where can . . ." he began, then thought about it. "Where will I find Paris?"

"In the palace keep, disguised as a common soldier. He'll be the one whose armor is clean."

Made sense. "Thank you. I'll see you again."

She smiled as if it hurt, or she was out of practice. "I hope not," she said, and winked.

He smiled back. For someone who had never lied, it was a good start.

Then he turned away to kill every grown man in Troy.

When she had her breath back, she raised her head and said, "I should have told the gods I musn't be granted divine stamina."

"Aha," he said. "So this is the world I started from?" he realized.

"They all are. I can't see into the other possibilities, but I know they're there. People made different decisions, and they made different worlds. This is one where I thought of telling people I hadn't been killed, that I musn't be given all possible aid in reaching Olympus, and I musn't be granted eternal youth or health. Help me up, my legs are like noodles," she said, laughing a little. "We'll take a real shower this time."

"How about a bath this time?" he said.

"Oh, poor thing, you haven't had a proper bath in years. Yes."

He carried her back to the bath, sat her on the edge, started filling it, and said, "You need to be the one who tests the temperature."

"It sets itself automatically."

"Nice. I've filled baths for people who thought I was making soup."

She laughed again, stronger this time. "One of the drawbacks of being a god is not realizing what hurts."

He frowned at her. "I'm not a god."

"Of course you are. You're the god of freedom."

"I've never *heard* of any god of freedom."

"You fight to end controls on people, and you want them to act from thought and not blind obedience. It's not a popular gig."

He considered this, then said, "It does explain why I can heal people. And why I end up in the worlds I do—though I still don't see how I get to them."

"Fate, of course."

"The Fates are still around?"

"There's actually only one of her," said Cassandra, and lowered herself into the tub. "Oh, that's good. She showed up as the three women to give others something they could understand: making, measuring, and cutting."

"How can she do it, anyway?"

"How can she not? She created Ouranos to be her lover, and when he turned to their daughter Gaea instead, she decided to replace him."

"Her plans aren't perfect," he muttered, settling into the tub.

"How so?"

"I was supposed to have either a short famous life, or a long anonymous one."

"You were foretold as having two destinies. It was only an assumption that it had to be one or the other. You were known to everyone at Troy, and that was the short part. This is the long part, where no mortal knows your name."

He gaped at her. Then he said, "Did you know this?"

"Not until after I saw you last. I do have to think about something to know it."

He frowned a little.

"You're not angry, are you?" she said, then relaxed. "No, you're not. You haven't lost your temper in almost four hundred years."

"Oh, yeah." He shrugged. "I was beginning to think I'd settled down at last. Mined silver, bought some land, and was called to the local government office to pay taxes on it. They kept me waiting three weeks for an appointment, then told me there was a fine because it was overdue. I went around the building throwing every tax official I could find out the windows."

"Thereby starting the Thirty Years' War," she said, smiling.

"I don't know, I moved on right afterward. Bad, I take it?"

"It killed two out of three men in the empire where it took place. But the peace treaty did result in nations ruling themselves and not being client states of religious authorities."

Freedom, in other words. "Just as well, I suppose. So Fate set things up so Ouranos would give way to Cronos? I'd hardly call him a worthy successor. Nor Zeus, when he overthrew Cronos."

"No. She set things in motion to produce another universe. And here you are."

He splashed a bit as he recoiled. "I'm no universe!"

"Not yet. But you're filled with the essence of all Creation. That's why you stopped being able to change shape when your mother held you by your hair and dipped you in her grandfather's blood: you were held in place by the pressure of the universe that already existed. The fact that you partake of all things is why nothing can hurt you."

"Huh. I thought it was because my shape couldn't change anymore. What do you mean, 'not yet'?"

"Ouranos isn't completely dead and won't be as long as the four primary forces have a meaningful effect. When this universe ends, you will expand to become the next one. And since your mind isn't dead, there'll be no need of an Atlas to hold the forces in place."

He wanted to ask if there would be an Athena but held his tongue. Instead he said, "Just how many times has Fate done this?"

"Once. She won't be in the next. She can't affect you directly."

"She does a fine job moving me from one universe to another."

"She does nothing of the kind. She moves the universes while you stay in place."

Lee stared at her. "Two universes together are easier to move than I am."

"You can't be moved at all against your will. You are irresistible force and immovable object in one, as takes your mood."

That had been his experience, certainly. He thought of something else and closed his eyes, feeling bitter.

"What is it?"

"I'm just tired of being lonely."

"Athena didn't kill herself. She dispersed. Prudence and innovation are everywhere."

He opened his eyes, not pleased. "I cannot talk with a concept. I surely cannot embrace one."

"Freedom and Justice are inseparable," said Cassandra.

And the universe began to fade around him.

But not before she said, "You won't be alone."

Good news. Just for once.

Unexplained, but good.

All Which It Inherit Shall Dissolve

M.R. Glass

Your mother wears the demon into the hospital room, its boneless body slung noose-like around her neck until it slithers off into a corner. Your father is awake, sitting up. Even a little chatty. His face is ruddy, but he seems mostly like himself, not the skeletal wreck your mother prepared you to see. You peer at the demon lurking in the shadows and hear the hiss of its breath, labored and raspy, mocking your father's illness. You wonder why your mother doesn't seem to notice it—first, beneath the chair, later, under your father's bed—doesn't react to the oily residue it deposited on her skin when it wound its body around hers and fed on her desperate hope.

The room is a sea of noise, for all that its occupant is so still: the steady chatter of the television in the background, the ping of monitors, and shrill tones of the IV pump. Washing over the top are choppy waves of conversation that gust and fade according to your father's wakefulness and the latest lab results. The medical staff are the tides—and there are so many, checking and testing. Waiting and watching. Like the demon: watching.

Your mother tenses whenever someone enters, wary of tone and body language. It occurs to you that even though she seems not to be able to see the demon, she's reacting to its influence and braces for the others she seems certain wait without knowing what terrors they will bring next.

You understand her vigilance when you meet the doctor on call. He is somber and looks nobody in the eye. It seems to you as if a cloud of darkness has woven itself into his skin, stretching itself beyond his body, fattening his shadow. You can barely tell where he ends and this other demon begins.

The thing under the bed hisses its welcome, and the stale air in the room shudders.

"Have you been eating?" the doctor asks, not looking at him.

"Not much," says your father.

"We've been trying to talk him into a milkshake," you say. "What could be bad about a milkshake?"

"Well," the doctor says, "he could be lactose intolerant." His demon grins, a string of drool trailing from its open mouth.

You are speechless. Rhetorical. It was *rhetorical*. You wish you could laugh at the absurdity. If you could, maybe the demon would be scorched by the heat of your disgust. The demons look at you and turn to eye your father. If you could, you would fling yourself across his body to keep those claws and fangs from his reddened skin.

Only when your mother leaves do you understand. They don't want *him*. They want *you*. All of you. You scour the corners for more of them, but the shadows are just shadows. At least for tonight.

A bruise blooms under your fingernail. You can't remember how you got it, a vague memory of a sharp edge and a stab of pain, all that's left of whatever marked you.

You were here.

Remember.

Just a souvenir of a time and place that rushes by so fast you can't keep track. You wonder where your father will be as the nail grows. When the bruise grows from the base to the tip, where will he be? Where will he have gone?

On good days, you imagine him home again. Fiddling with his laptop, picking at the meals your mother prepares. But then the demons crowd around, putrid, rubbing slick poison into your skin, and then you can't picture him here to see the bruise ever leaving your body at all.

Especially in the dark, you know their breathing—rough and heavy, and you prickle with dread. Just before sleep, you hear them stalking your dreams, whispering lies in your ear, the stuff of insecurity, born of fear and nurtured by the day's troubles. You've always thought they were yours alone.

But now you're home again—your childhood home—and instead of your mother, you see a demon from your worst nightmares. It awaits you, oozing and writhing in the space between her breaths. It coils around her neck and leaves her gasping. It drinks her tears.

You don't believe in demons.

You'll fight them if you have to. You may very well have to. The one on your mother can only be pried off for short moments. It's growing. When you get too close, you can smell it. See its teeth. It's laughing at you.

You think they must prefer the silences, the fear that comes in with the medical staff, so when you speak up, ask questions, sound hopeful, you do it to make them cringe. You do it more, and you smile. You hope they hate it when you laugh into their darkness.

"You can't have us," you tell them when you're alone. "We have too much to do here, and, frankly, you're distracting."

You hear nothing but the sound of an endless ocean. It makes you shiver, but you pretend you're only cold and turn over, praying for dreamless sleep.

Light fills the room again. Your sister is on the phone, her anxious voice throwing shadows toward the bed, but he's in a chair today, sitting up and talking to visitors. She's imagining a skeletal father, just as you did, and she's so far away. You suggest a video call. The demons have wound her so tight you wish you could stand with her, breathe with her, each breath deeper than the next.

The demons don't like networks, so it's a full hour before you manage a stable link. You and your mother hover around your father and the screen; your sister's voice relaxes. Your family talks about nonsense, smiling and laughing. But you catch a flash of red through the screen, an eye that is not your sister's. It sees you, and you hold its gaze until it blinks.

He's stable, and for now there's only more waiting. So you go home, your grown-up home, the one with job and husband and children and house. But your mind and heart are at the hospital, tracking every change, marking new shadows as they all grow. You try to dispel them with encouraging words and baseless hope. Time between phone calls brims with a hissing that seeps into your bones. Only contact silences it. A nurse's voice, reassuring. Your father's voice, tired, tight, increasingly breathless, but still his.

Even without the demons, you understand that being transferred into intensive care (crashing . . .) is not the desired direction (crashing . . .), and each moment between updates saturates with dread and the ceaseless trickle of barely-managed panic.

You're not sure why sometimes you can push the demons aside, denying them entry, if only for moments at a time. Maybe you are like your father, refusing anything but a happy ending. But sometimes all you can imagine is an ending. You're not sure which way is better, but in your calmer moments, you decide that you would rather be hopeful for as long as there is hope; never mind those other watchers oozing fetid sweat in the shadows. Besides, he's still here, isn't he? So sick, but still very much himself?

If he hasn't succumbed, you'll be damned if you do.

"Do you want me to come?" you ask. You don't want to go, but you don't want not to, either. What you really want is to have no reason at all to drop everything and get on the first available flight.

"Yes!" Your mother's answer is an agonized wail and, in it, a wounded animal.

"Let me talk to Dad," you say, wanting her animal out of your ear.

"I'm thinking of coming out to see you. What do you think?" you ask him, affecting a casualness you don't feel. You can't decide if he is as stoic as he seems or if he really does inhabit each present moment, refusing to address even the idea of a future. In the past, he would have brushed you off, told you to wait. "No need to come *now*," he would have said. "I'm not dying."

"You could come," he says instead, and your heart pounds, a frantic drum, as you book the ticket home. The only sound from your demon, its breath rasping in your ear.

This time it's different. No longer awake to watch television and refuse food. Immobile, a machine to help him breathe, sweat in a sheen on his forehead, his body working too hard to keep up with the technology that has spread like choking weeds. Apart from the whoosh of the ventilator and the muffled sobs of too many visitors grieving a man not yet dead, the room is silent.

When you walk into the darkened room, your first thought is that if you don't get out of there right *now*, you're going to hit somebody.

Even through the thick rubber glove, his skin is too hot.

"Hi Daddy," you say, but the sound of your voice tastes wrong behind the sterile mask you wear, carries oddly through air as thick as liquid. "I'm here." You pause. "Were you bored, because, you know, if you wanted more company, you could have just asked." Nobody laughs, but the more you chatter, retelling him everything you can think of about the five scant days you've been away, the more your voice crowds out the heavy air.

You won't let them win, those waiting presences, circling shark-like around and under the bed, sliding softly through the unseeing eyes and unfeeling skins of those too quick with too much life. You won't let them use all the oxygen until all that remains for filling your own lungs is death. You talk and talk until words lose their meaning and all you have left to give him is the sound of your voice through the mask.

He doesn't respond at all.

"If anybody can turn this around, you know it will be him," you tell your mother later, and it's so true even she has to nod, her neck stiff within her demon's stranglehold. It would be just like him to open his eyes again, even after crashing so far and so fast you can't imagine how they managed to catch him. It's midnight, and you're on your way to get your sister. She's been in the air an unbearably long time, and you cradle her terror in your chest, the fear that by the time she touches ground, it will be too late to ever see him alive again.

But he was, tentatively, when you left him, and despite the midnight hour, you go back there, all of you, and instead of goodbye, you find him steadier, quieter now, and you relax too, just a tiny bit.

You always were the optimistic one.

There is a world out there beyond the shuttered windows and fluorescent hallways where the demons stalk the halls with impunity as if they belong there just as much as the doctors and nurses. As much as you. More, even. Your eyes burn when you walk beneath the skylight, the sun pouring over you like honey. Compared with the world you've been inhabiting, the smiles and chatter and shrieking children feel false, like actors on a set. Only at night, shadows swallowing you as you leave to sleep, does the world feel familiar again.

Your choice is between horrible and terrible. To watch him all night long, waiting for the alarms, fighting the demons whose greatest joy is to jolt you awake from the sleeping nightmare to the waking one. Or to go to your room, where uncertainty rises in a tidal wave to batter you until you must call and check on him again. And again. And again. What are his numbers? Are there new lab results? Is it safe to go to sleep for a few hours? A half hour? Long fingers creep forward to clutch your throat more tightly with each step you take away from him. There is no safety anywhere.

After days in Intensive Care, you know the demons that inhabit this place. Coiled around the monitor you've all become expert at reading, their teeth gnashing in rhythm with the shrilling alarm when medicine runs out; rising, eager to feed on every accelerated heartbeat. Yours. Your father's. It only makes them stronger.

They know when you're vulnerable. You can feel them sidle up to you, pebbled skin rubbing against your arm, your cheek, foul breath burning your face, a slippery tongue dipping deep inside to taste your fear.

Inexplicably, tomorrow is better. You're confused. Cautious. Unsuccessfully quashing giddiness when his eyelids flicker just before he wakes.

You surround him like vultures. "Open your eyes," your mother commands, and he tries. He always did listen to her most and best. "You're okay," you tell him.

It doesn't escape you how very far your collective definition of "okay" has stretched in recent weeks. Still, you soothe and encourage, willing his eyes to open. Willing him to know you're all here with him. For him. When finally the lashless lids struggle and rise, you're yanked back in time to the weeks after your babies were born, too early, so small. Paper-thin eyelids, lashless, too, eyes glazed and confused, like his are now, opening warily to a too-bright world. Just as you did for your babies, you want to cheer when his eyes open.

"Hello there," you say. "It's so nice to see you." He blinks his agreement, and the effort exhausts him.

The sun shines through the window. You close the blinds against the painful brightness.

You see the enormous heads. Scaly. Nostrils flaring and dripping, eyes glowing malevolent red, but only after she begins to speak. Today she lingers in the doorway, students flanking her, not coming in all the way. Her eyes dart around like she can't find you, even though you're all sitting right there. You wonder if she'll bother to acknowledge your father. He's awake, after all.

You can barely make out her words, but then you understand. It's the demon speaking. Its voice has no sound, flooding the room with shadows. Both heads are gabbling a poison of misinformation and incomplete plans that spreads quickly and drowns out the light that had only just started to fill the space, leaving all of you blind, flattened, breathless.

She sweeps away, but the demon stays, clinging to the ceiling, scything its heads over you, exposing ulcerous gums pooling with acid.

Your father would appreciate the irony of discovering that there actually are demons when he is incapacitated and unable to enjoy the show.

But your father doesn't care about demons now. Their shadows only lie on you. He swims in his own pool of light and shade. You wonder what he dreams.

To everyone's surprise, he is increasingly awake, and you dare to imagine a future that extends beyond tonight, maybe even into tomorrow. He is responsive, interacting, for days in a row, a week; a nod of the head and his familiar expressions more newsworthy than anything in a hundred years.

So you begin to consider making plans. Such hubris, and yet you do.

"I'm thinking of going back home in a few days. Just for a little while. Is that okay?" you ask after he's been awake and responsive all morning. He looks at you, eyes less glazed now, his glasses making him look more like himself despite the ventilator tube. "Do you think it's okay?" you ask again. He nods. "Are you sure?" Again. He may be sure, but you're not.

But you have a job here, though you don't know it until they tell you.

It shouldn't be a surprise that you wonder what use you are here. Mother and sister understand one another; they always have. If you're honest, you've always been the odd one out.

It's only later, after the crying, that you feel the slime on the back of your neck. It got too close, its poison seeping beneath your skin even as you guarded against it.

But you don't know it yet, and so you sob there, in the kitchen with your mother and your sister, as alone as you've ever felt.

"I'm an alien creature," you tell them that night, all the tears you haven't shed for weeks still wet on your cheeks. "You don't need me here." But you don't want to leave, either, no matter how much they miss you at the grown-up home in that other world.

Your sister looks shocked. For the first time, you hear her say, "We do need you. You're the Yin to our Yang. Besides, who's going to call the nurses if you're gone?"

That makes you smile.

"You're the girl version of Daddy," your mother adds, affirming what you've always known: that you are the one most like your father. "I need that. I always have."

It reminds you of the days *between,* when you were the voice that anchored them both. Your job to call, to question, to assess and then to report. You, the one who kept the linkage between mother and sister from being swamped by the demons' venom.

You can still feel your sister's arms around you and the whisper: *Keep in touch.* It's not your best thing. *Keep in touch.* You know she's right, and so you promise.

But you know it's all a mistake the moment you enter the airport. Alone. Alone.

No. Apparently not entirely alone. A demon accompanies you, and you're so damned desperate, you're almost grateful for its company. You succumb to the grip of its bony fingers and the pollution of its breath as you race for the gate. If you didn't hate it so much, you might thank it for keeping you tethered to the family you're leaving behind.

Only two days, but it feels like a lifetime trapped on a faraway planet. You can't quite get back into the rhythm of life after nearly two weeks away, not with the demon sucking the air out of you and stirring your thoughts. You can't call often enough. Perversely, you miss the ventilator and the rustle of the nurse. You wish you were there to monitor, as if you had any control over the ending. So when it all goes to hell, you take it as definitive proof that you were, in fact, the only thing keeping your father alive.

Or so the demon tells you.

The doctor and her demon are both in attendance at the hospital while you are rushing back. More substantial this time, grown fat on its potent slurry of hope and dread, it oozes into the room without a glance at your father and declares the war over.

"He is going to code in the next day or two unless we get him back on dialysis," says one of the heads, "and it's clear he can't tolerate dialysis." The demon flashes yellow teeth in a grotesque smile. "Do you want us to use chest compressions?"

Your mother's demon rears its head, greedy. No longer satisfied to wade in the eddies of fear that flow through the room, it has become her second skin. She seems both smaller and larger in its clinging embrace.

The man in the bed is become just a set piece for the demons' drama.

"Yes," she says with the demon's voice. "Yes, I do."

Three minutes later, the two-headed demon is back, its second head leering, entirely obscuring the doctor, its host. "We've got the thumbs-up to put him back on dialysis," it says as if it hadn't just pronounced your father's imminent death with its other mouth, and your mother's demon salivates.

This is what you walk into when you return.

If you squint, you can see the wounds of the last few days. You were needed here and you left, the demon whispers.

How *could* you?

There isn't time, though, not yet, for regrets. Not now, when they won't even wake him up anymore. You're sure he can still hear you, and so you talk. You ask the nurse if you can unglove and touch his bare skin with yours, and he says, "Yes, of course you can." And that's how you know it's almost over.

Your sister tells him true versions of old stories and insists that if he wakes up, this never happened.

"I've been taking notes," says his nurse, joking, and you laugh. There are no demons here, not now, here in the room where your father lies, sweaty and exhausted. Maybe the nurse has chased them away with his calm efficiency and his compassion. Maybe it's the stories you tell one another and the memories you share.

"We're okay," your mother tells your father, holding his swollen hand in hers. "It's okay." To let go, she means, to stop fighting, and you can't quite bring yourself to chime in.

"You'll be okay, too," you tell him instead. "But it would be really great if you found a way to come back and let us know." Your mother and sister shake their heads, but you are sure he understands.

The morning before he dies, you meet with his doctor, the one who has known him longest and best. The one who cares about all of him, not just the cancer, or his lungs, or the infection raging through him. He is direct, but so terribly kind. He listens and alters the treatment plan when your mother asks him to.

"He's hung on much longer than I thought he would," he tells you. "But that could just be him giving me the middle finger." You all laugh, and then you cry. Together.

"It will probably be a few more days," he continues and describes what to expect in the clearest, gentlest terms.

All you care about—all anyone in the room cares about—is increasing your father's comfort and maybe, just maybe, finding a scant few moments more to talk with him, to be there together one last time. That is your last and greatest and only feeble hope.

The demons are nowhere to be found.

In the early morning before the sun rises, the phone rings, heralding your last, blind rush to the hospital. Time pulses forward and with it, the final beats of your father's heart. The streetlights flicker, and you wonder if you would stop time if you could. If you had the power, would you leave your father suspended in limbo for all eternity, rather than let him go?

The Intensive Care Unit is strange in the early morning dark. It echoes around you when you push through the doors, naked without the gloves and gown and mask you've grown accustomed to wearing. Fears gone now, taking with them all hopes but one: for a last moment. For peace. For rest.

"We're here," you each say, reaching for his bare skin with bare hands. "We love you."

You imagine his heart leaping as it accelerates for the first time that night. For the last time: *I love you, too.* There is silence broken only by the pounding of your father's heart as he leaves you. It's only a moment, though, before his pulse slows again and you watch the last beats fade until he is still.

"Middle finger again," you tell his doctor when he comes by to see you all before his rounds.

He laughs. "I'm really going to miss him," he says.

The only people there as the sun rises, bathing your father's motionless form with light, are the ones who cared for him. The ones who will remember. Those who already miss him the most.

There's nothing to do without an ICU to occupy your time. All those hours sitting, watching the monitors weigh and measure your father's life, crowd around you now, moments blurred together behind the glass, pressing against it as if they might reanimate if only they could get through. It was like occupying a foreign country, those weeks of watching and waiting. Time stretched and compressed until it was unrecognizable. Only the rhythms of the equipment that supported him and kept him from slipping away from here kept you tethered, too. But now you're without a compass, drifting on the current of today, and time stretches on like an endless ribbon only recently unfurled.

The funeral is almost as awful as you imagined it would be. From the car window, you can see people streaming onto the ragged lawn, walking slowly, heads bowed. The cemetery is small, and this section is nearly desolate, a bald stretch of brown grass, empty of stones. The reluctant sunlight casts almost no shadow, and the living look oddly sharp, like a black-clad honor guard thrusting up from the soil.

Behind the words of the service, the single, the communal, a trace of stench lingers, if only as memory, and idly you wonder what the demons will feed on now.

In this house filled with memory, there is no purchase for demons, so instead, they hide.

They hide behind the cloths covering the mirrors; you catch a glimpse of an errant tail, an extended claw. They hide behind the barriers, trying to lure you with the temptation of your own reflection. Haggard. Haunted.

Starving.

But you push the cloth back between the people and the shadows and return to the rooms full of people who have brought you photographs and stories of your father to stoke the memorial flame.

There is a picture of him on the school bus, his exuberant smile a shaft of warmth through the sadness.

They all come. Old friends, former rivals; a boy, now a man, grateful for your father's care when he was small and scared in a new place. People your own age sharing the impact he had on them, a power still felt so many years later. Stories weaving together to show you a tapestry of a life deeply lived.

The candle, lit with love and shared history, burns even brighter in the presence of your children, his grandchildren, and the legacy they carry. You feel the demons now, their weakening thoughts circling the candle, desperate to extinguish it.

With a thought, with intent, you push them in. You catch the scent of scorched wings, and you smile.

Heal Thyself

Bran Heatherby

"**W**hat's your name?"
Your simplistic, rudimentary human vocal apparatus cannot begin to pronounce it, let alone your mind comprehend. Flappy tissues and cartilage and air. You couldn't even try.

"Tara," she said.

OkCupid didn't have "I'm a Goddess stuck without magic and my ex is an arsehole" in any of its checkboxes. She looked for an alternative. Twice.

Instead, she filled in "feline veterinarian" and "business owner" and listed her favourite films in descending order of release date. She didn't know how any of this was going to help find someone to worship her, but she hoped it might pass the time.

After two thousand years of this shit, she was bored to tears.

The last time Tara had invented a ritual in an attempt to regain her magic, she'd ended up naked on the front lawn of a town hall, surrounded by pigeon feathers, so she'd decided—rightly or wrongly—to give it up for a while. That had been back in the 1980s, and she'd spent most her time since then learning the finer points of digital piracy and narrowing her focus to a viable treatment for Feline Infectious Peritonitis.

She'd had considerably more luck with the former than the latter.

Any powers she'd once had as a Goddess were well and truly gone. She'd retained rather more intuition than a human when it came to medical matters, but she still found herself regularly angered by the lack of magic. This .

.. this was one of those times.

The kitten had been found abandoned on a sidewalk and brought in. Tara stroked his downy side with the pad of her forefinger as she listened for a hum of life in his veins. He'd been a little fighter, and cats often survived all manner of things which defied explanation, but no matter how diligently she'd worked, no matter how hard she begged the universe for any sign—a tail twitch, a snuffle, a tiny, pin-toothed, perfect yawn—none ever came.

The universe was a bitch.

At least this time there probably hadn't been much pain. It was tough to tell, though. That was another sense the loss of power had robbed from her.

Exhausted, disheartened, depressed, she stumbled off to the back office to take a nap.

"It's Arthur," Molly said at the front desk the next morning. She held out the receiver.

"Who?"

Molly sighed. "The guy from two weeks ago. With the . . . you know. Loafers and no socks."

Tara scowled down at the post she was sorting through. Bill, bill, bill, ad, ad, drugs rep something-or-other, bill . . . "Who?"

"The one who ate the rest of your meal without asking. Who kept staring at your mouth."

Oh. Him. "How the hell do you remember all this?" Tara said, finally looking up from her task to blink at her.

"I enjoy eating the popcorn." Molly quirked a smile. "So here, or in the office?"

"Neither." He was annoying and likely to be clingy, and she'd yet to gather the strength to deal with him, just on the off-chance she'd get her magic back. "Maybe I'll phone back later."

"I'm shocked," Molly said, rolling her eyes. "Surgery's at 5, still?"

"As far as I know."

Tara scowled at the post as she considered phoning Arthur back. Truthfully, it seemed a bit pointless. Over time, fewer and fewer of her immortal cohort remained, slowly fading from existence as belief in them waned, until eventually Tara was convinced no one was left. She was old, alone, and done for, and had felt so for years. And no wonder; any belief people had now tasted subtly different—somehow more dense, yet more flighty— and the few times she'd felt herself getting close to regaining her magic, the person on whom she'd pinned her expectations had failed her.

So it wasn't necessarily Arthur's fault. Even *if* being revered was the key to getting back her power . . . well. Tara had just about given up hope of eliciting worship from anyone.

The cat was grey-haired and wiry as a grandmother. Her eyes were hazy golden slits, and one fang was hanging out of her mouth as if she couldn't be arsed to keep it in any more.

Tara stroked the cat's head. There was a complicated feedback loop going on between her pancreatic cancer and her liver function, and Tara had done all she could. Over time, she'd treated countless animals in similar positions, and the prognosis was never positive. Tara scratched below her ears. The old lady's tail twitched: her spirit was appreciative, her flesh weak.

Tara had some time alone with her, so she allowed the stoic veterinarian mask to fall. She was incredibly tired. With her powers, this wouldn't have been any trouble at all to fix, but instead she was stuck watching and waiting. Hoping that the surgery would do the trick. Expecting that it wouldn't. Tara placed both hands on the cat's side and blindly *willed*, pressing all the energy she could muster into the skinny body. She pushed and shook, mentally screaming down the walls at how unfair it was that she could do nothing. If only Robert had recognised her as a Goddess. Robert, or Michael, or Ashley, or Keshawn, or Samir. Any of them could have done the trick. But now Tara had to endure the agony of doing nothing when once she could have fixed it with a simple flare of magic.

She didn't necessarily want to heal everyone—back in the day, she'd save everyone indiscriminately, and even now thought fondly of the accolades she'd received for it while being aware it *probably* wasn't the best policy— but over the years that impulse had faded. Now, she'd be pleased if only she could give it a try once in a while and know she'd be successful. Lady Grey was one thing, but the kitten? What was the point to being a Goddess if you couldn't be assured you could save a kitten?

The uselessness made her feel . . . *mortal.*

After a few minutes of effort, straining so hard her eyes became damp, there was a noise out in the corridor. Tara let go. She stood by the sink and ran the water as Lady Grey's owner came in, hiding her face until she was certain the mask was back in place, then took a deep breath and turned.

"Okay. Let's talk about our options."

It never became second nature to deal lightly with death. Ever. But if Tara were honest with herself, it had eventually got a bit easier over time. But only a bit.

The fact that she had little say over it any more might have something to do with that.

She slammed a few boxes into the spaces in the shelf, restocking the shit out of their store of bandages. Molly came through to see what was going on.

"If you're back here, who's on the front desk right now?" Tara growled before Molly could open her mouth.

"You okay?" said Molly.

"Of course."

"Of course."

"I just . . ." Breathing heavily, Tara grabbed onto the shelf and stood, head bowed, trying to get a grip on her temper. "Sometimes I really *hate* this. I can't—" Tara bit her tongue. *I can't do anything about them dying,* she wanted to say. *I should be able to stop it, but I can't.* "Do you want to know what might help?"

"Definitely."

"Phone Arthur back for me."

"*Arthur?*" Molly said, pulling a face like someone had put a live mouse in her mouth.

"Yeah. Tell him if he's free tonight, I am, too."

"You're serious."

"Absolutely."

"You have the weirdest reactions to losing a patient I've ever—"

"Just. Please do it. For me."

For several seconds Molly just stared at her. Then she nodded, spun on her heel, and pushed open the double doors. "And this is my job," Tara heard her mutter just as the doors closed.

Well, this is my endless life, Tara thought, preparing herself. Annoyed or not, she was worn out. She needed her powers back. Now.

"Whoa," Arthur said, doe-eyed and astonished, as she took off her coat. "You look amazing."

"Better than last time?"

"You always look amazing."

"You're good at flattery, at least."

"But it's true. No flattery necessary."

Tara tried to preen without seeming like she was preening, which was always an awkward series of gestures. She was saved by the waitress coming over with their menus and a list of the specials.

She couldn't shake the flutter of hope born from the reverential look in his eye.

There was ordering, and there was dinner. The conversation wasn't even that bad.

". . . But now he's fine. Only a bit of stiffness in his back leg . . ." Tara realised the reason she was enjoying the conversation was that she'd fallen into a monologue. Arthur looked a little dazed. "Sorry. You don't want to hear about this. Tell me about . . ." There really wasn't enough about him to get a conversational foothold. Internally, she flailed. ". . . Work?"

"I don't mind," he said.

"Don't mind?"

"Talk all you want. You're amazing."

"Ah."

"Beautiful. Especially when you talk about your job."

"Huh."

"Your whole aspect shines. You talk about healing some poor little thing, and I just . . . You're a *Goddess.*"

Tara had expected that when it came there, would be some bolt of thunder, or the ground would shake. Or the lights would flicker, at least.

But someone had called her a Goddess and *meant it*, and there was no external shock to mark the occasion. No one even dropped a fork.

With a sinking sensation, she excused herself to the ladies'. On the way, she bumped into a waiter with a tray of drinks and used the ensuing ruckus to cover the fact that she'd snagged a lobster from the tank near the kitchen and bundled it into the toilets.

If she'd still been expecting her powers, she was bound to be disappointed; holding the lobster was as empty of information as touching a rock. She didn't understand. Surely someone's belief in her was the key. When it came to the powers of Gods and Goddesses, belief was *always* the key. And it was the only reasonable idea she had left.

She felt a pang of desperation. What if she were going down the wrong track entirely? What if being believed in wasn't the key she'd hoped it was?

Disgusted with herself for letting her hopes get so high, bereft, and more than a bit punchy with anger, Tara sulked out of the toilets and ran smack into a waiter. "I hope you're planning to pay for that," he said with an expression that said her very existence was curdling his soup.

Fuck off. "He's not a that, he's a he. And his name is Jim."

Nonplussed, the waiter opened his mouth, shut it again, and stepped aside as she pushed past and into the sea of diners.

"Don't bother with pudding," she called out, brandishing the live lobster. "I've got to make an emergency trip to the coast."

The next day, she closed the clinic for lunch and treated Molly to a meal. They sat out on the patio of a local bistro while Molly ate a sandwich and Tara picked at a salad, hoping for distraction. She was still bitter about her failure the previous evening—and still exhausted by her late-night trip to return the lobster to the sea—and she allowed her attention to be tugged to and fro by the city wandering past.

It was pulled to the gaggle of girls seated at the next table with a mountain of shopping bags piled at their feet. Each girl's hair was perfectly smooth and shiny, some like corn silk and some tumbling over their shoulders like dark rivers. Dark rivers tumbling over the mountains, quiet and serene before the dawn of industry. Tara realised she was a bit homesick.

It was true, what they said: you can never go home again. Especially nowhere where you're meant to be aging. Or old. Or dead.

"You deserve better than him," one of the girls said, to the humming acclaim of her companions.

"Yeah, you are so much better. You're a *goddess*," one said. She probably didn't even capitalise it in her head.

Tara stared down at the tomato speared on her fork. *Do you even know what that means?* "She's only a human," she muttered.

"No need to be petty," said Molly, and Tara could do nothing but sigh. Of course she was going to be petty. The worst thing these girls had ever experienced was not fitting all their shopping into their SUVs, while the worst thing Tara had experienced was overstaying her welcome during the Black Death and being pursued as a suspected witch. These girls couldn't imagine the pain of—

Her thought process was derailed by movement at the corner of her eye: a flash of orange and swing of long, dark, *incredibly familiar* hair as a back disappeared into the crowd.

Without a word to Molly, without even putting down her empty drinks cup, Tara exploded out of her seat and into pursuit. Down one side street, then another. Through a tiny gift shop full of stationery and tiny plastic figurines, then over the road, under an overpass, and through a crowd of people gathered round a busker performing an amped-up version of "Strawberry Fields" arranged for kick drum and accordion. Tara tried not to knock over too many people as she pinballed within the gathering, but it was inevitable, so by the time she got through, she had pissed most of them off. A large man snagged her by the upper arm and spun her to face him.

"Hey, watch where you're going!"

Immediately, fury filled her like scalding water, and she tried to burn him with her eyes. "Take your hand off me."

"Don't be such a bitch. We're just trying to watch the show."

"And I'm just trying to get through."

"Say excuse me."

"Excuse me," she said and shoved her empty cup into his free hand. He automatically grabbed it, confused, and she took the opportunity to slam her foot down on his instep. While he howled in pain, she dodged away and ran down the road, but the orange figure was nowhere to be seen.

Shit.

Winded, Tara slunk into a used clothing store and waited until she was certain the arsehole guy in the square wasn't limping after her, then took a meandering path back to the bistro. Molly watched Tara's approach with her chin propped in her hand, clearly amused and annoyed and finished with her meal. "Do I want to know what that was about?"

Tara brushed it away and plopped down into her seat. "Thought I saw someone."

"No kidding. It looked like they stole your purse."

"I don't carry a purse."

"I know. And you're sure you're fine?"

"Totally." Tara didn't look her in the eye. She stirred more dressing into her salad until it was pale and glistening and appeared just as unappetizing as it was. "I'm totally fine."

On the way back to the clinic, they stopped to pick up an order from the print shop. As they walked out the door, another flash of orange caught Tara's eye. Her head whipped round. She half expected it to be just a kid in a hoodie, but there was that same long, dark, familiar hair flowing behind as a figure turned the corner.

Alexandra.

She tried to dump the boxes of business cards onto Molly, but couldn't because *her* hands were already full of flyers. Frantic, Tara took a few steps to follow, but the burden of carrying the cards made catching up a lost cause. "Damn it." She considered dropping them, but realised that was ridiculous; she couldn't even be positive it was her. But if it was . . .

Alexandra.

Tara sagged.

"Again?" said Molly.

"Again."

"It wasn't her?"

"Couldn't tell." Tara swallowed down her curiosity and disappointment. "Doesn't matter."

"Sure." Molly, being sharp and having worked with Tara for years, didn't appear to believe her, but mercifully she kept quiet as they moved on.

It could very well not be Alexandra, of course. The flash of profile Tara had seen had only been a flash, after all, and there were any number of tall, svelte, dark-haired women walking around the city. But the profile was right, and the toss of her hair had always been distinctive. Even after two millennia without magic, Tara was still inclined to trust her instincts, and her instincts were screaming.

Alexandra.

They walked straight past a hole-in-the-wall music store without stopping in. Ordinarily, skipping a chance to peruse the vinyl would have aroused comment, but Molly was sufficiently plugged in to Tara's mood to let it go. "You don't want to tell me about this person?" asked Molly.

"Who?"

Molly sighed. "Who do you think?"

"No," said Tara. *What could she possibly be doing here?*

"Have it your way," Molly said, and she led them round the corner toward the clinic. For once, Tara appreciated being steered. It saved the brainpower for puzzling.

They paused under the awning as Molly fumbled for her keys, and Tara cast an eye over the facade of her building. She would need to get someone out to look at the crack in the foundation before winter, because it was worrisome, and—*Why the fuck is Alexandra here in my city?* Tara scowled. It had been a long damn time since she'd caught even so much as a whiff of another Immortal, and she wasn't sure if she was angry or relieved that, if anyone was left, it had to be *Alexandra.*

When they saw each other, what would Alexandra have to say? What would Tara? How was she meant to react? How *would* she react?

Furthermore, if Alexandra was in town, it meant nothing good. What kind of mischief was she planning? Would Tara be able to focus on anything else with her in the area? If Alexandra wasn't already inclined to, did Tara have a chance in hell of getting her to leave? Did Tara even want to be left alone again? Would it be better than being left alone with *her?*

Was there any way Tara could get work done while these questions hung over her head?

Tara at least knew that answer immediately: if Alexandra was around, it was clear Tara would have to find her and suss out her plan.

There was no way round it.

Unless, of course, Alexandra found her first.

The windows set into the door to the waiting room reflected orange only seconds before she pushed through. She was carrying a longhaired white thing which probably was a cat, but just as easily well could have been an angora rabbit or some sort of Swiffer. Tara blinked hard.

"Welcome to Cat's Cradle," said Molly, holding out a clipboard. "Walk in?"

"No, I have an appointment," said Alexandra. She tossed her hair. "3:15. Pritchard." As she spoke, she never stopped staring at Tara, but to be fair, Tara was staring right back. Her heart pounded as everything—memories two thousand years old—came flooding back.

"Ah, right. Here it is." Molly clipped some papers to a clipboard and held it out without taking her eyes from the screen. She didn't look up until she realised Alexandra wasn't taking the clipboard from her.

"Is that even your cat?" Tara said. And now she had the answer to at least one of her questions: now that she was face to face with Alexandra, her initial reaction was *anger*.

"Yes, as a matter of fact."

"Wouldn't have figured you for a cat person."

"No?"

"No. Maybe foxes. Goats. Or giant spiders. Tradition."

"That was never my thing, and you know it."

"Lots of things have changed since then." Understatement.

"Not this."

"Funny. You never indicated you liked cats before."

"And you never indicated you preferred cats over people before."

"Cats like to live."

"Then small wonder you see the appeal."

They just stared at each other, and Tara kept a sweaty grip on her temper. She felt Molly's attention flick back and forth between them. "Well." Tara swallowed. She realised the only way to figure out Alexandra's plan was to play along. "I guess . . . come on through." As they walked through the heavy door separating reception from the medical area, Tara looked at the pile of fluff in Alexandra's arms. "What happened to . . . her? his? carrier."

"What do I need a carrier for? He always obeys me perfectly."

"Oh, of course he does."

In the exam room, Tara arranged the Swiffer for inspection. He was well cared-for, for all that his owner was a horrible guttersnipe. A horrible guttersnipe with beautiful hair. Maybe they were groomed at the same time; after all, long hair *was* tough to maintain.

Tara bit the inside of her cheek to stifle a bitter smile and realised she had no idea what to say next. Best stick to the topic of the cat, right? She was afraid if she started asking questions she might not be able to stop, and she wasn't sure she wanted to know the answers. "What's the trouble?" The cat certainly *seemed* fine. It was following Tara with its eyes, baleful and distrusting. Reassuringly cat-like.

"He just seems . . . out of sorts."

Helpful. "Not eating? Drinking?"

"Oh, sure, he's doing all those."

"Elimination?"

"What, like, peeing?"

Tara sighed. "Yes. Like peeing. And having bowel movements."

"Fine."

"Then what's the—"

"He won't chase anything. Just sleeps all the time."

"And this is unusual behaviour?"

"Well . . ." Alexandra wouldn't look at her. She went to examine some charts on the wall, and Tara stopped poking at the cat to stare at her back. "No. Not really. He doesn't really play. But other cats do. And I was concerned."

Tara blinked. Her brain spun up, stopped, and started again, like a faulty hard drive. "Not all cats are the same, Alexandra."

"So you're saying I shouldn't worry about it?"

". . . That's why you brought him in here?"

Even from the back, Alexandra's half-shrug was eloquent. "I suppose."

"You brought your cat to the vet—to me, of all people—because he was exhibiting the same behaviours he always has?"

"Well . . . yeah."

Pinching between her eyes, Tara sighed. "'Did you come in here just to fuck with me?"

"Of course not."

"Oh, please. Don't pretend that's a ridiculous concept."

Finally, Alexandra turned. "Why do you assume I have an ulterior motive?"

"Because you always do."

"I could have changed."

"I doubt it."

The tiny quirking at the corner of Alexandra's well-formed mouth told Tara all she needed to know. "I just wanted to see you."

"After two thousand years?"

"I figured you might be settled in by now."

"I do have a phone."

"Which Molly answers."

"And a mobile."

"Would you have talked to me?"

Maybe. "No."

"There you go, then."

Tara grabbed up Swiffer and shoved him into Alexandra's arms. "Your cat is fine. Now get the hell out of my clinic."

Alexandra stopped and frowned at her, head cocked to the side. She looked genuinely sad. Tara wasn't buying the act for a second. She set her jaw and stared back, and finally after a moment Alexandra ceded the floor with a sharp nod. "Just putting things the way they're meant to be."

And with a dark splash of hair, Alexandra was gone, leaving Tara to stare after her with heavy foreboding, wondering what in the hell she'd meant by that. For the first time in many, *many* years, Tara was terrified.

The next day after lunch, Alexandra appeared again. This time she was holding a grey tabby with a weary expression on its face. Tara understood the feeling; she didn't have the energy to deal with Alexandra's shit either. She shook her head. "Oh, hell, no. Get the fuck out. Leave me alone."

"Language, language."

"You know I can get a lot worse. Want a reminder?"

"Didn't you take an oath to help all animals?"

"I didn't need a fucking oath. It went with the territor— Wait. Whose cat is this?"

"Mine."

"What are the odds you have two cats sick two days in a row?"

"Pretty good, when you have a lot of cats."

"Do I want to know how many?"

"No, probably not."

An image came to mind of a large palace, completely overrun. Tara wanted to ask if they were all being well cared for and how in hell Alexandra didn't know different cats behaved in different ways, but then she realised she didn't really want to have that conversation with her. Or any conversation, for that matter. "Get out."

"Piddles needs some tests run. He's having trouble. He's not drinking enough."

"Cats never drink enough."

"Too much, I mean. It's weird."

"And that's why you named him Piddles?"

"Coincidence."

Oh for fuck's sake.

"Listen, I have some information for you. If you look at Piddles, we can talk."

"So you're bribing me with info so I'll fix your cat? Or is it the other way round?"

"Whichever you like."

"Did you really think I wasn't going to look at him anyway?"

"No."

"You're a real dickhead, you know that?"

"Everybody knows that."

Tara sighed. She saw an older woman with a cat carrier and a harried expression coming up the walk and wanted to get out of the waiting room before they had company. "Come on," she gritted out.

Once back in the exam room, Alexandra cleared her throat before Tara could so much as touch the cat. "Listen, I just wanted to say—"

"Oh, here we go."

"I have an idea how you can get your magic back."

"No doubt you do."

"Listen. Our powers are directly related to the belief of a mortal, yes?"

Tara knew precisely where she was going with this. "And you thought 'Hey, if someone just believes in me hard enough, the magic is bound to come flooding back.' Nope, doesn't work. I think it's because people here don't believe the same way they used to."

"I was considering something different."

The cat between them on the exam table was staring at Tara. Alexandra smiled her familiar smile, and Tara distrusted it with the ease of long experience. "What."

"Your powers will come back if *you* believe."

"My powers will come back if I believe? If I believe I'm a Goddess? What a load of bullshit. I *know* I'm a Goddess."

"Belief is power. What if belief in yourself is stronger than the belief others have in you?"

"I'm a Goddess. The whole *point* is for people to believe in me."

"And how's that working out for you so far?"

Tara thought about how excited she'd been when she'd seen Peter Pan and first got the idea. But that had been so long ago, and thus far there hadn't been a tingle. She cleared her throat. "So. Tell me about his diet."

After an examination, she diagnosed Piddles with a probable UTI, wrote a prescription, and sent the two of them on their way. She breathed a sigh a relief when they were gone, but truthfully, it had been almost pleasant. Much more pleasant than common wisdom always said such reunions would be. And Alexandra seemed to be behaving herself. Tara strolled out toward the lobby, enjoying a few pleasant memories of ancient times and ancient affection. Then she heard a sickening squeal of brakes and a scream that sent her heart plunging to her stomach.

Shit.

Tara burst through the front doors with Molly close behind. Out on the pavement a crowd was gathering. At its center was Alexandra, huddled over a grey pile near the curb. She locked gazes with Tara, and her eyes were dark and brimming with horror.

"He just . . . jumped. Out of my arms. I don't know why—it's . . . it's never happened before."

Tara knelt beside him and felt for a pulse. Thready and diminishing. "What hit him?"

"A van. They didn't stop."

Tara spared a thought for what she would have done to the driver if she'd had her power—kill, then revive? Maybe just once; otherwise, it crosses into torture—but she only allowed the thought for a moment. She gritted her teeth. "This would be easier if I could . . ."

"Please. *Help him.*"

"Fuck."

Tara placed both hands on the cat and breathed deeply, palpating the cat's limbs to assess the damage. Without warning, a strange and familiar tingle started in the base of her spine, something like gold glitter stirred into water, cinnamon-warm and casting off a heat that grew and grew until it shot up her spine, out her arms, and filled her hands. It drove her like a horse driving a cart, and she felt the tissues beneath her hands knitting, felt the blood flowing, felt the heart begin to steady. The cat made a confused noise, and the end of its tail began to twitch. Its ear moved. So did its whiskers. In moments—before Tara could fully comprehend what was going on—the cat had leapt to its feet and growled at Tara. Alexandra knelt and held out her arms, and the cat sprang into them.

Just as quickly as the feeling had begun, it passed, leaving Tara even emptier than she had been before. She reeled, then realised what had happened. "What in the living fuck?" Tara said, furious. She grabbed Alexandra by the elbow and yanked her through the gathered bystanders and into the surgery. Tara towed Alexandra and her cat through the double door to the exam area. "What the hell was that?"

Alexandra was busy petting the cat, checking over its head for abrasions. "He's fine."

"God damn it." Tara scooped the cat from her and elbowed her out of the way. On the exam table and under the lights, Tara found nothing: no cuts, no broken bones. No thickened bladder, either. There was a bit of blood in the fur, but there was nothing to indicate the source of it. She'd seen this sort of thing before. Just not in a very, very long time.

To make matters worse, she was touching the cat but now felt nothing else. Her powers were clearly gone again.

"What did you do?"

"I didn't do anything." Alexandra indicated the cat.

"I don't believe you." *You're a goddamn Trickster.*

"You should."

"*Trickster.*"

Alexandra accepted her role with a shrug. "And yet, you did it."

"I can't have." Tara shook her head as if trying to get a mosquito to leave her be. "No, seriously. I can't. I've tried."

"Maybe you just didn't try hard enough."

Tara sneered. "Are you seriously saying that belief bullshit was true? Because I'm telling you: it's not. If it were, I would have got my power back already."

"Maybe you just didn't believe."

"Are you trying to tell me that I've been stuck like this because I *wanted* to be? That it's my fault?"

"I'm saying all you needed to do was look within yourself, and you would have known how to find the answer."

". . . So you're saying it *is* my fault."

"Well . . ."

"If I only *believed in myself,*" Tara shot through gritted teeth, "and kept my precious *heart open,* if I believed in *fairies,* the truth would be revealed."

"That's an over-simplified—"

"The power of *positive fucking thinking* can bite my arse." Tara balled up her fist, trying to decide precisely how and where to hit her.

"Tara . . ."

The cat between them made pugilism problematic. "The power was within me all the time? What kind of Somewhere-Over-the-Rainbow, Wizard-of-Fucking-Oz lesson is that?"

"To be fair, you did lose your powers two millennia before the film." Fury rose up behind Tara's eyes like a boiling tide. Apparently Alexandra remembered the visual, because she took a step back. "Wait. Tara—"

"No. Take the *bloody cat,* and GET OUT." It was a poor choice of words, but she couldn't muster any regret; he was alive, after all. She might have felt differently if he had died.

"What about the bill?"

Tara blinked at her. "You've got to be joking."

Alexandra stared back with her wide, brown, cow eyes for just a little too long, a little too disingenuously, before she flashed a quicksilver grin. "Usually," she said, and then she was gone. Winked out of existence as if she'd never been there.

Tara wondered how she was going to explain her disappearance to Molly.

It didn't turn out to be too difficult; Molly was easily sent away to pick up two lattes, and Tara expected she'd assume Alexandra had left while she was out. But while she was gone, Tara closed herself in the back office to do some science. Not having any lobsters handy this time, she'd have to settle for the clinic's blood donor cats. First, she laid hands on their Siamese called Radon, whose in utero exposure to the panleukopenia virus meant he was clumsy and twitchy and never quite able to jump. She *willed*, but nothing happened. She tried it next on their tiny, bossy marmalade called Lucas, who'd broken his jaw falling from a high rise, but the lazy thing remained asleep. She tried to feel how gracious she'd always felt when healing someone. She tried to remember how proud she'd been when they dedicated the fountain to her, when they called it the water of life, when they gathered as acolytes to drink and be saved. She remembered how it felt to be worshipped for taking away so much pain. She remembered what it was like to truly, *truly* feel like a Goddess. She believed in herself.

It did absolutely nothing.

Tara calmly walked down the corridor, out into the waiting area, back down the corridor and into the back office, shut the door, and *roared* as loudly as she could. It didn't help. She was still furious and confused. What if, behind all the arrogance and the condescension, there was some truth to what Alexandra had said?

What if the flaw in belief was her own?

That night was a horror show.

She dreamt of conducting symphonies of followers, both hands swishing and flicking as if they were broomsticks in an old Disney film. She went faster and faster until fireballs consumed her, and she woke drenched with sweat with a whimper in her throat. Rather than stay in bed sleepless, she got up at dawn and went into work. She had paperwork to do. She always had paperwork to do. But at least this way she could get started on her coffee intake early and beat the morning rush.

And if she was working, she didn't have to think about how it had felt—just for that brief, sweet moment—to have her power back.

That afternoon, Molly phoned into the back office from reception.

"Er, so. Your 3:15 is here, and you're not going to like it."

Tara set her jaw as premonition trickled in. *No.*

Sure enough, Alexandra was sitting primly in the waiting room, perfect hair and perfect teeth and another damned cat sitting perfectly in her lap. A sleek seal-point who looked just as smug as its owner.

"Didn't you do enough yesterday?" Tara said, letting the double doors slam behind her.

"Hello to you, too."

"What do you want?"

"Indigo is—"

"Let me guess. Constipation? Worms?"

"I just found her. I think she's pregnant."

The cat looked far more calm and clean than most feral cats recently adopted, and Tara narrowed her eyes. "I see."

"I'd like to have her looked over. I mean, if you're willing."

Tara had half a mind to send them both somewhere else, but she was so exhausted, she didn't even have the energy to tell Alexandra to fuck off. She just grunted and beckoned them back with a jerk of her head.

Back in the exam room, Tara breathed a moment before she handled the cat, just in case her powers were about to return at the touch. But there was nothing. Disappointed, but unsurprised—none of the other cats she'd touched that day had yielded any result either—she palpated the cat's gut while imagining Alexandra had just . . . disappeared.

It wasn't too difficult. After all, Alexandra had done it before.

"This is a nice place," Alexandra said into the silence, breaking Tara's fantasy of being alone in the room.

"Shut up."

"I should have said before."

"Shut all the fuck up." Tara adjusted the stethoscope and listened to the internal goings-on.

"So you decided to focus on cats because, without your magic, they were easier than trying to heal people?"

"I can't hear what I'm doing."

"Congratulations on almost getting your power back by the way. Have you had any luck since?"

"No, and you know what?" Tara gave up on trying to listen. "I think you really *are* just messing with me."

Alexandra looked pleased. "Oh?"

"Because the only other option is that you're telling the truth—and I know from experience how good you are at that, Ms 'I'll Say I'm Just Popping Out to the Market But What I Mean is I'm Not Ever Coming Back,' and my problems are all my fault. That the only reason I don't have my magic now is because I don't want it."

"That's not what I said."

"But that's what you meant. You said I had to look within myself and find the answer, and when I looked within myself, I found someone who needed her powers back. I joke, but I don't really give a shit about being declared the sainted patron of another fucking fountain. That's not the way the world works any more. Not the same way it used to. I just really . . . Look."

She led Alexandra into the back office where Radon was sleeping. "Look," Tara said and scratched his ears affectionately. "I can't heal him. I want to. I should be able to. But I can't. And it's killing me." She pointed to several photographs prominently displayed on the wall. "I couldn't save any of them, either. They didn't make it to old age. Not a one. I tried my hardest, but I failed. It's been two millennia of this shit, and it's killing me." She couldn't look at Alexandra; she didn't want her to see the expression on her face. "What the hell good's a Goddess who can't serve? I'm just living." Tara swallowed. "Which is more than I can say for all of them. I don't need to save every one. I just want to save a few more."

Behind her, the door closed. When she turned, Alexandra was gone.

Tara huffed a dry laugh. "Figures."

When she found her, Alexandra was back in the exam room, petting her cat with a look of serious consideration on her face. "You can help my cat, though," said Alexandra.

"Yeah." She sighed. "Probably." Well past drained by this point, Tara began examining the cat again.

"Let me tell you a story," Alexandra said.

"Please don't."

"Once upon a time—"

"Alexandra . . ."

"Once upon a time, there was an arrogant Goddess: beautiful, but cold and egotistical as the ocean."

Tara fought to keep working while all this shit was going on. "I hope you're not describing *me*."

"She had magnificent powers. Miraculous powers. But that was the trouble; they were miraculous, but she didn't use them wisely. She scattered them about in broad strokes, indiscriminately, casting the careful balance of the universe into chaos. She was selfish of the acclaim it brought her, and—"

"*What?*"

"And selfish of how good it made her feel to grant life. Which, above all, it did. This cannot be in doubt."

Tara let her hands fall and devoted all her attention to glaring. "What, dare I ask, is your point?"

"She saved people, and she saved animals, and she saved anything under the sun that was dying, whether or not she should. This might have been good for some of those she saved and certainly was good for her, but it was very, very bad for the natural cycle of living creatures."

If she scowled any harder, her face was going to ache the next day. "I know that."

"She couldn't abide saying no. So she didn't. And no matter how the other Gods and Goddesses tried to convince her otherwise, and no matter how her loved ones tried to convince her otherwise, she could not be swayed. Lifespans stretched beyond their natural expanse because she healed everyone who asked. Old people weary of life, unable to die because loved ones interceded on their behalf. Fountains of eternal life dedicated to her, waters that healed everyone who drank. And so time went on, and things that should have died didn't, and the world became a very confused, very off-kilter, very scary place."

"It wasn't *that* bad."

"It was."

Hindsight was more than 20/20. At this point, it might be 2000/2000. Tara could have kept arguing, but it would only have been for the sake of her ego, not for the sake of truth. She sighed, weary to her bones with Alexandra's penchant for stirring things up. She really hadn't missed it. "I suppose it got kind of bad. But I was young. I didn't really get what I was doing. It was too pleasant to fix everything."

"While causing problems on the other end."

"Though it caused problems on the other end."

"I get the feeling you'd make different choices now."

"My priorities aren't exactly the same any more. Fuck, the *world* isn't the same any more. But it doesn't matter, does it? It doesn't look like we're ever going to find out."

"Oh, I wouldn't say that so quickly."

Premonition dragged Tara's stomach down to her shoes. "Why."

A grin started on Alexandra's face. It started small, at the corner of her mouth, and little by little it spread out across it until she resembled a deranged jack-o'-lantern.

Fucking shapeshifters. Tara fantasised about lopping off her head. "Alexandra. *Why.*"

Alexandra's grin became so broad Tara could see all the way round her teeth into the sides of her mouth. "Because of this." And Alexandra grabbed both Tara's hands and pressed them to Indigo's fur. Immediately, the cinnamon-warm sensation started at the base of Tara's spine. It expanded until she felt incandescent with light and heat and brilliance. She gasped. Her palms buzzed. The entire time, Alexandra continued that terrifying grin. "Welcome back."

"What in the fuck?" said Tara. Her sense of touch was in hi-def; she could feel every single individual strand of fur and the precise temperature of the cat's skin and could instinctively gauge the blood pressure. When she focused, she could direct the power deeper into the animal, layer by layer, like an organic MRI. The cat seemed perfectly healthy and not pregnant at all, which solidified Tara's suspicion that Alexandra had been manipulating her.

She let go of the cat and curled one finger, then another, examining the knuckles and the nail beds and the stretched skin in between. In a second vision that she hadn't experienced for a very long time, she could see the healing power gathered in the centre of her palms, a fuzzy yellow glow limned in orange. The necessary synapses in her brain were rusted over, but if she focused very hard she could control the coalesced power. She let it expand outward from her hands until they were subsumed in a wild glow, then let it collapse down into itself until it lay quiescent in the center of her palms again. It was a bit like pushing mercury round on a table top.

Tara huffed out a breath as hot as an angry bull's. "What did you do?"

"I told you. I'm putting things back the way they should be," said Alexandra.

"How did you manage to—"

"It was simple."

"No need to sound so smug."

"You know how I said all you had to do was look within yourself?" Suspicion tickled the back of Tara's mind. ". . . Yes . . ."

"Well, that's not exactly true."

"I KNEW IT." Startled, the cat between them growled, then stalked in a circle before settling back down to stare at Tara. "So it was just *you*."

"Of course."

"You returned my powers, all by yourself."

"Yep."

Under the circumstances, Tara thought she was remaining tolerably calm. "You could have returned them at any point in the last *two thousand years*."

"Could have. Wouldn't have. You needed to get to this point in your evolution before it was a good idea."

The arrogance was staggering. "Who the fuck gave you the right to make that call?"

"Oh, love." Alexandra tilted her head in one of the most patronising displays Tara had seen in real life. "It was always going to be my call."

Something in the way she said it and the way the overhead lights shaded her face sparked a memory. A terrible, horrifying memory.

The horse showed up on Tara's doorstep without warning. Well, truth be told, the door was more of a portal and the home behind it more of a giant roundhouse, but the point was the same.

A small child melted out of the nearby underbrush and approached her.

"She's sick," said the child in a tiny voice. Her eyes were huge and incredibly dark. "Can you fix her?"

"Of course I can," said Tara. Gently, she touched the child's cheek then went to work. She laid hands on the side of the beast, sending her awareness down, layer by layer. When she reached her heart, she was jolted with a curious shock. She tried to lift up her hands, but they were stuck to the horse's flank. Then the wrenching sensation began.

It felt like tearing cloth, like something was being ripped away from her spine and pulled through her limbs. She tried to inhale, but her lungs were frozen. The burn of a fresh wound began prickling down in the pit of her, the tingle before the pain truly begins, and that was when the terror got a firm grip.

It lingered even after the ripping stopped, even after she'd collapsed to the ground, even after the horse had disappeared into thin air. Tara had one last sight of the child's devilish grin before she passed out.

When she woke, it was to Alexandra's face swimming into view. "What's happened, my love?" Her touch was gentle. She smoothed back Tara's hair and kissed her forehead.

"I was— I just—" Tara relived the sensation of her power being torn from her. She assessed the emptiness. She assessed the fear.

She buried her face against Alexandra's shoulder and began to cry.

"It was you, wasn't it." It didn't feel like a question. Tara compared her memory of the child's eyes and smile with the ones she saw before her. She wondered why she'd never considered it before. "It was you. The child with the horse."

"Yes."

"That's why it was your call to give them back. You took them away."

"Yes."

"You took them away because I was fouling things up."

"I took them away because in your search for outside validation, you were throwing everything off balance."

"You're a *monumental* shithead."

"When I need to be."

"Your ego really hasn't changed."

"Did you really expect different?"

It was difficult to swallow past the thickness in her throat. With the enhanced vision of Tara's powers flipped on, Alexandra looked like a darker, bonier version of Galadriel coveting the ring in *The Fellowship of the Ring*. Tara expected her hair to start blowing in a nonexistent wind. "I . . . I *trusted* you."

"You trusted a Trickster."

"I loved you."

"More fool you."

"Wait, this is *my* fault?"

"Well, it's certainly not mine."

But it was. It *was*. Tara growled.

Alexandra's expression flashed with delight. She scooped up the cat with one arm and pulled open the exam room door with the other. Then she blinked out of existence, leaving the door to swing slowly closed on its hydraulics.

Taking that as an invitation, Tara ran out into the lobby. Alexandra wasn't there, but through the glass doors to the clinic she saw the flick of her hair disappear into the stream of passers-by on the street. Tara chased her outside.

Everything seemed lit in bright pinks and greens, strange colours that made the world seem clownish. Unearthly. The crowd was thick and flowed past her five people deep, a gaggle completely unaware that among them, right at that very moment, was a Trickster who hadn't hesitated to torment her lover for two thousand goddamn years. And for what? A healthier source of self-esteem? Universal balance? Even as she had the thought, it occurred to Tara that, by moderating balance in the world, Alexandra had only been doing her job.

Nevertheless, Tara held onto her righteous anger, deciding it was all a terrible conflict of interest to have *Alexandra* be the one to keep Tara in check. She elbowed her way harder through the crowd. "We're not through here," she yelled to Alexandra. A few people stared.

Alexandra emerged about fifteen feet away and stood on the pavement. She smirked. "Look at it this way: being without magic meant you were sheltered. Everyone else faded away when mortals no longer believed, but not you. I might have actually saved you."

"Oh, I'm supposed to be thankful, now, am I?"

"It would make a nice change from the norm, I must say."

"I should kill you for this."

"What a wonderful Goddess of Healing you make."

"It's the least revenge for two thousand years of—"

"You don't really want to kill me."

"Everyone always wants to kill you."

"It goes with the territory."

"A manipulative, thieving, arrogant—"

"But you're too happy right now to kill me."

The trouble was, she wasn't wrong. Tara was blazingly angry, but there was a peculiar sort of joy sitting next to the fury in her chest. Her heart raced. She felt more alive than she had in aeons. More alive and way, *way* less bored. The future stretched out before her, and she didn't mind in the least. "So that's how you do it, then? You keep those you torment from killing you by buttering us up with something we want?"

"Usually."

"You're an arsehole."

Alexandra sparkled. "Usually." She disappeared again into the crowd.

Tara pushed after her like a salmon swimming upstream, unsure if she was hunting for a kill, being lured into a trap, or simply embattled in a demented game of kiss chase. When she emerged on a traffic island, an oasis in the centre of the throng, Alexandra was waiting.

"Where did you get the horse?" Tara asked.

"Ehhh, Pale Horse Stables."

"Are you fucking *kidding me?*"

"If there was anyone whose business it is when everything keeps living, it's a death deity."

"So he gave you a . . . Trojan horse to take me out."

"I wouldn't say *gave* it to me . . ."

"You stole it?"

"A Trojan horse is a pretty good description, actually."

"I meant a Trojan horse like in Troy, not . . ."

"I know what you meant. A computer virus is a good analogy. Too bad you couldn't physician-heal-thyself out of it, though. You would have got your magic back ages ago."

"But you wouldn't have wanted me to."

"Not until you'd learned your lesson."

"And what about what you did today? The thing with Indigo?"

"Same thing as before, but in reverse. And with a slight change in the mode of transference, since you only work on cats now. Besides which, I didn't think I could get a horse through the door."

While Tara tried to breathe deeply and control her temper, she examined Alexandra. She looked exactly the same: beautiful, graceful, shadowed, fascinating. But somewhere over time, the combination of features had lost its particular appeal, and now she was simply looking at an attractive person she used to know. *Did you almost kill that cat on purpose?* she almost asked, but decided she didn't really want the answer. "Why did you leave?"

Apparently, that wasn't a question Alexandra had anticipated—which just highlighted how low in her priorities emotion had always been. She shrugged. "I'd taken your magic."

"Years before."

"I waited so you wouldn't suspect me."

"You only stayed with me long enough that I wouldn't suspect you?"

"I didn't want you to know and be angry with me."

Tara took this in. If this was all in aid of Tara gaining the ability to find motivation from within herself instead of trading healing for devotion, well . . . it seemed Alexandra had actually got what she wanted. However, Tara now had her magic back, she had things to do, and she didn't need any of Alexandra's tricky bullshit to validate her self-worth. After a few long moments, she turned on her heel to leave Alexandra behind.

"Where are you going?" called Alexandra.

"Back to work," Tara said over her shoulder. It might be too late for Lady Grey with the pancreatic cancer, but there was a young patient with aggressive gastrointestinal lymphoma she could totally fix. And besides which: with all the advances in medicine since the last time she had magic, the possible combinations of the two were tantalising. She already had a very clear picture in her mind how to complete that cure for FIP she'd long since given up on. If she trod very carefully and worked very hard, she might even find a way to publish it.

She couldn't fix everyone and wasn't keen to try, but it would be nice to know she could succeed whenever she wanted to.

And eliminating the damn *kitten killer* was high on that list.

Sidetracked by the possibilities, she bumped into a man emerging from the cafe a few doors down from the clinic, knocking his steaming cup of coffee over his hand. He yelped.

"I'm so sorry," Tara said distractedly, laying a placating touch on his upper arm. She felt the pulse of healing scintillate down into her hand and into him. The bloom of redness on his skin cleared as quickly as a time-lapse video.

His astonishment was so loud she felt sure everyone on the pavement would notice. "You're . . ." He took her all in, hair to shoes. She felt ten-foot-tall and bulletproof. "You're a *Goddess*."

He meant it.

Tara threw back her head and laughed. With tremendous joy, she continued toward her clinic.

"*Absolutely*."

Seller's Market

Matthew Joseph Harrington

Tori Laster has endured as long as she has only by holding close to her heart the words of her friend Ishmael eleven years back, when she still hoped physical therapy would help her: "I don't have energy to squander; if I do anything, I want a return on investment."

This credo had kept her going ever since, but it has run out its string.

She actually has the gun to her head—muzzle behind the mastoid process, barrel aligned with a radius of the skull, punch through the Circle of Willis, and the lights will be *out*—when the pounding starts on her apartment door.

She considers firing anyway, but whoever it is will surely hear and might be fast and smart enough to get her onto life support if her aim is imperfect. Not good.

She considers shooting whoever is at the door and letting the State of California finish her off, but that would take too long, even if it worked. And she might get life—and on a suicide watch that would make it a really long life. Even worse.

She eases off the hammer, sets the gun down, forces herself to her feet, works her walker over to the door, opens it, and forgets what she was going to say. The blonde outside it is in a chauffeur's uniform, and though it isn't as tight as the ones Hollywood has always put women in, it is manifestly worn over a body of superb proportions. The woman has her cap under one arm and at 9 p.m. is wearing mirrorshades, which she leaves on. "Oh, I'm so glad I was in time!" she says.

"Huh?" says Tori.

The chauffeur takes a pressure injector out of her right jacket pocket. "I'd like to give you a shot that'll help with your illness."

"Cyanide?" Tori jokes.

"No, but if you're not happy with this I can get some." She seems to be quite serious.

"Fair enough," Tori says and presents her arm.

The woman takes her arm, swabs her inside elbow, and fires the injector into a vein with astonishing precision. Then she spits on the punctured skin and presses her thumb over it, and adds, a little contemptuously, "The idiot who originally made it up didn't think of it, but *I* added Demerol for your pain until it starts working."

Tori can tell.

The woman catches her as she staggers, cradles her in her arms, carries her through the apartment until she finds the keys, and says, "Any pets?"

"Sisters have them," Tori says with woozy enunciation.

"Okay, then," the chauffeur says and takes her into the hall, locking the door on the way out. She carries Tori downstairs with no evidence of strain, and Tori musters the coherence to be startled at this. One of the reasons she loathes being carried is that she is painfully overweight and has always been certain someone doing so would drop her.

She looks at the woman as she is being carried. The mirrorshades have the damnedest weird red highlights.

As she is being set gently in the limousine and her limbs arranged in the astronaut-grade seat for comfort, she says, "Who the hell *are* you?"

The chauffeur does not reply, unless you want to count uproarious laughter that persists long enough to delay the start of the trip, followed by occasional snorts and chuckles on the road.

The trip is long, and Tori falls asleep.

She awakens once, to be held up at the shoulders by another big fairhair in sunglasses, this one male, and given a great deal to drink. "You'll need a lot of liquid to wash the crud out of your system," she is told but needs little encouragement as she is parched. Also, the iced tea is fit to drink, which is not something she gets much outside her home—among other things, it contains no lemon, which she detests and was unsurprised to learn was introduced to cover the bitterness of tea that had gone rancid, like vinegar on fish and chips.

Later she is woken again by the blond man and this time notices his beautiful linen suit. He says, "You may want to visit the lavatory."

This is entirely correct. It is also a surprising experience; her back doesn't hurt as much as usual, and she feels something coming out that is not liquid but not painful. It is silt, as if her kidney stones have been reduced to powder.

She is a slow starter waking up, and it does not register until she is washing her hands that an airplane had not been involved when she went to sleep. She looks out a window, and it is very dark out there.

The man, who is apparently here solely to look after Tori, comes over and says, "Your driver is in the cockpit. She's good for driving, fetching and carrying, that sort of thing. You should buckle up."

"Does the treatment dissolve kidney stones?" she says.

"No, that's the sodium fluoride in the water for the tea."

"Isn't that a pesticide?" she says in alarm.

"It's used in them. If you breathe through spiracles like an insect you're a goner, because they're going to get brittle and cave in. Lungs should be okay." He raises his absurdly blond eyebrows over his shades, smiling faintly.

This is embarrassing, and she changes the subject. "Where are we?"

"About two thousand miles south of Hawaii," is the reply. "We're approaching Baldr Island. Used to be called Jarvis Island before all the work was done."

Unlike most of the people on Earth, Tori has heard of Jarvis Island. "Isn't that right on the Equator?"

"A shade south of it, but close enough, yes. The buildings all have heat exchangers, though. Come, sit."

Tori comes and sits, and the man buckles her in and takes a seat across from her. "I have little doubt I'd have questions if I were you," he says. It comes to her that his manner carries a faint but steady undertone of condescension. So, for that matter, had the chauffeur's. The highlights on their mirrorshades are no comfort, either.

"What am I doing here? I don't have a passport!"

"It's an American possession; you don't need one. The boss said go fetch the sick lady, so here we are. Your sisters have both been called, and if you want to stay, we can fetch your cats any time."

"Who's the boss?"

"He says you're the only one who's allowed to call him 'Ilp.'"

Tori opens her mouth and nothing comes out for a while. ILP. Ishmael Looing Pormber, whose words had sustained her for eleven long years. Finally, she manages, "When I knew him, I didn't know he was rich."

"He wasn't yet. He made a pile in the stock market a few years back—I don't understand this kind of thing, I just got the information he wanted—then brokered some kind of deal with the Department of the Interior, which was in charge of the island. Yes, six thousand miles out in the ocean, Department of Interior," the man says before Tori can interrupt. "They're not my rules. Anyway, he put up a small power plant and a seawater evaporator and went into the fertilizer and mineral business. Imported a lot of rock, laid new footing for a wider reef, does satellite launches for small countries."

"Holy crap."

"Well said. Oh, and he's part owner of a fishing fleet. The coolant water pumped up for the power plant is full of nutrients."

"What does he use for fuel, uranium?"

He grins again. There is something disturbing about his teeth, which are perfectly white and seem oddly sharp. "The evaporator doesn't produce that much. Hot surface water. The plant's basically an air conditioner running in reverse. And we are practically on the Equator. And here we go," he says as the plane begins to descend.

It turns out to be a seaplane, and as it first touches the wave tops, Tori's first impression is that something is dreadfully wrong. Then she figures it out.

He sees her expression and says, "Sorry. I'm used to it, I should have warned you; he'd have wanted me to. Your *driver* can't be bothered with *details*," he adds with a toss of his head. "Baldr doesn't have a lot of land area, and anyway, who wants planes landing on your roof?"

"I'm surprised he didn't buy the Spruce Goose."

"Evergreen wouldn't sell the Hercules, thank the Powers. It'd take over a day to get here. Have to refuel, too."

"Could put extra fuel tanks inside."

"How would that be fun?" he asks reasonably.

Tori considers. "Could also put in an arcade."

He tilts his head and studies Tori for a moment, then smiles on one side of his mouth. "I think I get why he sent for you." There is something downright lascivious about this.

This makes Tori extremely self-conscious, as she and Ishmael had not been at all romantically involved, and in any case, she does not consider herself attractive—though, be it said, he had sharply contradicted her a couple of times when the subject had rolled around. This consideration does not help with the self-consciousness issue at all. "Why did he import rock?" she says.

"For the reef footing and to fill in the hole from the guano mine. Jarvis and Howland and Baker were all annexed before the Civil War as a source of saltpeter. Amazing, the ingenuity human beings put into the concept of killing one another. Even humbling." He frowns for a moment then goes on. "They're about halfway to anywhere. Birds would stop, eat some bugs, take a dump, and keep going. The other two islands are even smaller than this one. Nowadays, it's all being bought up by organic farmers. He bought the rock from one of those former Soviet vassal states. Somebody in Ireland offered a better price, but the boss wasn't real comfortable with the idea of selling gunpowder ingredients to the Irish. Here we are."

The plane has come to a halt, and Tori realizes that the man, who had not been all that chatty before the landing began, has been distracting her from the disturbing noises of landing and docking. She gives him an appreciative smile. The one she gets in return is distinctly amused.

As she reaches the doorway and looks out into the walkway tube, which evidently connects to the shore atop a very superior pontoon bridge, judging by the lack of ripples in the floor, Tori suddenly realizes that her legs don't hurt despite the absence of her walker. "Holy crap, I can walk!" she exclaims.

"So can I," says the man approaching from the other end of the tube, "but I don't have to if I don't feel like it."

Tori stares.

This man is not obese, not in a power chair, and not suppressing reactions to awful pain, but she still recognizes him. "Ishmael?"

"Victoria," he says, the only person she knows who uses her full name. He comes to take her right hand in both of his.

"What the hell *is* this treatment, anyway?"

"A group of prions," he says, setting off sirens in her head as she thinks of Mad Cow. "Not like Mad Cow," he adds, turning to lead her into what looks like a fairly credible James Bond Villain Lair: broad rooms, high ceilings, the occasional unidentified machine done in Art Deco. "That's an unusual prion. Most prions are useful and necessary for cellular function. They shape enzymes that are almost like themselves to be the same configuration. Enzymes operate like elaborate clockwork. These are improved versions of some of the enzymes involved in the transport of materials through cell membranes. I came up with the idea of examining people who had survived things like freezing, metal poisoning, snakebite, and Ebola. *Lots* of people—many survivors were just lucky. The real trick was getting it done without hurting anybody. Talk about stress— Anyhow, these make your cells better at letting things out, putting things out, and keeping things out. I took the mix as soon as the crew came up with it, but I wasn't going to pass it around until we'd had a longer look at what the effects were. Seems fine so far, apart from a tendency to impatience, but you're the second guinea pig, I'm afraid."

"Why me?"

"Victoria, you're not stupid."

"Oh, come on, don't make it a guessing game."

"I'm not. That's why you. You're not stupid. I like that. It occurred to me much too recently that you were almost as sick as I was, so I sent the remedy as soon as I thought of it in hopes of catching you before you committed suicide. I understand I was barely in time, and I'm sorry it took so long."

"It's cool," she says, dazed.

"Thanks. Come on, let's get some protein into you."

She raises an eyebrow.

Ishmael looks conspicuously patient. "*That* is not primarily protein. You'll be burning lipids for fuel, but you need structural material for repairing a lifetime of damage. Protein. I wasn't even going to *mention* sex unless you showed an interest in me."

"That's an odd thing about him," says the blond man. It comes to her that he looks like the guy James Bond has to kill to reach the off switch, or a superhero in a comic book published by Illinois Nazis, but he doesn't act like either. Not exactly. "He's really serious about being really serious."

"Hey, I did the grunt job, work on your own pitch," says the chauffeur from behind Tori. Tori looks at her and sees that she is now wearing a pilot's uniform.

"What a rotten pun," says the blond man.

"Thank you," says the chauffeur, who now that Tori thinks about it looks like she might have come from the same comic book. She smiles, or anyway, shows lots of teeth. White, sharp, and disturbing.

"Credit where it's due," says the blond guy.

The lighting in here certainly brings out the highlights on their mirrorshades.

"Don't work it to death," says Ishmael. "Simple courtesy will suffice. Come on, Victoria; I'll whip up some steak and bacon."

"Anything for a vegetable?" she says, without much hope; he is a man.

"There's chicken," Ishmael says.

This actually sounds reasonable for a moment, before she cracks up. "That is *not* a vegetable," she gets out.

"We raise them here. If you decide to stay, you may change your mind about that," he replies, and leads her into a kitchen where cooks who please Gordon Ramsay go when they die.

He puts her onto a tall chair at one of the counters and works on this and that for perhaps eight minutes before presenting her with a salad of iceberg lettuce, spinach, bits of whatever kind of seaweed it is that's used to wrap sushi, sliced onions, shredded carrots, bacon, and eggs, with garlic ranch dressing on the side. This is the first thing that gets her out of the fugue she has been in since she saw the kitchen. It has all manner of appliances and working surfaces, and the layout is brilliant: three people could work in here and not be in each other's way at all.

Once the bowl is before her, he turns away to begin cooking.

She spears salad ingredients with her fork, dips it in the dressing, and eats the bite.

She does not think of anything else until the bowl is empty.

"How did you *do* all this?" is what she finally thinks of.

He has just finished turning over the steaks in the broiler, and he turns to her with a somewhat uncertain half-smile. "Well," he begins, "it all started when I decided not to commit suicide. . .."

Ishmael Looing Pormber believed in Hell. Given his childhood, he had no choice; the people he had had to cope with were too stupid for their elaborate cruelties to have had anything but outside inspiration. This belief kept him from killing himself for as long as he was certain that damnation would be worse than what he was already going through.

But what he was going through kept getting worse.

It was when he spent three consecutive days with his pain level above 5, the point where he was unable to concentrate long enough to read, that he decided that Hell would be a break.

But when he took enough painkillers—which themselves would have killed a healthy man—to start contemplating swift and certain methods, it came to him that he resented the choice he faced.

If he was going to damn his soul, he at least wanted something for it.

So he decided to sell it.

His sickness had forced him to be intensely methodical, since his physical resources were so limited he couldn't afford do-overs. He looked into the matter with great care.

It took years.

One of the first conclusions he reached (and this was not soon) was that no summoning ritual he found was, or indeed would ever be, complete or entirely accurate. It made sense to him; anyone who sought power of this nature would hardly be willing to share it and therefore would never make it easy for someone else to do the same thing. Very well; he was accustomed to attempts to keep him ignorant and knew the drill. He collected as many variations as he could find—which, given his proclivities, may have been all there were—and studied them for common factors. One summoner would hardly share information with another, so they would leave out or distort different things. Anything that was unique to a particular ritual would presumably be false.

What was left after omitting the deceptions wouldn't fit together. He sorted through the mess and came up with what seemed to be two different rituals, whose only common factor was a specially-prepared wand. A man with something to lose would have been upset. He simply worked out the two different rituals and spent most of a year constructing a wand that could be used in either.

Then he made his preparations for both.

He was at the limit of his resources financially as well as physically when he was ready. He worked his way through one ritual. There was no result. He worked his way through the other. Nothing.

After eight years' work, he'd still gotten it wrong somehow.

He screamed and snapped the wand over his knee.

There was a moment of utter silence, as if he had gone deaf.

Then *both* diagrams had an occupant apiece.

Tori can feel her eyes bugging out. "You summoned *two* demons?"

"Yep."

"You sold your *soul* to them?"

He smiles. "Nope."

"I don't understand. How did you get all this if they didn't do it?"

"They did. They're still here. You've met them."

"Captain Aryan and Axis Girl?" she guesses.

Ishmael bursts out laughing. He can't talk right away, but he nods vigorously. Finally, he wipes his eyes and says, "Yeah. Oh, that's good. Yes, that's them. They manifested in the shapes of the most monstrous evil known, of course. Back in the Middle Ages, that was the worst parts of vicious animals, all put together. Predator teeth and claws combined with the hooves and horns of herd animals, which are insanely aggressive. But you just can't beat your smiling damned villains for sheer—"

"*Why* did they give you all this?" she demands, cutting him off.

He is grinning in unmistakable delight. "You have to understand. Getting someone to sell his soul is a coup that hasn't been accomplished since Robespierre. They're staying here—which is a nice gig in itself—until one of them gets me to make a deal, and so they keep having to outdo each other. *It's a bidding situation.*" He awaits a response, which is not forthcoming any time soon, then turns back to check the broiler. "Rare?"

"I'd say unique," she says faintly.

"I was asking how you want your steak."

"Rare is good," she says.

Lines and Squares

Jae Eynon

Whenever I walk in a London street,
I'm ever so careful to watch my feet;
And I keep in the squares,
And the masses of bears,
Who wait at the corners all ready to eat
The sillies who tread on the lines of the street
Go back to their lairs,
And I say to them, 'Bears,
Just look how I'm walking in all the squares!'
                                          ~A.A. Milne

Breathing hard, Darshan strove for calm. The gap between platform and train reached for his feet as he rehearsed the energy-sapping litany of rational good sense that carried him over lines, edges and borders day after day. *Happy Birthday*, he thought bitterly. It had been no worse than any other work day—averagely corrupt clients on a quest to put one over on someone else, averagely annoying colleagues, no more than a few looks when he left the office on time on this October Monday just like any other, but which, to him, and particularly this year when he crossed the threshold from one decade to the next, needed to be a little special. He thought about the cards on a shelf at home: from his parents, his sister, his little brother away at university in the States, his aunties in India, and one from an ex he still kept in touch with. He would see his family at the week-end, but today seemed utterly detached from distant Saturday. A gulf of days intervened. A bottomless rift of time. By the weekend, the moment would have passed. He would have taken the step from one place to the next with no one to hold his hand; no one to catch him on the other side, in case he stumbled—in case he fell.

The crush on the train thinned, and Darshan dropped into a seat. There had been plenty of singles dotted around for the last couple of stops, but the English revulsion for sitting next to strangers, coupled with his own bulk, kept him on his feet until a double came free. And it had to be a double with a double cushion. Individual cushions meant a line down the middle, and when he overflowed the seat, he'd be on the line, which would be bad. Life would be simpler if he were smaller. If he fitted better into the spaces life gave him. His tiny mother always proudly introduced him as her "great big bear of a son," as if she alone was responsible for producing his wrestler's build, as if it were a good thing to be a man who'd sit *on* you if he tried to sit next to you.

He realised he was actually sitting on something and rummaged under his right buttock, producing a teddy dressed in a souvenir t-shirt. Too late to try to return it to the child who'd left it behind. There would be tears in someone's house tonight. Memories of the vast teddy bears' picnic in Hyde Park—another charity drive, all schools and celebrities and *Blue Peter* badges—would be nothing to the grief of losing one of a million identical Chinese-made toys. He straightened the bear's t-shirt and laid it on the seat next to him, swapping it for the *Evening Standard* someone else had dropped.

He opened the paper and leafed through, skimming headlines and bright adverts. One full page blared noxiously colourful hallelujahs about some touring US church group, a background of gaping choristers fronted by a row of preachers' portraits, all white, middle-aged, and rich: a rogue's gallery of slick smiles and Botox. Darshan thought he'd never seen a bunch of men he'd trust less to look after his wallet, let alone his soul. On the facing page, photos of gambolling teddies shaking desperate charity buckets illustrated a short article about the allegedly successful event. Below, yet more bloody bears. You couldn't get away from them. The star of the British Museum's new "Celtic London" exhibit: hard-muscled legs, bared breasts, and a snarling animal muzzle—some bronze statue they'd dug up years ago and kept in a box until they found more stuff to go with it. Hideous, but closer to what Darshan thought a real bear might be like. Dangerous, unpredictable, a mess of hot breath and animal stink. Nothing like a teddy.

Darshan leaned his temple against the window and let his head rock to the beat of the train. His reflection rocked in counterpoint, sickly against the near-dark outside, lights from blocks of flats blanking it in an off-rhythm flicker. Further back, a few other passengers peopled the dim otherworld of the glass. There was the unkempt man in denims and a soiled parka, who only rode the train to keep warm. As soon as the chill set in, there he was, riding from one terminus to the other and back again all autumn and winter, bumming change when he could be bothered to take his nose out of whatever half-mangled paperback he had in his hands. Beneath a publicity banner for "Celtic London", three young guys in cheap suits and shiny shoes too long in the toe boasted and compared notes about the girls they worked with. And there, just across from him, was the student teacher with the beaded plaits and a tiny pink jewel in her nose. Ear buds in and knee jigging to some unheard beat while her beautiful dark eyes remained fixed on the screen of an e-reader, she'd dumped her open bag of text books and lesson plans on the seat beside her to mark her space.

The train slowed, squealing into a station, the last before home. Elevated high above street level, the wind-swept platform sat opposite a row of windows in a red brick wall, too new to have gathered either grime or character. A light went on in a kitchen, and Darshan watched a middle-aged woman dump her handbag on a table and reach to turn the kettle on without looking. She shrugged out of her coat and slung it over the back of a chair, then reached up to take a mug from a cupboard. She set it down next to the kettle, dropped a teabag in, then moved across to stare unseeing out of the window, her hands massaging the small of her back. Between the straining buttons, her blouse gaped, shadowed flesh behind. It was like a play, every movement finely judged; repeated night after night, telling a story as securely removed from the observer as a TV show, the character slotted perfectly into her setting, every motion precisely timed, fiction as hyper-reality, but a construct nevertheless. Darshan wondered why it should be he that felt insubstantial.

The jerk of renewed motion and a clatter made him turn his head, and he was just in time to stop the girl's e-reader from sliding under his seat. He scooped it up and half-stood, reaching it out to her, politely angling the screen so as not to see. She accepted it with a glance that seemed to take his measure. He tried the smile he'd been saving for months. Too late and too stale. Her bright black eyes were down again, shutting Darshan out as effectively as the woman at the window with her tea and her backache. An ad for health insurance and a poster of the ancient figurine, ill-juxtaposed, slid past the window as the train gathered speed.

He picked up his briefcase and gloves and settled his scarf over his suit lapels, neatly under the front of his coat. His stop was next, not far away now. Preparing to stand, he noticed that the three young men had got off without him missing their chatter, and in their place sat a teenage boy in sunglasses and a hoodie with a clawed paw print motif on the front. A pair of green wires ran down to a pocket from inside the hood, where a tinny beat sounded and the boy's head bobbed. Darshan crooked his arm round the nearest pole and swung to his feet as the train slowed. It jolted again—was the driver asleep or the track faulty?—making him stumble, but only the down-and-out with the crumpled book looked up.

The button lit up blue and Darshan pushed it with the back of his wrist. He didn't like putting his fingers where thousands of other hands had been, where grime had settled possessively round the illuminated chevrons and the word "OPEN". With a rattle, the doors slid apart directly opposite another of those museum posters. The Celtic figurine, blown up to human size, was grotesquely female, the jaws gaping, elongated. It looked obscene with its throat open like that, not like any kind of goddess Darshan wanted to know.

As usual, he hesitated, intimidated by the hungry gap between the train and the platform. His mind slid down the well-worn tracks of its customary unspoken complaint that the components of the transport system never seemed to *fit* each other, and why couldn't they just *fit*? Surely it couldn't be that difficult to engineer things to *fit*? His hand tightened on his briefcase, and he stared down at the shadowed crevasse, willing his foot to move.

It wasn't as if it was a new problem. It wasn't as if it was particular to trains. Between one thing and another thing, one place and another, there was always a gap, a chasm. It might be as narrow as a line drawn with the finest pen—might even be invisible—but that material breach was to Darshan's eyes, to his absolute knowledge, full of its own particular terror. Something was in there; something was waiting. Waiting for him, drawing him to its ravenous constancy. But nobody knew what waited in those interstices. Worse—nobody cared. They'd put it down to a 'pathologically hyperactive imagination' until he learned to fake his way past, tiptoeing over the lines with his breath held, his heart pounding, and his eyes turned away from the pull of the void.

"Careful, now," said the tramp as Darshan's foot wavered over the gap.

The boy in the hoodie raised his head, then sprang out of his seat and charged past Darshan out of the train as the door mechanism started to rumble, his momentum carrying him right across the platform. He caught himself on the wall, one hand squarely on the idol's heart, and grinned at nobody in particular.

Darshan flinched, and the doors slid closed, almost catching his head. His stop retreated into the darkness.

"Gawd. That was out of order," the tramp muttered.

Darshan stared out at the gathering dark, his shoulders tight. He didn't turn his head when someone crashed through from the next carriage, lurching from one support pole to another. From the corner of his eye, Darshan could see the girl with the plaits curl her lip and hunch tighter over her e-reader. She was reading *Winnie the Pooh*. Lucky kids, to have that on the curriculum and her to teach it. Tigger was standing on Pooh's chest. Darshan had always envied Tigger's carelessness of boundaries, his insouciant bounce, so different from Darshan's own anxious footfall. A body reeking of alcohol and old food knocked against him and . . . sniffed, like a dog taking a scent. Darshan recoiled.

"Sorry, mate." The drunk staggered away and slumped down next to the tramp, splashing cheap cider from an open can onto his grimy sweatshirt. The tramp moved his book out of range and grunted unaggressively. "Wotcher, Arfur," slurred the newcomer amiably, but his eyes were on Darshan, hollow as the between places.

One stop past home, Darshan clenched and hurled himself onto the platform and down the steps that promised him an exit. At street level, an automatic barrier deposited him just inside the station archway, where he gripped his briefcase between his heels while he slipped his Oystercard into a pocket and buttoned himself into his coat. A crumpled napkin from the nearby coffee shop flapped on the wet tiles and the sound of market traders closing down their stalls drifted across the road.

It was the worst time of day. Shops neither open nor shut, pubs ready for business but empty of drinkers, people in transit with their minds elsewhere, absent from the moment. Everyone but Darshan himself, marooned in the between time and paying careful attention to where he put his feet, unwillingly present as he walked past the windows, some dark, some lit, all vacant.

He wished he hadn't missed his stop. The goddess gurned and flaunted her bronze breasts at him from a billboard across the road. He was beginning to resent her presence everywhere he looked. What had she to do with him, this Celtic demon with her relentless 'look-at-me'? What had she to do with any of the millions of people who walked over her land? He might only be second-generation, but in real terms, he was no further removed from her than the rest of modern London, so why wouldn't she leave him alone?

"Celtic Night!" proclaimed a poster in a pub window, a pint of Guinness Photoshopped into the goddess's hand. As if. Fake Irishmen playing tin whistles for crowds of drunken Brits who didn't have a drop of truly local blood in them. But the whole city had been caught up in the game since the dead goddess's temple and her grave-goods were resurrected by the workers on the new underground. Celtic this and Celtic that and pure idle speculation based on a few fragments of unexplained evidence, and what he wouldn't give for World Cup fever to begin and St George to paint his bloody cross all over everywhere.

He was passing the demolition site now. Progress had finished Hitler's work and torn down the tired remnants of Victorian London that remained in this spot, along with warehouses gutted by the downturn and colonised by drug addicts and other lost souls. Further along, a small church stood, bravely incongruous, but behind the graffitied boards along the pavement, silent diggers and cranes loomed over deep foundations and deeper tunnels reaching down to the new highway through the abyss.

The wind picked up. It plucked at Darshan's scarf and weaselled chill fingers down his collar. In the near distance, a motorbike growled. Somewhere closer, metal shutters rattled down over a shop front. Darshan's shoes, every step a witness to careful placement, thudded and scraped on the pavement, regular and deliberate under his weight. Across the road, a wash of orange street light illuminated a tessellation of snarling goddess figures badly pasted onto the work site hoardings, wrinkled and partly torn. The boards rattled under a fierce gust, roaring. *Lookatmelookatmelookatme.* Darshan pulled his eyes away just in time. These old pavements with their wide slabs of broken stone were hazardous—one step further and his foot would have been on a line. His momentum broken, breathing hard at how close he had come, he stopped to calculate his route along the cracked section of path, a matter of a few metres until the safety of cheap council tarmac took over, presenting no thresholds, no crossing points.

From behind, as the sky drew breath: the dull slap of trainers on stone.

Darshan glanced over his shoulder. There was just about enough light to recognise the tramp from the train and his cider-swilling friend.

The end of the street, where it joined a busier road ablaze with electricity and stinking of exhaust, was a matter of a couple of hundred metres away. Darshan picked up his pace, not caring how idiotic he might look dodging the cracks on the pavement, his coat flapping. His hand tightened on his briefcase—it was solid enough to slow someone down if swung with force. A small voice within told him he was being ridiculous. A sickly tramp and a drunk just happened to be taking the same route as him; he was bigger and stronger—*built like a bear, remember? said his mother while she ladled food into his bowl*; there was enough distance between them to guarantee his safety. But the small voice was quiet, and it wavered, and he didn't feel safe, and less so when a slim figure in a hoodie peeled away from a shadowed doorway ahead and stood waiting, its hands in its pockets and its head bobbing to a faint, tinny beat.

Behind him, the slap of trainers came on.

Darshan teetered on the fractured paving stones, his head swivelling. Blocked forward and back, there was only one direction to take. He vaulted the lines of the kerb onto the wet asphalt of the road, running heedless of cars towards the church. Barely registering the peeling gold letters on a black board proclaiming "St. Ursula's, Church of England", he dived past the doorless east end that faced the road and into a shadowed footpath that stank of stale urine and fresh earth. Away from the road, broken remnants of graveyard showed the limits of the developers' planning permission, though they had seen fit to pile equipment and rubbish inside the walls. Gravel crunched under Darshan's feet as he passed a shallow porch and broke into the empty shadows beyond the church. He skidded to an ungainly halt, nearly falling at the border drawn at his feet by the moon, full and harshly bright behind thinning clouds.

He dropped his briefcase and backed towards the high, grey stone wall under the west window. The sound of gravel made him such a target, but . . . He listened hard. There was nothing else. He was imagining things. His breath sobbed from his chest, and he strove to contain it. Two men got off the train at the same stop as him and happened to take the same route— there was no reason to think they were following him. Some boy in a hoodie and headphones could be any boy in a hoodie and headphones, waiting on the street to bum a cigarette or some such. It didn't have to be the boy from the train. And even if it was—so what? Why would three perfect strangers have any interest in him, just a big man in a suit on his way home from work?

Under the hollow moonlight, a mess of chest tombs and gravestones cast the blackest of shadows over the lumpy, untended grass. What kind of custom was it that consigned the dead to the ground, to rot and be walked on? So disrespectful, to let bones and flesh lie piled below, to be consumed by time and earth. He would wait a few minutes here, no more. Just long enough for those people to be on their way. He would not think about death, and what lay under the ground waiting to claw its way back to the light, and the great excavation just beyond the wall. He bent forward, hands on knees, while he silently chanted the mantras of good sense and hauled his thoughts away from corrupted flesh and the ravening darkness that consumed it. And the night . . .

. . . exhaled.

Dizzy, then, Darshan spun and fumbled, tripping, back towards the path, towards the orange glow of electric light at the end, which held, not hope, but dark shadows and the scuff of shoes. His shoulder struck the porch and he slung himself under its shelter, fingers scrabbling for a handle and meeting a twisted iron ring, whining until it turned with a rusty screech. He banged the door shut behind him and rested his forehead brief-ly against its panels. A key rested in the lock, but it would not turn, no mat-ter what force he applied. Something . . . something . . . Pews shoved haphazardly against the walls. He grabbed the end of one, his fingers snag-ging on the worm-eaten and splintered wood, and dragged it against the door, making nothing of its weight. Safe, maybe, for the moment.

"Thank you, thank you," he whispered, not sure to whom. What was it called? Sanctuary? Perhaps the Christian god wouldn't mind sheltering him from pursuit. Wasn't he supposed to be a kind god, after all?

The building smelt of dust and damp stone and something animal. Rats, perhaps, nesting in the kneelers. Darshan's eyes adjusted to the dim glow that bled through high windows, robbed of strength by stained glass that glowed monochrome in the night. What light there was gathered force at the end away from the road. Darshan moved towards the nave, carefully using the centres of the worn flags until he stood below the west window, where the moon shone through broken panes like an eye in the endless void.

What now? What to do? Heavy pillars and pitch-dark vaulting defined the echoing space and magnified his breaths to whispers. Was it safe in here? He didn't feel safe. Now he thought about it, why would the key be in the *inside* of the lock? Phone. He had a phone. This was London in the twenty-first century, full of help, full of police, who might laugh at rescuing a big man from a bunch of shadows, but laughter wouldn't kill him. He reached into his pocket and came up empty.

"Darshan."

Her voice was soft.

"I've been watching you, Darshan."

Wide-eyed before the breathing shadows, he could not move.

"Watching such a long time," she crooned. "And waiting."

Moonlight infused her brown skin, burnishing her breasts and slender belly, raising copper tints in her many plaits. A pink jewel sparkled in her nose as she approached from the cavernous east end, placing her feet me-ticulously on the centre of each flagstone in a mocking dance, drawing a cloak of shadows in her wake.

Darshan squeaked and fumbled at his other pockets.

"You didn't oughta keep valuables where they ain't safe, mate." It was the drunk who had taken his scent. He padded from the shadows still sniffing, dangling the phone just out of Darshan's reach.

Hands caught at his sleeves, holding him in place.

"Yo Artio," said the youth in the hoodie. "We brought him. Just like you wanted." His urban twang echoed in the dim spaces of the church. Bookish Arthur stayed silent, his grip firm.

"You have done well," she said. "Claw, Dogman, Arthur, my namesake—you have all done well. Have your reward, for you have brought me what is mine. Drink of me, my pets."

As she swept her arm forward, bronze and languid in the moonlight, her fingers drove claws of shadow hard and deep into the heart of each man. Crumpling, mouths agape and overflowing with darkness, they folded to the cold floor. Dispassionately, she watched them writhe and gasp. Darshan, though freed by their collapse, could neither breathe nor move as they twisted, ecstatic or in pain, then quieted. A last jerk of the Dogman's hand sent Darshan's phone clattering against a pillar. Then dust and darkness and the feeble moon that faded as the woman Artio folded the gloom around her, leaving only her eyes and bright, sharp teeth to steal what light remained.

She waited, and she smiled. Her lips—he remembered the lush, red lipgloss that had tempted his gaze on the long-ago train—curved and curled back. Too far, too red.

From somewhere, he found the will to turn away. The cracks between the flagstones seemed a net closing in, drawing him to the abyss behind.

"Don't you like my house, Darshan?" Her whisper came from right beside him; though he had not heard her move, her breath stirred the hair behind his ear. "How strange that they named it for me long after they forgot me." Fingers brushed his cheek, gentle and hot. So hot.

"I don't . . ."

"St. Ursula, my cub. 'Little Bear' they called me after they painted me in incense and crosses. They forgot . . ."

"What do you want?" His voice trembled. Soft curves pressed against his back as the shadows wreathed his waist.

"Come to me, Darshan," she said, laying her lips over the pulse in his neck. "You've stared at me enough when you thought I wasn't noticing. Don't you want to come closer and look properly?" She paused, teeth bared and feral, grazing his skin. "Don't you want to *fall?*"

He screwed his eyes shut but stayed still. Was he not, in any case, already fallen, constrained step by step to this place, this meeting?

"Are you going to kill me, too?" he whimpered.

"Too?" She glanced at the fallen men and shrugged. "They aren't dead. They're . . . full. They will wake and hunger again and be useful."

"Then you don't need me. You've got them. Why me?" He felt ashamed of his fear.

"It was always you," she said. "Born on my day, when they brought me back to the light. I chose you, Darshan. I *made* you. I swallowed your first cry. I nurtured you with my own strength. I singled you out and kept you apart. All I had to do was wait. And though I am very patient, my time of waiting is over."

"I don't understand."

"You know why today is special, dear Darshan, sweet Darshan? Today, out there, below in the darkness, today they uncovered my altar. Today, the day of your birth and my rebirth—today, I take what is mine."

"What do you want of me?" he whispered.

"Oh, Darshan." Her shadowed face took contour from the darkness. His knees buckled and came to a painful meeting with the floor. He cried out. "My Darshan. A goddess has needs, too."

Her eyes gleamed like polished obsidian above lengthening jaws. Her full breasts were so close to his face as she leaned down and slowly ran her tongue up his temple and into his hair, her smell musky and enticing. "You've seen it all along. You're the only one who can truly see it, but you've spent your entire life running away." She straightened and backed towards the thick dark around the altar.

"I still don't understand. I'm nobody. I have no connection with you, with this place."

"Silly Darshan. You have nothing but connection. I have called to you and you have refused me, running from the one truth in your life." She nudged one of the unconscious men with her foot. "These . . . These can see me, can see my darkness and hear my voice. But you . . ." She backed slowly towards the altar, her clawed hand held out to him. "You are the only one who can follow me. You've been marking time, staying out of the way until I came for you. But you've known the truth forever: you could be the first and greatest of my ascendancy, and a priest should answer his calling."

Careless of where the flagstones began and ended, she strolled into the shadows.

Darshan clambered off the floor. All around him, the flags extended into shadow, a sea of stepping stones back to safety. An ocean of bottomless darkness welling between them. He could rush back to that life, vindicated in his terror. He could be normal and spend his days teetering on the brink, feeling her eyes on him, her fingers clasped around his soul, her jaws ready to consume. Or . . . he could fall. He raised his foot, choice made.

Who Tricks the Tricksters?

Libby Weber

It all started when YHWH agreed to speak at the Trickster Caucus Annual Barbecue. Or perhaps it was actually when Buddha agreed to do it
two years prior, thus setting the precedent that primary figures of con-
temporary religions had nothing to lose by having a beer and some of
Nanabozho's smoked walleye with the lesser gods. The following year, Jesus delivered a selection of parables, which was a huge hit—so much so that
the Prince of Peace indulged in a spot of boasting at the monthly One True
Gods Brunch.

It was a pet peeve of YHWH's when other gods were put before him, so
He appeared to Ananse the Spider in a symbolic dream involving seven fat
houseflies and seven lean houseflies. Ananse could read the writing on the
wall. The next morning, the Trickster Caucus sent YHWH an invitation to
speak, and He accepted.

And so the G-d of the Hebrews appeared before them in the form of a
conflagration whose flickering tongues were composed of multifarious images, each one meaningful to a different trickster. Even a group of shapeshifters had to admit—it was pretty cool. His speech wasn't so much a
speech as individualized revelations in the minds and hearts of all, and He
was so flattered by the ovation He received that He soon found Himself
sharing a calabash of palm wine with Ananse and Prometheus, studiously
ignoring Kokopelli, Veles, and Huehuecoyotl playing a tune from *Porgy and
Bess* that He particularly loathed.

When the song ended, there was polite applause, and Ananse raised the
calabash to YHWH.

"Even if I lacked a raconteur's penchant for hyperbole," said Ananse,

247

stretching four of his legs toward the fire, "I would say that this has been, without a doubt, our best barbecue ever."

"Hear, hear," said Prometheus, half a beat late.

Ananse regarded him with a mild, eight-eyed gaze. "Liver giving you trouble?"

"No, it regenerated this morning, just in time for tonight," said Prometheus. "Truly, it's nothing."

"If not even Loki's mead can cheer you up, it must be something," said Ananse. "Come on, tell your Uncle Ananse and Grandpa Jehovah all about it."

"Self-indulgence, nothing more," said Prometheus.

"It can't be more self-indulgent than most of the requests for intercession I get," said YHWH's voice through the fire.

This startled a laugh out of Prometheus. "Fair enough. It's just that I finished composing an epic poem this morning. That always puts me in a melancholy mood."

"I didn't know you were writing again," said Mercury, slapping Prometheus on the back and sitting next to him by the fire.

"It may be the finest work I've ever written," said Prometheus, with a titanic smile. "It's the story of how I tricked Zeus into demanding the worthless parts of a sacrifice to the eternal benefit of mankind, all in heroic couplets."

"I've always liked that one," said Ananse, grinning. "It's the grandmother of all tricks. I think everybody's used it once or twice. Excepting those who have no need of such tricks, of course," he said, gesturing magnanimously at YHWH.

"Where will you be publishing it?" asked YHWH.

There was an uncomfortable silence.

"It's unpublishable, I'm afraid," said Prometheus. "But I shall be happy to burn you a copy and waft the smoke into your sanctuary."

"Balderdash!" said YHWH, who had finished off the calabash of palm wine and was sipping from the winged helmet that Hermes had slipped into His hand before sitting down next to Mercury. "If it's as good as you say, it should be available to everybody."

"You're right, of course," said Ananse delicately. "Unfortunately, such a thing would run afoul of the Decree."

"That's not the Decree's purpose," said YHWH through the fire.

"Of course it isn't," said Mercury, grinning in unison with Hermes. "All of us understand that. But Prometheus telling his own story, even in verse, is exactly the sort of thing that could be construed as inciting mortals to worship him, which the Decree expressly forbids."

"Surely the tribunal wouldn't apply the Decree to a work of literature." The fire flickered uncertainly as YHWH spoke.

"The same tribunal that judged Aristotle's *Comedics* to be unfairly influenced by Dionysus and ordered every copy destroyed?" asked Prometheus. "Times may have changed, but Osiris hasn't, and as long as he's in charge, the tribunal is going to continue as they always have. And it's not just published works they object to."

"How so?" asked YHWH, whose hiccup made sparks fly.

"They sent Ananse a cease-and-desist letter for joining mortal storytellers around the fire and telling stories about himself," said Mercury.

"Ridiculous!" said YHWH, burping mightily and taking another sip from Hermes's helmet. At some point Mercury's matching helmet had appeared on His head.

"I agree," said Ananse, "but you can't deny that telling my own stories around the fire violates the letter if not the spirit of the Decree. It's just the sort of thing that happens when you have a legislative body making one-size-fits-all laws that apply to all gods and goddesses, no matter how minor."

"Despite the little hiccups that a few of us have encountered along the way, I don't think anybody's saying that the Decree has outlived its usefulness," said Prometheus, giving Ananse a warning look.

"Definitely not," said Mercury, catching Hermes's eye. "It exists to protect small religions, not to persecute their deities."

"Not that Jesus and Moroni haven't gotten around the Decree by encouraging their followers to do the proselytizing for them," said Ananse, producing another calabash of palm wine and handing it to YHWH.

"Besides," said Prometheus, "even if they did amend or repeal the Decree, YHWH, Jesus, and Mohammed have a huge advantage in recruiting followers due to name recognition. It's not as if they need the help."

"Imagine," said Mercury, snickering, "Ananse going door-to-door to recruit followers. They'd call the police."

"Or pest control," said Prometheus.

"Enough shop talk," said Ananse, frowning. "Is this a party or isn't it?" He handed flagons of mead to YHWH, Mercury, Hermes, and Prometheus and raised his own in toast. "Ladies, Gentlemen, and Others; Friends, Enemies, and Nemeses: thank you all for observing tonight's détente, and aren't you glad you did? And we have the Almighty Himself to thank for a truly unforgettable evening! Raise your glasses, and let's drink: to YHWH!"

Enthusiastic cheers rang through the assembly, but though YHWH set a stunning rainbow in the night sky in thanks for the tricksters' hospitality, He remained in thoughtful silence for the rest of the evening.

The following month, the One True Gods Brunch was less fractious than usual, and the attendant cherubim and seraphim noticed that the guests' trips to the toilet were frequent, unusually long in duration, and tended to end in handshakes.

Nobody expected the 12,986[th] Congress of Deities to accomplish anything interesting, and for the most part it lived up to expectations. However, in the otherwise unremarkable bill extending the benefits and legal protections of god-hood to demigods, Titans, and three subclasses of miracle-worker for another millennium, there was a seemingly unremarkable clause clarifying the Decree's ban on proselytizing to exclude interactions with small groups of mortals, as well as works of art and literature clearly distinguishable from Divine revelations.

As with all bills that came before them, it had been certified by Mithra the Undeceivable, and since the bill had been sponsored by the notoriously stodgy Council of One True Gods, the bill passed with no opposition, apart from the Chaos Cabal, which as usual was split.

The next day, Articles of Organization for Glossosimi LLC were filed with the state of New York. Later that week, a small suite of offices in a Midtown high-rise overlooking Hell's Kitchen became the physical home of Glossosimi LLC. The neighbors, a medical software startup and a family law group, saw little and heard less of the new tenants, apart from the occasional scuttle of claws on hardwood late at night.

The following month, retirees were treated to a radiant photograph of Julia Roberts on the inside front cover of their AARP magazines. Her smile was dazzling, and a golden Om charm hung around her neck. The caption, in friendly-looking Avenir font, read "Hindu. Are you?"

Soon, the ad and other versions of it featuring notables from around the world had appeared in print and all over the internet. They all bore whimsical copy, like "Life is complicated. Your religion should be, too;" "Dharma for Greg;" and "Think you're innately divine? We do too!," a golden Om, and a link to a newsy-looking website with entertaining features like "Karma Calculator," "She Made an Offering to Ganesh—You'll Never Guess What Happened Next," "QUIZ: What Hindu god are You?," and "Ask Shiva the Destroyer," which also had its own Twitter feed.

It wasn't until one of Jesus' followers took his name spectacularly in vain at a Wal-Mart jewelry counter that any of the One True Gods took note of how quickly and thoroughly Hinduism had penetrated the market. Taking care to ensure that his stigmata were prominently displayed, Jesus himself appeared by the jewelry counter in question. The miracle was lost on the sales associate, who was busy helping a man find his fiancée a slightly more affordable engagement ring.

Jesus pretended to peruse one of the cases while listening for additional blasphemies but stopped short at the sight of a selection of Om necklaces next to the gold and silver crosses. His confusion must have shown on his face because the sales associate putting a display tray back into the next case took notice.

"Did you want to see something in the case, hon?"

"What's up with those?" he asked her, gesturing toward the offending pendants with a jerk of his head.

"They're Oms, sugar-pie," she said. "We've got them in sterling silver, 18 karat gold, and with diamond accents."

"I know what they are; I want to know what they're doing here."

"Selling like hotcakes," she said.

"But this is Alabama," said Jesus. "It's the Bible belt!"

"Shoot, every belt's got holes in it to hold it in place," she said, laughing. "Besides, it ain't just Yankees that're filled with sparks of the divine."

"Buying a necklace from Wal-Mart doesn't give you a spark of the divine," snapped Jesus, his temper getting the better of him.

"Do you want to see one or not?" she asked, crossing her arms.

Jesus scowled and briefly considered knocking over the jewelry counter, but it looked much sturdier than a money lender's table. He settled for leaving a dead fish hidden above a drop ceiling tile in the men's bathroom before he re-ascended to the heavens.

The following week, the Hindu gods received a warning letter from the tribunal that oversaw adherence to the Decree, to which they replied with a polite but firm request to back off, given that advertising was the antithesis of divine revelation and now a protected activity, according to recent legislation passed by the Congress of Divine Beings.

Osiris was unimpressed with this claim and sent a cease and desist order for all advertising, not on anti-proselytizing grounds, but because bribing supporters, even in small groups, was still banned.

The Hindu gods responded that though they had paid Glossosimi LLC a price beyond rubies (specifically, rubies and some superb Darjeeling tea), that payment was for services rendered, nothing more. There was also a tart suggestion that perhaps the tribunal might hire Glossosimi LLC themselves to help cast off their out-of-date reputation.

The Hindu gods received no more letters, which they took as a sign that their argument had been accepted.

The tribunal closed its file on the incident, but Osiris kept it on his desk.

The following week, a video featuring a trio of monks in saffron robes dancing to "Bust a Move" went viral, as did a series of photographs of Buddhist temples and monasteries by a DeviantArt user named Thirteenth_Incarnation. Several days later, a daredevil free-climbed Angkor Wat and meditated atop a spire in a Free Tibet shirt. His GoPro video was shared and re-shared on Facebook and Twitter, macro images spread like wildfire on Tumblr and Pinterest, and The Daily Sutra, which hosted the content, racked up millions of unique hits and subscribers.

Buddha had arrived on the social media scene.

The tribunal sent letters to Buddha similar to those that had been sent to the Hindu gods. Upon the advice of Glossosimi LLC, he responded exactly as the Hindu gods had.

Buddha received no more letters, which he celebrated by taking the

"How Enlightened Are You?" quiz that Glossosimi LLC had sent for review. He was delighted to score 15 out of 15.

The tribunal closed their file on the incident, but Osiris kept it on his desk after applying a bright red sticky flag to it.

It wasn't until Lucifer undertook a number of high-profile publicity stunts, like sending costumed picketers to the Westboro Baptist Church with signs that said "Satan Loves Hate" and "Fred Phelps Says Hi!" and airing infomercials advertising competitive adjustable-rate soul loans, that the tribunal realized that the problem wasn't going away.

Lucifer responded to their letters promptly and very much in the same way the Hindu gods and Buddha had. The tribunal sent no additional letters to Lucifer, since there had now been three incidents, but Osiris wrote up a report and sent it to the Fates, as a matter of procedure.

Nobody actually expected the Fates to get involved.

One Thursday afternoon, three elderly women entered the offices of Glossosimi LLC, all dressed in white business suits. The first wore enormous bifocals, the second carried a golden walking stick, and the third carried a briefcase and had short, fluffy white hair that made her look like a dandelion gone to seed. If they were surprised to find Coyote at the reception desk, they didn't show it.

"How may I help you ladies?" he asked, showing all of his teeth.

"We would speak with your partners," said the woman with the walking stick.

"Who are you?"

"This is Nona," she said, gesturing to the woman in the spectacles, "this is Maud," she indicated the woman with the dandelion hair, "and I'm Denise."

"Do you have an appointment?" asked Coyote, stretching his forelegs and yawning.

"How are we supposed to get an appointment when there's no contact information on your website?" asked Nona, glaring at Coyote through her thick lenses.

"If you're interested in our work, I can have one of our account representatives meet with you to discuss your needs, but I'm afraid Mr. Glosso and Ms. Simi are unavailable," said Coyote.

Maud glared at Coyote and plunked her briefcase on his desk, but Denise brought her cane down on top of the lid. "*Pax*, sister," she said in a quelling voice. "A meeting with any of your employees would be acceptable," she said to Coyote.

"Good," said Coyote, sniffing. "Have a seat. Someone will be with you shortly."

He skulked out through a doorway.

"I would only have cut off his tail," said Maud petulantly.

"You'd have given us away," said Nona, glaring through her spectacles.

"Isn't that the point?" asked Maud.

"Eventually," said Denise. "But not yet. For now, we observe."

The three sat down in unison.

Moments later, an enormously tall woman with wavy, waist-length black hair appeared in the doorway. "Excuse me, ladies. I'm Mamala, account representative. If you'll just step this way, we can speak privately."

The three allowed themselves to be ushered into a conference room that smelled faintly of wet paint. Plastic still covered the chairs along the wall, but someone had placed a pitcher of water, glasses, and a bowl of fruit on the table that ran the length of the room. There were silver folders sitting on the table, indicating where the women in white should sit.

Mamala poured them water and passed the fruit around the table. "Welcome to Glossosimi LLC," she said, smiling. "But before we start, may I offer you something else to drink? Wine? Juice? Ambrosia?"

"No, thank you," said Nona, taking a sip from her glass of water.

"As you wish," said Mamala. "Now, the folders in front of you contain our standard non-disclosure agreement that we ask all potential clients to sign, which protects your identities as well as ours, as well as our proprietary services. Please, take your time reading it and let me know if you have any questions."

Nona bent over the table and peered through her spectacles at the agreement. When she finished reading, she passed her spectacles to Denise, who did the same and passed the spectacles in turn to Maud, who harrumphed as she tracked each clause with her index finger.

"I don't see anything overly binding or unfair," said Maud at last, producing a fountain pen and signing the form.

"Our associates may have something of a reputation," said Mamala, "but our highest loyalty is to our clients."

"And their gold," muttered Maud, handing her form to Nona.

"We accept most major forms of payment," said Mamala, "including but not limited to gold, gems, precious oils, souls, and American Express."

Nona peered through her spectacles at the signed agreements. "They say the devil's in the details."

Mamala smiled, revealing several rows of razor-sharp teeth. "I'm sure he'd like that, but we have our own legal department."

This startled a laugh out of Maud, and the tense atmosphere in the room dissipated. Nona handed the signed contracts to Mamala who initialed them just before they disappeared in a burst of silver stars.

"Thank you very much, ladies," said Mamala, smiling warmly. "How may I serve you?"

"I'll get straight to the point," said Maud, jamming her thumbnail into the leathery skin of a pomegranate. "We used to be household names, and now we're not. We'd like to change that."

"Household?" said Mamala frowning. "I thought I knew all the members of the Home and Hearth Coalition."

"We never go to Congress," said Denise, giving Maud a quelling look.

"It doesn't really work with our ethos," said Nona. "We're what you might call, well . . ." she trailed off.

"Homebodies?" suggested Mamala.

"Yes, exactly!" said Denise.

"Sort of," said Maud, popping a handful of pomegranate seeds into her mouth.

"Mostly," said Nona.

"We were very impressed with your Hinduism ads," said Denise.

"Thank you," said Mamala. "We all agreed that the third largest religion in the world deserved more coherent representation."

"I loved what you did for Buddha, too," said Nona. "It was fun."

"Well, if you liked that," said Mamala as she pulled a sleek tablet computer out of her pile of forms and made a subtle gesture that lowered a screen behind her, "let me show you some of our different service levels for branding and marketing."

She tapped her tablet, and an empty Tumblr dash and Twitter feed appeared on the screen. "The most basic promotional service we offer is social media representation, including tie-ins between your brand and popular trends."

She tapped again and names of trickster gods appeared at the end of humorous Tweets, along with Tumblr dashes filled with beautiful drawings and digital images, each with tens of thousands of notes.

"As you can see, all it takes is a bit of careful content construction, and a million people will share it. A few viral successes can guarantee your presence on social media for years. This method has the advantage of being relatively inexpensive, since access to these markets is free."

"Do people know they're sharing paid advertisements?" asked Nona.

"They're not advertisements," said Mamala. "They're memes. But if you want to talk advertising—"

"No advertisements," said Nona.

"We offer hybrid packages," said Mamala, "like the one we did for Buddha. That campaign was social media-heavy but also included website design, news content, and sponsored aggregation by companies who collect the best of the web."

"That doesn't really work with our ethos, either," said Nona.

"What exactly is your ethos?" asked Mamala.

"We're prognosticators," said Denise. "People used to pray to us to know the future."

"Some people actually used to think that we controlled it, too," said Nona with a brittle laugh.

"But that's an outdated notion we want to shed," said Denise.

"Speak for yourself," muttered Maud, slurping up another section of pomegranate seeds.

Denise elbowed her.

"Well, does it work with your ethos to appear in comedy sketches?" asked Mamala. "That's one way to soften a draconian image. It worked for Nixon, it can certainly work for you."

"Definitely not," said Denise.

"Perhaps something with music," said Nona.

"A flash mob?" asked Mamala.

"Nothing funny," said Maud firmly.

"Homebodies, more aspirational than humorous," said Mamala, making a note. "I think, ladies, that Pinterest is the ideal platform for you."

Denise and Maud looked at one another in confusion, but Nona was nodding.

"That could work," she said.

"What in the name of Pluto is Pinterest?" asked Maud.

"And why do you know what it is?" asked Denise.

"I'm on Pinterest because my job is exactly the same, year after year," said Nona huffily. "I can do it with my eyes closed. I might as well do it with my eyes open and be entertained."

Mamala tapped her pen against her lips. "I'll put together a proposal for you for a basic social media package. If you like what you see, we can consider cross-platform campaigns according to your preferred holiday calendar. How does that sound?"

Maud shrugged and sucked noisily on her pomegranate.

Denise hesitated for a moment and then nodded.

"Perfect," said Nona, smiling broadly.

"Excellent!" said Mamala, handing each of them a business card. "You'll find rate sheets in your folders, and you can discuss payment with Coyote out front. He'll schedule a meeting for us next week. I'll e-mail you with any questions."

"In my day, we had proper messengers," grumbled Maud.

"We remember, dear," said Denise. "We were there, too."

"Thank you, Mamala," said Nona, rising. "We'll see ourselves out."

After Nona, Denise, and Maud made their way to the lobby, Mamala noticed that Maud's briefcase was still on the floor by the table. After glancing down the corridor to ensure that she was alone, Mamala put the briefcase on the table and flipped open its latches. On a bed of black velvet lay an enormous pair of golden shears that shone with dangerous magic.

'Kanapapiki,' swore Mamala. She slammed the briefcase shut and dashed to the lobby, where Denise and Nona were waiting for Maud outside the ladies' room. She pasted on a broad smile. "I think one of you left this in the conference room."

Nona tutted and took the case from Mamala. "I swear she's getting senile."

"Hush," said Denise. "You're as old as she is. Thank you, Mamala."

"Any time," said Mamala.

She held her smile until the door closed behind them then bolted off down the corridor in search of Mr. Glosso and Ms. Simi.

The following week found the three women in white sitting once more in the lobby of Glossosimi LLC, each wearing an expression that betrayed apprehension.

"I don't understand," said Nona in a low voice. "You left your shears for them to find. They know the tribunal's procedures at least as well as we do. They must know who we are. Why are they keeping us waiting?"

"They know," said Denise. "But shows of deference are anathema to their sort unless there's some kind of trick involved."

"I don't fancy being made a fool of," grumbled Maud, who appeared somewhat mollified by the bowl of pomegranates on the table.

"Appearing foolish is a small price to pay for restoring balance," said Denise. "If the tricksters are truly united in their opposition to the Decree, Osiris and the tribunal face an unprecedented challenge."

"But how can we be certain they recognize us?" asked Nona, polishing her spectacles for the fifth time.

At this, the lights in the reception area flickered and went out, and the room was plunged into darkness. There was a snap of fingers, and a floating ball of green light appeared suspended above a pale hand whose owner stood just outside the door frame. The sound of a flute pierced the silence. A moment later, it was joined by a thrumming drum.

"Don't worry. They know," said Maud, cracking open a pomegranate.

Nona's eyes went wide as the ball of green light began to bounce in time with the music, and a sonorous voice broke into song.

"Welcome, ladies, to our home, where wit and art reside
We're very glad you set your famous reticence aside."

Nona squeaked with excitement, and Denise relaxed, accepting half of

Maud's pomegranate. The music continued, and a slender man in a green suit with gold pinstripes slid out from behind the doorjamb. His eyes gleamed in the light cast by the ball in his hand, which burst into flame and danced on his fingertips. Denise let out a soft sound of recognition, for this could be none other than Loki, de facto leader of the Trickster Caucus.

> 'For I am Mr. Glosso, though you know my other name,
> And you may rest assured that we can also say the same."

The flames at Loki's fingertips swayed in time with the music, and he performed a quick pirouette, circling himself with a ring of fire. As the music to the second verse began, a tiny hand with perfectly tapered fingers appeared in the doorway, a ball of white light hovering above its palm. A sweet female voice began to sing.

> 'Your incognito entrance was a well-thought out conceit,
> And in this case, it was a trick disguised, and so, a treat.
> But subterfuge and camouflage and fear shall ever flee me,
> For I am called Uzume, but I answer to Ms. Simi."

The singer's other hand swept into view and snapped open a silk fan, which sent the ball of light bobbing into the air. A petite, perfectly proportioned woman in a light pink kimono stepped into the doorway and swept into the room, and as she danced, the fan and ball of light cast delicate shadows in the shapes of flowers and fanciful animals on the walls.

The music shifted from verse to chorus, and Loki and Uzume sang together in harmony.

> 'Together we have made ourselves a home,
> For all whose tongues sometimes outrun their wits,
> A company where every misfit fits,
> Our somewhat less than stately pleasure dome.
> There's nowhere we'd prefer to be
> Than Glossosimi LLC."

Nona began to bounce in her seat as four more arms appeared in the doorway, each holding a ball of light, but Maud simply chuckled and stuck her thumbnail into the tough skin of a second pomegranate.

"*Of course you know Ananse and his many sportive tricks!*" sang Ananse, stepping into the doorway and juggling the balls of light.

"*And Sun Wukong who shows that strength and mischief often mix!*" sang the Monkey King, stepping proudly into view and sending a jet of purple fire from his staff, lightly singeing one of the plants in the reception area.

> '*Our numerous associates from cultures far and wide,*
> *Have come up with a strategy we know you haven't tried,*"

sang a panoply of tricksters who poured from the doorway, including Mamala, Prometheus, Hermes, Mercury, Crow, Raven, Iktomi, Coyote, and the musicians, Veles, Kokopelli, and Huehuecoyotl.

Flickering lights and dancing bodies filled the reception area, and not even Maud could resist tapping her foot in time with the music. Nona was clapping her hands as Ananse's juggling grew more elaborate, and Denise stared at Uzume's shadow dance with a look of rapt attention on her face.

The tricksters formed three rows, with the smaller animals in front, and began to sing in unison.

> '*So now our cards and yours have all been laid upon the table,*
> *You know we'll represent you three as well as we are able.*
> *But there's a thing we think that you have not anticipated:*
> *It's just how well we work when we are keenly motivated.*"

This made Maud cackle aloud, which in turn made her sisters titter. Suddenly the balls of light went out, leaving Loki and Uzume standing in their own spotlights as the sprightly music faded to a solo flute.

> '*Together we endeavor to exceed*
> *All expectations and to make you laugh,*
> *At what we'll do to make sure you succeed,*
> *And all the tricks we'll pull on your behalf,*"

sang Uzume and Loki, facing the Fates with hands spread wide, giving every appearance of sincerity. Then, the drumming started up again, and the lights came up on the other tricksters.

"*So hire us!*" sang Hermes.

"*Fire us!*" Prometheus bellowed.

"*Shove us!*" yipped Coyote.

"*Love us!*" Mamala crooned.

"*Jeer us!*" hissed Iktomi.

"*Hear us!*" Ananse intoned.

"*Bleed us! Need us! Gain us! Retain us!*" chorused the tricksters, holding the final note until Loki cut them all off with an elegant gesture. Uzume raised her closed fan and conducted the final lines, and the tricksters sang in raucous harmony.

"*So take a chance with us, and you will see
The best of Glossosimi LLC!*"

Uzume cut off the singers, and the music picked up tempo. The company broke into frenzied dance as arcs of colored fire blazed across the reception area. When the music finally stopped, the room went dark, and the Fates broke into wild applause.

A moment later, the lights came up, and other than a few scorch marks on the walls and furnishings, nothing remained of the elaborate production number. Loki walked into the room in his green and gold business suit, holding a golden folder.

"Ladies," he said, smiling broadly. "It's a pleasure to make your acquaintance. I know you arrived this morning expecting to see Mamala's presentation for your Pinterest campaign, but I hope you won't mind terribly that, in accordance with a company-wide vote, I will personally be seeing to your account. I've come up with a bold, multi-platform vision for you, and I know you're going to love it."

The Fates looked at one another, "To be honest, we're not certain we want to go through with anything," said Denise, looking slightly abashed.

"Don't get us wrong, I haven't seen singing and dancing that wonderful since Jove was a boy," said Nona apologetically. "But we came here primarily to observe what sort of operation you were running."

"To see if we were in compliance with the Decree?" asked Loki.

"We don't give a fig for the laws of gods or men," scoffed Maud. "But seeing how you got up Osiris's nose was well worth the trip to the mortal realms."

"I see."

"If I may," said a melodious voice from the doorway, where Uzume stood dressed in a sky-blue business suit and cherry-colored pumps. "You've come all this way, and I'm sure the mortal realms weary you," she said, gesturing for Prometheus to enter and offer the Fates wine goblets filled with luminous ambrosia. "Let us at least show you what we've done for you."

"Well . . ." said Nona, looking imploringly at Denise and Maud.

"What the Hades," said Maud, tossing an empty pomegranate peel over her shoulder and grinning at Loki. "What could it hurt? Have you got a phone number, handsome?"

Two weeks later, the Fates' first television spot aired during *American Idol*. At first, it appeared to be one of the show's own promotions, informing viewers of when there would be auditions in their area, but then the music changed, and an entirely different message appeared: "Tempt Fate." Then, the no-nonsense sans serif font faded to black and two seconds of silence.

There was little response to this, apart from a few live-Tweeters who seized the opportunity to complain about their cable providers. But more "Tempt Fate" messages began to appear—during prime-time television, hiding in film trailers, flashing on Jumbotrons at baseball games, sponsored internet ads, and, in a move that got the internet buzzing, on the official swag bags at WonderCon. When a picture of one WonderCon attendee displaying his "Tempt Fate" bag whilst hanging from the bicycle rack of an OCTA bus was featured in a Nerdist convention report, satirical versions began to pop up on 4chan and Reddit. It didn't seem to matter that nobody knew what "Tempt Fate" was or what it meant.

Naturally, once a Fox News commentator opined that "Tempt Fate" was part of a liberal media conspiracy, "Tempt Fate" began to gain traction on social media. But it wasn't until George Takei shared a picture of himself and his husband parasailing accompanied by the #TemptFate hashtag that critical popularity was achieved. It was time for Phase Two.

Uzume, who was attending the American Association of Advertising Agencies' annual conference on the day that "Tempt Fate" went viral on Facebook, sent Loki a congratulatory text. She was surprised that he didn't respond but chalked it up to his being busy launching Phase Two. She had no idea how correct she was.

The following day, Loki summoned the account managers to the conference room. Given that Uzume, who usually tempered Loki's mercurial demands, was out of town, none of them expected anything pleasant. The fact that Loki arrived late to the meeting with his phone mashed against his ear and his face twisted into a rictus of fury lowered their collective expectations even further.

"That's certainly an idea," he was saying as he smoothed his rumpled tie, "but I'm afraid I have to go, I just walked into a meeting. Yes, of course we'll be discussing your account. No! You don't need to attend. Purely internal affairs. Nothing that would interest you. All right. Yes. Yes, fine."

"Twenty drachmas says it's the Fates again," said Prometheus quietly.

"No bet," said Crow.

Loki ended the call, tucked the phone into his jacket pocket, and adjusted his lapels. "Let's make this quick. I need to discuss some changes to upcoming—"

Loki's phone began to buzz and play the opening riff of Dire Straits's "Money for Nothing."

"Baldur's bunghole!" he swore.

Loki stomped into the hallway, which was separated from the conference room by a large pane of glass and slammed the door behind him. The account managers did their best not to be obvious about watching Loki pace and bite his cheek to keep from snapping at the person on the other end of the call.

"There but for the grace of Loki go I," Mamala muttered.

They all fell silent when Loki stalked back into the room, slamming the door behind him. "All right," he said crossly, looking at each of them in turn. "First things first: Ananse, as of now, the Fates' account is yours."

Ananse blinked all eight of his eyes in surprise. "We're in the middle of shooting Buddha's Kickstarter video—I can't be both places at once."

"Hermes and Mercury can take Buddha," said Loki.

Hermes and Mercury let out twin groans.

"We've both got our hands full trying to get the Hindu gods' approval for the next phase of their campaign," said Hermes. "Have you any idea how many signatures that requires?"

"If it's just signature gathering, brief Crow and have him do it," said Loki.

"What about Lucifer?" asked Crow. "I've built up an excellent working relationship with him, but I can't spend time grooming him if I'm flying all over the divine realms trying to hunt down every last Hindu god to initial forms in triplicate."

"I think Mamala can handle Lucifer, don't you?" said Loki.

Crow clicked his beak disapprovingly, but Loki ignored him.

"And what will you be doing?" asked Mamala, crossing her arms.

"I am going to think forgiving thoughts about why any of you should continue to have jobs," hissed Loki, effectively lowering the temperature of the room several degrees. "Mamala, get a proposal for Lucifer's next publicity stunt on my desk in three hours. Crow, if I see you without paperwork in your beak before every contract is signed, I'm removing all the shiny things from your office. Mercury and Hermes, I want Buddha's video wrapped by the end of the day, and Ananse, keep those cursed crones out of my way. I have things to attend to."

With that, Loki threw his phone into a nearby trash can and disappeared in a flash of green flames.

The account managers exchanged glances, none of them truly convinced that Loki had actually run away. It was a good ten minutes before any of them dared leave. In those ten minutes, the phone in the trash can played the guitar riff from "Money for Nothing" three times.

Several days later, Lucifer's Ask Me Anything webchat on Reddit got off to a rocky start when several sharp-eyed Redditors noticed an unfortunate typo on the banner that was supposed to read "Hail Satan, Lucifer, The Devil, Beelzebub, Lord of Hell" in the background of the image he'd posted to prove his identity. The AMA continued as planned, but #Beelzeboob was soon trending on Twitter. Mamala's first call was to the commercial printers. Her second was to Loki to allege sabotage of her event by a trickster or tricksters unknown.

Mamala forwarded Loki a scan that showed how the properly-spelled proof she'd initialed had been stamped with a dark purple infinity symbol over the "u" of "Beelzebub," which the printers had faithfully reproduced. The infinity stamp, as everybody at Glossosimi LLC knew, lived in the upper drawer of the reception desk, where it was used to endorse paper checks.

Fortunately for Mamala, it was obvious to everyone that someone had deliberately sabotaged her proof at some point in the two hours between the time she approved it and the time it was delivered by courier to the printers. Unfortunately for Mamala, everybody except her client was so amused by the trick that Crow, whom everybody knew had been responsible, went unpunished. And unfortunately for everybody else, Mamala was not known for her forgiving nature.

Thus it was that a print ad for the Hindu gods appeared in *Time* with the tagline "Have a steak in eternity," which spurred an outcry from practicing Hindus. Shortly thereafter, the Fates mysteriously came into possession of a contact list identifying the specialties of every employee at Glossosimi LLC. Soon, everyone was getting calls at all hours about everything from requesting the dimensions of Facebook cover photos to detailed instructions for making Vines. Mamala's revenge spurred additional acts of project sabotage, furniture literally walking out of offices, and exploding bowls of fruit. Coyote was on the receiving end of so many tongue-lashings from angry clients that he stopped answering the phone and circled the reception area with salt in hopes of reducing the number of furious gods manifesting in the lobby. By the time Uzume returned from her business trip, Glossosimi LLC was in such uproar that she found Loki hiding in her office, invisible.

"I know you're here," she said. "I can smell you."

Loki rippled into visibility with a self-deprecating laugh. "Of what do I smell, my dear?"

"Pride," said Uzume, sitting and folding her hands primly on the desk in front of her. "And shame. The whole floor reeks of it. And rotten fruit."

"Don't start," snarled Loki.

"I am disappointed," said Uzume.

"You agreed that the Fates' account should be handled by a senior partner," said Loki.

"I agreed to follow the will of the majority," said Uzume. "But judging by the number of empty mead bottles in the recycling bin, I think the majority followed your will and not their own."

Loki smiled. "I had a batch ready to bottle," he said. "Can I be blamed for the precise timing of wild yeast?"

Uzume frowned. "You do not yet understand."

"Understand what? That I ought to have let a minor demigod like Mamala sell a cheap service to the three most powerful women in existence?" sneered Loki. "I saw a golden opportunity for us all, and I seized it."

Uzume sighed. "When you told me you wished to thwart Osiris and the tribunal by making the Decree look ridiculous, I told you there was one thing we needed to do to succeed."

Loki raised his chin mutinously. "We needed to do good work for our clients."

"That part of the strategy was never in question," said Uzume.

When it became clear that she would not speak unless he did, Loki bared his teeth and turned his back to her, pretending to look out the window. "You said that we needed to unite our colleagues against a common enemy."

"Do you recall why?"

"So we would reserve our tricks for others and not ourselves," Loki muttered.

"Yes," said Uzume. "That's how the Fates out-tricked us."

"Those old women haven't enough cunning to find their way out of a cave in millennia," said Loki.

"They dangled prestige in front of you, and, in order to gain control of their account, you played a trick on the rest of us—the one thing I told you not to do," said Uzume. "And once you'd taken the bait, they made themselves intolerable until you chose to sacrifice the relationships our associates have built for your own convenience. Is it any wonder that the others ceased to be united?"

Loki pulled himself up to his full height and scowled down at Uzume. "I made the Fates a household name, just as I said I would."

"But you failed to see the trick they hid within their ruse," said Uzume.

"Fine!" snapped Loki, pacing along the wall of windows. "I made a tactical error. Is that what you wanted to hear? Now, cease these riddles and tell me what we should do."

"Nothing. Surely you can see that our game here is finished."

"What?" exclaimed Loki, whirling to face her.

"We knew our sun would set eventually, or at least by the next Congress," said Uzume gently. "But nightfall became inevitable the moment the Fates tricked you into breaking our accord. A djinn cannot go back into a shattered bottle."

Loki was silent for a moment, thinking. "Odin's bollocks," he swore softly. "We'll be playing tricks on one another for a hundred years after this. We have lost, haven't we?"

"The war, yes," said Uzume. "But we aren't worthy of our caucus if we can't win a few battles as we retreat. Come with me. We must meet with the account managers in five minutes, and we have a client meeting at two o'clock."

"What are you planning?"

"You will see," she said, reaching up to pat his cheek before proceeding through the door he held open for her.

When no buckets of water dropped on her from above, Loki followed her, only to receive a handful of pomegranate pulp to the face from an invisible assailant.

The two o'clock meeting was short and bitter. All of Glossosimi LLC's clients were gathered in a magically expanded room and ceremoniously dumped, with a literal passing of the torch, with which clients could choose to burn their own contracts or not. Of course, those who chose not to burn their paperwork could expect to find themselves mocked in every media channel at the tricksters' disposal.

Buddha failed to laugh. Shiva swore to raze the building. Lucifer, no stranger to contractual loopholes, saluted Loki and Uzume before returning to Hell. The others departed with promises to avenge themselves on the Trickster Caucus at the next meeting of Congress, until only the Fates and the senior partners remained.

Uzume clapped her hands, and Mamala entered with six golden goblets. She offered them to the Fates first and to Loki and Uzume second. She took the final goblet that remained and raised it.

"A toast," said Mamala, "to the finest bit of trickery ever seen."

Mamala, Loki, and Uzume raised their goblets and paused when it became clear that the Fates were not planning to drink.

"Is something wrong?" asked Loki.

"You tell us," said Maud, squinting suspiciously at her goblet.

"This isn't ambrosia," said Nona, sniffing the liquid.

"No, it's mead—my own special recipe," said Loki, smiling broadly and taking a drink.

"Delicious," said Uzume, sipping.

"Mmm," said Mamala, licking a lingering drop from her bottom lip. "Is this the same batch from the barbecue?"

"Same recipe, new batch," said Loki. He glanced at the Fates, who had all placed their goblets on the table in front of them. "For Frigg's sake," he said. "Take our goblets. We've already drunk from them, and you don't see us sprouting feathers or writhing on the ground in agony."

Denise sighed. "I hope you know that our interference wasn't personal."

"It's our job to maintain balance," said Nona, wringing the edge of her jacket. "Radical changes must be countered, no matter how much we like seeing Osiris annoyed."

"You out-tricked us," said Uzume placidly. "That is something we can respect."

"None of you are looking for trickster work on the side, are you?" asked Loki, rubbing his index finger along the edge of his goblet.

This made Maud snicker, and she switched her goblet for Mamala's. Denise took Uzume's, and Nona blushed faintly as she swapped hers for Loki's.

"To tempting Fate," said Loki.

This time, they all drank.

"So," said Mamala, sitting back in her chair. "What are you going to do now?"

"Go back to the cave. Wait a few millennia for the next time Osiris needs us to intervene," said Nona, gloomily, taking a deep pull from her goblet. "I say, this is good, isn't it?"

"Very good," said Denise.

"Not bad," said Maud, belching.

"At least we have internet access these days," said Denise. "Now, what about all of you?"

"Any plans we should be worried about?" said Maud, looking askance at the tricksters in turn.

"I don't know about the others, but I plan to take advantage of the Decree's loopholes for as long as they exist," said Mamala. "I'm headed for the islands—I haven't been surfing in Pele knows how long. I might share some of the old songs."

"That doesn't sound awful," said Maud, draining her goblet of mead.

"Ananse will tell stories around mortal campfires, I'm sure, and Prometheus will seek a publisher for his poetry," said Uzume. "As for myself, I think I shall go to Washington DC."

"For the cherry blossoms or for the politics?" asked Denise.

"Yes," said Uzume.

"I've always wanted to go on the stage," said Loki. "And I happen to know of a theater in the Poconos that's holding auditions next week."

"That sounds wonderful!" said Nona, sighing. "Performing for an audience always looks like such fun."

"Have you ever thought about taking some time off?" asked Mamala, taking another sip of mead. "Surely you could find someone to take your place for a few days."

Denise nearly sent a jet of mead out of her nose. "Out of the question!"

"It's never been done," said Maud.

"Well . . ." said Nona.

"No," said Denise and Maud in unison.

"Think about it," said Nona, her eyes going slightly misty behind her spectacles. "We've just handed Osiris and the rest of the tribunal a victory that's likely to discourage others from organized shenanigans until the Congress has the chance to revise or rescind changes to the Decree. Athena owes us favors, and Olympus knows she spins well enough to cover for me."

"They're doing *Pinafore*," said Loki, giving her a charming smile. "You'd make a splendid Buttercup."

Nona's cheeks flushed a deep pink. "Please, sisters?"

"It's not as if we can stop you," said Maud, scowling.

"Oh, thank you! Thank you!" cried Nona, kissing her sisters in turn.

"Veles has a piano in his office," said Loki holding the door open for her. "Let's find you an audition piece."

"Do you think something by Mesomedes of Crete would be too old hat?" asked Nona.

"Perhaps you might consider something from the show," said Loki tactfully, leading her down the hall.

"Persephone's pants," said Maud, hiccuping. "If she's going to do summer stock, I'm not going to sit around in the cave watching *telenovelas* and snipping threads. Mamala! I'm coming with you."

Mamala blinked. "Seriously?"

Maud rapped her knuckles on the briefcase that contained her shears, and it popped out of existence. "And the more scantily clad men the better."

Denise made an exasperated noise. "Just who do you think is going to cover for you? It's not going to be me!"

"Of course not—you practically severed your pinky the last time you picked up my shears," said Maud. "Death will do it. He's always telling me how tired he is of wandering the world collecting souls, so I'll give him the chance to do it from the comfort of our cave. Are you ready yet, girl?"

Mamala ripped off her suit and blouse, which left her nude but for a loincloth. "You bet I am," she said, taking Maud's arm. There was a sound of crashing waves as they disappeared.

Denise eyed Uzume warily. "I don't suppose I could convince you to go somewhere nicer than Washington?"

"You could ensure that I am otherwise occupied," said Uzume, reaching down to pick up Denise's golden walking stick, which had rolled under the table. She weighed it carefully in her hands. "There's little trouble I could make in the presence of Athena and Death."

"True," said Denise.

"And since Loki, Mamala, and I will be busy with other things, you needn't worry about the others organizing any elaborate mischief."

"Also true," said Denise. "But what's in it for you?"

"You are not the only ones who desire a break from business as usual," said Uzume, kicking off her pumps. "It is quite a lot of work to manage mischief makers. It would be a pleasure, I think, to focus on one thing at a time, such as one does watching cherry blossoms. Or measuring threads of life."

"It's not an exciting job," said Denise.

Uzume nodded gravely. "You accept my offer, then?"

"Promise me that you will measure the threads of life faithfully, no more and no less."

"I promise," said Uzume.

"Good," said Denise. "I'm off to Palm Springs."

"Before you go, may I ask how I shall find the way to your cave?"

"Oh, that's simple," said Denise. "Hold out the measuring rod."

Uzume did, and Denise wrapped her fingers around Uzume's.

"Measure truly," she said softly. "For you shall hold lives in your hands."

"I understand," said Uzume.

The world dissolved around her.

The Fates' Cave in the ether was every bit as desolate and gloomy as Uzume had imagined—mist-shrouded and dark but for the glow of the fire in the brazier and the blue LED of the wi-fi router. Athena tutted when Uzume introduced herself, and Death regarded her silently from under his hood, but the three of them soon found a rhythm in the Fates' work, with Athena spinning the threads of life, Uzume measuring, and Death cutting. Uzume sang as they worked, and they continued without incident for three days and three nights.

On the fourth morning, Athena paused in her spinning to yawn. "This is deadly dull."

"Recalling that each thread is a mortal life makes it less so," said Uzume.

Death set his scythe on the floor of the cave and stretched, which made all the bones in his spinal column and shoulders pop loudly.

"I suppose you're right," said Uzume, as if he had spoken. "It is a more novel experience for me than it is for either of you. Does it weary you to sit still for so long?"

Death shrugged and lurched to his feet, shaking his feet and arms and releasing another volley of cracks.

"It wearies me," said Athena, flexing her hands. "If I'd known this is how the Fates would call in favors, I would have tried harder not to be in their debt. How on earth did you end up here?" she asked Uzume. "Was it part of the deal for you to close your little PR firm?"

"No. I volunteered," said Uzume.

"Things must have been worse than they sounded," said Athena.

"I'm ready for you to cut these three threads, when you're ready," Uzume said, nodding at Death.

Death heaved a sigh before severing the threads with a graceful arc of his scythe.

"Even though our plans came to a premature end," said Uzume, "I believe that having a bit of responsibility made us all realize that tricksters are truly capable of anything."

"Like taking over for the Fates?" asked Athena shrewdly.

"Certainly," said Uzume. "Ananse is a spider—an expert spinner. Any number of tricksters could cut threads, though Crow would find the most pleasure in using the golden shears, for he adores things that shine. But this is idle speculation. You have both promised the Fates to do their work until such a time as they return, no matter how long."

Athena and Death exchanged glances.

"Do you think your friends would be willing to take over for us?" asked Athena. "I didn't volunteer to be the Fates' drudge indefinitely. And working hunched over like this is killing Death's back."

"What could I promise them if they agree to take your places?"

Death's shoulders shook in silent laughter, and Athena scowled. "I suppose I could talk the Mediterranean deities into following the tricksters' lead the next time they introduce legislation to the Congress."

"That would be quite satisfactory," said Uzume, smiling. "You have my word that I shall find competent replacements for you as soon as possible."

"Will you promise to do the Fates' work faithfully?" asked Athena, giving Uzume her most imperious look.

"I already have," said Uzume.

"Good," said Athena. "Now, do you happen to know the damned wi-fi password?"

A month into the Fates' vacation, Denise and Nona received an urgent summons from Maud, and they all manifested at the mouth of their cave.

"This had better be important," said Nona. "I was in rehearsal!"

Denise was rubbing greenish paste off of her face with a towel. "And I was in the middle of a very expensive treatment. I sincerely hope, sisters, that—" She stopped speaking abruptly as she looked at Maud.

Maud was brown as a nut from the tropical sun, but her eyes were red, and her mouth was set in a furious line.

"Something's gone horribly wrong," she said in a hoarse voice. "Who did you get to measure the threads?" she asked Denise.

"Uzume. But she swore to do the job properly."

"Well, she found some way around her vow," said Maud. "Mamala and I were surfing in the morning, like we always do. Conditions were perfect—strong surf and the water was crystal clear. That's how I know it was a mistake."

"What was?" asked Nona, taking her sister's hand.

"The shark," said Maud, angrily. "They only attack humans when visibility is bad. The boy was only eleven. Everything about it is completely wrong. I know they're up to something. They tricked us into leaving our posts, and now there will be a run in the tapestry because one of the threads was cut too short!"

"You don't really think they'd do that, do you?" asked Nona. "What benefit is there for them?"

"Tricksters have a long tradition of biting off more than they can chew," said Denise, her voice grave. "And if they've meddled with mortal lives, they have gone too far."

"I agree," said Nona softly. "That poor child."

The Fates wrapped themselves in their white robes and entered their cave to find Ananse, Uzume, and Crow spinning, measuring, and cutting the thread of life in companionable silence.

"What is this?" shouted Denise, her face going red. "Where are Athena and Death?"

"They wearied of the work," said Uzume. "Fortunately, Ananse and

Crow were kind enough to take over. Have your vacations been enjoyable?"

"You have a lot of nerve asking that, considering what your foolish actions have done!" shouted Maud.

"I don't have the pleasure of understanding you," said Ananse, his voice soft as silk. "What have we done?"

"You killed an innocent child," said Denise.

"I thought that was part of the job," said Crow, hopping on Maud's shears to sever the strand that Uzume had threaded through the blades.

"That's strange," said Nona, removing her spectacles, cleaning them on her robe, and bending down to examine the tricksters' handiwork. "I don't see any break in the pattern."

"I know what I saw," said Maud, crossing her arms.

Denise looked over Nona's shoulder. "She's not mistaken. Everything is as it should be."

"That can't be right," said Maud.

"The workings of fate are not right or wrong," said Uzume, her graceful hands pulling the thread of life taut against Denise's measuring rod. "They simply are."

"You think we don't know that?" snapped Maud.

"Of course you know it," said Ananse, spinning two threads simultaneously with four of his arms. "You have dispassionately executed the vagaries of fate since the beginning of time."

"But perhaps that is because you had no passion for anything other than your work. Certainly nothing in the mortal realms," said Uzume.

Maud gave Uzume a poisonous glare and bent over to examine the tapestry for herself. For several long minutes, she tugged at it and poked at the pattern, but there were no weaknesses in the tricksters' work. Finally, Maud let go of the tapestry with a growl to scrub angrily at her cheeks.

"I don't understand," said Nona. "Did they trick us or didn't they?"

"The trick is that there was no trick," said Denise.

"We merely strove to educate," said Uzume.

"After all, what harm can a little knowledge do?" asked Ananse.

"Or a little empathy," said Crow.

"Get out of our cave," said Maud.

"If you and your sisters wish," said Uzume, bowing with a touch of insouciance. She offered a handkerchief to Denise, who used it to wipe the last of the green paste from her face. "Be well," she said as Denise touched her arm, which caused her to fade into the ether.

"I'm sorry I won't have the pleasure of hearing you sing," said Ananse to Nona, who was rearranging the distaff to her liking. "I do hope your understudy is up to snuff."

Nona gave him a sad smile and touched his arm to return him to the divine realms.

"For what it's worth," said Crow to Maud, "I'm sorry about the boy. We didn't want to end his life, either."

Maud snapped the shears within inches of his flight feathers, and he took off with a caw.

In unison, the three Fates sat to resume the work that had been theirs since time immemorial.

In unison, three whoopee cushions filled the ether with the sound of three reverberant farts.

The 12,987[th] Congress of Deities was notable for several reasons. Firstly, the Trickster Caucus lacked a quorum, so they were unable to serve in an advisory capacity or in any kind of voting bloc, much to the consternation of the Chaos Cabal, who had hoped to gain their support for a resolution to dissolve the Congress. Secondly, there were so many proposed amendments to the Decree that none of them passed. However, one bill that had been authored by Osiris, banning all members of the Congress from owning, operating, or working for a business in the mortal realms passed by a simple majority. However, this was of little consolation to him, given the distressing news out of the underworld that overall mortality rates were down significantly.

Osiris strongly suspected that the tricksters were behind it, but he never did figure out just how.

Brother Æthelstan's Paintbrush

Bran Heatherby

The paintbrush which Brother Æthelstan found, he nearly didn't. In fact, if not for the curiosity of a cat and the strange illumination of a paintbrush, his tale might have had a much brighter ending.

Even such a sanctified place as a monastery must have its darknesses. The rest of the brethren were long since tucked up in bed, but Æthelstan had wanted to squeeze a few more hours of work out of the day after Compline—regardless of the regimented schedule of offices they were oath-bound to follow—so he'd braved disapproval and crept up the two flights to his tiny, doorless room off a drafty corridor, cat at his heels. He couldn't resist. It was still too novel to have a space to himself after the cramped quarters in which they'd all been creating their manuscript pages, and as he prepared some more ink, Æthelstan sent up his thousandth prayer of thanksgiving that the Father Abbot had finally granted his request to use one of the unoccupied rooms of the tower. Solitary. Serene. Silent. It was beautifully quiet with no one there to jog his elbow or borrow his tools—or, for that matter, to complain that Berengar was walking over their work.

Æthelstan loved it when Berengar walked over his work.

The candle and its dangerous, forbidden flame cast eerie yellow shadows, and the corners were all the darker for the light it gave, but the bright pleasure of Berengar's company was a defence against the falling gloom. As that night wore on, however, Æthelstan began to regret his choice of companion. Ordinarily, Ber would spend the time roaming a circuit of the room, inspecting corners for mice or milk or whatever cats searched for when they were on the prowl. But, instead, Ber was restless: weaving through Æthelstan's ankles, clawing his way up his robes, jarring his hand, upsetting the water cup with his tail, and pacing restlessly from one end of the room to the other. When he miaowed for a full five minutes at something in the corner, Æthelstan finally put his brush down to pay him some attention.

It took several seconds until his eyes adjusted to determine what Berengar was pawing at. Eventually, however, Æthelstan discovered that it was a paintbrush—dusty, old, forgotten—which had fallen into a crack between two stones. With a bit of work and the aid of his belt knife, he levered it up out of the dirt. It was in fairly good shape, all things considered; the brush still had all its hair, and it formed a remarkable point for the apparent age of the handle. Pleased, Æthelstan scratched Berengar's head and went back to work in blessed quiet.

His current project wasn't a carpet page, alas. Æthelstan had been deemed too inexperienced to be given that honour, so instead, he was illuminating a page from Revelations for which Brother Gerald had already handled the script. His hand was so much neater than Æthelstan's, and it had been proven long ago that it was easier to let someone else handle the calligraphy than to endure Æthelstan scraping down his mistakes so often that the vellum wore through. Æthelstan simply protected the words from smudging with a spare scrap of parchment, and that process suited him— and the rest of his brethren—well enough.

He decided acanthus was too lively for the subject matter, and roses were a bit too cheery. Instead, Æthelstan wound ivy and nightshade through a trellis of checks and dots and crowned the entire piece with a half-circle of illustration depicting a palace silhouetted in the moonlight. He surveyed his work and quashed his pride.

Yes. That would do.

Eventually, he needed to change brushes. He needed something finer, something as quick and adept as a rabbit hopping across snow. The brush he'd ordinarily switch to was missing from his toolbox, and he couldn't find it anywhere: not beneath the table, not beneath his chair. But when he bent down to search once again under the worktable, the old but new-found brush caught his eye, and he flushed with gladness at his luck.

After five minutes of cleaning and two minutes of painting, Æthelstan was in love; the brush was a marvel. It created a smoothness of line he had never before experienced. It held ink like a dream. The way it bounced off the end of a stroke was sublime, and its balance in the hand made painting effortless. Æthelstan found himself embellishing the nightshade which bordered the page, and in the flickering candlelight, the plants seemed to move in the breeze. He was entranced. In a matter of moments, it had become his favourite brush in all the world.

When it was time to tackle the main event, he stared at the blank space in the middle of the page. In his mind's eye, a crowd of people gathered round to watch the king sit in judgement, tall and proud on his throne. Æthelstan had already outlined the background diapering that made up the surrounding throne room, drawing the crossed lines and diamonds that he would colour in later. The room, the throne, and the crowd needed to be majestic, all the better to contrast with the fear-inspiring figure planned for the front:

The demon.

In his imagination it was terrifying—a writhing black thing, hairy as a spider, with yellow eyes that glowed like fire and slit black pupils. He wanted to capture the thrill of seeing a moving shadow out of the very corner of your eye and the simmer of fear that remained when you realised nothing was there. He wanted to capture the stomach-dropping flash of a cat's eyes on the stair in the middle of the night. He wanted to capture the terror of a waking nightmare and the horror of Satan's minions made flesh.

Æthelstan shivered with excitement. If he couldn't scare readers into better behaviour with a sight like that, he would be very much surprised. Surely then the elder brethren would recognise him, he thought. Surely then they'd see how skilled he could be, if only given half a chance.

Maybe then he'd be given a carpet page of his own to paint.

Æthelstan began outlining the figures in the crowd but was sidetracked when Berengar wove round his ankles, begging for attention. "Not now," Æthelstan murmured. "Patience." When Berengar butted his head into his calf, he smiled. "Once I've finished this page, I'll find you a snack." He yawned. "And then bed." If Æthelstan's calculations were correct, he'd be able to sneak just a bit of sleep before Prime. The illustration wavered before his eyes.

Impatient, he gave up on the crowd and started instead on the central figure.

Enjoying the dexterity of his new brush, Æthelstan outlined the beast's hairy head and shoulders. He gave it overlong arms and long, knife-sharp claws. The legs he shaped as muscular as a boar's, and with several flicks he drew ears as overgrown and upright as a wolf's.

Even the outline on its own was terrifying, and Æthelstan smiled at his work. He could almost feel the hot breath of the demon on the back of his neck. His arms broke out in gooseflesh, and he shivered before he realised it was only Berengar perched on the back of his chair. Laughing at his foolishness, he reloaded his brush with ink.

Out of nowhere, Berengar went mad. He yowled loudly enough that the sound echoed round the stone chamber then ran from one corner of the workroom and back before scaling Æthelstan's robes and sinking claws into his shoulder. Startled and in pain, Æthelstan jerked, splashing three drops of ink onto the beast's face: two next to each other, and one larger below.

And then there was nothing.

Æthelstan woke in the infirmary. He had a pain in his head unlike anything he'd ever felt before—an off-balance spinning, the moment before a fall or the disorientation of a fever—dull and bright and endless all at once. Brother Peter was whispering to someone in a hushed voice as loud as the bell tower.

"They told me he was working too late again," he said. "Prior Cormac found him on the floor beside his worktable, so I expect he fell asleep and slipped off his seat. Poor fool." Æthelstan groaned.

There was a rustle of fabric, and Brother Peter's bald-chicken face leaned into view. "What were you doing, working at that hour?" His voice was harsh, but his eyes were kind.

Nothing, Æthelstan wanted to say, but the better angel on his shoulder made him speak the truth. "I wanted to finish another page," he said.

Brother Peter clicked his judgement while he investigated under Æthelstan's tongue and asked him whether he'd been trying any of Brother Niall's new tisanes. "I'm not sure I'd trust him to fetch a drink for the cows," he said then added, "It's dangerous to be alone."

"So we're taught."

"The Devil speaks to us in seductive voices when we're alone."

"Yes."

Peter looked deeply into Æthelstan's eyes. "Have you anything you'd like to confess? I can arrange—"

"No," Æthelstan said, confused. "I don't know how I got here, either. I'm sure it wasn't sin that brought me here."

"It's always sin that brings a brother here," said Brother Peter, but he simply raised a knowing eyebrow at Æthelstan and left him to doze.

Æthelstan awoke again at midday, feeling much more himself. Brother Peter let him go with an admonition not to let constant work be his method of atonement as well as a reminder that even the Lord knew when to rest, and that was that. Rumpled and still bleary, Æthelstan slumped his way to the shared dormitory. He could just make it to the chapel in time for Nones if he didn't dally, so he changed quickly.

A few steps down the staircase, he was arrested by the sensation that something was following. He stood stock still for a moment as fear wound him like a top. When it let him go, it propelled him round the first corner, then the second. He lost his footing at the next landing, caught his fall against the banister, and used the momentum to carry him round and down the second flight to the ground floor. At the bottom, he crashed into something solid but soft.

Prior Cormac's huge, weighty hands steadied him. "Odd. Your robes don't appear to be on fire."

On any other day, Æthelstan would have appreciated the comfort of the Prior's sense of humour, but on that day he was too terrified for it to make much of a dent. "Sorry, I—I beg your, er, pardon."

Cormac stepped back, amused rather than affronted. "No harm was done." He held out one arm to gesture toward the cloister. "Clearly you know the service has already begun, what with all this running as though the Devil is behind you." Æthelstan stared at him wide-eyed. Cormac's phrasing clutched at him. "How are you feeling?"

Æthelstan shook it away. "I don't . . . want to be late," he said and pushed past him to the church. He slipped into his pew and into his role, setting any fear from his mind. He wanted familiarity and love and the comfort of the world beyond this. Besides which, if he truly was ill, the best thing to do was atone for his disobedience. And the ritual of the service had always brought him strength.

He refused to think on it further. He was overtired, that was all. He'd been sneaking in too many late nights of work and now he was paying the price. It wouldn't happen again.

Nones was a balm for his anxious soul. Æthelstan sang his heart out, praying with every note for some clarity. For some idea of what the hell—perhaps literally—was happening to him.

Afterward, still riding peacefully on the inner light of the service, Æthelstan headed up into the quiet of the tower to his cubicle. He stood in the doorway for a moment. Work could be a balm too, he repeated to himself. The simple pleasure of creation could always soothe him, and there was no reason today should be different. He sat, picked up his new favourite brush, and sent up the usual silent prayer before he began.

A chirrup echoed in the corridor. Berengar ran into the room, hopped up onto Æthelstan's lap, and, with the greedy impatience Æthelstan expected of him, butted his chin into his arm until Æthelstan put down the brush to pet him with both hands. His paws were so cold from the flagstones that Æthelstan could feel them through his robe.

As he petted, he noticed a curious thing on the page in front of him: in the centre of the illumination, right where he had begun painting the demon, there was nothing.

"I don't know what's happening to me," he said to Berengar. He buried his face in the cat's fur. "I thought I'd done more than that. I remember painting his claws." The warmth of Berengar's purr made the tension in Æthelstan's spine melt. Nonetheless, he still had work to do, especially now that he had only dreamt he'd started on the demon. Æthelstan reluctantly shifted to painting with one hand and petting with the other, willing Berengar not to leave.

An hour later, just when he had finished the terrifying profile of the demon, pairing its one yellowed eye with spindly claws and a body entirely covered with wiry hair, Æthelstan was overcome by a wave of dread.

It froze his muscles in place and pressed firmly on his chest, creating the sensation that all air had been driven from the room. He strained to hear an approach, a footfall, a sound, anything, but the corridor was as silent as the grave. Berengar had been curled up asleep on the corner of the table, but now he stood with one of his feet planted firmly in the ink, his back arched, letting out an unearthly growl that filled the room. His heart in his throat, Æthelstan crept step-by-silent-step toward the open doorway. He leaned out just far enough to peer round the corner.

There was nothing to see. Not to one side, nor to the other.

With his fur up, Berengar followed, half again his usual size and leaving a trail of footprints. He slunk out to investigate, but finding nothing of interest, he turned back to stare up at Æthelstan.

"I don't know, m'friend." He was starting to get his breath back. "I don't know what that was, either." He returned to his desk and stared for a long time. Somewhere out there in the outside world, did madness run in his family? Had he been poisoned? Or was it a punishment divine and sinister?

Something touched his thigh. He jumped as all the fear he had been suppressing came flooding back in a rush. Berengar flew across the cubicle with a yowl and glared at him, puffed up. Immediately, Æthelstan knelt down and put out one hand toward him. It shook.

"I'm so sorry, Ber." When Berengar consented to cross the room and butt his head into Æthelstan's palm, relief poured through him; not only was he relieved to have the cat's forgiveness, but the warmth and the softness of his fur improved Æthelstan's outlook enormously. He let Berengar climb all over him, and moment by moment he felt more able to appraise the terror without reliving it. There was something worrisome going on, and Æthelstan only hoped he figured it out before it got any worse.

When his heart rate had settled enough that it didn't make his hand jump, he picked up the paintbrush and got back to work. First of all, the border needed filling in. Æthelstan added some more nightshades and an explosion of thorn in one corner, then he sketched, creeping down the side, a snail-like creature with spidering legs. He gave it a cheery grin, large smiling mouth, one eye, then the other—

—and blinked awake, stunned and on the floor. From that angle, he was presented with a terrifying sight: not two feet away, Berengar was chittering and batting around a six-inch long, snail-like creature with a preternat-ural smile and four spidering legs. When it ran, its legs made tiny tap-tap-tap noises on the stones. Gooseflesh rose on Æthelstan's forearms. He pressed his back against the wall to stare, his breath heaving. The thing he'd created, the thing he'd just drawn, had . . .

With a decisive pounce, Berengar killed the snail creature. As he crunched through the outer shell, Æthelstan's gorge rose. He ran out into the corridor to breathe and think.

The thing he'd painted had come alive. And now was being eaten . . . with tremendous relish, if the sounds coming from inside the room were any indication. The thing he'd painted had come alive. It had been paint and paper until he finished it. He finished it by painting the face. The thing had come alive when he had given it a face. The thing he'd painted had come alive. The things he was painting were *becoming* alive. It explained the shimmer of movement he'd seen in the leaves when he first painted them, and it explained why they seemed to be wilting now. It explained how they seemed to wave in an invisible wind.

But didn't explain why the demon he'd painted that day remained paint and paper. Gingerly, Æthelstan crept back into the room. There were translucent bits of shell scattered round, and Berengar was cleaning him-self. Æthelstan did his best not to look at him or his mess but inspected his paper instead.

The demon was still there, and hadn't—

All of the blood in Æthelstan's body turned cold at once.

He picked up his brush and, trembling, painted another snail creature as he had before. Head, a spiral shell and two legs. Wide grin, one eye, anoth-er—

There was another flash of white, but Æthelstan was half expecting it this time. The shrug of the earth came and the strange sudden flatness of the air surrounding him, but his grip on the table edge held him upright. And crawling across the vellum was another snail-like being, real as life, leaving a trail as it pulled itself forward.

With a noise of pleasure, Berengar hopped up and began batting it about. It curled up into a tight ball, its legs wrapping somewhat round its shell. It made a scratching noise when it slid across the vellum, like autumn leaves crunched underfoot. Æthelstan bit down on a sob then pressed both hands against his mouth to hold in further reaction when the full realization crashed down upon him. He, a mortal man, had brought lives into the world with the paintbrush. Two small meals for Berengar and one . . .

An image of the demon flashed into Æthelstan's mind. Fear ran through his veins like spring water: thin and quick and cold.

He pocketed the brush and ran.

In the corridor, he nearly collided with Brother Niall but spun to avoid him. Ignoring Niall's cry of alarm, Æthelstan pelted down the stairs. Nearly at the bottom, he turned his ankle slightly, but at that point the staircase made an abrupt turn and he ricocheted harmlessly off the wall and into the corridor, where he made for the kitchens.

"Supper isn't for another hour," called Brother Everard when Æthelstan burst in and pushed headlong against the wall of steam and the scent of roasting vegetables.

"I only need to borrow your fire for a moment," he said. Shielding his motions from the rest of the room, he produced the brush from his sleeve and quickly dropped it into the centre of the flames. Sparks flew up and dissipated in tiny green flashes of light.

"What do you need it for?" said Everard, now an arm's-length from Æthelstan's back. Æthelstan spun.

"Just trying something."

"More of your paint creations?"

Æthelstan tried to look as bland as possible in spite of the pulsing, eager way his heart was throttling him. "Yes. Yes, that's right." His mind raced. "You see, some pigments are nicer when burnt, so I wondered if—"

"Oh, never mind." Everard waved it away. "It's all the same to me. Hurry up; you'll need to clear out before supper, or you'll be conscripted. Oh!" He knelt quickly and plucked up something from the hearth. "And you've dropped your brush."

When Æthelstan saw the condition the brush was in, he nearly ran screaming from the room; Everard was calm and expectant as he held it out, clearly unaware of the ghastly horror in his hand. But the paintbrush looked just as it had when Æthelstan first laid eyes upon it.

The fire had done nothing at all.

In an empty daze, Æthelstan took the brush and allowed himself to be chivvied from the room. He floated to the church, keeping far from the shadows the entire way.

Æthelstan hid in the sacristy, continuously reliving the unholy movements of his creation and the crunch of Berengar's teeth until he could flee to the refectory and take refuge in the comfort of supper. Its silence, its regimented rituals of gesture and food, and the constant recitation from Brother Gerbert in the corner might help to soothe his spiralling panic enough that he could swallow.

But midway through his stew, the feeling of an oncoming storm thickened the air in the room. Every hair on his body pricked on end.

Over the sound of the reader, a laugh echoed through the hall. A laugh like ripping parchment. A laugh like a dry quill scratch. Æthelstan froze, then slowly turned round to see if he could identify where it was coming from. His breath came quickly, and he fought to keep his seat. No one was laughing. Furthermore, no one appeared to be taking any notice of the sound whatsoever. He scanned the room, but everyone else was focusing on their food.

The laugh sounded again, nearer, more intimately, and once more he seemed to be the only one to hear. Panic rose in Æthelstan's throat. His mouth ran bone dry. Across the table, Brother Osric furrowed his brow and stared at him, his spoon arrested halfway to his mouth. Æthelstan shook his head in a rough jerking movement intended to convey that he was fine. Osric didn't seem to believe him, but he resumed eating nonetheless.

"And for this we give thanks . . ." read Brother Gerbert, his prayer intended to keep the brethren in holy thoughts throughout their meal, but Æthelstan rather thought there would be little chance of that for him. The laugh echoed down from the rafters and nearly drowned out the prayer.

Below it came another sound, just as terrifying: footsteps, loud enough to be heard over everything—laughter and reader alike. They were dry but resonant, like scraping hair off a hide. And just as with the laughter, it seemed Æthelstan was the only one who could hear.

Shhhk. Shhhk. Shhhk.

He gripped the table top and tried to look round without looking round. He glanced into the glossy pitcher to see the reflection of the space behind him, but the surface was too rippled and dark to be anything but frustrating.

Shhhk. Shhhk. Shhhk.

Æthelstan tried to breathe normally. He tried to swallow.

Just when Brother Osric's frown had turned the corners of his mouth down far enough to distort his face, and just when he had lifted his hand to call over the Prior, there was a ruckus at the far end of the refectory. Shouts went up and brothers dove after something running along the floor. When it rounded the corner towards Æthelstan, the relief made his guts watery.

It was Berengar.

The unearthly laughter that had filled the refectory disappeared, and with it went the fear. Æthelstan fumbled to catch the cat as it leapt into his arms.

How did you get in here? Æthelstan thought, scratching under Berengar's chin and ignoring the tremble in his own limbs. The atmosphere in the refectory now seemed just as it always had been.

"Æthelstan?" Prior Cormac said at his elbow. Æthelstan was suddenly unnerved by all the eyes looking on him, by all the thoughts focused on him. It seemed as if someone might *hear.*

"*I don't know,*" he gestured, mindful of the rule of silence.

"*Take him outside,*" the Prior gestured in reply.

Wishing with all his heart to become invisible, Æthelstan nodded. The Prior ambled away, and Æthelstan took a last swallow of his wine to wet his throat. He hoped no one would notice how his hand shook.

But Brother Osric was still staring, and his scrutiny was particularly horrible from so close. "You look as though you're seeing demons," he muttered under his breath.

There was nothing Æthelstan could think of to say in response. He twitched his mouth in a wan imitation of a smile and stood with Berengar still cradled in one arm. As he skulked from the refectory, he kept his eyes turned squarely downward. He abandoned the rest of his supper, needing a few moments to himself before Vespers for quiet reflection.

Thankfully, he heard neither the sound of the laughter nor the shuffle of feet, yet the creeping feeling of being observed still followed him as he dropped Berengar into the cloister and ran to the sanctuary. Æthelstan ensconced himself in the rear of the chapel to wait for the service. He didn't have long to wait, thank God, and the creeping feeling melted away in the comforting rhythm of prayer and the warm press of bodies around him. He was overcome with the same relief he always felt at the passing of pain. For a little while, he could forget the strange laughter and the bone-deep fear, and he could focus on singing out. He prayed for forgiveness, and he prayed for strength. He prayed for wisdom, and he prayed to be relieved of the burden of the unearthly paintbrush plaguing him. He prayed, most of all, to be safe. He tried not to fidget as he listened to the reading, and he tried for a while to lend his will to those listed in the intercessory prayers.

As the words washed over him, Æthelstan was struck with an idea so obvious he wondered that it hadn't occurred to him before. It was an idea that would cleanse the demonic presence from the paintbrush and his life. Relief flowed down his spine, and he smiled. The revelation freed him to sing from his gut, letting the words transport him somewhere untroubled. He felt better than he had in days. A feeling not unlike joy began to push to the corners all the worry and dread that gripped him. Caught up in the song, his spirit flew.

Once the service was over, he lingered in the shadows until the rest of the brethren had gone on to their next duties. When he was certain he was alone in the chapel, he slunk out to the front and held the brush up to the light. There was still no mark to show that it had been in the fire. He was overcome by a massive shiver.

Without further ceremony, he dropped the brush into the sanctified water.

If the world had been a fair place, the holy water would have boiled away as the devil was purged from it. But no, the damned thing only sank to the bottom. Æthelstan stared. Nothing more happened.

After a few minutes, he took a deep breath and said a prayer, then pushed up his sleeve to fish out the brush. Upon examination, it looked wet, but otherwise exactly the same as it always had. Frustrated, he took two steps sideways and dropped it into the deep crack in the flagstones next to the wall.

He quick-marched to the door, but leaden guilt weighed down his feet and he paused. It wouldn't be fair to leave it, he thought. It would only be passing the burden onto someone else. And if they came to be haunted by the same troubles Æthelstan was experiencing, he would never forgive himself. He levered the brush out of the crack, then knelt in the back of the church until the brethren filed in for Compline. He clutched the paintbrush and bowed his head over it, praying for further sanity and guidance and protection.

Why him? Where did the brush come from? Was it the brush itself that was waking these creatures, or something inside Æthelstan? Why did he have to be the one to find it? He'd done everything he was meant to, had followed all the precepts laid out by the church and his training, but here he was in this predicament regardless. Somehow, he'd been induced to sin, and the paintbrush was his punishment. He wanted to confess in hopes of absolution, but how would that go?

Father Abbot, I am being followed by a demon I created using this paintbrush I found in my cubicle.

Father Abbot, I am being followed by a demon, and I feel like one of our cats is defending me.

Father Abbot, I hear unholy footsteps whenever I leave the sanctuary of the chapel.

There was but one commonality shared between all these: Æthelstan himself. Each was caused by him, and all were happening to him. No, the core problem itself was his responsibility, and he was bound to be the one to fix it.

And surely he would succeed; after all, he had lived within the church since he was a boy. If anyone could find the solution, he could. His chest swelled. If this was a test, he was certain to emerge victorious.

But his brief moment of confidence was punctured immediately when he realised he'd not the foggiest idea how to begin. He set his jaw and took a deep breath, ignoring the rapid tightening of his throat.

Ora et labora, his brethren were instructed. To pray and to work. Prayer was easy; Æthelstan could do little *but* pray, sitting there in the back of the sanctuary and hoping for God to show him the way to fix what he'd done. *Labora,* on the other hand, *to work,* was less easy. For one thing, it would probably entail leaving the sanctuary of his own volition. He knew he'd been shirking his duties and hiding in the church, but so far it was the only place he'd been able to stay where he hadn't been interrupted by bowel-churning fear or the steady *shhhk-shhhk-shhhk* of dry footfalls. He needed to do more. The usual penance wasn't going to be enough to save him.

Ora et labora may have been sufficient for others, but they weren't haunted by the crunch of teeth biting down on something they'd accidentally created. He felt as if he'd hear that sound echoing in the back of his head for the rest of his life. Æthelstan bent his head and fought the urge to weep.

A hand on his shoulder made him shout.

"I didn't intend to startle you," said Prior Cormac, who appeared a bit surprised himself by Æthelstan's outburst. He smiled. "But you looked too lost in your own thoughts to notice we've left."

Heart racing, Æthelstan pushed to his feet. His knees felt like dry wood and rusted metal. He couldn't look Prior Cormac in the eye. "Thank you. I . . . er. I *was* lost, rather. Thanks, er, for . . ."

"You won't find much answer in starving yourself of rest. Asceticism can only go so far," he said, his round face soft with kindness. "No matter what others might say." He clasped Æthelstan's shoulder and led him out into the corridor. "Private contemplation is one thing, but if what troubles you isn't between you and God, and if you'd like an ear, I've found there's many a tangle that's been unbound when I've unburdened myself." His chatter enfolded them as they climbed the narrow stair up to the dormitory, and Cormac's steady serenity was a warm bubble of comfort that kept the strange crawling feeling from Æthelstan's neck, like a hood in the rain.

Æthelstan prepared himself for bed as quickly as possible, wanting his back to the wall and the thin blanket up to his chin. The solidity of the flagstones under his mattress was a small comfort.

For hours he lay and stared at the dark hole that was the door, hoping upon hope not to see a face there and not to hear the dreaded footfalls of the beast. He prayed for a quiet—if sleepless—night.

The room was filled with the familiar noise of sleeping men, the snoring and the farting and the turning over on their beds, but none of it masked the sound when it came.

Shhhk. Shhhk. Shhhk.

Fear solidified Æthelstan's muscles as the dusty smell of old parchment swept through the dormitory. Already burning too low, the room's lamps guttered in a sourceless breeze.

Shhhk. Shhhk. Shhhk.

The laugh came, turning Æthelstan's guts to water. Not another man in the room seemed to hear. Their rhythmic breath and gentle snores went on unbroken while the footfalls approached, closer and closer and closer. The nearer the sound came, the harder Æthelstan fought to move, but the more he fought the smaller was his range of motion. The smell stung as it slid down the back of his throat. His blood froze in his veins.

A bolt shot out of the darkness, a thing of fur and claw which was highlighted in a dark-bright-dark rhythm as it passed through the moonlight pouring in at the windows. It flickered past Æthelstan's feet and then back into shadow. He heard Berengar chitter. He heard Berengar yowl.

Then there was silence.

Scarcely a moment later Berengar strutted down the aisle between the beds, tail held high. When he reached Æthelstan he hopped onto the bed and curled up to clean himself. He was covered in some sort of powder and smelled like an old library, but he seemed content.

There was a murmur from the next bed over, and then the next one, and then the next. Someone lit another lamp, and soon the room was filled with the grumbles of waking men.

"Did I hear a cat?" someone asked.

Brother Osric peered over at Berengar. "Æthelstan, isn't that the same one from supper?"

Æthelstan thought quickly. "I, I was so cold last night, I thought—"

"He's not allowed in here. Put him outside," said Brother Niall, sounding still half asleep.

"Cold? Are you ill?" piped up someone from across the room.

"It's not cold," Niall said. "If you're ill, you should see Brother Peter."

Æthelstan fisted his hands in his blanket. He looked at Berengar and sighed, dread beginning to coalesce in his stomach. Nevertheless, he did as he was told. They stared at each other in the hall for several moments, then Berengar settled himself primly outside the door, his tail lashing expectantly as if he planned to stand guard until morning.

As he went back to bed, Æthelstan prayed with all his heart that he would. Still, sleep came only in fits and starts, and by the time Prime came he was so tired he wondered how he was meant to make it through the day.

When he shuffled from the dormitory with the rest of the brethren to start their morning, Æthelstan was soothed to see Berengar still waiting outside the door. Whether that explained the rest of the demon-less night remained to be seen.

Cat companion or no, the morning air weighed heavy on Æthelstan's shoulders, and each breath was thick and intentional. It felt as if someone had been sitting on his chest while he'd tried—and failed—to sleep. He stepped into the cloister on his way to the chapel and sucked in air. The cool dampness did something to ease his shattered nerves, but he knew it was only a matter of time before the creeping feeling on the back of his neck returned, as well as the certainty that something was *looking*. Watching.

Knowing.

He stared at the few lank roses that had survived this far into autumn. A few honeybees bumbled from empty bloom to empty bloom, looking for pollen and having little luck. Æthelstan ran his fingers over the lavender and crushed a few of the leaves. When he bent to breathe in some comfort, he heard the sound that had been pricking at him since supper the night before.

Shhhk. Shhhk. Shhhk.

Frantic, Æthelstan looked round for Berengar, but the cloister was un-characteristically empty, and instead of the rustle of leaves or the whistle of wind through the stones he could only hear the footsteps, getting louder, moment by moment. Louder. Closer.

Shhhk. Shhhk. Shhhk.

Æthelstan turned tail and fled.

The change in air was palpable once he crossed the threshold into the chapel. It was rarefied, holy, and as he took his place in the row his head was clearer than it had been all night. But with that clarity came the soul-deep certainty that he'd have to *do* something. Work, and not just prayer.

He needed to know where the brush had come from and why he'd been the one cursed to find it. Unfortunately, nothing he'd ever read, no spark of training, had ever addressed the topic of painted figures coming to life.

No wonder, really.

Prime went on round him as Æthelstan thought and prayed and thought some more. His hands had been clasped so tightly and for so long that by the time he came to a decision they slipped against each other, slick with sweat. As soon as the service was over, he would head directly to the library; since no answers were forthcoming from his own experience, he'd have to do some research until he found word of someone else's. Research had never been his strength, but if any situation called for an exercising of his meagre abilities, this was it.

The sound of his name yanked his attention back to the present.

"Æthelstan, walk with me," Prior Cormac said. Æthelstan looked round to find that Prime was over, and the church was emptying.

Laying a hand on his shoulder, Cormac steered him out and into the cloister. He launched them on a path along the walk which encircled the autumn-dead flowers and fading lawn. Æthelstan hadn't realised how cold it was getting. "Is there something that's been troubling you?"

Wide-eyed, Æthelstan's brain whirred, trying to decide what—if any-thing—he could say. This was just the opportunity he'd wished for, but he couldn't imagine the outcome would be any more favourable in real life than the tragedies he'd envisioned. "N-no," he said. "I can't think what that would be."

"You're certain? You seem distracted."

Æthelstan swallowed and shook his head. "I would tell you so."

The small smile that tinged the Brother Prior's face was just the same as it ever was. Æthelstan had been an eager child, and even before he was of age to become a novice he had been excited to impress the Prior with his interpretations of scripture and his willingness to work. Whenever he turned that careworn and quiet expression on Æthelstan, it always made him feel like he was home.

"I know you would," said Cormac. He squeezed Æthelstan's shoulder and nudged him in the direction of the library. "Go on. You know better than I do what you're called to do today. And you know how to find me should you change your mind."

Æthelstan took a deep breath. "I do."

In the library, his hopes started out high, but as the work period wound on without sign or sense of an answer Æthelstan felt the knot of fear turn tighter. In desperation, he climbed up to the dustier, older scrolls tucked away on the hard-to-reach shelves. The ones seldom looked for. The ones full of apocrypha and folk tales and myth.

There, in a scroll of Gnostic learning, he found a ray of light to pierce the darkness. If he'd ever read about it before, that time was so far beyond the reach of his day-to-day life that his knowledge had crumbled to dust. A scholar told the story:

"*Samael was born isolated and thereafter grew alone, imagining he was the only God. Blind and ignorant, he created the seven heavens as well as the material and animal world, but his was the source of evil, for he did not know the beauty of the spirit.*

"*The God of Grace, He whom we call Lord, breathed true life into all the creatures Samael created. In his jealousy, Samael raged and spat and swore his revenge, but no matter how he tried he could do nothing but create a simulacrum of life. Creatures he created lived, but were soulless, black things, cursed to an empty existence until the God of Grace planted them with true life. Ineffability was more than Samael could inspire.*

"*One day, Samael swore that he would trap true divinity into a material form. To that end, he plucked hairs from his own lion head, a quill from a golden goose, and a twig from a world tree, and together fashioned a brush with which he could paint into life anything his will desired. But it was not to be; still Samael lacked the spark necessary to create full life. Frustrated and furious, he threw the paintbrush into the darkness at the edge of space, and took his place as Samael, The Blind God.*"

Æthelstan pulled the paintbrush from his sleeve to examine it in the light of the lamp. The wood of the handle was dark, smoothed into a satin finish by the touch of years and hands. The ferrule was thin with age, yet still sturdy. The hairs were fine and elegantly sprung.

For a moment more Æthelstan stared at the brush, but he began to feel the creeping suspicion that the more he looked at the brush, the more the brush seemed to be looking back. Quickly he pocketed it then shook off his gooseflesh.

Impossible.

Then, from out of the dark, deep in the heart of the library, came the sound he'd never wanted to hear again—and this time it was louder than before.

Shhhk. Shhhk. Shhhk.

Humming under his breath, Brother Lambert hove into view at the end of the aisle. He carefully slid a book into its place, nodded genially but distractedly to Æthelstan, then wandered off, neither pinioned by fear nor aware of the demon's approach.

Shhhk. Shhhk. Shhhk.

An overpowering scent slammed into Æthelstan, a palpable wall of rotting parchment and mouldering ink. The smell clawed its way into his sinuses and dug in, and as he choked he heard a voice, rasping and dry as dust.

"*Æthelstan.*"

Æthelstan dropped the scroll and ran.

He bolted out of the library and ricocheted round the corner, nearly hitting two brothers but spinning out of their path and continuing his flight. It felt as if the demon were drawing its fingers up the back of his neck in a tender caress, and any moment he expected the shock of nails cutting open his throat from behind.

"*Æthelstan.*"

The dry-death smell and the sound of rasping footsteps echoed down the corridor towards him. The pricking feeling of its approach lifted all his hair on end. He skidded to a stop; he was pinned down like a cornered rabbit, with the source of the sound between him and the church doors. He couldn't think, and he couldn't move, and all he could do was wait for the demon to come nearer.

Shhhk. Shhhk. Shhhk.

With a flush of terror, he bolted in the opposite direction, away from the smell and the sound and, unfortunately, away from the church. He ran out into the cloister and down a side path, then back into the building on the other side with no idea where he was going, only hoping that if he ran fast enough he might be able to escape.

"Æthelstan."

When he reached the base of the tower, an idea struck him. He hesitated. Perhaps if he could get to his cubicle, he could—

He took the steps two at a time, even as a breeze pushed down at him carrying the scent of mouldering calfskin and rotting oak gall. He held his breath up three flights to his workroom. On his table, sitting directly on top of the illuminated page, was Berengar.

The cat stood silently and stretched. He chirruped and butted his head into Æthelstan's arm, and with the other Æthelstan swept the page onto the floor to reveal a blank sheet of parchment. He snatched up an ink bottle, shook it, and produced the infernal paintbrush from the sleeve of his robe.

His hand shaking, Æthelstan poised over the parchment. Now that he was in a position to do something, he wasn't certain how to begin.

"Æthelstan."

Fright spurred him on. Using Berengar as inspiration he drew the outline of a lion—large claws, large teeth—but it occurred to him that he had no easy way to indicate scale. He could be drawing a lion that was no bigger than a rat. Panic choked him. He drew a chair, then he drew a tree, but the tree only bent in the breeze and he had no idea if that was going to be enough.

"Æthelstan."

Tears made the figures blurry. Æthelstan dashed them away and blinked hard to clear his vision.

"Æthelstan."

The voice grew louder, and Æthelstan could hear the footsteps rasping up the stairs. There was breath now, a heavy sound with a click at the end like a knife trimming a quill. He was out of ideas; his mind spun in circles, and terror made his thoughts feel spongy. After throwing another sheet of parchment to the floor, he started again, this time beginning with a sketch of the room he was in and placing the lion within it. Panic made his hand shake, but still he painted bold, black strokes. He painted a lash-like tail. He painted sharp claws, long enough to curve into the floor.

"Æthelstan."

Next to him on the table, Berengar began chittering, that peculiar sound he made just before he went on the attack. He started to yowl, but instead of its usual shrillness this time the noise dropped in pitch as it got louder. The shift was unbearable. Berengar jumped to the floor and continued howling, and Æthelstan's lungs burned for air as he watched Berengar begin to grow.

He shifted taller, then longer, then darker, eventually turning more black than pitch: black as a starless, moonless night, black so dark that the light coming from the window was swallowed up by his fur. Berengar's tail became whip-like, his ruff grew longer, and his claws extended long enough to scrape against the floor. And his eyes . . . Æthelstan threw himself back against the wall and sent up every prayer he could summon. Berengar turned his glowing yellow eyes his way and grinned. His teeth were like blackthorn.

With a mighty scream and a lash of his tail, Berengar bounded out into the corridor. After a breath, Æthelstan followed.

Cresting the top of the stairs, whispering his name loud enough for the sound to echo off the stone, was the demon.

It looked unfinished. Unformed. Its face was smooth and white-yellow-grey, translucent, hairless and featureless but for three dark blots on its surface that formed a howling mask. When it moved, Æthelstan was reminded of puppets and scarecrows. An inky outline floated in the space surrounding it and defined its form. It flickered strangely, as if Æthelstan weren't meant to see it but out of the corner of his eye. The demon lifted its hand toward him. Its claws were long and sharp, just as Æthelstan had painted them.

"*Æthelstan.*"

When it opened its mouth, its lips ripped apart and oozed a black ichor that stained grey every fissure and torn edge. The pits of its eyes never blinked.

Berengar, even larger now than before, growled in a voice that shook the flagstones, then attacked. Claws and teeth flashing, he pounced at the demon's face. But the demon only batted him away as if he were no more than an insect, knocking him to the ground, then took another step closer to Æthelstan.

Slowly, Berengar got to his feet. Growling, he dragged himself forward to sink his teeth into the demon's boar-like leg and was kicked away with a power Æthelstan wouldn't have believed. In a smear of night, Berengar smacked against the opposite wall with a sickening crack. He slid down, and whimpered when he hit the floor.

Once more, the demon turned its soul-sucking gaze Æthelstan's way. Its feet made a scraping noise along the stones that lifted gooseflesh on Æthelstan's arms. He couldn't move. The demon was close enough that the smell of rot was overpowering; it stung his sinuses and closed his throat. He couldn't breathe, and his feet wouldn't move, and still the demon came closer. "*Berengar . . .*" Æthelstan gasped out. His heart beat so hard it hurt.

When the demon reached toward him again, Berengar let out an unearthly, broken keen. He threw himself forward, panting, wild, limping on three legs, and with a last-ditch effort slammed ineffectually into the demon's side. He fell to the ground in a crumpled lump.

The expression that stretched the demon's face was the most sickening thing Æthelstan had ever seen in his life. Its maw opened wide, stretching threads of flesh between its lips. Its teeth were in doubled inky-black rows, and as it reached down to snatch up Berengar's limp body, they glistened. In one strike it bit down on the back of Berengar's neck. There was a grating, crunching noise, and Berengar's legs dangled, lifeless. Nauseated with fear and loss, Æthelstan watched as the demon grew larger and larger while Berengar shrank. It appeared to be drinking him in, sucking him dry of all the power Æthelstan had just given him. The demon now filled the corridor in a hulking mass, and the stench of mouldering vellum was so strong Æthelstan's gorge rose. The demon shook its head, jiggling Berengar's tiny body, and dropped him to the floor. It turned Æthelstan's way to open its mouth as if laughing.

Æthelstan bolted for the stairs.

He flew down the first landing and slammed his shoulder into the corner at the bottom of the first flight, but he kept running. The demon's presence itched between his shoulder blades as it pursued. Æthelstan's breath was harsh as he turned the corner at the bottom of the second flight. He reached for the bannister to swing himself around the corner of the landing, but in his haste he misjudged the distance and fell into space, tumbling and twisting and spinning down the stone steps. His body flared with pain, and the darkness of the stairwell blazed a brilliant white.

At the bottom of the stairs he came to rest, twisted and shattered. The ringing in his ears increased as he watched the paintbrush tumble down one step, then another, then hit the bottom. Slowly it rolled along the floor towards a shadowed crack between the flagstones. It disappeared, and Æthelstan's vision went black.

Shhhk. Shhhk. Shhhk.

Human Resources

Antioch Grey

From: Luke Malton
To: Susan Maltravers
Subject: Application for Funding

Hi Susan

Now that the latest funding round for research has opened, I would like to put forward my application, so please see attached! I hope it speaks for itself, but if you have any queries, please let me know.

Luke

Attachment: Does Human Sacrifice Work? A double blind test proposal.

_____

From: Susan Maltravers
To: Luke Malton
Subject: Application for Funding

Luke

Are you serious? This is the goats all over again, and you know that you didn't get statistically significant results with them. This is just a waste of time.

Susan

From: Luke Malton
To: Susan Maltravers
Subject: Application for Funding

Susan

If you'd read the proposal, you would see that I had addressed those issues. It is my hypothesis that the very reason that the goat sacrifice experiments didn't work is that (a) the prayers were addressed to the wrong god, and (b) goats have insufficient soul value to attract the attention of the right sort of god. We need to step up both the quality and quantity of the sacrifices to develop the close working relationship with a deity that is necessary to obtain favours.

Luke

———————————————————

From: Susan Maltravers
To: Luke Malton
Subject: Application for Funding

Luke

Ok, I will concede that your new proposal does address these issues. However, I notice that it is very light on suggestions as to how to source human sacrifices? We can hardly abduct people from the street. And surely the costs of housing the sacrifices after acquisition and before sacrifice would be prohibitive? The straw bill alone last time was exorbitant.

I need assurances that you have costed this appropriately before I even look at methodology.

Susan

From: Luke Malton
To: Susan Maltravers
Subject: Application for Funding

Susan

Ok, the straw bill was a little larger than I expected last time, but whatever happened to science for science's sake?

Luke

———————————————

From: Susan Maltravers
To: Luke Malton
Subject: Application for Funding

Luke

You know what the current environment is like—I need proper costings and some suggestions as to how we can monetise the research afterwards.

Susan

———————————————

From: Luke Malton
To: Susan Maltravers
Subject: Application for Funding

Susan

I've reworked the costings and put together some ideas for putting the proposals up for sale if the research is successful. Frankly, even with a low correlation, some people will be so desperate for additional luck that they will take the chance that it does work.

Luke

Attachment: Cost/benefit analysis of double blind testing human sacrifice
    Attachment: Monetising human sacrifice: some suggestions

From: Susan Maltravers
To: Luke Malton
Subject: Application for Funding

Luke

Ok, that looks better. I can work with this. I'll run the numbers and see if I can cut costs somewhere along the line. The budget is still higher than our current grant limit, but the research looks intriguing.

I do like the analysis dealing with the combination of staff development/appraisals interfacing with a human sacrifice element. The big beasts in business studies are always interested in something new to take to the market—if we can get some cross-jurisdictional buzz going, maybe there would be some joint funding initiatives that we could tap into?

Susan

From: Luke Malton
To: Susan Maltravers
Subject: Application for Funding

Susan

Just as long as we get top billing on the publication of the research. I don't want that bunch of shysters taking the credit for my idea.

Luke

From: Susan Maltravers
To: Luke Malton
Subject: Application for Funding

Luke

Noted, and good points.

I've had a quick chat with William Percher, and I'll copy you in on the email suggesting we collaborate.

Susan

From: Susan Maltravers
To: William Percher
CC: Luke Malton
Subject: Co-Funding Project

William

As discussed, I attach the original proposal and Luke's update on costings and proposed monetisation.

What do you think?

Obviously, we would take the lead on publication, but if this comes off, there would be plenty of glory to go round.

Susan
Attachment: Does Human Sacrifice Work? A double blind test proposal.
Attachment: Cost/benefit analysis of double blind testing human sacrifice
Attachment: Monetising human sacrifice: some suggestions

From: William Percher
To: Susan Maltravers; Luke Malton
Subject: Co-Funding Project

Hi All

Yeah, this looks exciting, and we would be interested in taking it further. I can run it past Bob later today and get his buy in, which is key to progressing it higher up the department.

I think it might be helpful if I add some performance indicators to the Monetisation analysis, to show how you could really focus on individual staff performance on several key factors. The enhanced productivity through unnatural wastage on its own is impressive, but if we leverage the soul energy by rewarding key staff at no additional cost to the firm, the benefits triple, according to my numbers.

And hey, if the numbers don't look that good, we can always have a dry run and see if we can improve them! The office junior isn't exactly pulling his weight at the moment, so sourcing a 'volunteer' wouldn't be difficult.

Just kidding.

William

From: Susan Maltravers
To: Luke Malton
Subject: Kidding?

Luke

Just a quick suggestion—perhaps it would be better if you didn't share the precise details of your methodology with William? Just the protocols for the double blind testing.

Susan

From: Luke Malton
To: Susan Maltravers
Subject: Kidding?

Susan

Total agreement here. Don't want the bastards stealing our ideas.

Or our livers.

Luke

From: William Percher
To: Bob Summerson
Subject: FW: Co-Funding Project

Hi Bob

See below about the proposal we discussed yesterday.

If we can get the right contract with Luke . . .

William

From: Bob Summerson
To: William Percher
Subject: FW: Co-Funding Project

Hi William

Pull the personnel files of the department, and let's look at the last round of appraisals and get the lawyers working on something suitable to screw them over, yeah?

Bob

From: William Percher
To: Susan Maltravers; Luke Malton
BCC: Bob Summerson
Subject: FW: Co-Funding Project

Hi Susan/Luke

Ok, Bob is on board, depending on getting the right sort of contract in place. I will get my secretary to see when we all have a window and put something in the diary asap.

William

Diary Entry:

25 March 2016 2pm to 3.30 pm, tea and biscuits for four

Required: Susan Maltravers; Luke Malton; William Percher; Lara Belitre

Meeting to discuss legals

From: Susan Maltravers
To: Luke Malton
Subject: What the hell?

Luke

What the hell just happened there? I feel the urge to count my fingers after that meeting, as I'm not sure that they're still attached.

Susan

From: Luke Malton
To: Susan Maltravers
Subject: What the hell?

Susan

I'm just checking both my testicles are still attached.

Luke

———————————————

From: Susan Maltravers
To: Luke Malton
Subject: What the hell?

Luke

Ordinarily, I would tell you not to be so crude.

This is not ordinarily. We really need to watch our backs here, and our fronts, and our bollocks—whether actual or metaphorical.

Susan

———————————————

From: Luke Malton
To: Susan Maltravers
Subject: What the hell?

Susan

Agreed.

I'm looking through the Demonology Catalogue to see if Lara Belitre is listed, or some variant, or something that looks like her.

If not, perhaps there's something in there we can use on our side in the negotiations.

Luke

From:	William Percher
To:	Susan Maltravers; Luke Malton
BCC:	Bob Summerson
Subject: Co-Funding Legals

Hi Susan/Luke

I haven't had a response to our proposals on the legals—have you had any thoughts?

William

_____

From:	Susan Maltravers
To:	William Percher
CC:	Luke Malton; Bob Summerson
Subject: Co-Funding Legals

William

We are currently reviewing the proposals with our own legal advisers and will come back to you shortly—do you have a deadline you're working to?

Susan

_____

From:	William Percher
To:	Bob Summerson
Subject: FW: Co-Funding Legals

Bob

See below about the legals—they're getting it reviewed! Disaster.

What shall I say about a deadline? I can crank up the pressure, but we don't want to risk losing them.

William

From: Bob Summerson
To: William Percher
Subject: FW: Co-Funding Legals

William

I think we should work on a plan B. It's surely not hard to work out the proto-cols from this—it's just an extension of his work with goats, and a copy of that's filed in the library. Dig it out. Read it. Work out how to replicate it with people.

Then we don't need their research or their double blind protocols. We can sell it to the investment houses as is. They bought into all that nonsense about horoscopes last year and spent a fortune working out whether Leo rising and trine Uranus was good for business.

It was certainly good for our business, and the disclaimer meant they couldn't sue us about that SNAFU in the bond market, which just goes to show that Lara is worth her very large fees.

Bob

———————————————

From: William Percher
To: Bob Summerson
Subject: Goats

Bob

Apparently I will need a lot of goats—do I have your authorisation to buy some?

William

From: Bob Summerson
To: William Percher
Subject: Goats

William

See if there is a leasing option and if that is better value for money.

Bob

From: William Percher
To: Bob Summerson
Subject: Goats

Bob

There is a rental option. Who knew you could hire goats?

Thing is, if you don't return them in the condition they arrived in, there are penalties.

William

From: Bob Summerson
To: William Percher
Subject: Goats

William

Get Lara to opine on the contract.

Bob

From: William Percher
To: Lara Belitre
CC: Bob Summerson
Subject: Goats

Hi Lara

Bob has asked if you would cast an eye over this contract—we are looking to hire a herd for testing purposes and there may be some goat wastage. Are we liable for damages/costs of replacement?

William

Attachment: Contract for Hiring One (1) Herd of Goats

From: Lara Belitre
To: William Percher
CC: Bob Summerson
Subject: Goats

Hi William

See comments on the attached—basically nothing to worry about. There's no clause to restrict sacrificing the goats, and there is a drafting lacuna in the definition of 'same condition' which allows you to drive a coach and horses through their damages clause.

Same condition isn't defined as still alive.

So you should be fine.

Lara

Attachment: Contract for Hiring One (1) Herd of Goats—Redline copy

From: Bob Summerson
To: William Percher
CC: Lara Belitre
Subject: Goats

William

Order the goats.

Lara—thanks.

Bob

From: William Percher
To: BillyGoatGruff Goat Rentals
BCC: Bob Summerson

Hi

I would like to rent a herd of your goats for a period of a fortnight commencing Monday next.

I attach a copy of the signed agreement, as discussed, and we have paid the required deposit into your bank account.

We look forward to receiving our goats.

Regards

William Percher
Office Co-ordinator and Goat Herd

From: BillyGoatGruff Goat Rentals
To: William Percher

Hi

Dear Office Co-ordinator and Goat Herd

We will deliver the goats to the address provided on Monday as requested. This will consist of one male goat, Bertie, and six female goats: Bella, Susie, Sally, Beatrice, Alison, and Frederica. Please note that Bertie can be aggressive if you get between him and his lady friends but should otherwise be amiable enough. All goats have special dietary needs and please see attached note on their care and feeding.

If you have any problems, please let me know and we will arrange for our aftercare goat support staff to visit your premises.

Best regards

Billy Goat Gruff
Trit trotting over bridges since 2010

From: William Percher
To: Bob Summerson
Subject: Goat delivery

Hi Bob

The goats are here. Do you want to pop down and inspect them?

William

From: Bob Summerson
To: William Percher
Subject: Goat delivery

Hi William

No.

Bob

From: HR
To: William Percher
Subject: Files

Hi William

Please find attached the files requested re appraisals.

Could I just take this opportunity to mention that there are reports of a nasty smell coming from your office—do we need to make arrangements with facilities for a special clean?

Thanks

Sharon

Attachments: Appraisal_files.zip
                 Staff Manual, Section E—Clean Desk Policy

From: William Percher
To: HR
Subject: Mind your own business

Hi Sharon

Thanks for the Appraisals.

William

From: William Percher
To: Bob Summerson
Subject: Appraisal files

Hi Bob

I've got the appraisals. I have worked through them, converting them into a spreadsheet with cross references to their appraisal scores in the various categories. I assume that on the first pass we will go for a simple average and not weight particular aspects more highly?

Also, HR may get in contact in relation to the smell coming from my office. I don't think mentioning the goats would be entirely compatible with our desire to keep this all secret?

William

Attachments: Appraisal_Spreadsheet
_____

From: Bob Summerson
To: William Percher
Subject: Appraisals

William

Looking good. Take your point about unweighted averages but suggest we find some way to make sure that Mark ends up at the bottom of the class.

He's not really a company man, I feel. Not a solutions man.

Bob

From: William Percher
To: Bob Summerson
Subject: Little problem sorted

Hi Bob

Noted, see attached.

William

Attachments: Appraisal_Spreadsheet1
_____

From: Bob Summerson
To: William Percher
Subject: Little problem sorted

William

Spot on.

How are we doing on the contracts, now that we have our targets identified?

Bob

From: HR
To: William Percher
Subject: Smell

Hi William

We are still getting reports about the smell! Facilities will be inspecting your office tomorrow (Thursday morning) to determine whether we need to fumigate.

Thanks

Sharon
Attachments: Staff Manual, Section E—Clean Desk Policy

———————————————

From: William Percher
To: HR
Subject: Out of office

I will be out of the office on Thursday morning at a meeting. I will have intermittent access to emails but will respond on my return to the office in the afternoon.

If there is anything urgent, please speak to my secretary Anne Peters.

Best Regards

William

From: William Percher
To: HR
Subject: Out of office

Sharon

I hope you haven't been in my office whilst I was out at the lawyers!

William

Attachments: Staff Manual, Section P—Right to Privacy

From: HR
To: William Percher
Subject: Goats!

Hi William

Goats. There is a herd of goats in your office. What the hell do you think you're doing?

Sharon

Attachments: Staff Manual, New and Expanded Section E—Clean Desk Policy

From: William Percher
To: HR
Cc: Lara Belitre; Bob Summerson
Subject: Goats

Sharon

I will remind you that you have no right to inspect my office unless I am present.

Therefore it is not possible for you to have seen any goats.

William

Attachments: Staff Manual, Section P—Right to Privacy

_____

From: Lara Belitre
To: HR
Cc: William Percher; Bob Summerson
Subject: Goats

Dear Sharon

I understand that you are alleging that my client is keeping goats in his office.

Please provide details of the inspection process, together with the copies of the forms required to be submitted in triplicate to (1) his immediate line manager, (2) the managing director, and (3) his appointed lawyer.

Lara

Attachments: Staff Manual, Section P—Right to Privacy_redline copy

From: HR
To: Lara Belitre
Cc: Bob Summerson; William Percher
Subject: Goats

Hi Lara

I note your comments concerning the proposed inspection of William Percher's office.

I would point out, however, that no such inspection took place on Thursday morning, as William was not present to give permission.

However, it was not necessary to enter the office to detect the presence of goats due to (1) the aroma, and (2) the distinctive bleating.

Sharon

From: Lara Belitre
To: HR
Cc: Bob Summerson; William Percher
Subject: Goats

Sharon

I note your purported evidence which you claim is suggestive of evidence of goats.

However, my client has an unfortunate body odour problem that does cause him to give off an aroma which may, to the uninitiated, smell a trifle caprine.

He is rather sensitive about this, as you can imagine. I understand that he has been listening to sounds of the forest and nature to deal with the stress and, again, it is possible that some of those sounds would include bleating.

He would be prepared to allow an inspection of his office given seven days notice.

Regards

Lara

From: Lara Belitre
To: Bob Summerson; William Percher
Subject: Goats

Move the fucking goats!

Lara

From: William Percher
To: BillyGoatGruff Goat Rentals
BCC: Bob Summerson

Hi

As per clause ten of the agreement, I would like to give you seven days notice that I wish to terminate the contract and return your goats. In fact, although I appreciate that I need to pay the cancellation notice fee, I would be grateful if you could collect your goats rather sooner than that.

Please let me know what would be convenient for you.
Regards

William Percher
Office Co-ordinator and Goat Herd

From: BillyGoatGruff Goat Rentals
To: William Percher

Hi

Dear Office Co-ordinator and Goat Herd

We can arrange pick up of the goats tomorrow if that's convenient. There will be a surcharge for next day pick up however. Please confirm that this is acceptable.

Best regards

Billy Goat Gruff
Trit trotting over bridges since 2010

From: William Percher
To: BillyGoatGruff Goat Rentals
BCC: Bob Summerson

Hi

That would be great. Just send me the additional invoice and I will arrange payment.
Regards

William Percher
Office Co-ordinator and Goat Herd

From: BillyGoatGruff Goat Rentals
To: William Percher

Hi

Dear Office Co-ordinator and Goat Herd

We are one goat short on pick up. We have added the cost of a replacement to your bill.

We are very disappointed to find that you were not capable of caring for our goats and have added an additional surcharge to reflect this as well.

Best regards

Billy Goat Gruff
Trit trotting over bridges since 2010

Attachments: Invoice.docx, Invoice1.docx, Invoice2.docx

From: William Percher
To: BillyGoatGruff Goat Rentals
BCC: Bob Summerson

Hi

HOW MUCH!!!!!!!!

William Percher
Office Co-ordinator and Goat Herd

_____

From: BillyGoatGruff Goat Rentals
To: William Percher

Hi

Dear Office Co-ordinator and Goat Herd

The terms of our invoices are clear, and I would remind you that for any invoices outstanding after 30 days, we will add a supplementary interest charge.

Best regards

Billy Goat Gruff
Trit trotting over bridges since 2010

From: William Percher
To: Invoices
CC: Bob Summerson

Hi

Please see attached and arrange for their payment.

Don't ask.

Kind regards

William

Attachments: Invoice.docx, Invoice1.docx, Invoice2.docx

From: HR
To: Luke Malton
Subject: Goats

Luke

Do you know anything about William Percher keeping goats in his office?

I remember that you had to purchase some for one of your projects—did you use them all, or did you pass some onto William?

And why does he want the last year's appraisals?

Thanks

Sharon

From: Luke Malton
To: HR
Subject: Goats

Hi Sharon

I'm sorry I can't help you. All my goats were carefully disposed of, so if there are any stray goats about the place, they've nothing to do with me!

And I've the invoices to prove it!!!!

No idea on the appraisals. I would suggest that they were going to pay bonuses this year, but he's tighter than a duck's rear end.

Sorry I can't be more help.

Luke

From: Luke Malton
To: Susan Maltravers
Subject: FW: Goats

See below!!!!!

Bastards are trying to steal my ideas. We'd better get the legals sorted pronto, and I know just the bloke to help. He owes me a favour.

Luke

From: Luke Malton
To: Abaddon

Oi Mate

You know that favour you owe me, well I need a bit of legal help—do you want to meet up in the pub this evening so we can discuss?

The Single Malt

_____

From: Abaddon
To: Luke Malton

Malty Maltster

Yeah, if you're buying.

Abaddon, Spawn of Satan
LLM, DPhil, and Bastard to the Stars

_____

Diary Entry:

17 April 2016 4pm onwards, vodka, sausage rolls

Required: Susan Maltravers; Luke Malton; Abaddon, Spawn of Satan

Legals, tactics, world domination

From: Susan Maltravers
To: Luke Malton
Subject: Spawn of Satan?

Luke

That bloke wasn't really a demon was he? You didn't actually manage to summon something evil from the vasty deeps with all those goat sacrifices?

Susan

———————————————

From: Luke Malton
To: Susan Maltravers
Subject: Spawn of Satan?

Susan

Nah, we went to school together. I used to stop the other kids from nicking his lunch money.

I told you the goat stuff hadn't worked.

Luke

———————————————

Diary Entry:

20 April 2016 12am to 3.30 pm, sandwich lunch

Required: Susan Maltravers; Luke Malton; William Percher; Lara Belitre; Abaddon, Spawn of Satan

Follow up meeting to discuss legals

From: Luke Malton
To: Abaddon

Mate

Brilliant. I owe you.

The Single Malt

From: Abaddon
To: Luke Malton

Malty Maltster

You do—5% of the net to be precise. Sweet deal.

Abaddon, Spawn of Satan
LLM, DPhil, and Bastard to the Stars

From: Bob Summerson
To: Lara Belitre
CC: William Percher
Subject: Spawn of Satan?

Lara

What the hell happened there? Who was that bloke?

Bob

From: Lara Belitre
To: Bob Summerson
Cc: William Percher
Subject: Goats

Bob

Abaddon, Spawn of Satan is only one of the top company and commercial law-yers in the country. So good, he's retained by lots of the merchant banks, which is where he picked up the nickname. He liked it so much he changed his name by deed poll.

Which you would if your name was Derek, to be fair. Just count your fingers and your blessings that you got out there with most of the deal intact.

And don't even think about trying to cheat. Really.

Lara

From: Bob Summerson
To: William Percher
Subject: Goats

Gods beat demons.

From: William Percher
To: Susan Maltravers; Luke Malton
CC: Bob Summerson
Subject: Underway

Hi Susan/Luke

Ok, now that everything is in place, could I see the protocols please?

William

From: Susan Maltravers
To: William Percher
CC: Luke Malton
Subject: Gods and Goats Protocol

William

As discussed, I attach Luke's protocol.

Please let me know if you have any questions.

Susan

Attachment: Does Human Sacrifice Work? Protocol.
Attachment: Sacrificial Altars—development practice and costs
Attachment: Knives, axes, and swords—a guide to disembowelling

---

From: Bob Summerson
To: William Percher
Subject: Gods and Goats Protocol

William

Have you read the fucking thing?

You have to sacrifice the brightest and the best to the Gods, not the underper-forming?

How the hell are we going to monetise that with the investment bankers? They all think they're their brightest and the best, and none of them are going to want to volunteer to cut their own throat for the good of the company!

Well, you've clearly ruled yourself out from the list of potential victims quite neatly—this will be going down on your appraisal!

Regards

Bob

From: William Percher
To: Susan Maltravers; Luke Malton
Subject: Gods and Goats Protocol

Hi All

I am afraid that this department is no longer interested in taking the project further and we will be withdrawing from the strategic partnership as of midnight tonight, with the appropriate penalty payments of course.

We only had the one opportunity to test the protocol, which met with a degree of success but we really could not see a way of making the protocol commercially viable. However, if you can find a way of cutting costs and/or changing the target demographic, please let us know. To that end, see attached.

William
Head of department

Attachments:
Human Sacrifice.mp4
Bob Summerson—Announcement of departure from firm

PS: We've had a little whip round for Bob's wife, and there's a 'with sympathy' card being circulated—do you want me to pass it on to your department?

The Good Not Done, The Love Not Given

Wendy Worthington

It was the tiniest shard, a little sliver of crystal, barely big enough to distinguish with the naked eye. But lying in her chubby, little three-year-old palm, it felt enormous. The fiery eyes that opened suddenly, high up in the corner of her dark room, saw it at once. And they knew what she had done. Their knowing gaze made her shiver. She felt the room grow colder, and her shivering grew with it. She could feel the whimper begin to rise in her throat, and she could not stop it, though she knew it would summon Mama. Mama would come, and Mama would see that tiny shard of crystal, and Mama would know, as well.

Raelene took the shard and thrust it under the mattress, as far beneath it as her short little arm would reach. There was no time to carry it out to Julie Heatherton's trashcan next door where the rest of the pieces were hidden, wrapped in the remains of the Sunday newspaper. She would have to wait until morning. Mama would be here in a minute, and she would know what a bad girl she had been.

She turned to look into the high corner of the dark room and summoned what courage she could find, what little courage a three-year-old body could hold, and she looked into the fiery eyes. She dared them to keep her secret. The eyes stared down at her for a moment longer, and then they closed, leaving the room in darkness once again.

She did not tell her mama about the eyes. She kept it as secret as the fractured pieces of the crystal figurine she had buried deep in Julie's trashcan. She knew there were things she must never talk about, not to anyone. But from that night, the eyes watched her, even when the daylight turned them invisible, like stars chased away by the sun. They never left her again, even though she never told anyone about them.

The fall when she started kindergarten, she did not tell her best friend Susan MacKenzie, even though Susan confided to her about her own guardian angel. Susan told her that her angel stood by her every time things got bad.

"She has ginormous wings," Susan said. "She flapped them at the bad man and made him run away. And she has a kind face. She smiles nice."

Raelene put her hands on her hips and glared at Susan. "Your guardian angel is stupid," she said, and she watched impassively as Susan began to cry. "You made her up!" she yelled after her as Susan ran away. A guardian angel was so much better than a demon with fiery eyes. She longed for her own demon to have a nice smile beneath those burning eyes. Maybe then she could tell Susan about him, but no nice smile ever appeared. She kept silent all through kindergarten. She buried herself beneath her blankets when he made the room too cold, and she pretended the eyes did not know what she had said to Susan. She pretended Susan had never been her friend.

She did not tell Devon Braithwaite, not even when Devon announced to the whole second grade that he liked her more than the six-foot high dragon that used to keep him company.

"It's good having a friend other people can see," Devon said, and he put his arm around her. "Raelene is my bestest friend ever," he told the class.

She smiled in his embrace, but she knew not even a bestest friend would understand a demon. She liked the feel of Devon's embrace, but she didn't trust him. The eyes in her bedroom at night knew she was a bad girl. They knew what she had said about Devon when he wasn't there. If she kept quiet, she could at least pretend she was the way Devon thought she was. If the eyes never found a mouth, at least it meant they couldn't tell anyone how awful she really was.

She did not tell Bobby Zimmerman about the demon, despite the fact that Bobby painted his fingernails black and admitted to seeing demons of his own. He had the sexiest voice of any boy in the whole eighth grade. He made talking about demons sound sexy.

"I kind of like them," he told her. "They scare me, but they make me feel more normal sometimes," but she knew that *her* demon would not make anyone feel normal, not even Bobby.

She let Bobby kiss her behind the middle school auditorium one hazy spring afternoon, but she did not tell him about the burning eyes. His tongue felt slobbery on her mouth. Her bedroom grew very cold that night as she lay in bed, remembering that thick, moist tongue. The eyes up in the dark corner knew she should not have let him kiss her. They blazed their cold light down at her in the darkness. She shivered under the covers, trying not to see the eyes that knew where Bobby's mouth had been.

She did not tell Father Tim, not even at Mama's funeral, when he took the time to hold her hand and ask how she was feeling.

"Your mother is in a better place, Raelene," he said, "and someday you will get to see her again." But the eyes that watched her from the corner of her room that night told a different story. She did not want Father Tim to think she was crazy, and so she let him say words she knew were not true. After the funeral, she walked next door to accept her high school diploma and give the speech her mother had helped her write, and she did not talk about the demon in her room who would never let an evil girl like her see her mother ever again.

She did not tell Benny, not even after the wedding, when it was too late for him to divorce her for seeing a demon in the darkness. He liked the fact that she preferred to make love in other rooms. He thought it was exciting. She did not tell him it was just to avoid the burning eyes.

"You're kinky, Raelene," said Benny, and he smiled when he said it the first time. Later, the smile started to drain out of his eyes, but she was pretty sure it wasn't because of the fact that she tried to avoid the watching eyes by seducing him in the laundry room. The eyes didn't follow her there, but they always knew what she had been doing. They knew she had chased all the smiles out of Benny. They knew that everything he did was really her fault.

She did not tell baby William, even though she was sure he could see those eyes, too. She held him on her bed, terrified that he might break apart in her arms, and she saw his tiny eyes looking up into the high corner. She thought he might ask about the eyes as soon as he learned to talk, but he never did. Maybe he was waiting for her to admit that having a demon watching her every night proved she really was a terrible person. Maybe he didn't need to hear her admit it.

She did not tell Grandpa Milton, even though it was clear he had a demon just like hers. She visited him a couple of times in the nursing home and sat with him while he struggled to breathe. He kept pointing up into the corner of his room, and she let the nurses think he was just being crazy Grandpa Milton. His eyes begged her to be the voice he had lost and tell them what they both knew was there. But if he had a demon, too, it meant he was just as bad as she was. It wouldn't help if she told the nurses.

The burning eyes stayed with her when she ran away to Ohio, leaving Benny while he was upstairs helping William with his fourth-grade science project. They waited for her in the new bedroom in the crummy apartment she found in Toledo. The fiery eyes opened in the darkest hour of the first night and stared down at her. They knew what she had done. The eyes made her shiver.

They followed her into David's bedroom on the first night she slept with him, watching her new boyfriend with those burning, condemning eyes. David didn't like making love anywhere but in the bedroom, so she closed her own eyes and pretended the demon wasn't watching, and she never tried to make David understand.

She didn't talk about the eyes when William drove north on his way home from his first year of college. "I hate you, Mom," he said, but he let her give him all the money she had in her wallet. "You ran out on me." He pointedly did *not* look toward her bedroom when he walked out the door, though they both knew the demon was listening to that final goodbye.

The burning eyes were still there when David had his first heart attack, and they watched her call the paramedics each time, even the last time, when it was too late.

They moved with her again when she packed everything she had left into a large cardboard box and a small suitcase and moved into the assisted-care facility. They settled into the corner of the ceiling of her last bedroom as she unpacked, and they interrupted her sleep every night for the whole first week she was there. They observed Nurse Ellen, who knocked on her door every morning at nine and brought her a medicine cup filled with pills and waited while she swallowed each one, and they witnessed Nurse

Marco, who walked in every night at five without knocking and wrote things about her on a clipboard, even though Raelene never told him anything worth writing down. The eyes knew what he should have been writing.

And still she did not tell anyone about them, did not try to describe the glow of the eyes that always looked down at her before they let her drift off to sleep or the chill of the room that nearly always came with them or the deep regret that they brought her whenever they peered into her too-small heart and her too-weak soul. The eyes were fierce and fiery, cold and implacable. The eyes saw everything bad about her, every flaw and failure. The eyes were hate itself, the enemy that never left her.

But always before that last night, the eyes had always decided when to open, when to wake her, when to interrupt the soundless dark. On that last night, she made them open on her command.

She had been dead asleep, and for some reason she could not explain, she woke up quite abruptly and stared up into the corner of the room where the eyes always hung, watching her, judging her life. The eyes were closed. The room was warm. She was alone. And she decided that she did not want to be. She willed the eyes to come for the first time, and at first they refused her. But she didn't give up, and at last she felt the temperature in the room begin to drop. The eyes opened slowly and gazed down at her, cold and red and staring. Waiting.

She took a deep breath, and then she said, "I'm not frightened of you." She said it quietly.

She wasn't sure what she expected to happen, but nothing did.

So she spoke again. "Once . . ." She stopped and blinked at a sudden rush of the grief she had not experienced for a very long time. *Mama.* The memory of the soft voice and gentle hands came hurtling toward her, and she felt suddenly ashamed. There had been a time when she could not have gone to sleep without first thinking of her mother. When had she stopped? How could she have betrayed her so?

Mama, I'm sorry, she thought into the darkness.

She looked back up into the corner.

"You can get used to anything," she said, brushing away the unfamiliar tears. "If you wanted to keep me frightened, you should have left me alone once in a while." She forced herself to think past Mama. Her thoughts arrived at her marriage. She winced. "Benny knew how to keep me on guard. You could have learned from him."

She remembered how Benny had hidden himself from her sometimes, even when he was right in front of her. He would lull her into thinking he was gone for good, waiting until he saw her shoulders relax and her misgivings soften. He liked it when she was vulnerable. He liked when he could make her hurt. He always made her sorry when she let him in again, and it was always her fault.

"If you were trying to make me afraid of you, you shouldn't have been so reliable," she said to the watching eyes. "You've been the one thing I could always count on. I used to be afraid whenever I thought about you. And William sure seemed to have a problem with you."

William. The thought of his baby eyes staring up into the corner of her room flashed swiftly into her mind.

"William saw you, too," she whispered. "Why didn't he ever admit it?"

In her mind, she went back to the first day when she had seen his eyes go up to the corner of her bedroom. "I should have made him admit it as soon as he could talk," she murmured. "Maybe it would have changed something."

She thought back on William's last visit. *I hate you, Mom,* rang out in the room as though he was still right there in front of her. She blinked back the shame. "I didn't love him enough," she admitted. "I just wish he could find some way to be happy. I wish I could have learned it so I could have taught him how."

She stared up at the knowing eyes. "You watched it all, and I know you think I made a mess of things. I wasted my chances. I drove William away, and I lost Mama, and Benny . . . Well, Benny was what he was. That was just the way things were. But you never made any difference, one way *or* the other."

Raelene frowned up at the burning eyes. "So what did you want from me? If you didn't want my being afraid, what did you want instead? My love? My attention?" She gasped suddenly. "My life? Is that what you've been waiting for?"

The eyes burned steadily in the darkness, a red flare that did not light up the ceiling or the corner of the room but burned their way into her heart. Raelene pulled the covers up to her chin and wiggled her toes beneath them. "I'm not even sure if you understand anything you hear. For all I know, you're a Lithuanian demon, and you got lost, and you've stayed with me just because you didn't have any place else to go, but you never learned to understand English, and you've spent all this time just as confused by me as I have been with you. Wouldn't that be a funny thing?" She started to giggle. The idea of being watched by a Lithuanian demon all her life suddenly amused her, here in the darkness. She snuggled down under the covers, starting to feel sleepy again. She yawned hugely. Talking to a demon was a tiring business.

But something had shifted in the room. She froze, listening hard now. There was a sound in the darkness. There had never been sounds before. It was like breathing, like the raspy in-and-out of William's tiny chest when the asthma had begun. Her gaze flickered toward the window. Maybe the sound was coming from outside. But the windows were closed and locked tightly against the chill, fall air.

"Are you . . . are you okay?" she murmured, almost afraid to voice the question. What would she do if he answered?

Tentatively, she reached a hand up from under the covers, toward the corner of the ceiling. She saw that her fingers were trembling slightly. "It's only because it's chilly," she whispered. "It's only the cold." The tremble continued, and she wondered if it believed her. She wondered, actually, if she believed herself. Was she truly unafraid after all this time?

The breathing had begun to quiet, and now she had to strain to hear it, to pick it out from between the squeaks and sighs of the old building and the ambient noises of the middle of the night. She heard the distant fade and squeal of a siren, hurrying on its way to some emergency. It passed on, leaving her to the almost-sound of breath in the quiet room. She dropped her hand, wondering what she had expected in reaching out toward him.

"You have been with me all this time," she whispered. "You have never given me a reason, but I truly would like to know why."

It might have been just wishful thinking, but the breathy sound seemed to pause for just a moment, as though he was considering her request. She held her own breath, hoping to hear an answer.

But no answer came, and Raelene felt herself grow suddenly furious. She sat up, clasping handfuls of bedclothes in both fists. "That's it!" she announced, her voice echoing loudly in the darkness, "I know you're a demon, though come to think of it, I have no idea *how* I know that, but you're really kind of an annoying, stupid demon. I stopped being terrified of you a hundred years ago, you must know I did, and you never even do anything really terrifying anyway, you just sit up there and watch me and judge me and make it cold, and that could just be hot flashes passing off or a sudden weather front or something, nothing to do with you at all, really, just something you take credit for. I mean, you don't *do* anything, do you? You don't tempt me to be evil or challenge me to be good. You're just *useless!*"

She started to rise from the bed, reaching toward the cold, fiery eyes with clawing hands, but her foot caught in the sheets. She felt herself fall forward in an uncoordinated lurch toward the cold floor.

As she fell, all the things that had never happened, all the people she had not met, all the faces she had never said "I love you" to, all the moments that had not come before—everything flew through her mind as she fell. *Wait!* she thought. *I want to kiss William's tiny head one more time before it gets filled with too much nonsense. I want another chance to try to love him enough. I want to taste kimchee and see how vanilla beans grow. I want to remember why and smell one more rainstorm and never lose my temper again and hold a baby bird in the palm of my hand and know something. I want to be young again and start it all over and make better mistakes, and I want to be taller.*

And as she hit the floor, just as her face smashed into the hard tiles and the warm blood began to ebb out around her right ear, the breath of a voice she had never heard before but knew as well as her own settled into the dark air.

And all that it said was, "Come with me."

The Place to Be

Jae Eynon

You wouldn't know—unless you *knew*—what was behind the scrawled-on, warped and peeling, heavy-lock-sporting door. Not by looking. Just one of those doors between tatty shop fronts. One of those doors that leads nowhere you can see, not to the stinking chippy on the left, nor the laundrette on the right, its creaking machines belching detergent smells that never win the war against many-times-reused chip fat. If you notice the door at all, walking down the ungentrified street on your way to somewhere nicer, you might think there would be a stair behind it, up to the grime-curtained windows above: bedsits for migrants or a knocking-shop for the downwardly-mobile.

But then there's that lock.

The heavy, shiny, you-don't-mess-with-me lock that says 'drug dealers' or 'stolen goods'—or worse, if you have an imagination—and you're wondering why you took the short cut down this shabby street at all. So you're going to just hurry on down to the corner where the money ran out and the developers stopped developing and you'll put your nice shoes on the nice paving and you'll never notice the man in the laundrette draw deep on his cigarette and tap the ash on the floor while he watches you rush by, and you'll forget all about the door.

You might not know, but there are plenty who do. Or think they do. See, this is a university town, crouched on the howling north-east coast where the wind whips salt into the brickwork and picks the paint off doors like this one with its mean, persistent little fingernails. And university towns, they're full of students, and students, they're always looking for something a little edgy, a bit of shabby-chic with some darkness to the shab and some pique to the chic. The braver ones, the savvy ones, find their way there quite quickly; some never make it there at all—but they're the rare ones, the ones who don't even get a bit of a giggle out of hearing "Welcome to Hell!" from the guy with the key to the big shiny lock.

Right now, there's a guy with no key standing at the door, noticing it pretty hard, just like he noticed the peeling sign for Pukka Pies on one side and the drifts of fag ash weathering the rotting lino on the other. He's noticing the bleached wood where blue paint sloughed off like snake skin, and he's noticing that the door with the big shiny lock is a lot thicker than it seems. He's waiting for an answer to the knock that rattled the door in the frame not one jot. He's holding a photocopied flyer in his hand, and he checks it again for the address: 13 Haggs Lane. "Live Music. Real Drinks. Thursday Poetry Jam. Happy Hour 5-7 Fridays and Saturdays. The IN-FERNO." He crumples the paper into his pocket and pounds the door like an angry heart one-TWO one-TWO one-TWO. It's mid-afternoon, he's had no lunch, and the Pukka Pies are starting to look good when the shiny lock clicks and the door opens. The stairs behind it go down.

The guy with no key looks down at the girl with her hand on the latch. She's half his height, half made of black clothes and tangled hair, the rest is eyeliner round pale eyes reddened by late nights and bad contacts. She waits for half a minute then sighs and shifts her gum to a childish-round cheek.

"We're closed."

Far below, shifting crates make bottles chime. Tinkle-clatter. The music of the night to come; a discordant melody of alcohol and loose limbs, loose words, loose morals.

"I said. We're closed."

Her flat vowels ride charmlessly on the bottle song, but the guy without the key doesn't mind. He rather likes it, and he smiles—something she never gets, never expects, isn't sure she likes that much.

"Whatcha want?"

"I'm expected."

Now there's the kind of voice you don't hear very often, slinking down your nerves like cat fur, taking your breath like you've got an allergy but not bad enough to make you cough. Soft and scratchy, can't tune out a voice like that. She rubs her ear and snags an earring on her bracelet.

"Shit." She flushes. Can she swear in front of this guy? She feels she ought to think twice, thrice, maybe more, before hacking up careless words like that but her head's hurting and now her ear's hurting and the big man doesn't seem to care, so she keeps her hand on the shiny lock and her body in the doorway. "You got an appointment? The boss dun't see anyone out of hours without an appointment."

"I'm expected," he repeats.

He hefts something out of the folds of his long, loose coat and she notices he's carrying a battered case with a belled end. Another bloody musician, then, trying to get a hearing on spec. She's got her orders about them. She steps back so she can close the door. This is the moment they usually bull forward and push through, but the boss gave her the tools to deal with their sort and she's ready, she's strong. And she's off-balance when the big guy stays put.

"The boss . . ."

"Will see his brother, don't you think?"

She frowns. What did the boss say that night? It's hard to remember the details of some nights, especially the night he became her boss, took her on, took possession. He said a lot of things and sometimes he cried and sometimes he raged, and he devoured her from the inside out and the outside in and she hadn't taken anything and it was all so much and it's just hard to remember the details.

"You're not one of the brothers that wants to kill him, are you?"

The guy with no key is amused by her question. Since when has his brother liked them so naïve? Since always, and since never. Innocence has its uses.

"Not any more, sweetheart," he says. "Why don't you let me in and we'll find out if he's happy to see me. It's been a long time, and time, after all, heals all kinds of wounds. Put away your flaming sword, Michelle, and let me pass, yes?"

She relaxes. The boss must have talked to him if he knows her name, and if he talked to him, then he's expecting him. She steps aside with a shrug and pockets the flick knife. It's a pretty thing—mother of pearl handle, and she doesn't like getting it dirty, even if the boss says she's allowed to. This guy gets points for not getting the knife dirty. Flaming sword? Yeah, she likes that.

The stairs, they go down a long way. Longer than you might think a cellar is deep. They're narrow and they creak and the walls are close and crumbly with salt and damp held together by old posters layered back in time a long, long way. There's not much light on the stairs and less below. The electric bulbs aren't lit yet and it's only the grey day oozing through a dirty window above the door that shows the big man where to put his feet, but the second he's in he's so big he blocks the light and he's stepping down the creaking darkness blind. Further down he goes, trusting the steps not to betray him, and behind and above the big shiny lock snicks into place. More bottles clatter and he knows he's nearly at the deep end.

Up above, Michelle double triple quadruple checks the lock like she's supposed to and turns to follow the guy with no key. No key but he's in and on his back there's another case and it's long and slender and black and oh shit! she thinks as her mistake hurtles her down the stairs. He's armed and the boss, the boss, the boss, he's in danger and he's going to kill her and what the hell is she going to do? What the *hell*, she thinks, a trace of irony tickling her as she fails to catch the big man's coat tails before he's through the door at the bottom.

He's through the door at the bottom. No lock, neither big nor shiny, to bar entry to a large room, sparse and scruffy and harshly lit in the vacant daytime. There are scarred tables and cheap chairs, a small stage beyond a sticky dance floor, a bar where the handles of beer pumps poke up and the optics hang down round the cavern where bottles chink into shelves and fridges and a man in flowered shirt sleeves stands up to swing an empty crate onto the stack at the end.

"Well, this is a surprise," he says.

Chairs clatter as tiny Michelle bursts through, gasping a litany of sorries, throwing herself into the space between the men, her eyeliner two perfect 'O's of terror.

"He said you were expecting him!" she cries. Her knife is out. The tendons stand proud of her shaking fist.

"There's a difference between hope and expectation," says the boss.

"I thought you didn't approve of hope," says the guy without a key.

"It's true that I prefer to plan, to anticipate, but even I can't rid myself completely of those *finer* qualities," he says with a bitter twist. "I've been expecting you for a very long time, really. Expecting against all the evidence until it could really only be called the faintest of hopes. Not today, though. Not any day soon."

"Boss?" Her voice is a chihuahua growl, all teeth and trembling.

"Stand down, Michelle. It's not a dire mistake." He doesn't say anything about forgiveness, but then he never does, because it's not what he's into and she knows she'll have to make it up at some point but maybe not dearly, not the way he's looking at the other guy. She's glad he's not looking at her with those bleak eyes full of the greedy unseen energy of the universe. She slinks to a door at the far end of the room, back to the kitchens and her work there in the heat and the spices.

The boss spreads his arms wide, his hands flat on the bar. "So, Gabe, why've you come all this way to see me? You look half-starved. Have you finally managed to fall out of favour too?"

Gabe lifts a hand to pull the beanie from his head. Golden hair, real Christmastime chocolate coin gold, spills to his shoulders. "I haven't fallen," he says, and the boss stiffens. Fingernails gouge the surface of the bar.

He dumps the hat and his trumpet on the nearest table and unslings the long case from his back. The boss's eyes devour it, but he doesn't move. Not yet.

"No, I didn't fall. I jumped. That's why I'm here, Lou. I finally did it. You were right all along." There's a crumple in his cheeks as he spreads his arms in echo of the man before him. "And I'm bloody famished."

There's a moment there, where the air is still and void. Anything could happen. You could walk round Gabe, between him and Lou, jump up and down and wave and they'd never see you, they're so fixed on each other. There's a kind of fade-to-grey, everything so irrelevant it loses form, everything but the two men and the long, black case. Something rattles in the kitchen, and Gabe blinks.

"What'll you have?" Lou says, waving a hand at the beer pumps. "Best selection of real ale in Yorkshire."

Gabe doesn't move but there's a sense of change, like someone's put the pin back in the grenade and you know there's more than just the strength of a hand between you and death. He flips his long coat up so it flows over the back of a chair as he sits. Tired wood creaking cradles his body and he reaches out to drag two other chairs closer so he can lay the long case across them. He pats it and draws his hand away slowly slowly as if he's not quite sure it's going to stay quiet where he puts it. Lou's hair has fallen forward as he bends for a glass beneath the bar. Gabe remembers it as copper fire, brighter than his own, brighter than the new-made sun. But that was then and he hasn't seen Lou in an age, and age it seems has breathed ash into the flame and now the colour is equivocal, laid across his cheek and casting his face in shadow.

He watches Lou's forearm tense against the smooth wood of the pump—still able to wield a weapon, he's ready to bet, but why bother with means so crude when he's built something far more potent here?

Lou pulls a second pint and brings the brimming glasses to the table. He sets them down and finds a fourth chair—he won't ask to move the case; Gabe won't let him near it, he knows, but eyes dilated, hungry, greedy, knowing, slide across it before he sits.

Gabe strokes a spill of froth from the outside of his glass then raises it to his lips and drinks deep. The beer is cool and brown and rich and bears no malice as it blesses his throat and curls kindness through his shoulders. It's been a while since anyone thought to be kind to him. He doesn't seem the sort of man who needs it. His coat rustles as tension ebbs. He puts the glass down precisely on the wet circle it left and turns it slowly until the brewery logo faces him.

"It's good to see you, Lou."

"How did you find me?" Lou's glass is untouched; he is not yet complicit in whatever this is. He glances again at the long case, then leans back, lacing his fingers securely across his stomach.

"I looked." Gabe shifts his gaze away, round the big room full of yesterday's air. He knows it's not answer enough, but he's trying to see the allure of the place, to learn how Lou does it. "I . . ." He fiddles with the catch on his trumpet case. "You always did like them, didn't you?" he says. "You actually liked them just as they were—far more than the rest of us did."

"None of you liked them at all, if I remember correctly. Most of you thought they were vermin, or a new kind of toy for the collection."

The kitchen door thumps open on Gabe's indrawn breath. It's Michelle, bearing a platter laden with sandwiches and crudites, an impromptu of flavour and colour arranged for the boss and his guest. She's uncertain it's what's wanted but the boss is always hospitable to the ones who interest him. She sets it down with a tremble that fades as he catches her arm.

"But you're not vermin, are you?" he muses. "Not playthings."

She puzzles over this, struggling with the do-as-you're-told-or-else-you'll-go-to-the-devil of childhood, the crushing years of her teens, the damage that makes her thoughts stumble on the stones and thorns of punishment.

"I haven't got time to play," she says at last. "Got to get ready for the evening. You want anything else, boss?"

He releases her with a pat. "You're doing well," he tells her and she glows. A fragile comet tail of joy follows her back to the kitchen.

"Eat the food, Gabe. It's good. She has a real talent. And you wouldn't believe the mess she was in when I lured her away from those God-fearing folk." Gabe is looking at the kitchen door as it thuds gently to and fro and comes to rest. "Or perhaps you would believe it."

"And where will you send her?"

"Oh, I'm not sending this one anywhere. She's too broken and too valuable where she is. It's amazing what you can accomplish through good food." He waits for Gabe to take a sandwich. "Again: how did you find me?"

"I followed the signs." Gabe takes a bite. He's hungrier than he thought. "The signs . . ." He gestures inarticulately around the sandwich. Flavour swamps his mouth and takes his words until Lou's coal-black interrogating glare loosens his tongue again.

"I left no signs. I turned from those methods sometime since."

"Oh, not those kind of signs. Not lights and symbols and prophecies and that."

Lou leans forward abruptly. "Then what?"

"You went quiet. The portents and prophecies were still there, but they were all fake." Gabe finishes the sandwich but he doesn't take another. Instead, his hand splays on the stippled leather of the trumpet case, stroking, flexing, then finding the catch and releasing it. The trumpet curls into his hands like a cat, old and cared-for, familiar. He depresses the valves one-two-three-one-two-three. "Everywhere I played, I sought out the prophets, but they weren't yours any more; there weren't many that were His, either, but none of them were yours."

"Why've you been seeking the signs, following me?"

Gabe frowns. "It's my job," he snaps. "Was my job. Is. I don't know. I just need to know . . ."

Silence falls, and at last Lou reaches for his glass. "I missed you too, man. Especially when you stopped playing. I bought all your albums, from shellac on."

"You did?"

"Funny how they say the devil has all the best tunes, isn't it? Flattering, but untrue. Yours were some of the very best, Gabe. Why'd you stop re-cording?"

"I lost it. I . . . looked around and I saw all the rules being broken and all the boundaries being smashed, and . . ."

Lou's leaning back again and he's got that smug look Gabe remembers so well from the old days, when Lou got away with something, danced over the line and back again with all the confidence of the favoured son. But it's darker now, that look, and richer: spiced with cynicism and wisdom and ancient pain.

"And?" he prompts.

"And it's better."

"I'm glad someone's finally noticed."

Gabe's smile is bitter and he takes another drink to sweeten it. He nods.

"You've been clever, Lou. I've spent a while watching what you've been up to, and it's damned clever, if you'll excuse the pun."

Lou rolls his eyes and waits for Gabe to tell him what he's been noticing all this while.

"A place for people to breed and exchange ideas, that's all. But I reckon you put in the encouraging word here and there, don't you? You nurture the creativity, make this the place to be in this town. And this town—this town's a part of it too. Not fashionable, not admired, but it's got that core of toughness that draws the right ones here, to you. And you . . ."

"And I love them, as you so rightly pointed out. I love them for what they are, what they can do, what they can achieve if you just teach them how to see." He snags a slice of apple from the plate and grins. He takes over the story, unable to resist showing off for an audience that knows him. "And then I send them away to all walks of life, to all corners of the world. And they're not the flashy ones, not the ones who'll make the headlines. No. They're the quiet ones, the behind-the-scenes ones, the ones who don't get given what looks like real power, but they're the fulcrum for my lever, the point from which I can change . . ." He sets down his glass and looks directly into Gabe's eyes, his face a crash of lines and rage. ". . . *every-thing.*"

Gabe, in his turn, leans forward, his long coat rustling behind him. "I think I'm the only one that's traced you so far. But I'm not the only one who's noticed."

"So much for omniscience," snorts Lou. "Is that what you've come to tell me, messenger boy?"

"Not really." Gabe remembers how volatile Lou can be. "If you're clever enough to make them your weapons like this, then you're clever enough to have seen . . ."

"*My* weapons? All I do is arm them for their own war."

"Don't prevaricate. Don't you see? They're in danger. You're in danger. He's gathering armies and breeding ignorance and holy war again. He's matching you step for step, blinding two for every one you awaken."

Lou grabs both glasses and takes them to the bar—an excuse to turn his back. His broad, tense, unadorned back encased in stupid flowery fabric. It makes Gabe sad.

"So why aren't you mixed up in all that shit?" Lou throws over his shoulder. "You're supposed to be blowing that trumpet of yours in the generals' ears, aren't you?" It's not the instrument in Gabe's hands he's talking about, and Gabe knows it. "Aren't you wasting time down here? Better get your march on. Holy war, ta-ran ta-ra!"

It's getting chilly in the cellar space. This close to the sea, everything underground's a bit damp, a bit close, a lot dark and getting darker by the second. Gabe's first reaction is to tense for the fight Lou's offering him—it's a familiar dance, after all—but that's not what he's come for, not this time.

He stays in his chair and glances round the space again. Black walls, shabby furnishings, wall art painted over and re-done many times to pass the vicious gift of time. The current style echoes the fractured visions of the first industrialised war. Is it a commemoration? Or . . . Lou is reaching over the bar for something. Or is it a prophecy? Gabe's never been a peacemaker, but now he has to find the words.

Or maybe the music.

He brings his trumpet to his lips and blows a soft, melancholy fall of notes. He's been alone a long time. He started to be alone the night he took the message to the girl and saw her face, just an ordinary little face full of innocence and hope, crumple under the weight of obligation. It was his words that pushed her into position on the great game board, his words that sold her into slavery, his words. He breathes his guilt into melody. Would Lou remember this one? It's the one he used to play those nights when he kept his distance and let Lou talk to the boy, sow the seeds of iconoclasm, show him the path away from what was expected? The path that led to his death and the everlasting grief of his mother, that poor girl-child. Would Lou realise that Gabe had let him near the boy? Would he know it was that dereliction that drew him, finally, to the peeling door on the dirty street above?

"I can't do it any more," he says, breaking the tune. "I can't fight for the wrong side any more. That's why I'm here, brought it here . . ." He nestles his trumpet back into its velvet niche and locks it away. With shaking hands, he takes up the long case, feeling the power of the thing inside hum through his fingers. His coat rustles and shifts, rising as if lifted by invisible hands. "You know what it can do. It's never been sounded, but I can blow it for you. If you want."

Lou turns round and takes in the trembling body, the flowing tears, and the wings that struggle to unfurl beneath the grimy ceiling.

"Ah, Gabriel, you silly sod," he laughs. "You and your grand gestures. We haven't lost yet. In fact, we've barely begun." He's holding two tumblers. "I'll put it under the bar where we can get it in a hurry if we need to. Let's have a proper drink and discuss how your playing will draw more young souls here for a talking-to from yours truly. Imagine the draw: God's own herald playing in the Inferno . . ."

Lou's fingers are tight on the case as he takes it at last, swapping it for a glass, but his face remains smooth as the whisky Gabe's gulping like nectar. "I hope you can play drunk," is all he says, snagging a bottle and returning to the table.

"Where are your wings, Lou?" murmurs Gabe after a second shot. "Where did they go? Did He take them, too?"

Lucifer shrugs, light with indifference. No point telling Gabriel that his wings stretch as wide as this place—that they are this place. That Gabe stepped within their shade the moment he crossed the threshold.

Up on the street, the daylight is fading. The man in the laundrette lights another fag and doesn't notice the street light flickering on. In the chippy, a woman tops up the oil and checks that everything's ready for the evening shift. She'll be working on her own until the club next door gets going for the evening, once the pubs are close to chucking out. Outside, a group of new-minted students trot past in nice shoes. One of them says something and points at the shabby door with the peeling paint and the others do a double-take. Really? There? That's the cool place to be? Maybe they'll give it a try later if they can find it again. Honestly, you'd hardly notice it at all if it weren't for the big, shiny lock on the door.

About the Authors

Jae Eynon is still running a chaotic household in rural England, still mothering and spousing, and still British—though she generally drinks coffee rather than tea. Life sends her more story ideas than she can easily deal with, and some of them are even quite functional. She is also working on a modern fantasy novel but is easily distracted by ooh squirrel. She can be found at www.facebook.com/jae.eynon, but if you do find her there, please tell her to stop wasting time and get back to writing.

M.R. Glass has been escaping into fantastical worlds for as long as she can remember. Using the threads of myth, archetype, legend, and fairy tale to weave those worlds into words and images that others can share is one of her greatest joys. By day, she is a psychologist, helping others to overcome their trauma; at night, she achieves balance by subjecting her characters to the worst suffering she can conjure. She relaxes by tying herself into physical knots on a yoga mat. She lives in the US Midwest with her family and two extremely furry cats.
www.facebook.com/MR-Glass

Antioch Grey is a lawyer who lives outside of London and who now has to learn to drive. Which is a risk for everyone around her. One day she hopes to make enough money writing to be able to retire from the day job and spends a lot of her time composing her resignation letter. If anyone knows a cute blond who likes older women, let her know.
www.facebook.com/antioch.grey

Matthew Joseph Harrington, son of historian Joseph Daniel Harrington, born 1960, US Naval Hospital, Yokosuka, Japan. Taught himself to read at two. Enrolled in public schools in Bowie, Maryland, received education by skipping class to hang out in public library. At ten, pushed two-ton truck

355

uphill unassisted.

First story sold to Larry Niven for Man-Kzin Wars series—which, given that the authors up to then were handpicked, was not unlike showing up for draft physical and being inducted into Justice League. Third published story, "Soul Survivor", in Baen's Universe, recommended for the Nebula. Coauthor, with Larry Niven, of The Goliath Stone. Soul Survivor and Other Stories, and fantasy novel Godspawn available on Kindle.

Working on novel, *Indestructible,* of which "Fame" is a peripheral standalone.

Rewired house, which had no ground; rebuilt its sewer drain, which had burst in the crawlspace in which he had to work. Prayers always welcome.

Has fed a feral kitten from the palm of his hand. Has repeatedly been bitten on the palm by a kitten.

On two occasions was propositioned by women who turned out to be porn stars. Turned both down.

Currently living with fantasy artist Valerie Anne Shoemaker and 5 cats.

Does not drink beer.

Stay fannish, my friends.
harvey-rrit.livejournal.com

Bran Heatherby likes creating, however that may manifest; sometimes a writer, sometimes a graphic designer, and sometimes a musician. There are many ways to tell stories. He likes them all.

Bran has a fascination with century-old literature he can't effectively explain. His own fiction involves mythology and mystery, music and history, nimble dialogue, stubborn characters, subtle plots, fantasy, surreality, and illuminating dreams. Once upon a time, he wrote a romance novel or five. He prefers his narrators untrustworthy and his humour pawky. And he believes that when fiction holds a mirror up to the world, that reflection had better be as diverse as reality.

Bran delights in dead languages, winter trees, and the talent of passionate people to love something to distraction.

He has art from ancient cultures tattooed on his skin and can be found at branheatherby.com.

Murphy McCall is a worker bee by day and a writer by night. Her first published story, "The Freakshow File", appeared in J.L. Aldis's *Thoroughly Modern Monsters* (Story Spring Publishing, 2013). She is a displaced Southern Belle who avoids animal shelters (too heartbreaking) and never trusts a man who's prettier than she is. You may visit her at https://www.facebook.com/murphy.mccall.3.

Spring Strahm is a ranger-class adventurer in southern California. A biologist by day, she has traipsed the foothills of southern California, the salted low lands of Death Valley, the caliche flats of New Mexico, the taiga of central Alaska, and across the summer tundra. When not on the trail, she prepares for the zombie apocalypse and/or eventual heat death of the universe with her husband, dog, cat and four chickens. She can be found at springsgoodthings.com.

Raised in Hollywood, **Lin Thornhill** traveled extensively with her family. She attended school in Wales and rural Norway, and remembers learning to ski under the midnight sun.

Lin has loved the written word since watching her mother's fingers trace letters on a page, luxuriating in riveting tales and well-turned phrases. Many a night she read until dawn, a plastic flashlight hidden under the covers illuminating the pages as she raced the rising sun to finish her latest must-read.

Her early professional forays were in the entertainment business, where she received encouragement from such notables as Albert Maltz, Ernest Lehman, and Stanley Kubrick. She is part of a writing team whose trilogy *Bitter Seed, Bitter Fruit* has garnered critical attention, and her documentary *Unlikely Hero: Jake McNiece and the Filthy Thirteen* is in its final editing stages.

Finding the screenplay format constraining, Lin has turned to prose. She discovered fanfiction as an excellent environment in which to develop her talent. To date, she has won more than fifty awards, including Best Author, Reader's Choice, and Favorite Overall Story.

Lin's original story, "Verisimilitude," was published in *Thoroughly Modern Monsters* (Story Spring Publishing, 2013). She is particularly thrilled to publish "Fixation" in this collection, as it anchors the *Messengers of Inari* novel series she has been developing for the past year.
Lin can be found at www.linthornhill.com.

Jonathan Waite, a humble cleaner employed at a highly secret scientific research establishment, found himself one fateful day accidentally sealed inside the testing chamber during a daring experiment in molecular disintegration. The experiment was aborted due to an unexpected power cut, but Jonathan refused to believe that something had not happened to him in those few terrifying seconds. For a time he went about calling himself Dr. Old-Fashioned and claiming to have secret powers, such as the power to predict the immediate past and to be far more unphotogenic than he is in real life, but nobody paid any attention, so he vowed to take revenge upon the world by turning to the writing of fantasy and science fiction, a "skill" which he also applies to his author bios. Some of his stories can be found at http://www.avevale.org/, while others . . . cannot.

Libby Weber was raised in a log cabin in rural Illinois and spent her childhood climbing trees, catching toads, and building up immunity to poison ivy. After earning a degree in theatre, four varsity letters in fencing, and a

spectacularly rude nickname from her fellow trombone players in the Northwestern University Marching Band, she followed her heart to San Diego, where she lives with her much-beloved husband/in-house editor and two dogs. In addition to writing fiction and poetry and occasionally blogging about the arts, Libby is a classically-trained singer who performs frequently with San Diego Master Chorale, Folklore, SACRA/PROFANA, and Downbeat Big Band. Recently, she was in the chorus for La Jolla Play-house's US premiere of Alan Menken and Stephen Schwartz's stage adaptation of The Hunchback of Notre Dame and wrote a sonnet every day for a year.
http://libbyweber.wordpress.com
http://libbyweber.tumblr.com/

Wendy Worthington is that rarity in Hollywood: a working actor. Her first union film was that great cinematic classic, "Mannequin II," and she earned her Screen Actors Guild card working with Tom Hanks and Jonathan Demme on "Philadelphia"—where she had her first (but not last) experience ending up on the cutting room floor. Moving to Los Angeles in 1993, she quickly established herself in guest roles in dozens of TV shows, starting with an appearance on "Murphy Brown." She played recurring roles on "Suddenly Susan," "Ally McBeal," "So Little Time," "Ghost Whisperer," "Desperate Housewives," "Bones," and numerous sketches on "Jimmy Kimmel Live." Under Joss Whedon's direction, she sang on "Glee." In films, she has worked with Steven Spielberg ("Catch Me If You Can"), Robert Zemeckis ("Cast Away"), and Clint Eastwood ("Changeling"). She was seen putting rat poison in the stew on "Buffy the Vampire Slayer" and was beaten up by Buffy herself as a result. This appearance (one in a long line of cafeteria ladies) was marked with its own trading card.

She has written radio plays, grant proposals, short film scripts, research papers, and even a ten-minute play, "Company Business" (which was a finalist at the prestigious Ten-Minute Play Competition at Louisville Rep for 2010-11), as well as numerous short stories. Her works have been included in several anthologies, including Story Spring's *Thoroughly Modern Monsters*.

She is currently part of the national tour of WICKED, playing Madame Morrible across the country. Demons are some of her best friends.

About the Editors

J.L. Aldis's background is in the study and teaching of literature, though she has also worked as a teacher of English as a foreign language and as a translator. Putting her academic skills to work in a real-world setting is a source of delight to her, especially with the publication of Immanence, her second anthology of original short fiction after *Thoroughly Modern Monsters* (Story Spring Publishing, 2013). She has once again found it a huge pleasure to work with such a talented and gracious group of authors and extends her thanks to them all, as well as to Story Spring for bringing this book to the reading public.

E.E. Weber is a writer and editor based in San Diego, CA. Her editorial interests include fiction, verse, drama, scientific writing, and providing useful feedback to fledgling writers. Her mantra for all words that pass through her hands, be they her own or someone else's, comes from Nobel laureate Max Delbrück, who encouraged all who attempt to communicate complicated concepts to "[i]magine that your audience has zero knowledge but infinite intelligence."

www.ingramcontent.com/pod-product-compliance
Lightning Source LLC
Chambersburg PA
CBHW070839260626
47170CB00007B/2431